PERDITA

HILARY SCHARPER

Published by Sourcebooks Landmark, an imprint of Sourcebooks, Inc.
P.O. Box 4410, Naperville, Illinois 60567-4410
(630) 961-3900
Fax: (630) 961-2168
www.sourcebooks.com

Originally published in 2013 in Canada by Touchstone, a division of Simon and Schuster, Inc.

Library of Congress Cataloging-in-Publication data is on file with the publisher.

Printed and bound in the United States of America.
VP 10 9 8 7 6 5 4 3 2 1

You will wonder who we are.
But that is getting ahead of the story.
We can only say that it was through Marged that
the thought of Perdita came to us.

To be sure it was a foolish and wonderful thought.
Did we do the right thing?
There are some of us, to this day, who disapprove of what we did.
Yet there is not a blade of grass, a bird, or a cloud in these parts
who does not know of Perdita.
It is the men and the women who live here—they do not know her.
It is for them that this story is told.

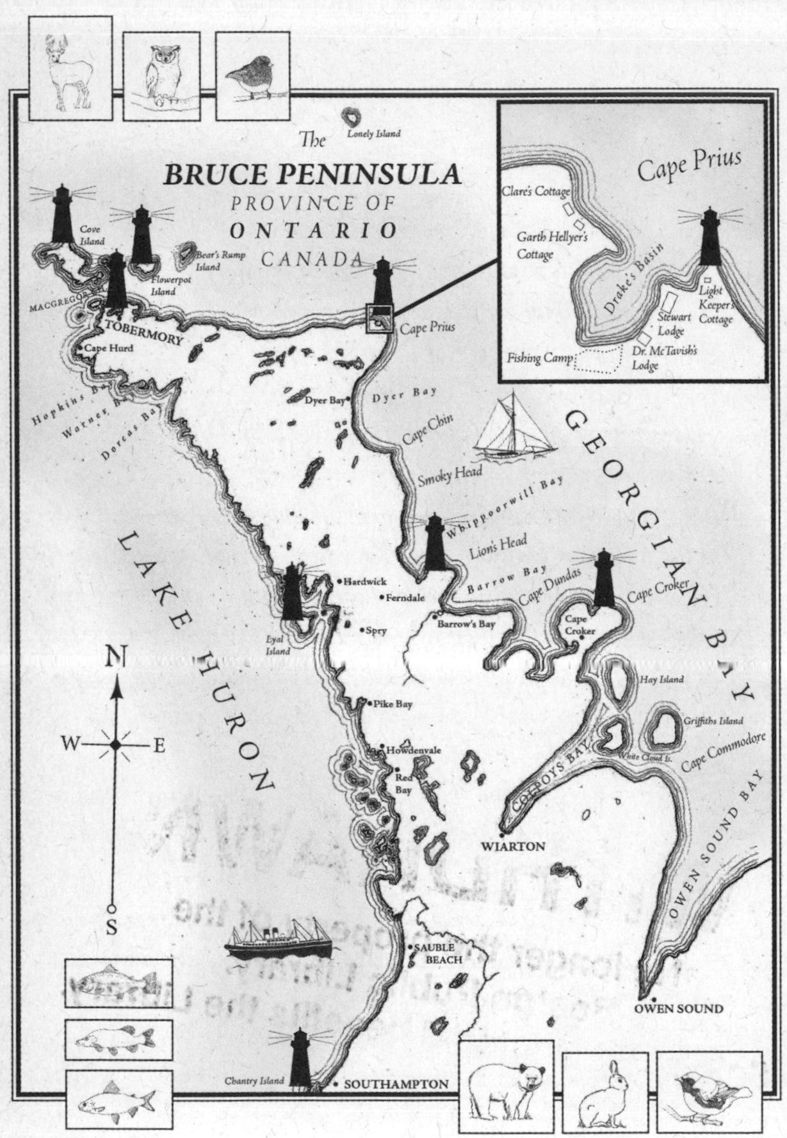

The
BRUCE PENINSULA
PROVINCE OF
ONTARIO
CANADA
Lonely Island
Cove Island
Bear's Rump Island
Flowerpot Island
MACGREGOR
TOBERMORY
Cape Hurd
Hopkins Bay
Warner Bay
Dorcas Bay
Cape Prius
Dyer Bay
Dyer Bay
Cape Chin
Smoky Head
Whippoorwill Bay
Lion's Head
Barrow Bay
Hardwick
Ferndale
Barrow's Bay
Spry
Eyal Island
Cape Dundas
Cape Croker
Cape Croker
Hay Island
Griffiths Island
White Cloud Is.
Cape Commodore
COLPOYS BAY
WIARTON
OWEN SOUND BAY
OWEN SOUND
Pike Bay
Howdenvale
Red Bay
SAUBLE BEACH
Chantry Island
SOUTHAMPTON
LAKE HURON
GEORGIAN BAY
N
W
E
S
Cape Prius
Clare's Cottage
Garth Hellyer's Cottage
Drake's Basin
Light Keeper's Cottage
Stewart Lodge
Fishing Camp
Dr. McTavish's Lodge

One

I WAS ABOUT TO knock, when I heard someone talking on the other side of the door.

"You mustn't run downstairs like that!" a woman insisted. The vigor of her voice surprised me; I'd been told that Marged Brice was quite elderly and rather frail.

Then I thought I heard a little girl's muffled laugh.

"You'll frighten people. You wouldn't want to do that, would you?" This time the woman spoke more gently. "Come now, promise me that you won't."

I heard a soft thud and then the sound of small feet pattering on the floor. What was a child doing in her room? Edna had said Miss Brice would be alone for the interview.

I gave the door a few quick raps and then slowly pushed it open. "Hello," I called out. "May I come in? It's Professor—it's Garth Hellyer."

There was no answer. I stood awkwardly in the doorway, peering into the dimness. After a few seconds my eyes spotted a shadowy figure in the corner of the room. A woman was sitting quietly in a wheelchair by a large window with her face turned toward the trees outside. She seemed to be stroking the screen lightly with her fingertips. A branch on the other side was tapping against the glass above her—almost as if it were trying to warn her that someone had entered the room.

Suddenly she looked over at me, very startled, and reached into her pocket. She hastily drew out a dark-colored scarf, pulling it up over her head and then drawing it down so that only her mouth was visible.

I took a step toward her when I felt something soft and sticky brush against my hand; a second later the door slammed shut.

"Oh dear," the woman murmured. "I'm so sorry. There are so many new people here, and it's a bit confusing for her."

"No need to apologize," I said pleasantly, shaking off what appeared to be clumps of hair on my hand. "I'm well acquainted with Cookie. She's a very skittish cat and probably thought I had my dog with me. Actually, I almost did bring Farley up to meet you."

"Farley?"

"Yes, he's Cookie's canine counterpart at the Clarkson—very friendly and very spoiled by everyone here. Maybe I'll bring him up to meet you sometime."

There was a soft rustle of wind and then a light tapping sound as a bough rubbed against the glass. I pulled up a chair and sat down, laying my briefcase to one side. "How are you this morning, Miss Brice?"

She appeared to be scrutinizing me carefully, so I let her take her time. It was hard to tell just how old she was, and I wondered how I might get her to remove the scarf.

"They told me you would be coming today," she announced after a short pause. "But I was expecting an older man. When Edna said you were a historian and a professor, I thought you would be in your sixties. But you—you couldn't be much more than forty."

"That's an excellent guess. As a matter of fact, I'm turning forty next month."

"Ah, then you're still just a young man."

I laughed and told her that I liked coming to the Clarkson because its residents often told me I was *young*.

"Oh, but you are young," she asserted. "Your best years are still ahead of you." She leaned toward me, peering intently at my face. "Why...you remind me very much of Andrew!" This time her tone was friendlier. "You're taller, though, like George. But dark," she mused. "Dark like Andrew."

"Tall? Dark?" I jested, "Don't I get 'handsome,' too?"

She eyed me for a few seconds and then nodded, placing a hand on the arm of her chair; I was struck by how long and supple her fingers were.

"And you're a single man from what I'm told?" she continued.

I couldn't help grinning—so she wasn't all that different from the other grannies at the home. Most of them were intensely interested in my matrimonial prospects. "Who's given away my secret?" I asked.

"Isn't it true?" she retorted icily.

"Yes, it's true. At the moment I'm still available. Can the same be said of you?"

She let me wait a few seconds. "I'm afraid I must disappoint you. I might be single, but I'm certainly not *available*."

"A disappointment, indeed," I shot back, and watched her mouth curve into a reluctant smile.

We sat there eyeing each other for a minute or so. Obviously she wasn't going to make this easy for me. "Miss Brice," I began gently, "I'm here on behalf of the Longevity Project."

"Longevity Project? Oh, yes, they told me about it. About some group wanting to find the oldest living person in the world."

"Well, yes, although there's more to it than that." I briefly told her about my research at the home and explained that I had been asked to follow up with her because Edna—the Clarkson's director—thought there had been some sort of mix-up with her date of birth.

"There's no *mix-up*," she told me calmly. "I have my birth certificate. I just didn't want to leave it downstairs in that office. I have it here."

"May I see it, please?"

She hesitated and then reached into her pocket, this time taking out a letter-size envelope. "I know all about your interviews with war veterans here at the home," she said, handing me a yellowed sheet of paper. "But the main thing is that Edna said I could trust you."

I looked down and saw that I was holding the birth certificate of a person named Marged Granger Brice, born November 13, 1878. The document had been issued by L'Église Sainte-Anne in Montreal.

"Whose birth certificate is this?" I asked.

She looked at me steadily. "It's *mine*."

I did a quick calculation: the birth certificate had been issued one hundred thirty-four years ago.

"There must be some mistake," I started to say.

She laughed and lifted up the edge of her scarf; clearly she was enjoying my confusion. "I told you—you *are* young! Imagine being my age. But, of course, my circumstances are somewhat unusual."

"Unusual?" I echoed. "'Unusual' would be an understatement if you were one hundred and thirty-four. Miraculous would be more like it. The average life expectancy for an adult female in Canada is between eighty and eighty-two years old."

"Oh, I was eighty ages ago." She waved a hand airily. "That was in—1958, I believe. I remember because I met the prime minister that year—Mr. Diefenbaker. Such a gracious man…"

"Miss Brice, I might be young in your eyes, but I certainly wasn't born yesterday. Now, whose birth certificate is this?"

"Professor Hellyer—" she addressed me crisply, straightening her shoulders and beginning to bristle.

"Please, call me Garth."

"Garth," she continued, even more crisply. "That is *my* birth certificate." Then she folded her arms and pursed her lips.

She began to tap the arm of her chair impatiently. "You'd like me to remove this scarf, wouldn't you? All right, then, let's see if I at least *look* one hundred and thirty-four years old!" Without any warning she abruptly pushed her scarf back from her face.

For a few seconds I was speechless.

"I'm sorry," she murmured contritely, keeping her eyes lowered. "I don't mean to startle you. It's not what one might expect, is it?"

I hardly knew what to say. I had interviewed dozens of elderly people, some of them well over a hundred, but I had never seen anything like her face before. There were several prominent seams that ran down each of her cheeks, but the rest of her face was literally bereft of wrinkles. Her skin appeared tautly stretched, giving the impression of polished stone. As the light from the window cast soft shadows across her features, Marged Brice suddenly seemed made of marble…but a warm, subtle, tractable marble.

"Don't ask me to explain it," Miss Brice was saying as I tried to stop myself from staring at her. "I looked very much like one of those apple-faced dolls for a brief period, but then my wrinkles steadily began to disappear. By my one hundred and thirty-first birthday, they were all gone, and since then my face has remained remarkably smooth." She ran a finger lightly across one of the deep furrows by her mouth. "I haven't lost my character lines, though—but I rather like them." Then she pushed her scarf farther back, releasing an astonishingly thick mane of glossy white hair that came to a soft point in the middle of her forehead.

"The only things that haven't changed are my eyes, not in one hundred and thirty-four years. I can still see perfectly—well, almost perfectly. They're not an old woman's eyes, are they?" She lifted her gaze proudly to mine.

This time I really did gasp. For several seconds I was unable to look away from two very beautiful, piercingly blue eyes. It almost seemed as if a soft light were revolving deep inside her head and casting searching beams of a luminous blue out at me every few seconds.

"No, they're not at all like an old woman's eyes," I repeated awkwardly, even admiringly. What was it I could see in them? Their vividness fascinated me, but I could also discern a lively intelligence in their expression. And an innocence, too. Yes, there was an open vulnerability in her eyes, despite Marged Brice's apparent reserve.

She smiled, evidently very pleased with my reaction. "George called my eyes a Great Lakes blue. But they're not always quite this bright. My eyes always grow brighter with the phases of the moon, and then they fade." She looked away. "That is Perdita. She does it. I don't know why she does it, but you've caught my eyes at their brightest because tonight's a full moon."

I just sat there, silently trying to estimate how old she might be.

"You do understand, don't you, Professor Hellyer?" she continued apologetically. "I really do have to keep this scarf on hand. It's not because I'm hopelessly old-fashioned. I'm more worried my eyes will scare the people here. I had to do it at my home, too, although my nephew Gregory never minded. But I certainly don't want to frighten any of the staff at the Clarkson." She drew her breath in quickly and returned her gaze to the trees outside. "I didn't frighten *you*, did I?"

"Garth," I reminded her and assured her that I wasn't at all frightened—just surprised. I fumbled around, telling her that one didn't usually meet women—of her age—with eyes quite so intense and—

"Yes, of course. You needn't explain. I've been around elderly people, too. But you see, it's not really me who does it. It's Perdita." Miss Brice sighed deeply. "I know it might sound odd, but I wish I could just age as a normal person does. I used to enjoy the brightness of my eyes and watching my face change from year to year. But I've been ready to die for a long time now. I've even resolved to die, but I just don't seem to be able to."

"Aren't *able* to?"

"Oh, I dearly want to pass on." She gripped the sides of her chair. "Especially now that I have no home. It would make Ava and her son very happy if I died. In fact, I'm sure they wish for my death. What is it you say when you want something in a hurry? ASAP." She frowned, and I saw a look of deep distress ripple across her face. "Believe me, I'd oblige her if I could, but there's no one who will take Perdita. And I cannot leave her."

It was the third time that she had mentioned the name. "Miss Brice, who's this—?" I swallowed, the words catching strangely in my throat. "Who's Perdita?" I asked, forcing them out.

We both looked up to see the trees bending and twisting in a sudden commotion outside her window.

"Please, I would prefer that you call me Marged."

"Marged—who's Perdita?"

She continued to stare at the trees and remained silent.

I stole a glance at my watch. I hadn't expected this, but I would give it just one more try. "Marged, could we go back to your date of birth? Do you happen to have any other documents with you? Say your health card or something along those lines?"

"My health card!" She looked at me in utter astonishment. "Do you think that Ava would leave me with anything like that? They took everything! Ava's lawyers are very clever people, you know. You won't find a record of me anywhere. Not even you—a historian—even you won't be able to find anything!" Then she began to twist her hands together fretfully.

"Maybe I should come back another time." I started to get up from my chair, thinking that I'd better get more background information from Edna.

"No!" she cried out, and then immediately calmed her voice. "It's not that I don't want to help you, or your Longevity Project. It's just that my situation sometimes frustrates me. I don't want to be the world's oldest living person—truly I don't! But I can't help it. *I just am.*"

"That's fine," I said soothingly.

She gave me a very hard stare. "But that's not why I wanted to see you, Professor Hellyer."

"You wanted to see *me*?"

"Perdita," she called out gently. "We could try again. Perhaps we could try again with *him*." I heard a faint, rustling sound behind me and turned, but I saw nothing.

For the third time I asked, "Who is this Perdita you keep mentioning?"

Miss Brice shook her head and put a finger to her lips. "Wait. You're too impatient, Garth. I must do this at my own pace." She motioned toward her bed, and I was surprised to see my World War II trilogy sitting on her night table. "It's wonderful writing," she said softly. "I think you might be able to help me—just as you helped all those war veterans tell *their* stories." She reached forward and took the birth certificate back from me. "But this time—this time I'll go one step at a time. I'll go more slowly; that way there will be less danger."

She ran her eyes rapidly across my face. "Do you—do you have a heart condition? Or anything like that?" she asked faintly.

I was a little taken aback by her question, but confirmed that I was in excellent health. Then she carefully pulled open the top drawer of the bureau next to her and stared down into it. "You rely a great deal on people's diaries and letters in your writing," she remarked, drawing out several small, leather-bound books. "All those veterans—and their wives and families—they must have trusted you very much to give you their war journals and letters." She passed two of the books over to me, watching my expression intently.

I took the volumes from her and gingerly lifted the cover of the top one. The pages were filled with handwritten entries—

"I'd like you to read my diaries," she said eagerly. "And then perhaps we could ask Perdita to come to you."

"Miss Brice," I interjected, "really, I'm just here to—"

"I was turning nineteen when I began the diary you just opened," she continued eagerly. "That's the one you are to read first. It was over one hundred and fifteen years ago, but I can still remember everything so vividly. That is where my Perdita began. It was that summer when the Bay knew it could no longer treat me as a child..." Her voice trailed off, and I could see the faint shimmer of tears in her eyes.

Just then I heard Farley barking downstairs; he sounded unusually excited. "That's my dog, Miss Brice." This time I put the diaries down on the table beside her. "I think I'd better go get him."

"Wait! I'd like to—to compensate you for reading them, but you see my nephew's wife, Ava, took all my money,.every cent of it."

"Don't worry about that," I said quickly, picking up the two volumes again.

"It was quite a lot of money. I won't tell you how much, because you probably wouldn't believe me." Miss Brice leaned forward earnestly. "George understood, you see. Somehow he knew, and he was very worried about what would happen if I outlived Allan. He even asked Andrew to take care of me..." Her eyes suddenly narrowed, and then her face hardened. "But Ava...George could never have anticipated what she has done. She told everyone that I had hallucinations. She said I would be put in a mental hospital if I didn't sign those papers. And she told the lawyer I was an impostor—that I wanted to defraud George's estate."

"An impostor?"

Marged took up her scarf, placing it lightly on her head, and then trained her remarkable eyes on mine. "Of course no one expected me to live this long. But none of them know I've still got my birth certificate. Even if no one believes me—even if *you* don't—it doesn't change the fact that *I am Marged Brice*."

She waited for me to speak.

I hesitated. "Of course I'd be happy to look at your diaries, Miss Brice—I mean Marged. But really, the main reason I'm here is to look into the record of your age."

"Oh, please! Can't you see I'm asking for help! I've never had to say that to a stranger before, and believe me it doesn't come easily to me. But I must."

Again I hesitated for a split second—and then half kicking myself, I slipped the two journals into my briefcase.

"Thank you," she breathed. "Thank you." She stretched out a pale hand toward me. "I knew you would," she continued softly. "You see, I asked my trees about you."

"Your trees," I echoed vaguely. Farley's barking was growing more frenzied.

"Yes. But I want to know—and you must tell me. What would *your* trees say about you?" she demanded. "Would *your* trees tell me to trust you?"

Now the light from her eyes was so piercing that I almost winced. "Oh, I think my trees would give me a good reference," I replied, surprised at how easily the answer came.

"You'll come back—soon? You'll come back to see me soon?" she asked, withdrawing her hand.

"Yes, of course," I promised. "It'll probably take me a few days, but I'll come as soon as I've read your diaries. Why don't we say by the end of the week?"

"I shall *trust you*, then," she whispered, pulling her scarf down over her face. "I shall trust to your return."

Two

"EDNA, YOU CAN'T BE serious." I was trying to keep my tone patient. "There's no way she could be the Marged Brice of that birth certificate."

"Do you mind if I smoke?" Edna got up to open the window and then furtively looked around for any of the staff nurses. "They think I've quit," she explained.

"Don't worry, I won't give you away." I took the chair by her desk and watched her take a few hurried puffs.

"Garth, I know what you're going to say. I did the math, too. If it's hers, it says she's one hundred and thirty-four years old. Impossible, right?"

For the second time I explained how extremely unlikely it was. We went back and forth with that for a while, Edna insisting that it was at least *possible* for a human being to live to 134. At last I decided to change the subject; had a psychologist assessed Miss Brice yet?

"You mean because of her so-called hallucinations." She took a long drag. "That's why she's been put in a nursing home. We're to keep an eye on her."

I reminded her that the Clarkson wasn't set up to do that.

Edna gave me a withering look. "Don't even think of suggesting a transfer. That's out of the question. This isn't the big city, Garth. They'll cut my funding if I don't keep my beds filled." She looked out the window gloomily.

"How did Miss Brice end up here?" I asked. "Is she from the area?"

"I'm really not supposed to talk about this." Edna stubbed out her cigarette. "But it would be a relief to tell you, because the whole thing has been a bit weird."

Edna recounted how, ten days earlier, a very "swanky-looking" limousine had dropped off Miss Brice. The "whole thing" had happened pretty fast. A lawyer had contacted her on behalf of the family. He had the papers ready and said the family didn't want to wait, that they'd take a bed if one were available. Any bed, but it had to be in a private room. The lawyer had also said it would be best if she were kept away from the other residents.

"Why?" I asked. "She seems pretty harmless to me—maybe a little eccentric."

"She's not violent or anything like that." Edna insisted that the Clarkson would never have taken her if that were the case. The lawyer explained that Miss Brice sometimes had hallucinations and that she could become very upset during these episodes. "But that's not what bothers me," Edna explained. "After we got her all settled upstairs, she made some peculiar comments."

"Such as?"

"Well…she suggested she's been forced to come here."

I reminded Edna that she probably got that kind of thing all the time.

"Yes, but I've gotten to know Miss Brice a little. She won't say much about it, but it seems she's been taken care of by her family for a very long time—like fifty years. At first a relative named Allan took care of her and then his son, Gregory, took over. Gregory just died, and now his widow, Ava, has power of attorney for her. I've gathered that Ava and Marged don't get along."

I asked her what she meant by that. Edna frowned and put her glasses back on, blinking at me like an owl. "It's those hallucinations. So far, we've seen no evidence of them, but the lawyer implied they've become so bad that no caregiver will stay on. I think that's why Ava wants Marged in a nursing home."

"Did you discuss Marged Brice with Ava directly?"

Edna shook her head. "There's more, Garth. The really weird part is that the family's identity is to remain strictly confidential. I even had to sign an agreement about it. No one here is supposed to know who sent her to the home. Even I don't know all the details because most of my dealings were with this lawyer."

"Then who brought Miss Brice here?"

"I already told you." Edna was growing a little cranky. "She came alone in a limo. There was the driver, of course, but he was totally uncommunicative. He wouldn't even carry that heavy trunk of hers upstairs."

I couldn't believe Marged Brice's paperwork didn't contain some information about her; surely an age was listed somewhere?

Edna just scowled. "The letter from the lawyer says the lady upstairs was born May 1, 1920—so she's supposed to be ninety-three years old. But that's just his letter. There was no official document. When I asked him about it, I got a long-winded spiel about how it wasn't necessary when a person's expenses are covered by private funds."

"I'm assuming the name is the same in the lawyer's letter."

She lit another cigarette. "It's Margaret Brice in the letter. But on the phone, the lawyer kept referring to her as Marged. When I pointed this out, he just laughed it off—saying that Margaret and Marged are really the same name."

I shrugged my shoulders. The two names were pretty close, and practically anyone might mistake them.

"By the way, the family also gave the Clarkson a generous donation," Edna said. "But I'm not supposed to disclose the amount," she added hurriedly. "It's a large amount, and believe me, we can use it. But I don't like it, Garth. All the conditions they've insisted on—it just doesn't smell right."

I was silent for a few seconds. "I wonder where she got that birth certificate, then?"

"She refused to have it put in her file, but I'm positive it's an authentic document. It must belong to somebody." Edna was now avoiding my eyes. "Miss Brice told me a little about her family. She said she moved to the Bruce Peninsula when she was a baby. Her father—she always refers to him as 'Tad.' That's Irish, isn't it?"

"I believe 'Tad' is Welsh for 'Dad.'"

"Miss Brice says her Tad had a one-hundred-acre farm north of Wiarton, but it was destroyed in a fire. After that her father became the lightkeeper at Cape Prius out on Georgian Bay."

I sat up. *Cape Prius*. My cottage was about half a mile down the coast from the light station. A local community group had recently taken over the light tower and was now running it as a heritage site.

Edna looked down at some notes on her desk. "I called up the curator of that museum they have at the lighthouse. Hugh Brice was hired in 1888, and he lived there as lightkeeper with his wife for more than thirty years. Mr. Brice had a sister, Alis, and she came over from Wales to live with them. Alis married a local man, and then her husband, Gil Barclay, became the assistant lightkeeper. But more to the point, the Brices had only one child—a daughter they named Marged." Then she stared at me pointedly. "You saw that birth certificate," she hinted.

"What are you getting at?"

"I can't explain it. It's just a nagging feeling I have, but I think she might really be that Marged Brice. I mean, the Marged Brice of the birth certificate."

I laughed. "Edna, is that tobacco you're smoking? We've been over all that. I don't think it's even physically possible for a person to live to one hundred and thirty-four."

"But did you see her face? I've never seen anything like it before!"

"Look." I adopted a more serious tone. "Don't you think it's more likely that there's been some sort of mistake?"

"But she insists she's the one and only Marged Brice."

"Maybe she's suffering from memory loss," I speculated. "Or maybe she's confusing her own identity with her grandmother's, or something like that. Sounds like she might have dementia."

"I don't think so." Edna shook her head firmly. "I'm not a doctor, but I've seen all kinds of dementia. She forgets things here and there, just as you or I might, but she's not disoriented the way people with dementia are." Then she laughed cryptically. "Well," she threw back, "what do you make of our mystery woman?"

I waited for a minute, choosing my words carefully. "I think you're understandably excited by the idea of having the world's oldest living person here at the Clarkson. But I'll be frank with you. There's no one at the Longevity Project who would go for this. A birth certificate without any other supporting documentation is not a credible lead."

"Do you really think so?" She sighed. "But what if she really is—"

I shook my head emphatically. "The LP requires us to verify a person's age based on very strict guidelines. There have to be at least three official documents that correlate a person's age and name, and that's just for starters. Then there's positive identification by living sources and the census data."

"But," Edna said, her eyes beginning to glint. "What if *you* investigated? You would be able to clear up this whole thing. I know you would! You're a historian—a distinguished university professor. You would know how to figure out who she really is."

I stood up, annoyed with myself for getting trapped so easily. "You know I'm trying to finish a book this summer, and I've got—"

"But I don't think it would take all that long, do you?"

She was probably right, but I wasn't quite ready to throw in the towel. "Why don't you just ask someone in her family? There's got to be someone in her family who could clear up this question of her age."

She shook her head vigorously. "That's not an option. I'm not to get in touch with anyone in the family—absolutely not. I'm only to notify them of her death, but otherwise, there's to be no contact with them."

"That's pretty strange."

"Garth." Edna looked me straight in the eye. "Just think of what this might mean for the home. We're facing closure, as you well know. But the government wouldn't dare shut us down. They'd never do it if we had the world's oldest living person right here under our roof!" Again she hesitated, watching my reaction. "Couldn't you just try to find out for us? Couldn't you just try? It's only that—I trust you. We all trust you here."

We both heard Farley scratching at the door, and I got up to let him in. I'd given him a good scolding for the ruckus he'd made, and he gave me an injured look. He was still covered in dust and what looked like cobwebs, and immediately waddled over to Edna for sympathy. She seemed not to notice and immediately scooped him up, beginning to rub his fat, little belly.

"Would you do it—for us? For the home, I mean?" she asked, fondling Farley's ears. She had taken off her glasses, and now I had two sets of large, imploring eyes trained on me. Just then Farley gave one of his awful sneezes, and Edna was left spattered in an unsightly ooze.

"Okay," I said, hastily handing her a box of Kleenex. "I'll tell you what—I'll look into this. But I'm going to have to do it my way. I'll need to know the name of the family who put her here."

"Stewart," she blurted out. "I know I shouldn't tell you, but the family are *the* Stewarts. You know, the really rich ones—the Montreal banking family."

"The family of the painter, George Stewart?"

"Yes, I believe so. But remember, you didn't hear it from me."

I stared back at her in surprise. Now why, I wondered, would the celebrated Stewart family shuffle an elderly woman off to a nursing home on the Bruce Peninsula? And hadn't Miss Brice mentioned a George during our interview?

"And you didn't get Miss Brice's file from me either." Edna handed me a folder. "I think you should take a look at the paperwork that came with her. If you start asking around about her, you're only repeating what Miss Brice told you herself. Agreed?"

I snapped my fingers for Farley to come down.

Edna gave him an affectionate hug before setting him on the floor. "You've been a naughty boy this morning, haven't you? He's been chasing squirrels in the garden again."

"At least he wasn't bothering that unauthorized feline of yours. It was a very good thing I didn't bring him upstairs with me, because Cookie was hiding out in Miss Brice's room."

Edna looked at me quizzically. "But Cookie couldn't have been up there. I took her to the vet yesterday. They're boarding her for a few days while she has some tests done."

"That's strange—" I started to say.

Just then her phone rang.

"Hello—yes?"

She rolled her eyes and then covered the mouthpiece with her hand. "It's the health inspector. You won't forget to bring back that file?"

Three

It would make Ava and her son very happy if I died...

I looked up from my desk and stared out the window at two loons bobbing past my dock. The file from Edna made it pretty clear that the Stewart family expected Miss Brice to die at the Clarkson Home, and preferably in the not-too-distant future. But that wasn't what bothered me. It was more that Miss Brice's care arrangement included a two hundred thousand dollar "donation" divided into two installments. Half had been given when she was admitted to the home and the rest was to be received "at her death."

At her death—balance on delivery? No wonder Edna was uneasy about the whole thing.

I had found no verification of the birth date of May 1, 1920, for the "Margaret" G. Brice mentioned in the lawyer's letter. There was no social insurance number, no health card or driver's license, not even a credit card number that I could use to confirm her name. There wasn't even a previous address or contact information for a doctor in the event of an illness. There was absolutely nothing that I could use to verify the alleged birth date the Stewarts' solicitor had provided for the woman at the Clarkson Home.

Yet there had to be a trail, I reasoned—everybody was on record somewhere.

I picked up the journals Miss Brice had given me that morning, finally admitting that this was going to take more time than I had anticipated. And all because of two sets of eyes, I thought ruefully—one belonging to a spoiled dog and the other to a portly spinster. Actually, there had been three sets of eyes; Marged's orbs had been pretty formidable, too.

I stood up and stretched—there *was* something else. It had been gnawing at me all afternoon. It was the name Marged Brice had mentioned, *Perdita*. I knew that I'd heard it somewhere before and in relation to my father. Had it been something he was working on before he died?

I began tidying up the papers on my desk when I noticed two Montreal telephone numbers at the bottom of the contract Edna had signed—numbers she was to immediately call in the event of Miss Brice's death.

The first number listed an extension—probably the lawyers.

I wondered about the second number. Would I get Edna into trouble if I called it?

I looked at my watch; it was a few minutes before 8:00 p.m. I could always say Miss Brice had given the number to me. It would be a long shot—

An elderly woman with a raspy voice answered the phone.

"Ava?" I inquired, taking a gamble. "Ava Stewart?"

There was a long pause. "Yes, who is this?"

"This is Professor Garth Hellyer." Then I rattled off something about the Clarkson Home and the Longevity Project.

"Clarkson Home? Could you speak up? I can't hear you."

I raised my voice. "Mrs. Stewart, I would like to speak to you about Marged Brice."

"Marged!" she cried. "Is she dead? Are you calling to tell me she's dead?"

"No, Mrs. Stewart. I saw Marged this morning."

There was another pause. I could hear her breathing heavily. "Why won't she die? Why won't she?" Ava Stewart wailed softly.

"She told me she'd like to die, but that—well, she says she can't."

"You didn't believe her, did you?"

I hesitated.

"You haven't seen *it*, have you?" she whispered fearfully.

"Seen what?"

"That thing—that thing she has with her."

"What do you mean?"

"It's that—*thing*! Marged's always talking to it. She made it come to me while I was sleeping. Just to scare me—it woke me up!"

She began to cough.

"Mrs. Stewart, I'd like to come to Montreal to talk to you about Marged Brice."

"No," she put in quickly. "You can't come here. That's out of the question!"

"Then could you tell me something about Marged? Did you know she came to the home with someone else's birth certificate? Was her mother's name also Marged?"

"Her mother—no. She had a French name. My father-in-law knew Marged's mother. He said she was very beautiful." Her thoughts seemed to be wandering, and then I sensed her growing nervous.

"Could you tell me anything about Miss Brice that would help me?" I was afraid she might hang up. "Could you tell me how old she is?"

"How old? Oh, she's very old. Very, very old. She's much older than you think. But—"

"But?"

"I shouldn't be talking like this! My son..."

I heard an angry voice in the background. "Mother! Who are you talking to? Give me that phone!"

A second later a man's voice barked, "Who is this?"

I took a deep breath, but before I could answer there was a click and then dead air.

Four

I HEADED DOWN TO the beach, Ava Stewart's words ringing in my ears.

She's much older than you think.

"This whole thing is becoming a bit bizarre, isn't it, Farley?" I bent down to give him a scratch behind the ears. There were no lights on at the neighboring cottages, and I paused to inhale the cool night air. A deep purple haze was just beginning to form above the horizon, and the Bay stretched out before me, silent and glasslike.

I needed a swim—an instantly bracing plunge.

I didn't bother to hunt around for my swimming trunks, but grabbed a towel and stripped down by the boathouse. I strode briskly into the water, diving in after I was waist deep. My skin was immediately seared by the frigid cold, and the scar on my back felt like it was on fire, but when I resurfaced, my head was wonderfully cleared.

A minute later, my body adjusted to the water's temperature, and I felt the Bay rippling around me. It seemed to be trying to pick me up, the long, low swells first pushing and then pulling at my legs. I stretched out on my back, finding the sensation very soothing and trying to remember when I had last experienced it. It hadn't been for years, I thought as I let the current take me. Not since I was a young man. Certainly before I met Evienne...

I don't know how long I drifted—probably only a few minutes—but my memory flew back to myself as a boy...pretending that I was a fish and that I'd been drawn to the surface by the changing colors of the night sky...

Suddenly I heard Farley barking. I flipped over, realizing the wind had shifted and an offshore breeze was carrying me out. I called out reassuringly to him as I swam back and then clambered out, wrapping the towel around my waist.

I lingered at the water's edge, still admiring the beauty of the night sky and marking the first stars as they began to appear. A soft loneliness stole over me, but it wasn't an unwelcome one. I reminded myself that I had come up to the cottage for some solitude, some time to think a few things over. Of course, there was also my book…

Farley suddenly ran behind me, whining anxiously. I looked up to see a huge German shepherd bounding toward us. It was coming so fast that I braced myself for its impact, but the dog skidded to a clumsy stop just inches away and then curled back his lips in a menacing snarl.

I remained perfectly still, but within seconds the shepherd started pawing the ground, and I realized that what he really wanted was to make friends. Farley, however, was absolutely outraged and ran behind him, nipping at his tail.

Then I heard a woman's voice. "Mars! Mars!" She was picking her way awkwardly across the rocks and hurrying toward us. Farley froze and stared at her with interest before abandoning the German shepherd and rushing off eagerly to meet her. I called out to him, but he snapped at her legs, and I was certain that she was going to take a nasty spill onto the rocks.

"Farley!" I yelled, rushing over and grabbing the woman to steady her. She gripped my arms and looked up into my face, her expression startled.

"Garth!"

I stared at her in surprise. Then she took a deep breath. "But you've *always* been away when I've come back. Every single time, you've been away…" She shook her head, as if to make sure of what she was seeing.

The German shepherd growled low in his throat, but she seemed not to notice.

"You don't recognize me, do you?" The woman was now smiling shyly at me.

I stepped back a little, trying to get a better look at her face. Was she was one of my new neighbors? I had met a young couple earlier in the week and lent them my kayak. The woman laughed at my puzzled expression. "Maybe I'm not being entirely fair. It *is* getting dark, but even so, I knew you immediately!"

There was something I recognized in her voice, in her tone.

She left me waiting for a half a second. "Shall I give you a hint?"

I nodded, playing along, rather intrigued by her friendliness.

She tilted her head to one side and said very sweetly, "Would you let me do a coming about? I'll be very careful. I promise. Would you, *please*?"

"Clare! It can't be!" I had a sudden image of myself at twelve, taking the new boy from the cottage next door out in our sailboat and all our parents watching from the shore. And Doug's six-year-old sister tagging along. A scrawny little girl who had capsized us on our first voyage because in a moment of weakness—or sheer and utter insanity, as Doug later said—I let her take the helm.

"But I just spoke to Doug last week," I said, now smiling broadly. "He told me you were still on the job at the British Museum."

"Oh—that job's over now. I decided to take a break and come home for a rest. I'm so sorry if Mars annoyed you," she added, lowering her eyes. "The first thing Douglas did was to dump me with Dad's new dog. He's the one who's supposed to be training this enormous beast, but Dad wants me to have him while I'm up here."

I continued to stare at her while she spoke, completely forgetting Farley and the German shepherd. "Clare," I softly repeated her name. It was such an unexpected and pleasant surprise to see her. Then I stepped back, slowly releasing her.

"You're looking very well," she said, her eyes scanning my face and her voice warm.

"And you're looking very well, too. In fact, you look wonderful!" How long had it been since I'd last seen her? "Doug never mentioned you were going to be up here." I could just make out the soft blue of her eyes.

"I always try to get up here as soon as I can: I miss the Bay so terribly when I'm away!" She looked out over the water. "Mum's actually given me the cottage for the whole summer—if I want it. Douglas said he's coming up in a few days. We're to have a big brother–little sister weekend, and he's absolutely promised not to be the Grand Inquisitor." Then her face brightened. "But you, Garth. Fancy meeting you like this!"

The wind started to pick up, and I suddenly remembered that I was wearing only a towel. Clare rubbed her bare arms as if she were growing chilly. "Clare, why don't you… Would you like to come up for a drink?"

She hesitated, looking back toward her cottage, and then shivered slightly. "That's very nice of you. I've really just arrived. Of course I absolutely *had* to come down to the beach first, and I haven't even gone inside the cottage yet—but I'd like a drink. It was a long drive."

I led her up my steps and across the deck, relieved to see that the place wasn't too much of a mess. Once inside, she took my father's old chair by the fireplace while Mars settled himself at her feet.

Farley planted himself in front of her, eyeing Mars warily.

I quickly ducked into the bedroom and pulled on some clothes, calling out to ask what she'd like. By the time I brought her a glass of wine, Farley had ensconced himself in her lap and she was petting him as if they were old friends.

She looked at me and then laughed outright. "That couldn't be! It couldn't be the same shirt. Not the one you and Douglas got that summer you became Grateful Dead fans?"

"No." I grinned back, enjoying her smile. What was the nickname my father had given her smile? Aurora borealis. He had always referred to Clare as his northern lights.

"This is a second edition," I explained. "I wore the original into rags quite a few years ago."

Clare shifted Farley in her lap to stroke him under the chin. "I wouldn't be surprised if Douglas had his original embalmed or bronzed, or something like that!"

"She's changed," I thought, taking a sip of wine and silently observing her. She was much more poised than I remembered, more at ease. More "in her own skin," as my father would have said.

She leaned back in the chair, and Farley reared up on his hind legs, attempting to lick her nose. "He's such a lovely little dog!" she exclaimed. "He's part pug, isn't he? Isn't that the breed your mother liked?"

"Yes, Farley was really her dog. I've just inherited him."

"You mean he's inherited you!" Farley began to emit sounds like an old motor boat running out of fuel, and Clare froze, looking at me quizzically.

"Believe it or not, that's Farley purring," I explained.

She laughed and held Farley's face between her hands. "Well, I think I should trade you. Farley's so much more my type. Mars is supposed to protect me from things that go bump in the night and I do love him, but he's such a handful!"

"I'm trying to remember," I said, still watching her, "when we last saw each other."

She looked over at me quickly—and then away just as quickly. "It was… It's been several years."

"That's right." I frowned, remembering. It had been four years ago, at Evienne's funeral. I had been in bad shape, still cut up and bruised from the accident, and hadn't really been able to talk to anyone. "I completely forgot—"

"But I haven't changed that much," she interrupted, keeping her tone light. "Now, what's your real excuse for not recognizing me?"

"Let's see." I folded my arms. "You must be—hmm, let me see, around forty or forty-one now."

"What!" She lifted a pillow and tossed it at me. "You know perfectly well I'm six years younger than you are, almost to the day!"

"Will you believe me if I say it's because you're prettier?" I teased, reaching out to catch the pillow. "Honestly, Clare, I mean it. You really do look wonderful."

She placed her hand lightly on Mars's collar and smiled over at me. "That's such a nice thing for you to say. But you were always nice to me."

"Who wouldn't be nice to you? You were a very sweet little girl, always my father's favorite."

She sighed. "Those were the days!" Her voice sounded just a little bitter. "I've managed to make a few enemies since then."

"I can hardly believe that."

"Oh, it's a long story," she said quickly. "I shouldn't have said anything. It's just been on my mind."

"I thought most long stories had a short version."

"Hmm, the short version is senior woman hates upcoming junior woman. Executive summary: she had it in for me. Unfortunately she was on the museum's board of directors, and I was but a lowly curator on contract. I only stayed to finish that exhibit because of Stuart."

"Stuart?"

"Stuart Bretford." She paused. "One of the trustees. He was my guardian angel, my swain of the museum world. You probably won't believe this, but the museum world can be pretty cutthroat."

"Just up for a holiday, then?" I asked.

"In a way, yes. A holiday and a retreat. I've got something I need to think through." She got up and went to the screen door and stood staring out into the darkness for a few seconds. "I so love it here! I've come back up here almost every summer," she said softly, her back to me. "Some summers I've come up in July and sometimes in August. But you were never up, Garth. I always saw your dad—and sometimes your mother—but never you. Do you come up very often now?"

I told her that after my father died, I had started coming to the cottage more regularly.

She turned around to look at me. "I'm so sorry, because I really wanted to come to his funeral. But I was stuck in Moscow. Literally stuck. There were no outgoing flights for days and days because of the snow. I always thought it must have been a bit rough losing him so soon after your mother."

I admitted it had been an adjustment. Clare walked around me as I spoke, pausing to rest her hand briefly on my shoulder. "I'm so glad you've kept the cottage, Garth," she said, her eyes meeting mine.

"I don't think I could ever sell it." The very thought made me shudder. "At least, I hope I never have to. This year I've even decided to spend my sabbatical here. Doctor's orders. Your brother's orders, in fact."

"Is Douglas actually your MD?"

I pretended to be shocked by her expression. "Why? Is there something I should know about his professional practice?"

"He never told me! He said that after the accident...but I shouldn't ask, should I?"

"I'm in perfect health," I said quickly. "I've just been overworking, or so Doug claims. I'm supposed to take it easy. But even so, I plan to get a good chunk of writing done."

Now she was moving around the room, pausing to look at some of the pictures on the walls. "You know Mum and Granny were thrilled by your success," she said. "They were ecstatic over you winning the Governor General's award. Dad loved your World War II trilogy: he said he's seen quite a bit of you lately."

"Yes, since I'm up at the cottage more, we've become neighbors in a way." I smiled. "Your grandmother gave me quite a lecture a few weeks ago."

"Really, about what?"

"About Doug."

"Douglas? Now why would she…?"

"It seems she feels quite strongly that Doug and Ellen should be having kids by now."

Clare stared at me in surprise. "And just what are *you* supposed to do about *that*?"

We both laughed.

"So what's on the horizon for you?" I asked casually. She still hadn't told me what she meant by *something to think through*. "Do you have another job lined up?"

"No. I've got something far more complicated on my plate: something in the romance department." She pushed a few strands of hair back from her face. "I need a quiet place to think about it. A beautifully quiet, inspirational place, a place that I can trust…"

"I can't imagine how you've managed to stay single for so long," I ventured.

"I've sometimes wondered the same of you," she said abruptly, picking up her wineglass. "You at least got very close—" Then she caught herself and flushed. "I'm sorry, I didn't mean that the way it sounded. You must think—"

"I only think it's wonderful to see you after all these years."

Just then a moth hit the screen with a loud thud, and Mars sprang to his feet, snarling fiercely. Clare grabbed his collar, and then, crouching down, she began to growl loudly in his ear.

"What on earth are you doing?" I asked, taken aback.

"Showing him I'm the *alpha* dog. It's a new way—you know, a new technique to get your dog to obey you."

I had to laugh. Her slender wrists and hands seemed no match for the dog's power.

"I felt a little silly at first," she explained, "but Douglas says that I'm to keep at it. Dad, of course, thinks it's all ridiculous."

Mars hesitated, submitting to the "new technique" for half a second, but he was clearly in the throes of a forceful instinct.

"Do you mind if I try the old-fashioned way?" Clare looked at me doubtfully. "Stay," I commanded sternly. Mars froze, but remained on his feet. "Stay." This time I said it in a quieter tone, but still firmly.

Mars immediately sat down.

Clare looked at me, tilting her head to one side and smiling whimsically. "You know, Douglas is paying all this money to some trainer who's teaching him how to growl properly. I can't wait to tell him about this!"

"I was merely protecting my property," I protested. "Mars looks like he could take that screen out in a single bound."

We both took a few sips of wine. I could tell that she was growing a little edgy—but was she eager to get back to her cottage or reluctant to leave? She wandered over to my desk, her hands lightly touching my chair.

I stood up and offered to help her open up the cottage.

"Are you sure?" She flashed me a grateful smile. "I hope you don't think I'm rude. I'd like to stay and chat, but I'm anxious to get organized. I feel bad imposing on you like this."

I walked over to my desk and carefully picked up Marged Brice's diaries. I felt her eyes following me as I locked them in a drawer.

"I'm not keeping you from something, am I?"

I assured her that it would keep until tomorrow.

"Those looked like very old books," she said as we walked down the steps.

I nodded and then smiled—remembering how she'd always wanted to know what Doug and I were up to. He'd teased her mercilessly about it.

"Do you mind me asking what they are?" She paused at the bottom step.

"They're diaries." I kept my expression noncommittal. "They belong to a woman who claims to be one hundred and thirty-four years old, and she's asked me to read them."

Clare looked at me closely, then she slowly grinned, her eyes sparkling. "I'm not quite as gullible as I used to be, Professor Hellyer. At least that's one thing that's changed."

Five

"I'm sorry, it's all I have. I've still got to get groceries: thank goodness Mum made me a care package! I dearly hope it's not a false rumor that you like this."

Clare was taking one of her mother's chicken potpies out of the oven.

"Did she make it for me?" I was surprised.

"Well, yes," Clare said slowly. "I mean, Mum said *if* you were up, I was to give it to you. You do like it, don't you?"

I said I was a very willing recipient of anything Donna might cook up.

"Besides, it's the least I can do," Clare continued briskly. "You spent all day helping me. I wouldn't have running water if it weren't for you. Dad and Douglas always dealt with that pump. I should have paid more attention."

I took the plates from her while she fetched two glasses. "Let's eat out on the deck," she suggested. "It's such a glorious evening."

Clare barely touched her food, but watched me swallow several mouthfuls. "So you weren't pulling my leg yesterday," she began, "when you said Miss Brice is one hundred and thirty-four years old."

"She claims she's one hundred and thirty-four," I corrected. "But she's probably in her nineties."

"Why would she lie?" Clare looked at me doubtfully. "I thought women always fibbed the other way around—about being younger than they really are."

"I'm sure it's just a mix-up. It's probably someone else's birth certificate."

"Why are you so certain?"

"Well, for one thing, it's extremely unlikely anyone could live that long."

"Is there a maximum age that we can live to, then?"

I explained that our genes tended to give up on us after we reached eighty, largely because we were pretty much irrelevant to survival of the species by that point. Then I told her the oldest person on record was a French woman who'd lived to be 122 years old.

"One hundred and twenty-two!"

I smiled at her puzzled expression. She had placed her elbows on the table and was resting her chin in her hands as she looked out across the Bay. "Do you think there's a secret to longevity?" she asked. "Maybe it's your diet—or stress levels, or something like that."

"The best advice for longevity I ever heard was from Li Ching-Yuen."

"Who?"

"He was a Chinese herbalist. Rumor has it that he was born in 1736, but others placed his birth at 1677. He died in 1933, so he was either one hundred and ninety-seven or two hundred and fifty-six years old."

"You're joking!"

I shook my head. "No. Of course his age was never verified."

"Did he ever share his secret formula for longevity? No doubt it involved ginseng."

"No ginseng, but Li Ching said that a person must do three things." I waited for a few seconds, swallowing a mouthful of pie.

"Well?"

I cleared my throat and assumed a solemn expression. "He said we should sit like a tortoise, walk sprightly like a pigeon, and sleep like a dog."

Clare burst out laughing. "Garth Hellyer! I am totally inured to Douglas's teasing, but you—"

"I kid you not. That's exactly what he said."

She pushed her plate aside, still grinning. "It's probably very good advice, then. Don't some animals grow to be very old, too? I seem to remember something about a whale that was two hundred years old."

I nodded. "That's right, a bowhead whale. They found harpoons from the 1860s in the carcass, and then tissue tests showed it was even older."

"I wonder if your Miss Brice swallowed a button or something like that when she was little?" she mused. "You know, a distinctly late nineteenth-century button. Or a coin with the date stamped on it. Then maybe you could x-ray her."

I smiled, saying that she'd make an excellent longevity sleuth.

"At least you have her diaries," she said, shooing Mars away from the table. "Surely they'll help you clear up who she is."

"I don't think the diaries are actually hers." I watched her fill up my water glass. "But I've agreed to read them. And since she seems a bit anxious about it, I'll probably start tonight."

Then I thought of something. "Clare, you were an English major, weren't you? When I spoke with her, Miss Brice kept mentioning a name. Perdita."

"Perdita. That's from Shakespeare's *The Winter's Tale.*"

"Do you remember it?" I took another mouthful of the pie, determined that she send Donna a good report. "Even the bare bones of the plot might help me."

"Oh, I know the story quite well. It's a rather complicated plot, but the story begins with a jealous king: King Leontes of Sicilia. He accuses his beautiful and virtuous wife of having an affair with another king—Polixenes—who happens to be visiting. Queen Hermione is innocent, but the king doesn't believe her."

I slipped Mars a piece of crust and surreptitiously dropped a wedge of chicken for Farley by my foot.

"The jealous king unsuccessfully tries to poison his suspected rival," Clare continued, "and he throws poor Queen Hermione into prison. He then sends emissaries to the Oracle of Delphi to verify his suspicions. In the meantime, Hermione has a baby in prison, and her maid, Paulina, brings it to the king, hoping that he will soften at the sight of the baby."

"And does he?"

"That would make things much too easy! King Leontes is furious, convinced it's not his child, and sends the baby off with his servant, Antigonus—ordering him to get rid of it."

"I'm assuming the baby survives?"

"Yes. Antigonus leaves the infant on the coast of Bohemia—with a nice, big bag of gold—and she is rescued by a kindhearted shepherd and given the name Perdita. Her name means the 'lost one.'"

"Don't tell me this all has a happy ending."

"Oh, Shakespeare was pretty skilled at reconciling the impossible threads of an impossible plot!"

"Go on," I said, intrigued by the idea of a "lost" child.

"Well, much to the king's consternation, the Oracle confirms that the queen and Polixenes are innocent. Then Paulina tells him that his wife has died in prison. The king is heartbroken and terribly remorseful. He also learns his son has just died and now he will have no heir unless the daughter he has just abandoned is found. It gets even more complicated but—"

"Maybe you should just tell me what happens to Perdita."

"Perdita grows up to be a beautiful young woman. Her true identity as a princess is eventually revealed, and she's reunited with her parents."

"Reunited? With a father who wanted to get rid of her? And I thought her mother was dead."

"Oh, His Royal Highness is very, very sorry for all his misdeeds..."

"Ah, the remorse of tyrants!"

"...and as for the Queen, she was never *really* dead, but hidden away by her faithful maid. Perdita eventually marries a handsome prince, Florizel, who also happens to be the son of Polixenes—"

"Good grief!" I interrupted. "What a plot!"

Clare laughed and began gathering up the plates. "It's actually a wonderful play. I was in two productions of it at college. I played Perdita as a frosh and then Hermione in my senior year."

"Two leading roles!" I was impressed. "Which did you like better?"

"I don't know," she said, suddenly stopping. "You know, I've never asked myself that question before." She looked past me, frowning. "There's a truly wonderful scene at the very end; in the garden of Paulina's house. Queen Hermione appears as a statue, and at the sight of her, King Leontes falls to his knees, wildly distraught and deeply repentant. But much to his joy, she comes to life..." She hesitated.

"And forgives him," I finished for her.

Clare shrugged her shoulders. "That, however, is only Shakespeare's Perdita." She smiled archly. "Of course you *must* remember Pongo and Perdita."

"Who?"

"Perdita from *101 Dalmatians*, Pongo's mate." Clare looked at me impishly. "Don't you remember her? Really, Shakespeare is one thing, but not knowing your Disney! Now, that's inexcusable."

I got up to hold the screen door open for her.

"I should let you get to those journals," she said over her shoulder. "Otherwise I'm going to feel guilty about keeping you from them."

"Those sound like marching orders."

"Not at all. And thank you so much for your help today. At least that pie will fortify you for the task ahead. I can take some comfort in that."

We both walked back out to the deck and she looked up at me, holding my gaze for a few seconds. "Her eyes aren't as piercingly blue as Marged's," I thought, but I liked their softness better.

"I think I'll leave the rest of my unpacking until tomorrow," she said, stifling a yawn. "My plan is to add to my longevity by sleeping like a dog tonight, but I suppose you'll be sitting like a tortoise with those diaries."

"Yes, I'll be up for a few hours—but only after a sprightly-as-a-pigeon walk with Farley."

Mars followed me down the steps, and I played a quick game of fetch with him on the beach while Farley watched. After several minutes of ordering Farley to "come" and then scolding him for refusing to obey, I finally picked him up and carried him over the rocks, telling myself that at least I had discovered one of Farley's secrets for extending *his* longevity.

I thought longingly of bed, but I knew that I had to get to Marged Brice's journals.

I poured myself a glass of scotch and sat down at my desk

MARGED BRICE
Cape Prius—1897

April 16

At last our supplies have arrived!

I ran to get Father as soon as I saw the boat. Uncle Gil came, too, when he heard my cries for Tad. Both of them were so relieved, and Auntie Alis almost started to cry as we unpacked the crates. I had not been aware that our stores were so very low. She said this has been the worst year yet because the road was impassable, even to Mr. Brown's farm. I do not think it likely that we will ever try to winter here again.

Tonight we had some of the bacon, and it was lovely not to have the aftertaste of vinegar in my mouth. I did not notice just how awful it was until today when we partook of our fresh provisions. Even Mother seemed to smile a little. I am sure that when she closed her eyes, it was not so much a savoring of its wonderful flavor, but more that she was giving a prayer of thanksgiving for our deliverance.

I am so glad that winter is finally ending. There are still bits of ice in the Bay, and it still looks very cold. But the long stretches of silence are gone. That long, deep, frozen silence that the winter brings and now the water is moving again and making so much noise.

Indeed, I am grateful to hear the water roaring again. For days it has been only the wind, dry and bitterly cold, moving about us as if the world were a great hollow place. The wind becomes such a rogue in the winter—or perhaps I am too harsh. Perhaps it is only lonely, left behind in restless, unending motion while the others sleep, oblivious to the dreary, bitter months of cold.

April 17

After supper I took the path down through the forest and out to the Basin to watch the lights on the boats. There are four anchored there tonight, each with a lantern fore and aft. They are setting up their camps on the shore, and then the men will be up early in the morning and off out into the Bay fishing.

In the darkness, I sometimes feel like an animal observing them, hidden from their view and my obscurity gives me a certain sense of…powerful invisibility, though I surprise myself in expressing it thus. The boats seem so safe in the Basin, like children nestled cozily in bed while the wind roars beyond the channel and howls at its own impotence to reach them. Indeed, I could hear the surf pounding beyond the Point; it seems just a stone's throw from the boats and their tranquillity. How fragile does their peaceful repose look from my vantage!

It is still bitter cold in the evenings, and I borrowed Auntie Alis's gray shawl to keep me warm. I love the sound of my skirts swishing through the dry grasses—as if I grow here, too, and am a part of this place, its flesh and blood. They were having a bonfire on the shore, near the Lodge, but I could not hear any voices. Sometimes it is so still I can hear a single whisper, but that won't be until later in the summer. Now everything is thawing and stirring and returning to life in a grand cacophony of whispers.

I cut Father's hair today—a sure sign that the summer season is coming. His hands are dreadful, filthy from the paraffin, and they smell dreadful, too. They will be like that for the next seven months. He and Uncle Gil have been cleaning and cleaning and getting the Light ready. I helped them with the glass, but honestly I know they came and polished again after me. Uncle Gil handed me an enormous pile of rags to be washed, and I have hidden half of them from Auntie A. She will begin her complaining, and then we will have seven months of that, too!

I begged Tad to let me trim his mustache. I can hardly see his mouth. But of course he will not let me. Tad is very particular about his mustache, and no one will ever be able to persuade him to grow a beard. Mother does not like them. That's what he told me, and I am somehow pleased that he should still think of her wishes. He is always so kind to her—especially since her seizure—so gentle and attentive.

I love my Tad's face. He ever seems to be smiling, and his eyes twinkle so. Maybe Tad's mustache hides his sadness, but to us he is always bright and safe and sturdy. This winter we almost ran out of food, but he never once betrayed any anxiety. I only knew of his worry when the supply ship came yesterday and I saw him bent over the table, his shoulders twitching slightly. The ice was so terrible this year! I don't know how the men came through it, but Tad was grateful and they knew it, though they would not let him show his gratitude and they joked about the five skeletons they expected to find. Men are very fine sometimes—and sometimes very terrible, too.

Now Tad will be up all night—and Uncle Gil, as well. I shall have to be quiet in the mornings when he is asleep. I shall make Auntie walk with me and keep her from making noise, for she has grown a little clumsy with age—though I should never dare to even suggest such a thing. We will go to her little Luke's grave, and we shall make it tidy, and I think while she is praying I will make up a story for him, just as if he were a living boy. Auntie A. will like to go—it comforts her. And of course we can leave Mother quiet—she always is restful in the mornings.

But I—I am so restless with all these familiar things! I will be nineteen this year. Will I spend all of my days here? Living through the seasons like a blade of grass or one of the rocks down below? I feel as if I am waiting for something to happen and all the world around is poised, expectant—and yet it is only the spring coming. And the boats, and the boaters from the city, and the fishermen… They all come year after year. And yet, why do I feel this expectancy—for something! For someone?

April 24

Everyone is in such a foul temper today. The mantle would not light properly and Tad and Uncle G. have been growling at each other like two old dogs. Tad says Uncle Gil got the oil hot too quickly and Uncle G. is so sullen under criticism. Oh, they are like this every spring!

The problem with everyone is that they get so…so preoccupied with that Light. It is such an exacting master. Or a spoiled child, I cannot decide. Tad wouldn't walk out with me to see the boats, and I so wanted him to see them. No doubt I shall have to spend all my evenings in the company of trees now that the Light must be tended, but of this I can hardly complain. I am sure the trees see and know everything. They will tell my thoughts to the wind, who will carry them to the Bay, and then they are taken everywhere, as far as the waves will travel. Sometimes I recite snippets of poems to them, and then I know it goes around the entire world, and every tree that is will hear it. And I think that perhaps they send their poems back to me… as if their swaying and stirring were a recitation. I like to think that this might be so.

Am I too fanciful? I wonder if George would understand me? He might. Perhaps it is because he is a painter and I have seen his pictures of the trees and they are beautiful—though Auntie Alis says they don't look very much like trees at all and she can't imagine who in his right mind would pay good money for such things. She makes me laugh. Thank goodness for her! I sometimes think I would drift off up into the clouds and out to the stars if it weren't for her good sense. And she is so attached to Mother. She is never rough with her body. I caught a glimpse of them this morning, and she bathes her like a child, kind and yet no-nonsense either. Mother is ever docile in her hands. It has been almost two years since her seizure, and yet surely we must not lose hope, surely its effects are not permanent. If only she might speak again!

Tad and I went over to Dr. Clowes to pick up our mail, and there was a letter for Mother from Montreal, from Aunt Louise, as it looked to be her handwriting. Flore had to pull us through a veritable bog, poor creature; the road is still almost impassible. The wagon swung about wildly, and Tad broke off some branches that got in our way. I put my hand on his arm to stop him; it just seems cruel to me, though he does not mean it so. Tad is a good man.

It is just that the saplings are always curious to see us—that's why they get in the way. I am sure that when I was little, I must have bothered Mother countless times by hanging on to her skirts; it was such a habit of mine. But she has ever been so gentle with me. I can't imagine Auntie Alis putting up with such nonsense. But I do think that sometimes the wind pushes the branches in front of me, just to cause mischief and make me feel that they do not want me to be here among them. Oh, the wind can be difficult. It is the one I understand the least. At times it truly hates me—I feel it so. Sometimes I put out my arms to catch it, just to say that I am not like those cruel men, but it won't let me.

April 28

I went out to the Point today—unaccountable occurrence! At first the wind was gentle, as if it were pleased to see me. But then, suddenly, it stopped and there was a strange stillness, as if there were some awkwardness between myself and the Bay. I grew constrained and anxious, and then without any warning, the wind came back but with such force it knocked me down.

It swept up my skirts and pushed back my hair—so vehement did it rush at me that I began to scramble toward the trees. But then I stopped and turned, asking it why it was so rough with me. It seemed almost ashamed and quieted instantly.

I sat there for some time, eyeing the Bay—somehow we are changed to each other this year. Perhaps it is just me that is changing, or perhaps I have become a little altered to it. I cannot explain it. But I felt it there, in our contemplation of each other. As if I am no longer a child…

I do not wish to remain a child, and yet my heart cried out to it that I was not changed, that I loved it still and could never bear to part with it!

May 1

More boats were supposed to come today, and Mr. Samuels was here from town. He brought Tad his usual supply of tobacco, and after a very long inspection and much frowning, Auntie A. agreed to purchase a new kettle. Then Mr. Samuels teased Tad and said that he had better not fall asleep but keep the Light going these next few nights because he heard at Owen Sound that Mr. Clarkson has become president of the Lake Carriers Association and will send out his boats no matter what the weather bodes. Indeed, Tad would never fall asleep and leave the Light unattended! Besides, he and Uncle Gilbert share the shifts, and even Auntie Alis and I are ever thinking of it. Living here as we do, not one of us can escape the Light, not for an instant. Sometimes it oppresses me. Last night I watched its revolutions flickering in my mirror until I fell asleep. I fancied that it was the piece of coal that Prometheus stole and that Zeus will see it and remember the theft afresh—and send us terrible, vengeful storms this summer.

I am glad that we have our own cottage and that Auntie A. and Uncle Gil are in the lighthouse. It seems like a great, towering beast to me sometimes, and I do not like to go into it—as if it swallows us alive. And then the chains and the rasping of the crank as Tad mounts the weights—it sounds like grating teeth and cracking jaws!

Mr. Samuels stayed for supper and told us of many accidents and fires because of boat collisions down at the docks. He said that last week the wind broke the moorings of the *Beverley* when the crew was still on board and that the tug had a hard time pulling her back, but the men were rescued from certain death. He says lots of boats have been drifting because of the strong currents. Mr. S. doesn't approve of the private yachts—he says that they should be prohibited from the commercial docks because they are such a menace. The Stewarts' boat is the *Coup de Grâce*; it hasn't arrived yet. I am relieved. The waters are still too dangerous.

Mr. Samuels thinks the Three Sisters are in a fearsome mood, having fought with one another all winter under the ice, and that there will be more than one terrible storm this summer. That's what the men call the huge waves that sometimes sink their boats, but I think they must be thinking of the Erinyes—the three Furies that came of Gaia and the blood of Ouranos. I am sure they must be the same. The men here think that it is their story, but I know that it belonged to the Greeks long ago. When I was little, one of the fishermen told me the Three Sisters are filled with a jealous hatred of each other, and that as one sister comes crashing down upon a boat, the others follow, coveting the vessel. But the other two come so fast behind the first that it gives the boat no time to steady itself—each sister trying to outdo the other in force and damage.

But it strikes me that perhaps I am wrong; perhaps they are the three Graiae sharing only one eye. Then it would be blindness and frustration, jealousy of the one who has the eye, and not the inexorable punishment of the Furies, that drive the sister waves to act thus. And yet, as such, still they are to be feared.

I think I have felt them—when I am swimming out farther than I should, out to where the waves get rough and then mistake me for a sea creature because no human should dare to swim out so far into the Bay.

Sometimes I imagine the Three Sisters, tied to each other as if cursed to do so long ago, and doomed eternally to stay bound together. Three temperaments, each nursing a great jealousy, and then the other two must follow the first's fury, adding her own. And always, not one, but three occasions for rage. No wonder there are so many storms in this Bay—my wonderful, dangerous Bay.

But this means that the boats are not likely to come today. Nor tomorrow perhaps. I wonder if he has changed since the fall. I am sorely aware that my imagination has created a form where only an outline was. His absence has prompted me to give him characteristics that perhaps are of my own making.

Sometimes I am appalled by how foolish I can be.

May 5

I am so provoked! Auntie Alis should stop her teasing. She says that I speak too freely and that a woman must bide her words around men, and that sometimes it is best to let a man find his own words without a woman interfering. Tad said nothing! I cannot believe it! Besides, those men are such great fools; Donald Brown is the worst of all of them, and I am sickened that Auntie should urge me to favor him.

She is afraid that I will never find a husband, and what would I do without one up here? It's not a place for a woman to live alone, she says. But I will be alone if I wish it. I wonder sometimes about that Mrs. Edwards and her strong words about women and the dignity of female work. I saw her picture in the newspaper, and I must admit I liked her face, though it was not pretty. Yet it was strong and intelligent. Not ugly. I have heard some men talking and they say she is ugly, but I think it is her intelligence that they dislike. To be sure, she is quick and sharp, and she sees things before they do, and that is why men do not like her, because it is not they who have shown her what to think.

Sometimes I think that I do not have such a high opinion of men as a general class, though it is important to make distinctions. There is, of course, Tad and Uncle Gilbert—and Dr. Latham was a distinguished scholar, respected by everyone. Even Miss Crabbage respected him—and we all feared her. She, in particular, puts me to thinking of snakes in grasses. Tad says that if you leave the snakes alone, they will not bother you—but sometimes the snakes do seek one out.

I am so thankful for Tad and Uncle Gil. And of course Dr. McTavish and Mr. Samuels and—oh, I contradict myself. George, too, I think. But Tad most of all. I like to look at his face the same way I like to look at the Bay. The Bay is best in the evening, just as the sun is sinking and a sort of deep gray begins to spread across it, and somehow it is both reasonable and beautiful all at the same time. Tad seems wise and impenetrable to me, and yet somehow I am not disturbed by my ignorance of all that he must know about the world.

Auntie Alis says that I am both pretty and smart, but it always sounds as a criticism coming from her!

I sound like a child today, sniveling and complaining. It is that Light! Tad says it is still burning the fuel too quickly and that we will be in trouble if he has to ask for more than our allotment. There are times when I wish the Bay would take that Light in one mighty wave and remove it forever.

Oh, I should not say that!

I do not mean it!

May 6

There are times when I wish that I did not write down my thoughts because then, when I read my scribblings over, I see how ridiculous I am. Yet Mr. Muir said I had a fine sensibility for the world around me. I am thrilled by the thought that his hands touched the pages of my letter and now I have touched the paper that his hands held as he wrote back to me. In this way our hands have touched, as have our thoughts. If I were ever to meet him, I think he would know that I understand his trees and would love them as much as he does. His trees must be beautiful, tall, graceful trees, all of them old and wise. My trees are much wilder, I think. They're a bit unruly sometimes—especially the cedars—more like sailors I suppose.

May 7

Mother fell asleep while I combed her hair this afternoon, and then I dressed it—just as she used to wear it—that it might be a surprise. When Tad came to get her, I heard him catch his breath, though I was careful to be fussing with the brushes at the bureau and have my back to him. How beautiful she looked!

Sometimes Tad is such a mystery to me. Mother's beauty is so exquisite, and yet I know him to prefer things that are a bit rough and unpolished. Except for the lens—that must be perfect and gleam like a diamond! I think it must be because he feels for the people so, out there on the water and if there should be trouble.

Once Auntie Alis told me that Tad is this way because their father had been a seaman and that he had impressed upon them both a respect for the power of the sea. Her father died rescuing people from the sea—when she was a little girl and Tad was just a young man.

How I hate it when Tad and Uncle Gil have to take the boat out in a storm. Auntie hugs him so fiercely when he comes back, and he must pet her until she quiets and releases him. It is the only time I ever see her affection for Uncle Gil. Tad says it is his duty as lightkeeper, but I am glad when the waves are so strong that they push the boats back to the shore. I am!

For a man, Tad is very neat and tidy and orderly, but he does not like fancy things. He doesn't like the Stewarts very well. I don't think he'll ever go to tea, though they invite him every year. I don't think he likes any of the families that come here for the holidays. It *is* rather odd to see them with their servants and all the baskets. Mrs. Stewart brings her own maid and crates and crates of china. I love the cups and the silver tea set, though I am afraid to drink my tea. Imagine if I were to break a cup. I should be ashamed, and yet I still love them so; they are absurdly fragile.

May 8

I think I will go to the Basin after supper to see if there are any boats. Yet if Allan is there, how shall I greet him? He kissed me on the lips when he left last fall, and I was so surprised. It was really only a peck, I suppose. He will be thirteen years old this year, and I think that I will not be able to tutor him for much longer. It was so sudden. What did he mean by it?

I didn't expect him to do such a thing, and now I cannot tell whether I am displeased or not. There is a part of me that is a little sad to see him grow up. I am only six years older, but still I am a young woman and he has become…a youth. He will want a man now to teach him.

Allan is a fine-looking lad. He is very fair, and his eyes are a curious and lively blue. But his feet are enormous and his boots sometimes so clumsy. He is a playful rascal at times, and sometimes I must be wary to be the prim teacher. Especially around George. But I think I must call him Mr. Stewart and not George any longer; he is very…reserved in some ways, even though I have known him since I was ten. I remember Allan, too, when he was a very little boy and Mrs. Stewart asked Mother if I would watch him. Allan has always been like a puppy, and sometimes I have a terrible time keeping him out of trouble. I am sure George thought I was party to the untying of his boat last year. It was terrible! Five of his canvases were lost—completely ruined!—but it was one of Allan's ill-advised pranks. I could not condemn him in front of their stepfather—he is so awful with his punishments! But I am sure that George thinks I am a foolish, irresponsible person.

I do hope the Stewarts won't come until the storms are over. Mr. Samuels says we are due for a big one for certain. He says that whenever his legs start aching in a certain way, he can tell a storm is brewing. I think Tad half believes him. I certainly believe him.

"Not like November '81, though," he always says. "There'll never be a storm like that one again in my day." And then that awful story about all the bodies from the *Fairweather* and the boy he found, drowned.

I can see the Bay from my window, and that dark blue color is unmistakably ominous. Besides, the leaves of the aspen are trembling and revealing their silvery underbellies—a sure sign of a storm.

The trees always warn us, if only we would heed them.

May 11

I wish that George's paintings had not been lost last summer. I am sure he must still think poorly of me.

Sometimes my own insignificance oppresses me. I am like the trees in this, am I not? We pay so little attention to them. And yet, how beautiful they are. How unpredictable and moody and wonderful and intelligent…

I think I will go down to the Basin when Uncle Gil goes this afternoon and perhaps walk over to the Lodge, just to see if the boats are in or if any are coming. I do hope that the Stewarts will wait, for it is far too dangerous to sail.

May 15

The Stewarts came early this morning! The Bay was quite rough, and they had a few anxious moments navigating the channel into the Basin. Not Mrs. Stewart though, or Effie with her new baby—they will come in a few days. But George and Allan, and their stepfather, have all arrived safely. They brought a cow again this year and two horses. The poor beasts seemed quite glad to be on land once again and were all quite docile. There is a new man to take care of the horses, and it seems Susan has agreed to be the Lodge's housekeeper for the summer. She brought her daughter, Charlotte, to help with the housework. Charlotte is just a little thing, only eight, and quite shy.

Allan is almost as tall as I am! I was quite astounded. He will tower over me by the end of the summer, I am sure of it. At first I was confused about how to behave with him. No doubt initially I was a little cool, but honestly I think he has quite forgotten his improper kiss. He whooped and whistled and pumped my hand up and down when he saw me; it was quite a display, and I was embarrassed in front of George. He shook hands with me quietly and asked after Tad and Mother, and then attended to the boats. Old Mr. Stewart was in a terrible mood, and he spoke quite roughly to Uncle G., as if he were a boat hand.

There seem to be even more baskets and crates this year, if that is possible. There is quite a stack of furniture and many carpets all rolled up, and Susan had two of her heavy irons in her bag instead of crating them. She is such a funny one about pressing her precious linens.

Auntie A. thinks that Mrs. Stewart pines for her first husband—George and Allan's real father. He died of influenza many years ago, when Allan was still a little baby. But she must be very rich to come on holiday here year after year. I do not care at all for their stepfather. He is harsh and very stern-looking, and terribly grim in his demeanor. I was truly reassured to discover that there is no shared blood between George and old Mr. Stewart, though he is cousin to Mrs. Stewart's first husband and that is why he shares the same last name. I am so glad he isn't their blood father. Am I uncharitable? George is almost twenty years older than Allan, and I think he tries to be a good brother. Allan is really quite wild—not in a bad sort of way but...in an animal sort of way. His stepfather is very severe, and so I cannot in good conscience betray Allan, in any of his pranks, to such a rigid and exacting disciplinarian.

May 16

Mrs. Stewart and Effie—I must remember to call her Mrs. Ferguson the first time I see her—will come in two days with her little girl. Allan says that George is going to do a great deal of painting and that he, Allan, is going to catch the largest fish that ever was seen on Georgian Bay. George laughed and said that if a reputable source confirmed the catch, he would give him a dollar. Allan jumped about as if he already had his dollar, and of course he upset one of the boats, and then suddenly he was in the water. The Basin is not so deep near the shore, but Allan is not a strong swimmer, and I rushed to help him. I did not realize it, but George was close behind me, and he pulled me back a little roughly. Then he stepped into the water to rescue Allan, who was bellowing that he was drowning and thoroughly enjoying all the commotion.

I must have been nursing my arm, though I don't recall that it was really hurting me—but Uncle Gil saw me and asked me about it. I so wished he hadn't, but I think Uncle Gil was vexed at George's rough manner. George was very sorry for pulling me back so hard, and he apologized twice. And then he inquired if I were wet and seemed anxious that I should be dry, for there was a wind stirring, and it is true that the air is still a little chill. I am sure that I was brusque in my response and awkward. I do not like to be fussed over.

When I started to walk back, he escorted me to the gate and seemed so anxious that I truly regretted revealing my discomfort. I suppose that my arm did hurt a little, but it was an inconsequential thing, and I was sorry for Uncle G.'s remark. George peered anxiously into my face—it was very peculiar—and he said, "You are not really injured, are you?" I was strangely pleased but also embarrassed by these inquiries. And then I could not look at him and said I had to get back home. I ran all the way back to our cottage like a fool!

May 17

Uncle Gil says the Stewarts always bring trouble with them. He says the Peninsula is no place for the cottagers and the holiday boaters, and that they should take their amusements to safer waters and not endanger the lives of the men who have to fish them out of the Bay when their boats capsize.

But I don't care what he says. I am glad the holiday families are here. It means the summer is coming.

Uncle Gil can be quite severe about the boaters, but I think it is because of his time at French River. Auntie

Alis told me that he was a river man there, and that in the spring he used to herd the logs into booms as the ice was melting. She said that was how he injured his back so badly one year—that he fell one time and the logs crushed him. But he is still very strong—Tad says that he is stronger than Flore even, and it is true, I think. I have seen him unhitch her and pull our sled through the snow by himself.

Tad says the blackflies will be bad this year—he feels it in *his* bones. Honestly, between Father and Mr. Samuels's bones, we shall have a forecast for the entire summer!

May 18

Mrs. Stewart arrived today with Effie and her newborn girl. Oh, she is an adorable little baby, and Effie has become so fat and pleased with herself. I cannot believe she is just two years older than I am and now she has a baby! She is like a ripe, red berry and looked quite funny in her tight clothes. Effie is Mrs. Stewart's cousin—or her cousin's daughter rather, but she calls her Aunt. Her husband owns several ships, and his business is mostly in Owen Sound. Auntie Alis says Effie married well and that they are quite wealthy.

I suppose that we are poor. I haven't thought about it very much, but it is true that Effie has many more dresses than I do, and I have only one really fancy dress. It was Mother's, and she said it is from Paris—I adore it. It is so mysterious—a dark blue velvet, almost black. Auntie Alis told me Mother comes from money.

It was my grandfather who paid for my schooling. But why doesn't he come to us, then? Auntie A. won't tell me, but I think he and Tad do not care for each other. Perhaps he blames Tad for Mother's illness.

Effie gave me a beautiful shawl—it is a wonderful, mysterious green color and fringed. It is so soft and very warm. I dearly love it! Effie has ever been generous to me. She let me hold the baby—just for a minute—and Corrie (that is her nickname for Corine) patted my nose with her little hands. We all laughed, and Effie said that she liked me. She is such a darling, little, little thing.

But Allan…oh dear, it was awful. He snatched her from me and began bouncing her about. Effie screamed and George had to be quite stern with him. I wondered—it's a silly idea really, but it did cross my mind—that Allan might be a little jealous of our attentions to the baby. He protested that he meant no harm, and I had to soothe him. I took him down to the old delivery dock to see if the beavers were there, I think he knew it was all a pretext to get him away as he was quite grumpy.

Mrs. Stewart gave me a little gold necklace and tiny, black pearl earrings that she says come all the way from a market in Peking. She, too, is so kind to me. I put them in my ears, and she seemed pleased. Effie says they make my eyes look very blue. She also gave me some lace and a bolt of a very nice gray silk for Mother, and I could tell Auntie Alis was pleased to receive it, though she would not say so. Auntie is proud, I think. Tad wrote a note of thanks, and I am to take it to them tomorrow. Auntie A. says there is enough to make two dresses—one will be for me, and I think I can persuade her to add some lace to the throat and cuffs.

I do wish Father would come for tea and see the inside of the Lodge. It is very beautiful! And Mrs. Stewart's carpets and all the wood make it seem very rich somehow. George always brings some of his pictures, and he has a kind of studio library off the front hallway. But I have only seen it from the doorway. It reminds me a little of the library at St. Edmund's, though there are paintbrushes and rags all over the desk and not half so many books. This year I caught a glimpse of the painting he put up over the fireplace—I think it is of a copse of trees at the Point, but I am too shy to ask if I might go closer to look. It is one of my favorite places; the cedars form a kind of archway, and it feels as if one were in a chapel, and if I look up, it seems as if all the trees are swaying as they sing hymns of praise to the sky.

May 19

I almost forgot to tell Mother—but Effie brought her sister-in-law, Caroline, with her. I am to call her Miss Ferguson. She is quite beautiful in an aloof kind of way, and she is a few years older than Effie, and I find her quite haughty. I do not think that I will like her. She was very chilly when I met her and would not take my hand, and it felt quite awkward to have it left hanging in midair like that. But perhaps she is not used to shaking hands. It is our way—Tad says that in the old country you must always take a person's hand in greeting, and that women must always give a little press with their thumb to another woman's hand, as it is a sign of goodwill. How they teased me at St. E.'s for this habit of mine!

I do not think that Effie is entirely at ease around her sister-in-law. For one thing, Miss Ferguson is constantly correcting her grammar. It is true that Effie is not well spoken—which is odd since her name comes from the Latin for "eloquence"! But it makes her flustered to be corrected all the time. Miss Ferguson seemed surprised I had taken two years at college and quizzed me on my studies. I gather she is well read, and we spoke in French for a few minutes. I am so glad Mother tutored me all those years before she became ill. I was not in the least intimidated by Miss Ferguson, and her French pronunciations are correct but lifeless. She aggravated me somehow—it was not as if she were truly interested in me, but wished to find out some weakness, some inadequacy in me.

I was tempted to ask her a question in Latin or even Greek, but I did not. I am glad I did not—though I grew hot with indignation under her scrutiny. She turned to George and said that my French was really quite good. She expressed surprise, and he nodded. I was so angry! I left right afterward and am afraid I did not thank Mrs. Stewart properly for her gifts. I will have to make sure that I do so.

May 23

Dr. McTavish arrived on Wednesday and will be in the smaller lodge. I think all of *his* crates but one are filled with books. I am always so glad to see him, though I wonder if the birds are quite so sanguine about his return, especially as the nets appear. But he does them no harm and is very conscientious about checking the nets. He has brought a young man with him, Mr. Thompson, who is to help him. I am relieved I will not have to do all the assisting this summer, as I found it quite taxing last year—though Allan and I always profit from Dr. McTavish's commentary on the birds. He says he will finish his book this year, but I have heard that for three summers at least.

Allan is quite awful—he can do such an imitation of Dr. McTavish and will pull at a beard just in his manner and drop all his h's and roll his r's and wave an imaginary grrreebe about in his hand. I shouldn't laugh, but I cannot help it; it is so like Dr. McTavish, and Allan looks at me with such triumph when he gets me to laugh in spite of myself. In a way I am responsible, since I was the one to imitate Dr. McT. first one afternoon last summer—indeed, what was I thinking, knowing how impressionable Allan is and his penchant for mischief? Now it is a kind of secret joke between us. Allan still teases me about it. He says I am a bad influence and that I have not set the proper tone of behavior appropriate to the teaching and guidance of a young boy's mind, and that I encourage all his bad ways, and that as a result he is not responsible for his actions. And then I am laughing again. Honestly, he is becoming quite a handful.

Mr. Thompson is a most peculiar-looking person. He is quite bald (Allan says that he shaves his head; he has seen him do it) and is very tall and very thin. He is an ornithologist and is extremely polite and a little taciturn. He seems to seek out George's company. I saw him standing near George's easel, and George was explaining something about his painting to him. I think he is doing a picture of the two buoys that mark the entrance to the Basin. Allan says he is calling it *Good and Evil,* and I am curious to see it, though I dare not ask.

May 30

We have had a most tumultuous week. Mr. Thompson was lost on the escarpment for three days and two nights, and the men had to search and search for him. It turned out he was only a mile or so away, but the forest is so thick that I can easily understand how he might get lost. He is covered in terrible bites from being in the bush, and Dr. McTavish is furious with him. I am sorry for him. I took him one of Auntie Alis's ointments and told him about the time that Dr. McTavish was lost for a week and how we had given him up for dead. He seemed a little comforted. But oh, his poor bald head with all those bites!

And then the government inspectors came! We had to feed them for three whole days, and all at Tad's expense. I do not see why they had to stay with us and did not remain aboard their ship. I have had to sleep in Mother's room, and she has been terribly agitated by all the commotion. And they looked at everything—everything! Tad had to wind and unwind the cranks, and Uncle Gilbert stood to attention like a soldier while they checked the stores, and then in their sly way implied that he had secretly been selling the supplies. I was so afraid that Uncle G. would strike the man—and he would have deserved it! And then one of them pored over the log for ever so long that I thought he must have found something amiss. They were not at all like the previous inspectors—those men were quite jolly and not the least interested in the lighthouse.

But I think we are finally returning to calm.

We have been invited to tea tomorrow with Mrs. Stewart, and Auntie Alis and I will go. She has almost completed my dress, and I have promised to do all the housework if she will only finish it. I think it suits me. Auntie A. says it sets off my hair and eyes, and she has made it so cleverly, just like the picture I gave her. She did not even object to the lace!

June 2

I was so angry that I could not write yesterday. I was afraid of what words I might put down. She is truly nasty and spiteful. Poor Allan! Innocent fool, he had no idea of what he was getting himself into. And I am utterly wretched.

Auntie A. and I went to tea. Mr. Thompson was there, too, though Dr. McTavish and old Mr. Stewart were not in attendance. Auntie A. was nervous but pleased to be there, and I felt splendid in my new dress. Though I was slightly ashamed that I had made sure to peruse Mother's books of French poetry for ammunition against Miss Ferguson should the need arise. I could tell I looked becoming by the way that Mr. Thompson bowed to me, and even George seemed to approve as he took my hand.

Mrs. Stewart is rather formal about her tea, so we waited while her housekeeper supervised the dishware and the setting out of the scones and cakes. Susan and Auntie Alis do not get along at all. I am sure that Susan looks down upon us and thinks that we have no business at all coming to tea.

I chatted with Mr. Thompson about his nets and the birds he and Dr. McT. had caught and examined when George asked me if I was going to tutor Allan again this summer. Truly I still feel sorry for him. Miss Ferguson seemed engrossed in a conversation with George, and I don't know why, but for some reason I felt my spirits growing a bit depressed. Eventually George joined us. Mr. Thompson had just finished instructing me on how to tell the difference between the pileated woodpecker (*Dryocopus pileatus*) and the yellow-bellied sapsucker (*Sphyrapicus varius*). I already knew the difference quite well, but I allowed this instruction since he meant it so kindly.

I didn't quite know how to answer George's question, as there was a part of me that had assumed I would continue with his studies, and yet I wasn't sure the Stewarts would wish it. So there was an awkward silence. Allan finally broke it by saying somewhat sheepishly that he was getting too old to be tutored, and besides, these were his summer holidays. I smiled and said that I would give him one examination and that if he remembered his Latin declensions and recited them correctly, then he could have the rest of the summer off. Allan brightened, and he came over to me.

"Truly," he said. "Do you mean it truly?"

"Yes," I said, still smiling. He is such a scamp! And I knew quite well how unlikely his success would be. I must admit that I had already planned to introduce him to more of the classics this summer and had begun to do some reading in preparation.

"All right. I'll do it!" he exclaimed. "Latin is of no use to anyone anyway! I don't see why I must study it."

It was then that Mr. Thompson broke in and discoursed quite earnestly and at length on the importance of learning Latin for the sciences, and so forth. He was so serious that I had to smile just a little—he pronounces his words with ever so tiny a lisp that at times I have to work hard to keep the corners of my mouth from curling upward.

Then Allan began to clown and started to name everything and everyone in the room in the most absurd Latin.

He called Corrie an *infans adoranda*.

George was an *artistus robustus* and I, his *magistra formidalae*. Indeed I had to bite my tongue to prevent myself from correcting his vocabulary and egregious disagreements in gender, number, and case!

Then he expounded upon our habits as if we were all birds and gave us all sorts of ridiculous characteristics. He made Effie smile when he said that she was either a mourning dove (a cooing and gentle creature) or the sora, I think referencing her surprisingly large feet for someone of so short a stature—though I was more than a little scandalized by his boldness. Fortunately, Effie has the best of temperaments, and she laughed quite heartily at him.

But still, there was something in Allan, the edge of something that I could not quite place, and it troubled me.

He said that his mother—bowing to her—was the tundra swan, beautiful and noble. His stepfather was an eastern kingbird—"known in the scientific world as the *Tyrannus tyrannus*." Mr. Thompson coughed slightly at this, but did not contradict him. Effie giggled a bit nervously, and so Allan took this as encouragement to continue.

Auntie Alis was the ruffed grouse, respectable, dignified, and to be heard thumping her carpets in the spring. Mr. Thompson was the Wilson's snipe, whose erratic takeoff made it difficult for hunters to follow him through the woods—rather heartlessly referencing, I thought, the poor man's recent mishap!

I pretended to glower at him when he said that I was the dark-eyed junco, preferring solitude to the company of other birds.

But then—oh my! He said Miss Ferguson was a shrike, possessed of extraordinary eyesight and known to impale its prey upon thorns and barbs, and then leave them there for future consumption. She truly did glower at him for that!

"And George," Allan said quietly, turning to him last, and looking first to him and then to me. "George is the great horned owl of the Lodge. Silent, mysterious, searching for his mate as he passes above us in soundless flight, under a moonlit sky."

It was quite a poetic statement coming from Allan! And almost against my will I turned to look at George. It was then I noticed that his eyes are indeed an amber-gray, flecked with tiny spots of gold—just like an owl's.

There was a pause.

"*Bubo virginianus*," quipped Mr. Thompson, breaking the silence. Then Allan laughed harshly and turned away from us sharply.

"Allan, you are quite a skilled dramatist," said Miss Ferguson quietly, and immediately I sensed danger. She smiled and moved closer to him. "Do you perform—impersonations?"

I felt my body freeze. *Allan, you mustn't*, I whispered to myself. But it was too late. There was a strange recklessness in him.

"Of course I do," he said.

"Do someone for us," purred Miss Ferguson.

"Who would you like?" demanded Allan boldly.

I think she knew that Dr. McTavish and Mr. Stewart were close by. But Allan couldn't see them because they were still in conference and were standing back in the hallway.

"Your best one," said Miss Ferguson, shrugging her shoulders. Somehow she must have known!

I sat filled with an awful foreboding—paralyzed with dread. Oh, that I might have stopped him! Why did I not think of some interruption? Allan, of course, did Dr. McTavish. It was an extravagant performance—terrible! In Allan's strange mood, it came out as cruel and mocking, a gross insult to the great man.

The rest of us could see Mr. Stewart and Dr. McTavish pause in the doorway and watch his performance. Old Mr. Stewart's face was a vivid red, and I don't think I have ever seen him look so angry before.

"Wherever did you learn to roll your r's like that?" Miss Ferguson gushed, pretending not to see Dr. McTavish, nor Mr. Stewart glaring at Allan from the doorway.

"Margie taught me!" Allan said ingenuously. "You should see *her* do Dr. McTavish!"

And then Caroline turned to me and said quite sweetly, "It seems that Allan's studies encompass much more than Latin, do they not, Miss Brice?"

It was then that Allan saw Dr. McTavish with his stepfather in the doorway, and his face fell.

I did not answer her.

Auntie A. and I got up immediately. I thanked Mrs. Stewart for a lovely afternoon, but I am sure I did it abruptly. I blurted out something to Dr. McTavish, but I could not look at George. As I was leaving, I took Allan's hand briefly. I could not help but feel sorry for him. He looked utterly crushed, and my mortification seemed to pale in comparison to his.

"I am still going to test you on your Latin," I whispered, pressing his hand firmly. "And for heaven's sake—behave yourself!"

Shrike indeed! Mr. Thompson has since told me that it is the only truly carnivorous songbird.

June 4

It has been two days since Mrs. Stewart's tea, and I am still filled with mortification. I know that I must apologize to Dr. McTavish, but I have lacked the courage, and I know that I cannot avoid this for many days longer, else the wound will fester and the insult grow worse.

Allan's words keep ringing in my ears. "Margie taught me!" And my face still burns with shame.

All this has had a strange effect on me. It is as if there is some deeper, sterner voice within me that will not let me hide away and wait out the storm. Auntie A. has said that I have taken it too seriously, that it sits too heavily with me—though I know she is not pleased.

But I felt strongly that I must seek out serious reflection, and so yesterday morning I decided to saddle Flore and ride over to Clootie's Point, taking the trail that the foresters have cut. I had to use the Mill Road, and my heart is still so broken to think what they have done! It is not as bad here at the light station as in other places, but along the Mill Road, the stumps are scattered everywhere. It is the beautiful white pines—they have killed all the tall, straight pines and left only their unwanted remains! Tad says they have cut down and gathered every stick of serviceable wood from the Peninsula—that the men who did this were mad for lumber.

Yet even though I am loathe to traverse the Mill Road, I felt that I must go—and to Clootie's especially. I felt that I might find my courage there; not just the courage to make the apology that I know is required of me, but something truer and stronger. Something that might instruct me on the lesson I must take from these strange events.

And Clootie's is such a stark place, perfectly suited to my meditations: there is no turf, but just great sheets of rock that stretch for miles in either direction. It is a lonely, rough spot, and I think one feels the company of the soul there. I do not think it is a place that abides deception, and it is certainly no place to seek easy comfort for a guilty conscience.

Tad once told me that Clootie means "devil," and that this is one of the most treacherous stretches of the

Bay because of the shoals that hide beneath the water and give no warning to a ship. Without a doubt, it is a grim and bleak spot, but I have always thought perhaps the devil brings the worst of temptations here, and that in seeing them, one might discern the truth and be made strong and whole again.

I am quite in earnest when I say that I seek to conduct myself differently toward Allan. I realize now that I regard him very much as a brother, as both my ward and companion, and that he does look up to me. It is true that I am only one person in a larger constellation—which includes the good influences of George, but sadly also Allan's weak mother and his exacting, cruel stepfather. I know that to be a truly good influence, I must behave differently. I have felt such a great shame, and I wince when I think of his recent performance—the fruit of a seed that I cannot deny is of my sowing. I seem such a silly and frivolous creature in my own eyes. And no doubt in those of others.

But perhaps I should not have gone to Clootie's. For now I feel more wretched than ever!

I tied Flore to a branch, making sure she had a patch of shade, and then walked down toward the water. I did not intend to stay for so long, but the day was clear and still—all grays. Even the sky looked at me as a dour Puritan might. I felt no disapproval from the rocks, but more a somber seriousness—as if the lessons of the soul were no light matter here. I looked around me and saw the stunted trees, the stern outcroppings, and the stubborn brush pushing up between the cracks. I listened to the waves and the wind, and I shivered, for I could not help but think that perhaps I had wandered into

Tartaros and that I might never return should I stray too far. And yet I knew my way along the rocks. I knew them all to be part of the wildness, and yet strangely they are dutiful—true to a course and to a place. They did not coddle or soothe me.

Perhaps Clootie's is a hard, dour place, but it, too, is part of this Bay and is truly one of my teachers. I think I must have just sat there for an hour, perhaps more—crouched on a large, flat rock, hugging my knees to my chest, watching the water and letting my thoughts spread out across the ledges and settle in amongst all the cracks and crevices. I cannot remember what I thought about, but I felt my resolve returning and—it is so hard to explain!—but I know I emerged with a sense of purpose, and I was no longer afraid to speak to Dr. McTavish.

I should have gone back then, but instead I wandered out onto the beach for a while, and I took off my boots to feel the water, as I always do. At length I grew hungry, and I went to Flore to get the food that I had packed in her saddlebag. I ate it, and as I felt my hunger easing, my mind became so clear and flat that it seemed to stretch out with the sheets of rock and go on endlessly. Just as I was finishing, I heard a voice behind me saying, "This is a strange place to find a young lady taking her lunch."

I started and whirled around to find George standing behind me, a sketchbook under his arm and a canvas bag over his shoulder. I had no warning of his approach, and he had caught me unawares. I hid my bare feet beneath me and moved closer to Flore, not in the least prepared to meet anyone—least of all George.

I felt flustered, and before I could catch the words, they were out of my mouth.

"What are *you* doing here, Mr. Stewart!"

I regretted my tone almost immediately, for I did not mean the words to sound the way they did; I said it like an accusation, as if he were an intruder trespassing on *my* land. Nor did I know why I addressed him so formally—

"I could ask the same of you," he replied mildly.

He paused and we looked at each other awkwardly. Somehow I managed to get my boots on as he stood there watching me. I grew quite furious with him, but he seemed impervious to my discomfort, even amused.

"What brings you to Clootie's?" he asked. "Such a forlorn spot." Then he hesitated. "Allan has called you a dark-eyed junco, but even so, this is a rather isolated place, don't you think?"

I don't know why—perhaps it was the bidding of the rocks—but I simply told him the truth.

"I wanted the courage to apologize to Dr. McTavish, and so I came out here to find it."

"Well, did you? Did you find it?"

"Yes," I said. And that was all. I turned away from him.

I shortened the stirrup, thinking to sit sidesaddle until I was out of view—but still, I was not at my ease with him. I took Flore's reins and swung myself up onto the saddle.

He watched me with some uneasiness, and before I could pull away, he took Flore's bridle and held her.

He tried to smile and said, "Now, Marged." He

used my Christian name, as he has always done, though I had called him Mr. Stewart. "Don't take this too hard. It is not quite so bad as you think, is it?"

"Do you really mean that?" I demanded. It was Clootie's talking again, daring him to speak untruths in its presence.

He looked grave all of a sudden, as if discerning my real mood for the first time. "Don't you think it was…just a bit of…Allan's foolishness?"

"No, it was not," I answered quickly.

I bent forward and tried to lift his hand from Flore's bridle, but he would not let me.

"What is it that troubles Miss Brice?" he asked. I thought I heard derision in his tone.

I don't know why I said it, but it came out of me as if in a torrent. It angered me to think of him treating me like a child, as if he thought I was to be mollified.

"You think I am a silly young girl, don't you?" I told him. "Perhaps my life is small and unimportant in your eyes. But I have had more experience of the world than you might think. I have seen little compromises that poison people a drop at a time, each day, as they rise and go about their work and share the day together. And I have seen something more foul—something that destroys innocence and goodness by violating a sacred trust."

I think I was crying as I said this and furious with myself, but still I did not stop.

"I will not encourage Allan's—thoughtlessness—because I am weak and afraid that—that I will be lonely without his company. If he must grow up and be a man, then I must help him to it through my own conduct."

Suddenly I understood Tad and the Light, and before me I saw his tired, haggard face and his eyes, always oriented toward that beacon.

I knew it was Clootie's speaking through me and out into my words. George stepped back, a little astonished, but still he did not release his hand from Flore.

I did not like to be held there that way, and I think I must have scowled fiercely. I am sure that the frown that soon appeared on his brow only mirrored my own. There was a pause, and I pulled my hat down to evade his eyes. He spoke his next words abruptly, almost harshly.

"Why did you leave the College? Why did you not finish your degree?"

I gasped. I was not prepared for such a question! He seemed to ask it in such an unfriendly way, as if to wound me. What gossip had he heard? Was he mocking me? I blushed with shame thinking of Miss Crabbage—and her evil insinuations. George could not think that I was guilty of them! I could not bear that George should think it true!

I drew Flore back sharply, finally forcing him to let go of her bridle. I wished to defend myself against the false imputations I read in his question! But my pride prevented me.

I rode away from him at a gallop. Once I turned back to see if he was still standing there, but I saw no one. I shivered and wondered if it had really been George—or if an apparition had been sent to tempt me with something I could not fathom.

June 6

Dr. McTavish and I are friends again. I am so relieved!

I could not go to him yesterday because Auntie Alis wanted me to accompany her to church and that took up all of the day, but I went right after breakfast this morning.

Mr. Thompson answered my knock and then removed to the back room, listening to everything, I am sure. But Dr. McTavish wouldn't let me speak first. When I came in, he just took my two hands in his own and said in his gruff but tender way, "Now, now. We're to be friends, aren't we? Haven't we always been so?" He wouldn't let me apologize. I think he knew how full my heart was. He gave me a linen to wipe my eyes, and then he showed me his exquisite drawing of a Bohemian waxwing (*Bombycilla garrulus*) and whispered to me that Mr. Thompson was quite jealous of its plumage (it does have a rather full head of feathers) and that he's had to keep it hidden from him.

I didn't stay long, and Mr. Thompson escorted me to the gate. He kept muttering, "Splendid! Just splendid."

I am so grateful. Dr. McTavish is a dear, dear man!

June 8

I have been true to my word. Yesterday Allan and I began our studies of the classics, and I had all my old books and worksheets down, with Dr. Latham's funny notations all over them. Allan, of course, did not pass his Latin examination, though he did better than

I expected. But forgetting how to conjugate *poner* was really quite inexcusable.

I have also wanted to study some of the Greek classic texts with him, and so yesterday we began to read parts of *The Iliad* down in front of the old boathouse, but before I knew it, we were discussing Homer, and then he wished to hear more about mythology and then we were on to the labors of Hercules. I am quite content to introduce him to the Greek works—perhaps it might be best to set our Latin grammar aside for now.

Allan has a good ear for languages. If he puts his mind to it, he can recall and repeat almost everything he has heard, often after only one lesson. After two hours or so, we walked leisurely back to the Lodge, and I told him about my correspondence with Mr. Muir. He seemed quite interested, and he told me of a former tutor of his and of his interest in natural history. I have never seen Allan so animated about any subject, and indeed I am now wondering if he is not more suited to scientific pursuits. I should be delighted if this were the case, though I have so little to offer him by way of instruction on this topic. But he was very eager to explain the classifications of all sorts of animals (becoming my instructor for once!), and I took the opportunity to echo Mr. Thompson's point about the importance of Latin for such studies.

I am amazed at his easy memory of such voluminous detail. I think we must perhaps set aside my beloved Horace—and even Hesiod and Aeschylus for a time. I shall ask Dr. Clowes to see if he might obtain the works of Mr. Darwin by post, since Allan is interested in these things. I think it wise to follow in the steps of his interests and to nurture a sense of scholarly discipline based on his natural inclinations. The Stewarts are planning to stay through to October, so it will be well for Allan to have these occupations. Old Mr. Stewart has taken charge of his other lessons, and they are going rather dreadfully, or so Allan says. Mr. Stewart has not forbidden his lessons with me, but Allan tells me that they have advertised for a tutor. Perhaps no one will care to come such a distance. But I am not offended—I have deserved it!

June 13

It is quite late, but I must chronicle yet another of my follies! Will they ever cease?

Today, after our walk, Allan and I returned to the Lodge, and he went off in search of Susan to see if he could persuade her to "release from bondage" some of her biscuits. I paused in the hallway when I saw that the door to George's studio was open. There was no one in the room, and the house was quiet and still. I could see his easel set up near the window, and a space had been cleared by the fireplace for a chair. I observed that he had been working on a large canvas; it seemed to be a portrait of a woman, but I could not tell of whom. My curiosity got the better of me and I slipped silently into the room, planning only to take a peek and then step back out.

Upon closer inspection, I recognized the outlines of Miss Ferguson on the canvas. He had painted in the background with rough, bold strokes and had blocked in the red fabric of the chair. Her dress, too, was painted in strong lines, and George had sketched in the outlines of a pearl necklace at her throat. He had started to detail her hair, and though the contours of her face were still unfinished, they were strangely precise—he had caught the cold, glittering gray of her eyes and the thin lines of her mouth. I wondered if she were pleased with it.

I should have left immediately, but I thought I might have a closer look at the canvas over the fireplace and determine whether or not it was my grove of trees that he had painted. I had begun to suspect that George and I had frequented some of the same nooks and crannies of Cape Prius, but without the other knowing. I had always thought of the cedar chapel as my secret, but looking at the painting, I realized that it was not. George had gone there and painted their smooth, twisting trunks and the dusky, damp shadows cast by their branches upon the forest floor. Somehow he had also painted the light in its sudden stillness. Even more remarkable, I knew the trees to be moving—gently trying to tease the light into laughter, and the light playfully refusing to move even a muscle…

I was entranced by the painting. I am quite sure that I pressed my hands together, and, holding my breath, I stood before it just as if I were in the copse and saying my prayers among the cedars. I thought it a most beautiful painting!

He must have come in without me knowing it, for I am sure that the room was empty when I entered. I do not know how long George stood there before saying in a low voice, "What are *you* doing here, Miss Brice?"

It was an echo of my address to him at Clootie's Point—I recognized it immediately. It sounded so unfriendly! Yet I suppose that I did deserve it. His voice was so unexpected that it made me jump, and I looked at him, horrified—as if I had been caught in a terrible act. His eyes were so dark and burning that they seemed to accuse me of trespassing into his private studio and—I don't know what else!

I stepped back unthinkingly, and without intending it—truly it was an accident!—I backed up against his easel, tripping over his box of paints and brushes. Before I knew it, I had fallen, taking the easel and thc painting with me onto the floor. I lay sprawled in a disastrous heap, the smell of oils and turpentine filling the air with a terrible pungency. I don't think that I have ever been so horrified at my own clumsiness! I was sure that I had ruined Miss Ferguson's portrait and that George would hate me for it—and be justified. In my mind, I saw the other canvases that Allan had destroyed—and myself by association. I could only think that George would believe me to be deliberately careless around his work—and the thought left me paralyzed.

It was George who lifted me off the floor, for I was not capable of any movement, so appalled was I at what I had done.

My face must have twisted as a sharp pain shot through my ankle.

"I've ruined it, haven't I?" I cried. "I've ruined her picture! I didn't mean to—please believe that I didn't mean to!" My eyes were blinded with tears, so I could not read his expression.

"Damn the picture!" he growled. "Have you hurt yourself?"

There was a sound of footsteps in the hallway, and Allan and Effie came rushing into the room. Effie let out a little scream, and Allan nearly dropped his biscuits when he saw the heap behind me. He gave out a long, low whistle.

"Oh, Margie," he said. "Now you've done it."

George told him to shut up—and to run and get Dr. McTavish.

Effie took me to her room. She helped to bathe my ankle in cold water. I am to do this three times a day until the swelling has gone down. I've really twisted it, and it is quite painful if I place any weight on it. Uncle Gil came and carried me home, and Auntie Alis says that I am not to go outside until I am properly healed.

I told Tad and Mother how it all happened. I knew Mother was sympathetic and that she understood my distress though of course she cannot speak. Tad didn't say a word about it, but just patted my head and then told me to go to bed.

But I don't think I shall be able to. I keep seeing the canvas on the floor—and that awful smell! To be sure, I have ruined Miss Ferguson's picture!

Six

"Did you get some sleep?" Clare was handing me a bottle of wine and smiling up into my face.

"I slept almost all afternoon," I said as I led her out to the deck. "My apologies if I seemed a bit groggy this morning."

"You did look pretty beat. Am I allowed to ask you about the diaries, now that you're properly awake?"

"Allowed?"

"Didn't Miss Brice swear you to secrecy?"

I smiled. "No, Clare—this isn't exactly top-secret stuff."

"Good! Because I've been dying to ask you. Is your Perdita mystery solved?"

"I only got through the first diary." I paused, enjoying her suspense while I extended the awning.

She eyed me wryly. "You know, these days you've only about five seconds before you lose your audience."

I laughed. "The less-than-five-second answer is no. There's not even mention of a Perdita in the first diary."

She looked disappointed but then grew very interested as I told her about the Brices and Marged's relationship with Allan and George Stewart. "Not the painter!" she exclaimed.

"The same. As you may know, his family once owned all the land around here. We've the Stewart family to thank for those beautiful, very old white pines in our backyards."

"Hmm. I seem to remember something about the Stewarts

having lots of run-ins with the logging companies. But I knew about George Stewart being up here through my grandfather. He saw him, you know, after he was supposed to be dead."

"You mean after Stewart disappeared?"

"Yes, it happened before I was born, but I vividly remember my grandfather talking about it. It was sort of eerie—it was just before the war. He and two of his hunting buddies saw an elderly man sketching on a rock outcropping. The man scurried off as soon as he saw their canoe, but they found the embers of a fire and some food and a bottle of brandy that he left behind. My grandfather always claimed that George Stewart's disappearance was staged. They never found his body, you know."

I wondered why Stewart would disappear like that, but Clare shrugged. "Even before that, he'd become reclusive, not even attending his own shows. But the Group of Seven always acknowledged him. Did you know that Tom Thomson went on camping trips with him and sort of studied under him?"

I shook my head. I knew next to nothing about George Stewart—except that he was probably Canada's most famous painter, and his canvases were worth small fortunes.

"You'll keep me posted about what comes next, won't you?" she said eagerly. I couldn't help grinning. "It would be cruel not to," she urged, smiling back, "especially if there's a romance involved..."

Romance? But I hadn't said anything—

"Have you ever seen a photograph of George Stewart?" she asked, guessing my thoughts. "He's incredibly good-looking, and there's a rumor he was secretly married. Wouldn't it be something if your Miss Brice turned out to be a clandestine bride or his mistress or something like that?"

I reminded her that the Miss Brice of the Clarkson Home was almost certainly not the author of the diaries.

"But you'll at least keep me posted?"

I promised—and then told her that I was planning to go to the county archives in the morning, possibly to clear up the whole mystery.

"What do you hope to find there?"

"A record of death for Marged Brice," I said quietly.

Clare picked up Farley, her expression thoughtful. "But a record of death would only explain who she *isn't*. It wouldn't explain who she is."

"You've a point there, but it would get me off the hook as far as Edna and the Longevity Project is concerned."

"Don't you want to read her diaries?"

Clare's comments about George Stewart had certainly sharpened my interest, but I told her that I planned to follow a pretty tight writing schedule for my book.

"And if you don't find a record of death at the archives?" she asked.

"Then I'll be back at square one, I guess, and I'll have to read the next diary."

Just then we both heard a deep roll of thunder in the distance.

"Garth, I'm afraid I'll have to cut out. I've left all the windows open."

"You'd better go the back way, then."

She followed me through the cottage to the back door, and I invited her to hitch a ride into town with me if she liked. "We can take my car, and you could do those errands you mentioned," I suggested. "Then we could meet for lunch."

"That would work perfectly! I've got to get Mars to the vet ASAP. I think he's got fleas or something. He's been biting and scratching himself constantly."

I handed her a rain poncho, and Farley let out one of his piercing howls as she disappeared beneath the cape of plastic. Before I could grab him, he darted between her legs and she lost her balance, knocking a framed photograph off the wall.

"Sorry about that," I said, helping her up. "Farley's terrified of storms. Don't worry about the picture. I've been meaning to tidy up back here."

"It *is* a bit of a booby trap." Clare bent down to retrieve the picture. Then—"Oh no! It looks like I've broken the frame."

I was surprised by her concerned expression and gently took the photograph from her. It was an old shot taken in front of the boathouse. I had my arm around Evienne's waist as she smiled coyly into the camera. Doug was there, too—and Davey Sullivan, the third musketeer of our summer gang. We all had cans of beer outstretched in our hands and Evi was holding up an extremely large whitefish.

I grimaced involuntarily—that had been a happier time—and then I placed the photograph facedown on the side table.

"I'm sorry." Clare was looking at me apprehensively. "I hope I haven't ruined it."

"No," I assured her. "It's not ruined at all. Please don't worry."

Before I could stop her, she was crouching down, trying to pick up the broken glass.

"Clare!" I exclaimed—but it was too late, she had cut herself.

I insisted that she bandage her hand.

"It's strange about that picture," she mused as we taped up her finger.

"What do you mean?"

"I've always hated it. I'm actually in it, you know. You probably never noticed, but the picture frame covers me up. I'm actually standing at the end of the row. If you look, you'll see part of my leg."

I went back to the side table and lifted the photograph out of the frame. There she was—standing off to the left, next to Davey Sullivan. Her towel lay in a heap on the ground at her feet and her long hair fell almost to her waist.

"I must have been about eighteen then—almost nineteen, because wasn't that your twenty-fifth birthday, Garth?"

"Yes, I believe it was. But why do you hate this picture? I think it's very—well, it's certainly flattering of you."

"Oh, no, it's not that. It was your mother; she was always framing me out of your family photos. Douglas sometimes got in them, but not me! It used to really annoy me, but I never said anything about it."

I was a little taken aback, but I knew that my mother had been rough on Clare—on everyone really—especially when she'd been drinking.

"And I bet you've forgotten it was me who caught that fish," she said, opening the door.

"I always thought Doug caught it."

"I guess you award-winning historians sometimes forget the little details, don't you?" She gave me a funny smile as she stepped out into the rain. "I'll see you in the morning!"

I watched her walk swiftly down the driveway and then disappear beyond the cedar hedge. Then I went back to the table to take a closer look at the photograph.

Had it really been a happier time?

Evienne was bending forward, her head thrown back—only a miracle of gravity keeping the top of her bathing suit up. We had been together for about a month at that point and I'd been unsure of the whole thing. I recalled that she had gotten somewhat drunk that weekend and flirted with Doug, later insisting she'd only done it to make me jealous. Why did I buy it? I could see it all in retrospect; all the signs of a disaster brewing.

I looked at Clare. Her expression was hard to read, but she certainly seemed withdrawn—standing at the edge of our group, her face guarded. She had a fishing pole in one hand and her other arm was raised, as if the camera had caught her in the act of pushing her hair back and away from her face.

Suddenly I peered closer.

I had always wondered what Davey Sullivan was staring off at in that picture, but now I knew.

It was Clare, standing next to him. He was giving her a very penetrating gaze—almost wolfish—and it looked as if he was just about to place one of his hands on her bare shoulder.

Seven

I CHECKED MY WATCH, surprised to find that it was almost noon. There was no sign of the archivist.

I made my way toward the front desk and returned a large stack of books to the librarian. She handed me a note: Dr. Elliot was almost finished searching the death indexes and would be back after lunch.

I walked out to the parking lot just as Clare pulled up, and we drove into town for a bite at a local diner. It took a very long time for the middle-aged waitress who usually served me to come take our order. She greeted me warmly but glared at Clare with undisguised hostility.

"Coffee?" Rachel asked her brusquely.

"We'll start with water." Clare didn't look up from her menu. "I'm trying to get my brother to cut back on his caffeine." I stared at her in surprise. Rachel looked from one of us to the other and then ambled off.

"Clare? What the—?"

"Didn't you see?" Her eyes followed Rachel's surly retreat to the counter. "I'd guess you're a favorite of hers, and she's just a mite possessive. And besides, I practically am your sister."

"You're nothing of the sort!"

"Well, I'm hungry then," she retorted. "And I have a feeling that as your sister, I'll get my lunch faster."

The service did seem to pick up after that.

"Did you find a death certificate for Marged Brice?" Clare examined her tuna sandwich doubtfully.

"Not yet, but the archivist is still working on it for me. He'll probably have something for me after lunch."

"Then what did you do all morning?"

"I've been reading up on James T. McTavish. He's also mentioned in the diary. Do you know him?"

"McTavish? I seem to associate birds with him."

"That's right—every serious birder knows about Dr. McTavish. He's a kind of Canadian Audubon."

She took a bite of her sandwich and began to chew it carefully.

"Clare, is your food okay? I don't think Rachel's up to poisoning anyone."

"Don't mind me." She laughed. "It's been a while since I've been in a diner."

"I'm sorry." I frowned. "I should have taken you somewhere else. The only real attraction here is—well, the coffee."

"Stop," she protested. "I'm perfectly fine. Now, what were you saying—serious birders. Do you remember how I used to pester your father to do his birdcalls? I especially loved his chickadee. Didn't he once say something about getting a higher pitch if you whistled out the side of your mouth?"

"My dad was pretty good, but he wasn't in the same league as McTavish. Apparently the doctor had an extraordinary repertoire of birdcalls." I told her about McTavish's famous performance of a robin searching for worms on the lawn of Buckingham Palace. Queen Victoria had been delighted with it, and so with royal approval, he became an instant celebrity.

"A stuffy, proper Victorian pretending to be a robin? I can hardly imagine it—"

"I don't think McTavish was all that stuffy, though no doubt he was proper. But there's also a mystery associated with him."

"A mystery?"

I waited as Rachel drifted past and then explained that when he was in his fifties, McTavish began to suffer from arthritis in his fingers and eventually had to hire assistants. There was one particular artist who worked for him for many years—someone who painted under the initials of DEJ. "Practically all of McTavish's illustrations after 1898 are signed McTavish/DEJ."

"Who was DEJ?" Clare asked.

"That's the mystery. No one knows. But there's been quite a bit of speculation."

Clare waved at Rachel. "Could we have our coffee now?" she called out sweetly.

I told her about one theory that intrigued me: several art historians had speculated that DEJ was McTavish's mistress, a much younger woman whom McTavish fell for in "a moment of indiscretion."

"Hmm. Are you thinking of Marged Brice?" Clare asked.

I nodded. "But the *mistress* bit doesn't fit. McTavish was very much—well, an avuncular presence in her life."

"Perhaps it developed into something more romantic later on?"

I shrugged. "My guess is that it didn't. But it seems that there are quite a few art historians who would give their front teeth to know who DEJ was."

We drove back to the archives, and I invited Clare to come in with me, promising her that I wouldn't be long.

Dr. Elliot met us in the reception area. "I've done a search of all the online death registries," he announced, giving Clare an appreciative glance as he handed me copies of the death records for Hugh Brice and his wife, Fabienne, as well as those for Alis and Gilbert Barclay.

"Anything for a Marged Brice?" I asked hopefully.

"No, I'm sorry. There's no record of death for a *Marged* Brice or a *Margaret* Brice. I've done a complete search, just as you requested."

"Would you mind doing a national search as well?"

"I've done that—or rather, a colleague of mine in Ottawa did it as a favor to me. There's no existing record of death for her in any of the death indexes. And I called the district office—there's nothing in the county's hard files either."

My face must have showed my disappointment. "Of course," he added, "death records are occasionally misplaced."

Clare glanced at me and raised her eyebrows. "Square one?"

"Would you wait here for a few minutes?" Dr. Elliot asked politely. "I think I have something that might interest you."

Clare started flipping through a book that Dr. Elliot had left out for me. "Garth, come look: here's a plate of Stewart's *Sylvan Chapel.* Isn't it gorgeous?"

"Yes," I said absently, looking over her shoulder—then it suddenly hit me. Could the painting of the cedar grove mentioned in the diary be George Stewart's famous *Sylvan Chapel*? It was almost inconceivable, but Marged's description of the painting above George's studio fireplace was uncannily close to the reproduction before me. How had she expressed it? A grove of trees with smooth, twisting trunks—the tops of the trees seeming to move…

Clare turned a page, and suddenly we were both looking at a grainy photograph of the artist himself. Stewart was around forty years old and cut a ruggedly handsome figure as he stood before an easel at an undisclosed location. Standing to his right was a young woman. He was holding her hand, but her features were maddeningly blurred.

"Clare, do you think the woman's hair comes to a point in the middle of her forehead?"

She peered closely at the photograph—and then looked up nodding. "Yes, she definitely has a widow's peak."

The caption underneath the photograph read, *Canadian artist George Stewart with model, 1900.*

"He's holding her hand rather affectionately, don't you think?" I looked up and caught her smiling softly. "Didn't I tell you he was very good-looking," Clare murmured. "Maybe you should also do a search for a marriage certificate."

"Professor Hellyer." It was Dr. Elliot coming up from the basement. "I wanted to show you these. Just for interest's sake. I found them quite by accident; they were in our newspaper files." He gave me two photographs.

Together Clare and I examined the first one. It was a black-and-white shot of the November 25, 1958, installation of *Sylvan Chapel* at the National Gallery of Canada. George Stewart's younger brother, Allan, was shaking hands with Prime Minister John Diefenbaker while Governor-General Vincent Massey looked on.

"Allan was tutored by Marged Brice," I explained to Clare. "He's probably well into his seventies in this picture."

"How much older was Marged Brice?"

"She was five or six years older than Allan."

"So she would have been in her early eighties in this picture." She bent over the photograph. "Here's a woman who looks to be about that old." She pointed to a white-haired woman sitting in the front row of dignitaries. The woman's eyes were riveted on Allan Stewart, and her hands rested quietly in her lap. There was something eerily familiar about her long, sinuous fingers.

"I think she has a widow's peak!" Clare exclaimed. Then she turned to me and said in a lowered voice, "I'm guessing that your Miss Brice at the Clarkson Home also has a widow's peak, doesn't she?"

"Yes. But—lots of people do."

"How many?" she challenged. "And besides, isn't it a genetic trait that skips generations or something like that?"

"Let's look at the second picture," I suggested.

The other photograph was dated June 22, 2006—again taken in front of *Sylvan Chapel* at the National Gallery. This time the caption underneath identified Gregory Stewart at the center. He was leaning on a cane and presenting an envelope to a very pleased-looking director. The event announced a thirty-million-dollar endowment for a new "Stewart Wing" at the gallery.

"Gregory is Allan Stewart's son," I explained. "Apparently he's the relative who took care of Miss Brice before she came to the Clarkson Home—" Then I stopped. Miss Brice had referred to Gregory as her nephew—wouldn't that make Allan Stewart her brother-in-law?

"There she is!" Clare whispered, her voice betraying her excitement. "It's the same woman. I'm positive!"

This time the white-haired woman was in a wheelchair.

"She looks much thinner," observed Clare, "but I think I can still see her widow's peak."

I slumped back, frowning. It just wasn't possible!

Clare was leaning closely against me as she studied the photograph. "Are you absolutely sure she couldn't be the writer of that diary you just read?"

I did a quick calculation. "This is silly," I muttered. "She'd be one hundred and twenty-seven years old in this picture if that were the case."

Clare drew back, looking at me guardedly.

"I'm sorry. I didn't mean that the way it sounded." I gently took her hand. "I didn't mean that *you're* silly. It's just that it's not possible for her to be the same woman."

"You're sure? Positively sure?" This time her voice was hesitant.

I didn't answer.

It was raining torrentially as we stepped out into the parking lot. I took off my jacket and turned it into a makeshift umbrella, Clare huddling close to me as we sprinted toward the car.

We retrieved a very clean and glossy Mars from the vet and then headed back up the Peninsula. Mars kept sticking his head over my shoulder and licking my face while I drove.

"What in God's name did they do to him?" I asked, almost choking.

"Don't you like the smell of eucalyptus?"

"For a dog?"

"Eucalyptus is supposed to be a natural flea repellent." She said it pertly, but looked at me sideways. "Besides, I'm sure Farley would love it."

"You've got me there. Farley loves anything involving a good 'rub,'" I conceded.

I peered through the large water droplets coursing down my windshield, my eyes watching for the cutoff to Cape Prius. I was just able to see the road bend before me when suddenly I hit the brakes and came to a complete stop.

"Is anything wrong?" Clare asked nervously.

I swallowed. "It just hit me—the initials *DEJ*."

"What about them?"

"They're the same as Allan Stewart's playful bird name for Marged Brice."

"Yes?"

"Allan called her a *dark-eyed junco*."

Clare's eyes lit up. "Oh my! And now you're the only other person in the whole wide world—besides your Miss Brice at the Clarkson—who knows who DEJ is!"

I was silent for a few seconds.

"Of course, now *I* know, too," she added softly.

June 19

Allan has been making great progress with his studies. We have borrowed a few books on botany from Dr. McTavish, and he has been coming here to our cottage to spare me walking out to the Basin, though my ankle is much stronger and I have assured him that it is almost completely healed. But I suspect another reason for this; Allan has taken a great interest in our light station. Uncle Gil has shown him how the weights are wound, and Allan has become quite an expert already. He has set up an ingenious method by which Tad and Uncle G. can watch the Light without leaving our kitchen. It is through a mirror fastened to the window on the inside, and most wonderful of all, when the weather is bad, Tad will be able watch the reflection of the light in the warmth of our back kitchen. Really Allan is such a clever fellow!

I have not seen George these few days. Allan brings reports of the household. He tells me that the portrait was not ruined and that George was able to salvage it. Apparently Miss Ferguson is quite pleased with it. Allan implies Effie is tired of her sister-in-law and wishes that she would go away, but he says that George and Miss Ferguson spend a great deal of time together. He seems very pleased with this, and has already predicted a brilliant career for George as an artist. I did not know it, but Caroline Ferguson is an heiress of sorts—Allan says the Fergusons are even richer than his stepfather and that they have "oodles of money."

June 23

I saw him today. It was quite by accident.

Allan and I were out for a walk—not a very long one because my ankle is still a little tender. But we went out, down by the north gate because Dr. McTavish had told us that there were two sandhill cranes (*Grus canadensis*) near the marsh. It was a breezy afternoon, and as the road is shaded by trees on either side, we both felt, I think, a lovely sort of idleness.

We rather foolishly came back by the woods, and Allan ran ahead laughing that I was too slow. Indeed I was picking my way rather carefully. But I came to a point in the path where a large tree had fallen, and its rotting trunk barred my advance. I realized that I would have to mount it and walk its length to reach the clearing. I was so vexed with Allan for going on ahead, for I was not sure of my footing and very mindful of what a false step would bring to my ankle. But I had no choice, and so I began to traverse it gingerly, taking very small steps.

I was about halfway across when I heard a ripping sound and I stopped because my skirt had caught on a branch. I was annoyed at first, but then I became aware of the stillness of the forest, and I felt a lovely warm solitude envelop me, without feeling any loneliness. I heard a chickadee let out a *fee-bee, fee-bee*—warning me that I was in its territory. Then of a sudden George was there, stepping out of a thicket. He does seem to emerge like an animal out of the woods sometimes! He had his sketchbook again and his satchel, and he looked at me with what seemed to me to be good humor. He put his hand to his chin, cocked his head, and pretended to eye me dubiously, as if he were studying a rather strange and unexpected sight.

"You look like a bird that has been caught in a shaft of sunlight and it will not release her," he remarked. "But I dare not make a sudden movement, else I frighten you, and then you will fly away and deprive me of your presence."

His voice was kind, and he looked very manly standing there, the sun giving golden lights to his dark hair, and his hands, strong and tanned, resting on his walking stick. He looked like a lord of the forest, and I—oh, ever perverse to him!—I bristled just a little under his easy self-possession.

I would not meet his good humor directly, nor would I be his bird! I put my hands on my hips and said a little crossly, "Is Allan with you?"

I regretted the question as soon as it flew from my lips.

George paused, and his expression changed almost imperceptibly. "No," he said rather quietly. "I have sent Allan on ahead."

I did not move from my somewhat perilous position on the log but began to press my palms together, betraying, no doubt, my agitation; now the tears were ready, almost brimming over as I remembered his question at Clootie's and the portrait lying in ruins about me. I despised myself for being so weak, but I was at such a loss as to how to compose my features. I surely wished in that moment that I had a mask, a veil, to hide my face so that he would not see its emotions.

He studied me closely and looked bewildered—a frown appeared, but it did not seem to me to express displeasure. He gazed at me intently, and it was as if he were trying to read something that moved too swiftly for him, as if the rapidity of thoughts that moved across my face puzzled him.

"Miss Brice—" he began. I drew my breath in sharply and he stopped. "I have ever called you Marged. Would you permit me to do so now?"

I nodded, as if to say that he could do as he pleased. He had the upper hand with me: *I* was disgraced before him.

"A few days ago, I intruded into the privacy of your life with a question and manners that were—shall we say—ill-suited to a gentleman. I have regretted them ever since I uttered them. I do not excuse myself, but I do ask your forgiveness."

While he spoke, I studied his features with a scrutiny I had not yet permitted myself. It is a strong face, I thought, and I remarked the square line of his jaw and the shadow of where a beard was beginning to show. His voice was deep but clear, and the forest seemed to hush around it. His words lingered in the air momentarily before falling to the forest floor and joining the other leaves that had gathered there.

"But—it is I," I stammered. "I who have—imperiled—one of your beautiful paintings. It is I who must ask for your forgiveness."

He smiled gently. Was he mocking me?

"Did you really think it was a beautiful painting?" he asked.

I was confused. I could not tell if he were teasing me or not.

"Well..." I faltered. "It was not finished when I saw it—"

He interrupted me. "Did you like the one over the mantel? The one you were looking at when I came in?"

I stood silent for a minute, my heart pounding so.

Then, hesitating a little, I clasped my hands together, just as I had done in his studio, and I nodded—it was the only way that I could tell him how truly beautiful it was.

He coughed and seemed a little embarrassed by my gesture. He shuffled slightly, as if the ground beneath his feet had shifted unexpectedly. But I do think it pleased him.

Then he looked at me again and said earnestly, "Do you forgive me?"

I nodded again, for still I could not speak. And I did forgive him. I forgave him fully and completely. I held nothing back—nothing for a future time when I might find fault against him. Again he seemed to recognize all this, and his face showed a not entirely reluctant appreciation. I saw him grateful to *me*—a foolish young girl, standing on a fallen log with her skirt caught in its branches! But I felt like a queen in that moment, surrounded by my court of faithful trees.

He came to get me, and I could not look at him as he lifted me off the fallen trunk, my face was burning so! My skirt tore; there was an unmistakable sound of ripping fabric, but I pretended not to notice it.

Is he amused by me, by all my silly antics? I don't care! I think his apology was sincere.

I am afraid I will betray what is in my heart. I do not think that I have owned even to myself what is there.

June 28

The fox is back—he showed himself to Allan and me as we rounded the cottage, and he stared at us for a few seconds before bolting into the hedge. Dewi has been barking furiously all night, and Auntie Alis says that we must keep the cat in. Agnes will stay with Mother, though Tad doesn't like an animal to be on the bed and will object, I am sure.

Allan has some strange ideas about this fox. He says it has come to warn us, but he won't say of what. He says that the last time we saw the fox, Mr. Burton fell off his boat and drowned. It is true: it was a terrible accident, and I remember hearing Uncle Gil tell Auntie A. that Mr. Burton was a drinker, and that the government inspector suspected that he fell because he was intoxicated. That was why no one heard him, for perhaps he made no effort to save himself. Allan is sure it was murder, and I have to plug my ears to make him stop!

We are getting along very well these days. Allan is interested in his studies and seems to enjoy the work we do together. But I think he likes to be around Uncle Gil and Tad the most. They do not seem to mind his company and he is somehow more—serious—when he is with them. Older, I suppose. Oh, he is still playful! I don't think he will ever be otherwise. He is always very polite to Mother and teases Auntie A. interminably, and even tricks her into giving him all kinds of treats. At first I was astonished to see it, but then I remembered that Luke might be close to Allan's age if he had lived, and of course Auntie would fancy her son and spoil him just a little as long as it brought no harm. Indeed, she scolds Allan all the time as if to make up for her moments of weak indulgence.

We have had some truly astonishing news today. Mrs. McTavish is coming! She has never joined Dr. McTavish on his excursions to the Basin before, and why she has decided to come this season is a great mystery to us. Mr. Thompson says that Dr. McTavish is in an awful state about it and is quite put out by the thought of his Emmeline visiting him while he is on the verge of completing his book. Allan informed me that Mr. Thompson has met her, and he says that she is quite beautiful but a terror. For my part, I am rather curious now. She is coming on the *Mary Jane* on Tuesday with the holiday boaters; first they will take an excursion to Adam's Rock and the Hotel, and then Dr. McTavish will send a boat to fetch her. No doubt the holidayers will carve their names on the stones again. How I hate to think of it! I wish the water would erase it all!

July 1

It has been quite an extraordinary day. Poor Dr. McTavish!

To be truthful, I cannot tell if he is vexed or relieved at the strange turn the day has taken.

We heard in the early afternoon from one of the Indian fishermen that a large steamer had gone aground on a shoal. Further reports confirmed that it was the *Mary Jane,* and we all grew quite concerned, for Mrs. McTavish is said to be on board. But strangest of all, the fishermen say that the passengers do not wish to be rescued—that they are all strolling about on deck and taking their tea, and some have even gone off the boat and are walking about on the rocks.

I could tell by the manner in which he frowned that Tad was not pleased with this news, and Uncle Gil positively scowled with displeasure. I think I must share their disapproval, for though the day is clear and there is not a cloud in the sky—still—it seems as if these holidayers will provoke the Bay. They seem to goad it with their carefree airs. They have not seen it as we have. To be sure, it is one thing to be on the shore in a storm, but to be out there in the water…I shudder to think of it.

They do not understand: one can never see the Bay completely. One never knows its full face. Those passengers have not seen, as we have, how a day may suddenly change.

I do feel sometimes as if I live next to some great, slumbering beast that lulls me into thinking of it as just rocks and water. And then, every once in a while, it awakens and I realize that it is alive and powerful and that I am a tiny, helpless creature next to it! It could swallow me up—and Tad and Uncle Gil and Auntie

Alis. And Mother, too! Without remorse. Just as an animal might, sating its prodigious hunger.

Where is *its* heart? I wonder. Whence do its passions arise? I cannot tell if it is right in the center, deep, deep down, deeper even than where the fish can go. Or is it in the north, where the great jagged cliffs jut out and direct the bitter winds that sting us and whip the rain against our faces? Or in the south, like an animal withdrawn in its lair, back in the shadows and dozing until awakened by hunger or a sense of intruders…

I think we will all be greatly relieved when these passengers safely reach their destinations.

Mrs. McTavish refuses to come! Indeed, I am thinking that perhaps she is a bit of a "terror." Apparently she has asserted in no uncertain terms that she will wait until the other steamer comes to collect her and the other passengers, and that she is determined to visit the Hotel first. George and Mr. Stewart and two of the fishermen took a small boat out to fetch her, but she insists that it is not safe. Mr. Stewart is quite a skilled boater, and he is furious at this insult. He says that Dr. McTavish can go get his wife the next time. George was laughing and shaking his head. Allan asked him if she were really a terror, and I nudged him to be quiet because Dr. McTavish might hear him. George said nothing, but his eyes twinkled as if to say that is only the start of it.

Now I am not sure whether I wish to meet her or no!

July 3

I have only a little time before the dawn, but I cannot sleep. Auntie Alis has insisted that I rest, but I cannot! I must write the day's events out, even if just to stop my thoughts from swirling so in my head.

It is all very terrible—as if Allan's forebodings about the fox have come true.

It was yesterday…the morning started out quietly, but it was overcast and the wind would gust so strangely, bursting as if out of nowhere and then disappearing as suddenly. I think I could tell that the day had not decided how it would proceed, but there was also something else. I was restless, and so I arose early and took a walk out to the Point. It was the water in the Basin that made me anxious. It is usually very still there, but I could see the boats drifting about, their masts bobbing up and down, and I could hear the men moving restively in their camps. The fishermen and some of the boaters knew, I am certain—that was why they had not yet gone out. From my side of the Basin, I could see, down at one of the fires, the same Indian man who went out yesterday with Mr. Stewart and George. He was standing with a small circle of fishermen around him, and as he talked, he kept gesturing out toward the Bay.

I hugged my body, watching them—it seemed terribly ominous! And though I was not cold, I began to shiver. I went to the Lodge, why I am not sure, but I felt very apprehensive. George and Dr. McTavish and two of the boaters were on the front porch looking out at the water and talking in serious tones.

"Marged," George said when he saw me. "Can you get your father—and Gilbert, too? There is going to be a storm, and we will have to go out and get the passengers from the *Mary Jane*."

I looked into his face, speechless with terrible apprehension. But I could not say it! I had no right to! I could not say that I did not want him to go out onto the water that day. That it was too, too dangerous!

His eyes bored into mine, and he took both my hands and pressed them.

"Quickly now," he said softly.

I turned and ran back to our cottage. Tad and Uncle Gil were standing by the side entrance, and Mr. Brown, Donald, and a few of the farmhands were with them. By now the wind had picked up, and I could see an ugly dark cloud edging along the eastern skyline.

I told Tad that some of the men and George and Mr. Stewart were going to go out in boats to get the passengers.

Tad nodded and picked up his cap.

"There's not much time, boys, is there?" I heard him say, and then the men grunted in assent.

Tad turned to us. "Alis—you and Marged must tend the mantle if we are not returned in time. Whatever happens, you must tend to the Light!"

Auntie nodded quietly, and she crossed herself and gave the men a blessing that they accepted in somber silence. Uncle Gil kissed her on the cheek, and she stood as if made of stone, her eyes not even blinking.

"Oh, Tad." I was so frightened. "Do be careful!"

He hushed me and folded me in his arms, and I clung to him. He told me to watch Mother and to get

Allan to help us with the Light. He kissed me and then they were gone—all the men.

The whole morning, I flew back and forth between our cottage and the Lodge. There was a peculiar apprehension in our movements. I told Allan that Father wanted him to manage the Light if he were not back before dark, and he came back with me and saw that all was made ready.

I kept reckoning the minutes in my mind. I knew that it would take at least two hours to get to the shoal and then perhaps thirty minutes to get the passengers in the boats—and then another two hours coming back. And then if the water were rough…

Seven hours passed, and the waves were—Mr. Thompson said they were fifteen feet or more in front of the Lodge. The rain had not ceased, but the sky had turned an evil gray, and we heard thunder far off in the distance.

Mr. Thompson had his field glasses trained on the water for any sign of the boats, and we gathered on the front porch with our eyes straining to the same spot on the horizon. Even Effie was there, standing in the doorway with Corrie, and the baby began to cry as if she sensed our mood.

"The storm is moving fast," said Mr. Thompson, and he shook his head glumly.

I began to pray fervently. It was but three o'clock in the afternoon, but the entire sky had turned a livid gray, and it seemed as if night had dropped upon us like a curtain falling. Now we could see lightning blaze across the horizon, and the wind took on a shriller aspect, knocking over the table and seizing the wicker chairs that we had neglected to take inside, battering them against the Lodge's stone walls. The rain came down in sheets, and the waves took on an even more ominous and angry aspect. My heart sank as I thought of the boats in that water.

Then—

"There," shouted Mr. Thompson, gesturing toward the eastern skyline.

And appearing suddenly from around the Point, we could see the outline of a large boat. Its foremast was rolling horribly—up and down, back and forth—and we could see, as it neared, that the first jib sheet was ripped to pieces. The mainsail was shredding rapidly in the wind, and the waves were pushing it toward the shore, where it would surely be smashed into pieces against the rocks. We saw the men lowering the lifeboats and then push off, desperately making for shore.

"Allan," I cried. He had run out into the storm without warning toward the boats, and I leaped out after him.

The waves took two of the boats and shot them as if from a cannon toward the shore, but the rowers were skillful and with much effort were able to guide them away from the treacherous rocks and then into the protection of the Basin.

George stumbled from one of the boats, and I ran to him. I looked around wildly, but I could not see my father or uncle.

"George," I cried. "Where is my father? Where is Tad?" I clung to his sleeve desperately. It could not be that *he* had drowned!

George stopped, bending over and catching his

breath. He placed his hands on my shoulders and leaned on me heavily. With an effort he swallowed. His face showed terrible exhaustion, and his jacket was torn—there was a smear of blood across his forehead.

"Back," he panted. "They are—I think"—a fit of coughing interrupted him—"going ashore at the Light..."

I knew immediately what he meant. There were mooring spikes that Tad had driven into the rocks down below the light station—positioned in such a way that a boat could be tied to them without coming too close to the sharp ledges, and hence beyond the crashing waves that might crack its hull and seize any unfortunate passengers.

Without a word, I turned from him and flew down the beach. It was raining fiercely by this time, and I hastened but poorly along the shore, picking my way back to the outcropping below the light station. It was foolish and reckless of me to take this route in such a storm, but I knew that it was fastest. I could hear George calling my name hoarsely behind me, but I did not stop.

As I got closer, I could see Tad in his boat, and Uncle Gil and Dr. McTavish on the stone landing. Uncle G. had secured a second boat, and there were several women huddled against the rock face. My first thought was that one of them must be Mrs. McTavish. Uncle G. was crouched low on the ledge, struggling against the wind to get to Tad—his boat was still tossing in the terrible water, and it seemed that it would capsize at any moment. Tad kept casting a rope out to him, but Uncle Gil was too far away to reach it, and then the waves would drag it down, and the rowers had to fight again to find a position near enough to the rocks.

From my vantage, it seemed that I might have a better chance to secure the rope, and so I beckoned for Tad to throw it to me. I could barely see for the rain, but suddenly I felt a rope in my hands and I grasped it. The mooring was not more than a few paces away from me, but it seemed a mile! The boat heaved and rocked, and the rope would not obey me. I struggled with it, pulling and pulling, and I could feel my ankle start to give way.

Still I persisted. I wrapped my hands in my skirt and tugged with all my might. Uncle Gil could not reach me, and I could see him fall against the rocks as a blast of wind took him down with a cruel ferocity.

I bit my lips against the pain that shot through my arms, and I pulled with all my strength on the rope, but ever did the mooring remain out of my reach.

It was the wind—it was the wind who wanted him.

"I will not give him to you," I shrieked out to it. "You cannot have him!"

And then—I do not know how to express it otherwise—it seemed as if two strong hands were next to mine and the Bay gave way. The rope slackened momentarily in my hands, and I quickly looped it around the mooring, tying it firmly in the way that Tad had taught me.

And then he was there, his face grim and his chest heaving from his exertions. He said my name, and I placed my hands alongside his neck, feeling the warmth of his body through my frozen fingers. I did not know it until later, but the rope had cut through my hands, and I left blood all over him.

But he is safe! And Uncle Gil! I am ashamed to be so thankful when so many others have perished—but I cannot help it.

July 4

Between them, Tad and Uncle Gilbert have saved eighteen passengers. George and Mr. Stewart have saved another nine. Dr. McTavish, too—but still I do not know if his wife is among those rescued. The boats of the other fishermen have also come in, and there are little children and women, all cold and crying, throughout the cottage. I have been of little use, but Auntie A. has done her best to make them warm, and I have tried to comfort the littlest ones. Tad and Uncle Gilbert cannot go back out—the storm is too fierce—and my heart is broken for these children. Will they learn tomorrow that they have mothers and fathers no more?

When will we know what has become of Mrs. McTavish?

July 7

There is to be a search. The inspectors have come, and there is an officer from the Royal Navy who has organized the men into crews.

It is all quite dreadful. For three days, we have had debris washed ashore, though thankfully there have been no bodies as yet in the Basin, or indeed below the light station. Mr. Stewart says that there were 150 people aboard the *Mary Jane* and that, so far, only eighty are accounted for. The worst have been the children's things: I found a tiny baby's bonnet and a little boot no bigger than my hand! There are two newspaper reporters staying at the Lodge, and each day, more people come hoping to get word of their relations. But it is now the third day, and our hopes are dwindling—Dr. McTavish seems to grow older with each day, and I can do nothing for him, except take his hand and hold it. He lets me do this at least, and when I asked him if he would drink his tea, he took a few sips, though he says hardly a word. I think she must be drowned...but I cannot tell if poor Dr. McTavish knows that it must be so.

July 9

The government inspectors have returned, and they had a long conference with Tad, Uncle Gilbert, George, and Mr. Stewart. The officer from the Royal Navy is here too, a Captain Howarth. Auntie Alis remarked that he is a handsome man, but I find his visage quite fierce. He has burning black eyes, and when he looks at me, I find them quite unnerving. He is very correct and stands quite straight and tall in his uniform, but he is displeased, it seems, with something and insists that Tad come with him to the Lonely Island light station.

The keeper there is Mr. Doric. He was here at Cape Prius before Tad, but then he was moved to the Lonely Island Light—why, I do not know. It is a terribly isolated, stark place and thus is well named. The island, too, is filled with snakes.

Captain Howarth has assembled two crews and has asked Tad to bring our dogs, though why I can't imagine. Allan has insisted on accompanying the men, and Tad says that I, too, can come with Dewi and keep an eye on Allan.

Allan says that he is not sure why we are returning to the island since they have already searched it and Mr. Doric reports no bodies or effects—but Tad seems evasive. We will go early tomorrow.

July 10

I do not know if I have the strength to write of my travails today, but I must try.

We left for Lonely Island just as dawn was breaking and the weather was clear and calm. Indeed, no one would guess that the Bay had been a monster but a few days before, for it spread before us so soft and pleasant. A light wind allowed us to raise both sails, and we made our way there in good time.

Tad and I, Captain Howarth, Mr. Stewart, George, and Allan were in one sloop, while six other men took a second, larger one. I was almost sure that Captain Howarth suspected some ill of me, for ever did he cast his black eyes in my direction, and I kept pulling my hat lower, so keen was I to avoid them!

Allan was almost quivering with excitement, and I had to talk to him in a calm, low voice to cool his impetuousness. George was very quiet; his mind seemed to be elsewhere as his eyes roved, resting now upon Captain Howarth and then on Tad. He looked at me, too, but did not seem to see me and would not answer the anxious inquiry in my eyes by word or gesture.

When we got to the island, Tad tied the boat and Captain Howarth turned to help me step ashore. Again his eyes seemed to bore right into me. Dewi snapped peevishly at him, but it gave me a chance to stoop down and scold him for being such a bad creature and thus evade that dark stare.

Mr. Doric came out from the lighthouse. He was in only his shirtsleeves, and he seemed angry to see us. I stepped away from them and drew Allan's arm into my own. I heard Mr. Doric raise his voice, protesting that there were no bodies that had washed ashore and that if there were, he would have reported them. Captain Howarth said something in a low voice that I could not hear, and then there was an argument. I heard Tad say that it could not hurt to look a second time.

I was filled with a strange dread, but I was glad to take Allan away from the men and their angry voices. We left the two hounds near the boats and took Dewi, who pulled us along, his nose to the ground, sniffing furiously. I was careful to keep his leash in my left hand, as my right was still bandaged and smarting from the exertions of the storm. Allan asked me if I thought that Mr. Doric might be hiding something, and I looked at him in surprise. Had he heard something that I had not?

Allan remarked he had overheard George and his stepfather talking, and it seemed that Mr. Doric had sent away some of the fishermen who had come two days before rather rudely.

"But it may have been—just his way," I exclaimed. "He is not a sociable man. That, at least, is no secret."

No, Allan indicated, shaking his head—they thought something more was amiss. Mr. Doric told them that no debris had washed up, but as the fishermen were leaving, they saw what looked to be some furniture: part of a table and a battered deck chair, such as one would see on a pleasure boat.

I was more than a little unsettled, and I stopped dead in my tracks. I did not like to think of what Allan was insinuating, and I remembered that we had to be wary of the snakes that infested the place.

Dewi was pulling vigorously on his leash, and Allan's eyes brightened.

"He's found something," he cried exultantly and yanked the lead from me.

"Allan," I protested, "stop!"

I could hear the men behind us with the other dogs; one of the hounds was yelping, and then there were loud scraping sounds as if they were moving some heavy object. A chill crept up my spine, and all of a sudden, I was afraid.

"You see," I heard Mr. Doric exclaim, "there's nothing here!"

"Margie!"

Allan motioned toward a pile of driftwood that had been bleaching in the sun for many months, or even years perhaps.

He paused before it and then said, "Come," very quietly.

Again, a wave of dread passed over me, but I drew in my breath and moved closer.

Dewi was tugging on a piece of cloth, and to my horror, when we pulled him away, I saw a hand protruding from what looked to be the sleeve of a woman's garment.

I must have screamed!

I do not know if seconds or minutes passed, but it seemed that Captain Howarth was there very quickly, with his hands on my waist, gently pulling me back from the pile of wood, speaking very softly to me, "Step away now—I've got you."

Allan was transfixed.

I closed my eyes and covered my mouth, for there was a terrible stench that arose from the body. Then Tad was behind me, and I turned and pressed my face against his coat.

"There, Marged. There," he said. And I swallowed and gathered myself, for I did not wish to shame him and have the men think him possessed of a weak daughter.

"Allan," said Tad sharply, "come here and look to Marged."

I am sure that he did this in part to draw Allan away from the grisly pyre. The men lifted up the pieces of wood, and I saw the form of a woman's body emerge. Her face was horrible—the lips drawn back and her eyes staring wildly. Her arms were crossed at her chest, as if clutching some object, and her dress was torn in several places.

"There's a wee babe with her," one of the men said, stooping over her body. "Aye, it's just a wee child."

It was then that I realized that the woman could not have been put there by the storm, for she was too far from the shore. Nor could the storm have placed the branches upon her body, so carefully concealing her. But how had it happened?

I turned slowly and looked at Mr. Doric as it dawned upon me that someone—someone on the island—must have placed her so.

Captain Howarth stood up abruptly from his crouched position above the corpse and said, "This indentation shows that this woman was wearing a ring. And it seems that something has been wrenched from around her neck. Mr. Doric, can you explain this?"

Mr. Doric stood as if turned to stone, his eyes staring vacantly before him.

"Robbing the dead," muttered one of the men.

Tad walked over to Mr. Doric and took his arm. "Come, James," he said, and he led him, unresisting, back to the light station. One of Captain Howarth's men stayed behind with the body, and Allan and I could do nothing except return to the dock, where our boats were tied and waiting.

"There are probably more—" began Allan, but I interrupted him.

"Don't," I said. "Let's not talk of it. Not just yet."

George and Mr. Stewart took us back to the mainland. We were all silent the whole way. I could not talk to the reporter either, though he came twice to see me.

When Tad came back, I heard Uncle Gilbert say, "They'll hang him"—and Tad offered no contradiction.

July 11

They found more debris from the *Mary Jane* in Mr. Doric's yard, and what Captain Howarth described as "personal effects." It seems that Mr. Doric has taken things from many of the dead, and they are discovering the other bodies that he has hidden throughout the island. I do not think that I could ever bear to go back to that lonely spot after this; perhaps it was the isolation that twisted him and induced him to commit such heinous deeds!

July 15

We buried Mrs. McTavish today. They found her body early yesterday morning; I cannot write much of this. My heart is breaking for Dr. McTavish—I heard Tad say to Uncle Gil that she was almost unrecognizable. How terrible! I am filled with sadness and regret. There will be five new graves in our little cemetery. One of them will be for a boy who is thought to be eight, and one for a little girl of three.

I don't think any of us will ever forget this summer.

Eight

I WALKED OVER TO Clare's after dinner, heading along the road rather than picking my way across the beach. I stopped at the overlook; there were dark clouds gathering on the horizon, and I found myself scanning the Bay for boats. Sure enough, a small yacht was making its way toward the two buoys that marked the entrance to Drake's Basin.

"Cutting it a little close," I said under my breath.

As I rounded the bend, I saw a second car parked in the driveway. "Doug's arrived!" I quickened my step. It had been ages since I'd seen him up at the cottage.

I knocked on the back door, but there was no answer, so I followed the side path around to the front. I could hear their voices coming out through the screened windows as I approached.

"Okay. Just one more question." Doug's tone was playful, but I detected a note of seriousness in it.

"All right." Clare laughed. "But this has to be it! After this, my personal life is off-limits for the rest of the weekend. Agreed?"

I stopped and turned around, annoyed to see that Farley had disappeared. Then I heard Doug say, "What about *Garth*?" He said it so quietly, emphasizing my name in such an unusual way that I stopped dead in my tracks.

"You've been talking to Mum!" Clare exclaimed.

"Yes, I had a long talk with Mum before coming up. She's worried about you."

"Oh." Clare sounded edgy. "She's probably told you some nonsense about me being in love with Garth—ever since I was sixteen or something like that. She did, didn't she?"

I felt I should cough or signal my presence somehow.

"Well?" Doug asked softly.

"I plead the Fifth—or whichever one it is," she tossed back.

"You know that only works in the States." Doug had moved closer to the window, very near to where I was standing, and paused with his back to me. I became very still, helpless to slip away without his hearing me.

"Come on, Clare. I'm not completely blind. Didn't you once—?"

"That was all a long time ago," she interrupted. "Once Evienne got her hooks into him, I didn't stand a chance."

"You weren't exactly without your own charms, you know," Doug said mildly.

"You know I'm not like that! Women who get men that way—it's hard to explain—but they never get the full man. There must be parts of Garth that Evienne never knew, maybe even didn't want to know."

"Did you sense that Garth wasn't entirely happy, then?" Doug asked tentatively.

I took a cautious step backward, but froze at the sound of a stick cracking under my foot.

"How could I possibly know?" Now Clare's voice sounded defensive. "I wasn't really around them, not after I left for Cambridge. But why all these questions about Garth? I know Mum's not keen on Stuart, but you've no idea how wonderful he was through all that awful hullabaloo at the Museum. Besides, it really isn't anyone else's business. Even Dad is looking at me so…pensively!"

"Mum doesn't think you're really—well—really in love with Stuart—or Lord Becksmith."

"It's Baron Bretford! Baron Bretford of Blackheath!"

Doug guffawed. "I beg your pardon, milady. I grant you his lordship might be a great guy. Even so, Mum might be right. She has a nose for these things, and she thinks you've got the let's-get-married-because-we're-good-friends syndrome. That and the fact you've put off the Baron for so long."

"Ellen took three years to marry you!"

"Fair enough. But that was different. Ellen and I were very much in love with each other. She just wanted to wait until I'd finished medical school." I could tell that Doug was being careful to keep his tone neutral.

"Douglas, you know perfectly well how old-fashioned Mum is! We shouldn't, either of us, listen to her about any of this stuff."

There was a long silence. A cool wind was coming in off the Bay, and I could hear the tops of the trees beginning to stir above me. If I timed my retreat carefully, I might be able to sneak away...

Then Doug started up again. "Did Garth ever—"

"No! Of course not! Don't be an idiot."

Now, I thought—*now* is the time to retrace my steps, but Doug had moved closer to the screen.

"Never?" he persisted.

"Garth doesn't—" She inhaled quickly. "Listen, he doesn't even *see* me."

"Doesn't see you? What do you mean?"

"I'm not sure if I can explain! After more than four years, I literally bump into him down on the beach. It almost took my breath away to see him like that again. Mum hinted that he might come up, but I thought it would be later in the summer."

"It must have been a surprise for him, too."

"I suppose it was. But he didn't even recognize me, not at first anyway. Douglas, I think I've just got to accept that he doesn't *see* me."

"I still don't understand—"

"I can tell: any woman could. Garth thinks of me as your kid sister. Period." She paused and swallowed. "Douglas, I'm going to be thirty-four in a few weeks! But he's always seen me simply as your kid sister—and always will."

"Well, you are my kid sister," Doug said softly. They were both in shadow, and I saw Doug move forward and put his arm around her. It seemed to me—I wasn't sure—that Clare had started to cry.

"Clare," Doug murmured, hugging her shoulders. "Don't…"

"I'm just being stupid." I could hear her voice choking a little. "Sometimes I don't even know what I'm saying."

Doug said something that I couldn't catch, but I heard Clare say, "Please don't pay any attention to any of this! I'm actually a bit raw from all that stuff at the Museum. Still overtired and emotionally bruised, I think."

I took a careful step back, but had to lean against the side of the house, feeling angry with myself for listening for so long. She'd never forgive me, if she knew…

"I'll be fine. Really I will." Clare had calmed her voice. "Mum's right. At one time I absolutely adored Garth. But that was long ago, and I've grown older and wiser since those days. And frankly, I can tell—any woman could. He just doesn't—*see* me that way."

I straightened up, absolutely determined to leave them.

"Then why have you come back up here, practically every summer?" Doug asked quietly.

She didn't answer, and I hardly dared to breathe—then I heard a chair creak as Doug sat down and muttered, "Oh, Clare!"

I stole another glance through the screen: Doug was leaning forward, his chin in his hands. "Garth didn't swear me to secrecy. But I wonder if I should have told you."

"Told me what? What are you talking about?" Clare dropped into the chair next to him.

Now I had to stay.

"I've not even told Ellen about what really happened," Doug began, "because—listen—Evienne was not—she was not the easiest person to get along with."

"I know that it wasn't all perfect between them. It never is," Clare said quietly. "But what do you mean, 'what really happened'?" This time her tone was startled. "Everyone knows what a tragedy the accident was. It was awful—only a few months before their wedding. Garth's mother always went on about how heartbroken he was."

"Evienne almost killed Garth in that accident. It's a miracle he survived." Doug's voice was shaking slightly as he said it.

"What?" Clare gasped. "But wasn't Garth the driver?"

"No. Evienne was driving—and she was loaded. Drunk, stoned—you name it. Why Garth ever got into the car with her, I'll never know. But he promised Evienne's father to take the blame as long as there were no criminal charges. Supposedly it would have killed her mother to know Evienne was an addict. Thankfully no one else was hurt, but I never liked the whole thing. Garth claimed it was easier that way."

"Easier! How terrible! How did Garth ever—? And everyone thinking it was his fault, and those awful journalists bringing it up again when he got his award!"

"He's pretty thick-skinned, but that's not all of it. Very few people know this, but he'd called off the wedding. You've no idea just how bad things had become. I could tell you some things that would—"

"Stop!" she cried, jumping up. "You've told me enough. I don't want you to break your word to Garth!" She moved away from him abruptly, and I saw her in profile, staring out at the Bay and hugging her arms around her body.

"I think you should talk to him about Evienne," Doug insisted quietly. "It might really help him."

"Talk to him about Evienne?" Clare echoed. "How could I possibly do that?"

I looked down; Mars was licking my hand and Farley was sitting on the ground at my feet, staring up at me inquisitively. Before I could grab him, he ran around to the front and whimpered to be let in.

I heard Doug rise and slide the door open.

"That's Garth's dog," Clare said quickly. "He must be coming up from the beach. I'm going to go splash some cold water on my face." I heard her hurry back inside the cottage.

I waited for a few seconds—then I took a deep breath and walked around to the front.

"Garth!" Doug exclaimed warmly, looking up as I tapped on the screen. He opened the door, and I smiled, taking his outstretched hand and grasping it firmly.

We both looked full into each other's eyes for a split second, and then, stepping back, he offered me a glass of scotch.

MARGED BRICE
Cape Prius—1897

July 20

I have so wanted to stay near the cottage—to be near Auntie Alis and Mother, and Tad and Uncle Gil. I am anxious if away from them, and I do not know why. Perhaps it was the terrible storm and its devastation.

Allan is here almost every day, and Mr. Thompson visits us, too. But he stays and stays and won't leave. Finally, Auntie became quite exasperated and tied an apron around his waist and had him kneading dough. I don't think he minded at all, although I certainly did not care to see him thus employed. So I had him come upstairs and read to Mother; he has a fine sensibility for poetry, and she seemed quite pleased to have his company. Poor Mother. She must be lonely at times, though I do try to be with her as much as I possibly can.

Mr. Thompson seems a little dazed and says that Dr. McTavish is in a very bad way indeed. Allan confirms this and informs us that George is with him frequently and that they have had long talks and that George is urging him to continue with his book. But Dr. McTavish won't go near his library, and the nets have been neglected.

Allan says that he saw Dr. McTavish weeping, and I told him to hush and never to tell anyone of it. I told him that sometimes one sees things—a moment of weakness in another person perhaps—but that these must be kept a secret and not used against him. That such a secret is a sacred trust and that it would be unmanly to betray these confidences.

He asked me if I thought Miss Ferguson would agree, and I looked at him in surprise, wondering at his question.

"She is very clever," Allan continued, and he looked at me a little slyly, as if trying to read my features for some reaction.

"She talks to George all the time about art—oh, for hours," he added, noting no doubt my involuntary frown. "She is very knowledgeable about it."

"She says her father can help George," he added. "He is a patron or some such thing and takes her to Europe with him and buys all kinds of expensive things—all the new art, she says. She wants her father to arrange for a show of George's work. She says that he is a great artist."

"What does George say to this?" I asked, in spite of myself.

"Oh, he listens," said Allan. "George is really quite ambitious. He's had a rough go of it with some of the critics. They go after him because he doesn't—you know—paint pictures like they're supposed to be. The realish sort. His colors are always so muddled in a way. Hey, do you like his pictures?" he asked me suddenly, looking up from where he was sprawled on the grass.

I flushed. I thought of all George's canvases floating in the Basin and the portrait that I had jeopardized through my clumsiness.

"Yes," I said, hesitating a little, and then thinking of the grove of trees. "Some of them are quite beautiful."

"Have you seen his picture of Miss Ferguson?" he

asked. "She adores it and says he could be a famous portrait painter if he really wanted to. She said he could meet other famous artists—if he wanted—if he went to New York—"

"I suppose they get along rather well?" I interrupted him in what I intended to be an unconcerned tone, though I was burning with curiosity.

"Oh, smashingly!" said Allan, and got up, brushing off his trousers.

And now I am cross and cannot sleep. I should not let Allan speak to me so and encourage such gossip! It is not my affair, and I should exert myself to pay more attention to our studies.

Which we have sorely neglected, I might add, since the storm.

July 25

Captain Howarth has been back several times to talk with Tad, and it seems that there is discussion of a foghorn being installed. Father and Uncle Gilbert would have to man it. For my part, I do not like to have Captain Howarth around us, though of course I am polite and would not wish him to think me discourteous.

It seems there has been quite a fuss in the papers about the *Mary Jane,* and indeed we have read some of these reports. There are strong opinions expressed against the government for its inattention to the light stations, and Mr. Ferguson—Effie's husband—has been quoted at length about how there must be support for shipping on the Great Lakes.

Effie's baby has taken ill, and Dr. Clowes was out to the Lodge, though it is nothing serious. But none of us are to visit until the coast is clear: Effie has such ideas about contagion!

July 28

Today I went to see Dr. McTavish, and I am very glad that I did. He seems to have aged so and is thin and terribly wretched. I had tea with him, and he seemed glad of my company, and I promised to come back if it would suit him. He nodded so vigorously that I felt ashamed that I had not gone before. Mr. Thompson looked quite pleased and hovered near us as we sipped our tea, and Dr. McTavish even growled at him a bit in his old way, and this seemed to give Mr. Thompson great pleasure.

Perhaps it was perverse of me, but I saw Dr. McTavish so lonely and desolate—and indeed my heart gave all its sympathy to him—that I could not but feel grateful that we were, just there, in that moment, together and alive. That I could look out at the Bay—so glorious and sparkling, though but three weeks ago it had been a fiend—and that I would go home to Tad and Auntie and Uncle Gilbert, and we would sit down to dinner. And then I would take Mother her tray and help her to eat her supper and then read to her while Dewi rested at her feet and Agnes purred in her lap. I felt so grateful, and I wanted to walk under the trees and see the stars come out. I felt such a quiet joy that the storm had passed, and I think my mood must have communicated itself to Dr. McTavish somehow, for he brightened and he took my hand and said that my visit had done him a world of good.

I met George coming in as I was leaving, and I think I must have smiled my gratitude at him, and he could not but help return it.

We talked a little, and he said something about Effie's sterilizing spoons and I laughed—it was the first time since the *Mary Jane* went down that I think I have laughed, and it came out of me as a song might, its notes filling the room and spilling out through the windows.

"You at least are full of sunshine today," George remarked.

And then somehow I had to explain, lest he think me heartless and uncaring.

"Oh, George," I said. "It is *so* very terrible. My heart breaks for the families who have lost their dear ones. But I am glad somehow that we were spared. It seems a miracle that none of the men from Cape Prius were drowned. Don't you think we should be glad to be alive. Is it wrong to feel so? Would the dead really begrudge me my thankfulness for the lives of my father and Uncle Gil and Dr. McTavish?" I might have added George's name, but I dared not.

I don't know what possessed me. Tonight as I sit here, it strikes me as such a strange thing for me to say to him.

And then Dr. McTavish came in, and he looked at me in the most penetrating fashion, peering at me over the top of his glasses. I felt that he had heard my words, and I blushed.

"Yes, you are quite right," he said. And then he walked over to his library and Mr. Thompson was there looking at me strangely, too!

George watched the doctor go, and he tapped his finger against my cheek lightly. "You're a strange girl," he said. "What looks to be stumbles are, in fact, the steps of an impenetrable design!"

"Like your brushstrokes?" I shot back at him, but there was no rancor in it. It was true. The magic of his brushstrokes appears to be in the accident of his placing them on the canvas—seemingly careless—and yet I know that it takes great skill.

He looked at me thoughtfully and then walked to the front porch, beckoning me to join him. I could feel Mr. Thompson's eyes following us out of the room.

George has asked me if I would come each day and help Dr. McTavish order his papers and encourage him (without seeming to) to return to his work. I am delighted by this suggestion! Allan and I can hardly resume our studies after such unsettling events, and it will do us both good to assist him. We will go back to our old custom of setting out the nets, and Dr. McTavish can discourse to us on his beloved birds.

I have not seen Miss Ferguson for days and did not detect her presence anywhere about the Lodge.

August 1

Captain Howarth has been here again. Indeed my misgivings about his visits have proved to have some foundation.

There is no mistake that he is a handsome man, in a dark, brooding sort of way. I suppose there are some who would find him comely, but I have never been at my ease with him; his eyes burn into one so! He is tall and so straight in his uniform that I must tilt my head back to look up at him, and then his eyes seem to blaze right through me. I have made it a point of honor not to look away, but it has been a sore test at times.

Today he came late in the afternoon, and I was at the back of the cottage, taking the sheets from the line and folding them, for it was washing day, and though Auntie usually does this task, she had been called away to some other undertaking. George and Allan had come by and were talking with Tad about the fog house, and Allan was quite animated about it all. I could hear him on the front porch discussing where it should be built, and Tad patiently explaining that the government men would determine that.

Captain Howarth did not approach the house from the front yard, but must have taken the side path so as not to be seen by Tad. He addressed me with a pleasant enough "Good afternoon, Miss Brice," and I returned his greeting but kept on with my task, indicating with a nod that he could proceed to the cottage where the men were.

He did not move but kept a watch over me, uttering not a word. The minutes passed, and I labored away silently. By and by, I grew uneasy with his strange deportment, and I felt his eyes upon my body, intently watching, or so it seemed to me, the movement of my arms as I reached to the sheets and took them down. I began to feel a great discomfort, as if he had intruded upon me as I was bathing and I stood in front of him naked and exposed. Finally I could stand it no longer. I drew in my breath sharply and moved behind one of the sheets, my face aflame. He had not said a word, but neither did he back away or look contrite that I had discovered him engaged in an inspection so unbecoming to his station. I felt that I could have slapped his face, so indignant was I!

He seemed to read my thoughts. But then, he had the audacity to grin at me! A slow and deliberate grin that gave his expression an evil cast. I recoiled, for his meaning did not escape me, and though I was outraged by his boldness, I grew increasingly uneasy under his unmistakably salacious gaze. It was then that I looked over to see that Tad and George had come down from the porch and were watching him—George with his hands clenched at his sides and my father with his eyes an angry black.

Tad said little at supper, but he did mention as he left to fetch the wood for Auntie that he did not think that we would be bothered by visits from Captain Howarth anymore. Auntie Alis looked at me questioningly, but I stared at my plate until she had finished with hers.

I do hope that Captain Howarth stays away, for I think that, between them, Tad and Uncle Gil would kill him if he were to bring harm to any of us!

August 7

I am so chilled tonight! I have wrapped myself in a warm quilt and am sitting close to the stove downstairs.

Mother was quite agitated by my absence, and Auntie Alis is angry with me for staying out in the fog, but I have not yet told her of what detained me.

This evening, after supper, I took Flore over to the old cemetery. Since the *Mary Jane* went down, I have ever had the image of those graves in my mind, and I thought I might place some flowers next to each one and tidy them a little so that they are not neglected. And I have been remiss in tending to little Luke's grave and did not like that Auntie A. should think me callous and indifferent to her grief. It still sits with her through all these years, and though Auntie is quite stoic and people will say she is hard, I believe her heart bleeds yet for this loss—her only child.

Twilight was just descending when I arrived, and there was no one else about the cemetery. It is a very old one, and few of the families bury their dead there anymore. It is but a small expanse of grass on a windy knoll that overlooks the Bay. At night, any spirits who might linger there surely have the clearest view of the light station and its ever-revolving orb. We buried Mrs. McTavish in a quiet corner, just as Dr. McTavish wished. Seven of the passengers from the *Mary Jane* are also here; these were the bodies too far decomposed to be sent back home. Theirs are the newest graves, and they looked to me somehow still uneasy and restive, as if the earth, turned over and dug out, is reluctant to receive these new and so violently acquired remains. I swept the debris from Luke's grave and then smoothed the turf upon the graves of the two children from the *Mary Jane*.

It was very quiet and still in the cemetery. Indeed,

at times I am drawn to its air of soft melancholia. There is a very old grave—a child's grave that is recessed deep in a corner. No other graves are near it, and the headstone is weathered white, so that it looks almost like a bone protruding from the earth. Its isolation from the others gives it quite a forlorn aspect. For reasons I cannot explain, I am drawn to this little tomb, and I like to sit and place my hand on the turf and hum a lullaby to it, as if the child might hear me and take comfort. The stone has only a *P* carved into it, and the date below is so worn that it is no longer legible. I have taken to calling the child Perdita because she is buried all alone and with none of her family nearby. I sense that the child must have been a girl, and though I know she must be with the angels in heaven, queer sensations come over me near her grave, and I begin to believe that it is a little lost creature and that it would be forgotten if even my infrequent attentions ceased. It is my fancy, I suppose!

I found the quiet of the graveyard strangely soothing, and though the light grew dim, I did not like to move. As I sat thus, an evening fog came up over the hill and spread downward over all the stones and enveloped me in a moist cloud. Still I did not move, and my mind wandered as if in a dream over nothing in particular, and I felt an incongruous but pleasing stupor steal over me.

I must have lingered by the grave for nearly an hour, but was finally roused by Flore's impatient whinnying and the feeling of a chill settling in my chest. I rose and stamped my feet and saw that the fog had grown denser. It gave the place a cold, gloomy cast, and all of a sudden, I wished to leave it. The fog disoriented me, though, and as it thickened I could not tell which was the way to the bluff and which the way back to the iron gate. I became rather disconcerted as the fog quickened its descent and swirled around me, for I realized that I could see only a few paces in front of me. This advantage soon vanished in the churning fog, and I looked about as a blind person might.

I turned to touch Flore's flank, and I drew myself up and away from the grave. It was then that I thought I felt a little hand, ice cold, take my fingers and give a tug to them. I cried out in fear and drew my hand away quickly, urging Flore forward while I walked at her side. My heart was racing so! She led me up and out of the graveyard, and as we cleared the gate, I chastised myself for my imagination. I mounted Flore quickly and we rode off toward the cottage, taking the longer but surer road.

The fog had lifted a little when I was a mile or so from home. I passed by Mr. Brown's farm and saw that three men were stopped in conversation by his gate. The darkness was descending fast, but by the rising moon, I could make out the outlines of Mr. Brown, his son Donald, and Captain Howarth, who was standing next to a black mount. Donald stepped out a few paces and raised his arm in greeting, but I only nodded and hastened forward, for I had no desire to stop in conversation with Captain Howarth.

I rode on quickly, but it was with a strange anxiety. I had stayed on the main road because of the fog, but I knew that if I remained on it, Captain Howarth could, without much effort on his faster horse, overtake me and force his company upon me for the remainder of my journey. Deciding to take a path that edged the woods, I urged Flore off the road.

Ere ten minutes had passed when I heard the faint sound of horse hooves behind me. I dismounted quickly and pulled Flore with haste into a thicket of trees, and there I waited, winded from my exertions and dismayed that it was perhaps Captain Howarth, and that he had guessed my detour and was following me.

I thought that it must be nine o'clock or thereabouts, but the fog had made the evening so dark that I strained my eyes into the blackness. Soon I saw the form of Captain Howarth—I could tell him by his officer's cap—guiding his horse slowly along the path, the reins held tightly in one hand. He was just a silhouette, yet I felt a strange dread come over me and grew still. I felt as a tiny animal might in the presence of a larger predator, hardly daring to breathe or move.

I watched him, my eyes never leaving his dark outline, and I thought of how I would escape into the forest and what direction my flight would take should Flore's breathing betray me. But she was as silent as I, and he—as if he knew we were close by—halted but a few paces away.

My nerves were sorely tested in those few minutes, and I took a deep and soundless breath to steady my trembling and calm my inner turmoil. Indeed I felt him to be a dangerous man!

I do not know how long he stood there, but at last he stirred his horse and, giving it a vicious kick, made his way in the direction of the main road. Even then I did not trust that my safe passage was assured, and so Flore and I remained hidden for several minutes longer. At last I felt that I might creep forward. I led Flore soundlessly across the meadow, and upon reaching the other end, I rode quickly the last half mile home along the track, seeing and hearing no one.

I have not told Tad, but I am disturbed by these events, though I think the chill I feel deep in my bones is perhaps more of the fog's doing than Captain Howarth's.

August 14

I have not felt quite myself for the past few days, and a dry, hot cough disturbs me at night. My dreams, too, sometimes disturb me. It is that little girl—my Perdita. I do not know why she comes to me in my dreams. Have I beckoned her forth—awakened her and drawn her from her grave?

But I grow so very tired, and even the walk to the Lodge seems to fatigue me. But still I have gone. Allan and I have spent most of our time helping Dr. McTavish organize his papers—or so we call the afternoon's activities. We always seem to start with good intentions, but somehow a conversation commences, and then we are deeply engrossed in listening to Dr. McTavish describe the habits of his birds, and then he always has something to show us. Next we are off, following a trail in the woods. Indeed, he is very disorganized, but we have found some of the most marvelous treasures in his piles of papers and notes—wondrous illustrations that he has done of birds, male and female. I rather suspect that he has forgotten about them, for he becomes so enthusiastic about the next project that the former one is quickly pushed aside.

But his knowledge of birds is truly formidable! Today he told us about the chimney swift (*Chaetura pelagica*).

Allan thought that he had espied a family of them in the ruins of the old barn, and Mr. Thompson told us this was quite unusual as swifts are usually city birds and rarely venture out into a forested area. Dr. McTavish expressed skepticism (he never says a word but just looks at Mr. Thompson over his glasses in a pointed fashion), and so we all trekked out to the barn with field glasses in hand and waited for the swifts to return. We went at twilight, as Dr. McTavish said that this would be the best time to catch the birds returning to their roost.

The forest was quite beautiful, and there was just a hint of change in the air—something I feel at this time of year and yet can hardly describe. It is the light, I suppose. It loses its bold, summertime quality and is somehow more muted and languorous. It is as if it knows the fall is coming and signals us—and yet there is no need for hurry, it seems to say.

We waited for half an hour in silence, hidden from view behind a thicket of cedars. It was Allan who saw them first. The swifts are not nesting in the old barn at all but in the cavity of a rotting tree. Mr. Thompson explained in a whisper that these creatures are possessed of very weak legs and so are ever reluctant to land. They feed and mate and even sleep while flying!

I expressed disbelief at the latter, but Dr. McTavish confirmed that indeed they do sleep while flying, giving themselves over to the wind currents while they rest. I believe I should like to be one of them if I were a bird—for once airborne, I think that I might wish to ride the wind as long as I could, like a cloud.

We made our way back to the doctor's lodge, rather rapidly, for the mosquitoes found us just as the darkness set in and they pursued us with vigor, though we all had our netting on. Dr. McTavish's abode is quite a cozy place—in a rumpled, dare I say untidy, masculine sort of way. By this, I suppose I mean that no feminine touch has ever ordered it, at least to my knowledge. Dr. McTavish will not have a housekeeper, and it is Mr. Thompson who serves as assistant, valet, cook, and house servant. He is, in appearance, an extremely neat man, fastidious as to his clothes and person, and I have often noted that his hands are ever clean and well manicured in spite of all the work he does with them.

Mr. Thompson is quite an enigma: he is always surprising us, just as he did this evening. After we returned, Dr. McTavish insisted that we light a fire, and he poured us all a glass of sherry. Before long we were pleasantly encamped around the hearth with his two dogs, Bruce and Clem, at our feet. He says they are named after two of his adversaries at the university and it is his revenge to treat them "as dogs"! He only chuckles when I point out how kind a master he is, and he says that kindness *is* his revenge. Unfathomable man!

We ate a dinner of bread and cheese, though Allan burnt the toast dreadfully. I don't know how we quite got upon the subject—perhaps it was the sherry that prompted it—but Dr. McTavish as ever began to discuss birds and before long was discoursing on his favorite, the cedar waxwing, his darling *Bombycilla cedrorum*. I rather think that Dr. McTavish is drawn to this bird because of its somewhat unusual but rather gentlemanly personality. He explained that the male is apt to gorge himself on fermenting berries in the spring and the result is a remarkable, if rather wobbly, courtship dance. Allan and I expressed disbelief and refused to have our legs pulled, or so we said. And then, of course, Dr. McTavish had to demonstrate the dance—his face and eyes becoming instantly like that of a bird—and he moved about like a slightly tipsy courtier, now proudly puffing out his chest and then tilting his head in what we gathered would be an alluring fashion to a female waxwing.

We were transfixed by his performance, and before long, and to our delight, we were subject to a wondrous repertoire of birdcalls and behaviors. Mr. Thompson is himself quite talented in this regard, though he is not as advanced in his skills as Dr. McTavish. Still, his rendition of a blue jay was remarkable, and even Dr. McTavish admitted that he had never heard better. The evening progressed from birds to poetry, and—I rather think a few glasses of sherry later—Mr. Thompson, to our utter astonishment and at no instigation, rose solemnly and recited Tennyson's "Charge of the Light Brigade" from memory. Not only did he recite it, but he performed it with dramatic gestures and theatrical tones. It was a Mr. Thompson that we had never seen before, and I found myself wondering if some secret twin had crept into the room, spirited the real Mr. Thompson away, and taken his place!

When he had finished, Allan and I stared at him, quite speechless. I think we clapped a little awkwardly but with genuine appreciation. Then, with barely a moment's pause, Mr. Thompson strode to the front of the fireplace, placed his thumbs in the top two buttonholes of his jacket, and fixed his eyes on a distant point behind us. He cleared his throat and then proceeded to recite "The Rime of the Ancient Mariner," in its entirety! I practically held my breath as he beautifully narrated the familiar stanzas. When he had finished, we sprang up spontaneously and applauded loudly. We spoke all at once, Dr. McTavish intoning deep "bravos" and Allan whooping shrilly as if his school team had just scored at a rugby match. Mr. Thompson turned to me to see my response. I, of course, smiled and indicated my appreciation, and he seemed quite gratified.

We must have made quite a racket, for George strode in and found us all in animated conversation. I think that the sherry had much to do with Mr. Thompson's spontaneous performance, for we had to lead him back to his chair, as he seemed almost on the verge of physical collapse. We praised his performance over and over again to George, who assumed a gently cynical expression, as if he wished to tease us with his disbelief. This, of course, only made us argue our case more energetically, and his smile turned into a wide grin when he espied the bottle of sherry sitting calmly on the mantelpiece. He picked the bottle up and held it to the light as if measuring its contents, and I could not help but laugh at his insinuation.

"Dr. McTavish," he began. "I am shocked, sir. Truly shocked to find that audiences are being plied with spirits to elicit favorable responses for your theatricals."

We all laughed, especially at Dr. McTavish's sheepish grin and at George's mocking refusal to share a glass with him. George pretended to turn his nose up at the sherry but said that he might be able to find some interest for the doctor's scotch. I did not know it, but Dr. McTavish has a very fine supply in his "cellar," that is, a crate carefully preserved in his library. Then he and George had a glass of the amber fluid, but I absolutely would not let Allan have any; I did not think that they would really allow it, but it was better that I, a woman, refused it on his behalf.

I had not heeded the clock, but the hour had gotten late when much to our surprise there was a knock at the door. It was Tad come to get me, and I immediately jumped up, vexed with myself for causing him undue worry and the inconvenience of the walk from the lighthouse. He smiled, though.

"Sit, daughter," he said. "Gil may watch the Light for a time without me."

We stayed for half an hour, and Tad had just a small glass of scotch with the others—though not Mr. Thompson, for he retired soon after Tad arrived.

I sat by the fire with Allan, who had grown quite sleepy, and I listened to the men talking, drawn to the sound of their voices. I could tell that they liked each other—though perhaps without each man knowing the other well. Their words tested each other in a way that intrigued me: each man with his own hammer striking the other's surface with skill and listening for the true ring of steel. At times they did it with seriousness and at others with humor, but I felt them drawing out that deep sound from one another...the sound of a good man.

I could hear Tad's resonant, solid strength so clearly and the doctor's, too—but George's was a little softer. I took note of him, for he did not speak as much as the others, as if deferring to the older men. It was peculiar to see him as the youngest man, for to me he has always been so much older than I. But this evening I saw him as a young man next to Tad. I felt, I think for the first time in my life, the true and manly beauty of my father's life.

We walked home, Tad and I, with my arm in his. The night air had turned chill, and we spoke but little. When he reached the cottage, he turned to me and patted my arm.

"No need to tell Alis about my visit," he said. "It would only fret her."

He grinned impishly, and I could see his eyes twinkling in the darkness. I knew he was referencing the scotch, and I smiled thinking of how Auntie A. would respond to my own, *single* glass of sherry.

August 18

Dr. McTavish's hands are not as steady as they once were, and he has had me helping him with his drawings. Today I worked upon an illustration of a male purple martin (*Progne subis*), and he was so pleased with my efforts that he says he will teach me to do more of the illustrations. In this fashion, then, I may be of great assistance to his book. I must admit that I am very pleased with his confidence, for I have never thought of my fingers as skilled in artistic pursuits.

Perhaps it is a result of my work with him, but I feel that I can depend upon Dr. McTavish's judgment and that he will respect my confidence. I told him about my nighttime encounter with Captain Howarth. To be sure I have been a little preoccupied and I am strangely reluctant to tell Tad about it. The doctor listened gravely and asked me a few questions. He wanted to know particularly if the detour I had chosen was visible from the Brown farm, and I said that I thought not. Then he asked me if the roads were muddy and if Flore might have left tracks, and I recollected that it was wet and damp owing to the fog and that perhaps we had, if someone cared to look closely. Then I told how Captain Howarth had stopped but five paces away and seemed to be searching for something.

Dr. McTavish listened most carefully, and then he shook his head and muttered that it was not the behavior of an honest man.

I did not mention the previous incident at our cottage, but Dr. McTavish grew rather serious and looked at me in an anxious way over the rim of his glasses. Mr. Thompson must have been listening from the other room, for he entered the library as I was finishing and wore a very grave and worried expression.

I almost immediately regretted relating these events to Dr. McTavish and do not know what possessed me to do so, for now I suspect that he will wish me to be prudent in my choice of walks and excursions, especially when alone. And yet I am so resentful of these precautions. I have ever been free in my movements here, and I cannot—I will not—be circumscribed by the likes of a Captain Howarth!

August 22

I worked with Dr. McTavish until late in the evening, taking my dinner with him. Mr. Thompson cooked a simple but quite tasty meal of sausages and a kind of sliced potato that he says is a family recipe. They both eat by the fire with plates on their laps, and so I joined them, though I was rather preoccupied with not spilling the sauce that Mr. Thompson heaped upon my potatoes. I began to help Mr. Thompson clear the dishes, but he seemed so embarrassed by my presence in the kitchen that I left him to complete the task alone.

I sat with Dr. McTavish for a while, and from his window we could see lights at the Stewarts' lodge grow dim. At one point, I fancied that I saw Allan gamboling about on the back porch, and then we heard old Mr. Stewart's voice calling him in harshly. And then a half hour later, George came by—I suppose he does quite frequently in the evenings—and he talked with the doctor while I finished my work and tidied our drawing materials. I heard them talking about Miss Ferguson and her enthusiasm for George's paintings. George seems quite animated about the prospect of a show in New York.

I wonder if George wishes to be famous; I suppose that I have not contemplated this, at least as regards to myself. I have always thought of fame as something that comes to a person because of what he does—like Mr. Muir, I assume. But Allan has mentioned the great difficulties George has faced with his paintings and his restlessness at his own insignificance because the critics do not appreciate his work. To be sure, this seems to be the lot of many artists. It brings to my mind stories I have heard about painters working alone, in poverty and isolation, and then going mad little by little, day by day. Oh, I do not think George will pursue that route! I dearly pray that he might not!

I cannot express it well, but I know that some of his paintings are timeless, beautiful; they will be recognized as such, of that I am sure. But I do not know when. I hope that it is in his lifetime so that he may experience being recognized. This would be a great blessing. But I also feel that he must risk that it might not be so—perhaps not unlike the chance a tree takes as it grows to be three hundred years old even as its fellows are mercilessly felled. Otherwise George's paintings will not be...true. Not true to himself, not true to this place. Oh, I express it but poorly!

I know from Allan that Miss Ferguson encourages George to be more...active, I suppose, in making people aware of his art. She says that he must have a sponsor—that all the great artists have had one—and that without one he is doomed to obscurity. Could this be true?

This evening Mr. Thompson offered to escort me home, but George insisted that he had a matter to discuss with Tad. He was distracted and even a little strained with me as we walked back together. I think he was not pleased to hear of my nocturnal flight from

Captain Howarth, for he mentioned that Dr. McTavish had told him of it. I bristled at what I saw as his interference. It is not just a reckless perversity in me. Nor am I insensitive to the kind interest that he takes in my welfare. It is just that I am wary of having my movements restricted by anyone! I could not bear it to be so! I told him as much, though I do not know if he really heard me.

I feel as if I must take the dangers of this place as part of my freedom here; a bear, a man, a snake—any might disturb me, and yet I do not feel as if harm would come to me. Is this a reckless confidence? Did the trees, too, grow in innocence, trusting to the future, only to be cut down so brutally by the axes and greed of men?

George stopped me before we entered the cottage gate and said that I must consider those who might worry as a result of my indifference to their concerns. He said this rather sternly, and I shrank from his tone. I asked him if he would have stayed back in the storm from rescuing the *Mary Jane*'s passengers because of our worry for his life?

He said it was not the same but—I cannot explain—somehow it is for me. Are women to have no courage, too? I must have my freedom to move, to be alive—here! I assured him that I was not careless but that I should detest the fear—the fear of…and then I could not entirely describe it.

There have been times when I have walked toward the water, out into the blackness at night right below the light station: it is so dark that I cannot tell where the water begins and the land ends. And my heart is always thumping wildly. It feels as if I am being swallowed alive by something enormous and terrifying. I know that if I give in to my fear, I can turn back and run away to safety, and yet I go on, refusing my fear. Then, when I am there at the edge, with the water almost at my feet and the vastness of the sky making me feel smaller and yet smaller, and the Bay unseen and waiting in front of me—I know to stop. I come to rest just past the moment where my fear might prevent me from taking another step. And then I feel truly in the company of the stones who have only true fear. The Bay seems so old to me then—older than even I can imagine, old enough to be eternal.

Of course I did not tell George all this. I am sure he thinks me contrary. He spent a good hour alone with Tad, and now I am vexed because I do not know what they discussed.

August 26

We have a new dog—a great big beast named Claude, and Tad has asked me to take charge of him. He is one of Mr. Samuels's dogs, a mastiff, and he is such a large brute with wide, watery eyes. I think he has taken a fancy to me, for he follows me everywhere and waits outside without as much as a whimper while I am occupied. Clem and Bruce sniffed him from head to tail and then left off, as if to say that he was acceptable, but barely so! At first Dewi would not even condescend to acknowledge Claude's existence, and of course—as an infinitely superior feline—Agnes won't deign to notice a dog.

Tad says that Claude did not get along well with

Mr. Samuels's other dogs, though I am puzzled as to how such a lugubrious animal could incite animosity in another creature. His spirits are so…melancholic and yet so endearing. Claude is quite appreciative in his way and most painfully loyal; he has made me feel as if I have an obligation to keep *him* company!

I think that Dewi is secretly very pleased to have a companion, but only after his authority was established. It is really quite funny to see Claude, who is a great, hulking thing, deferring to little, energetic Dewi. After one day they were the best of friends.

I brought Claude up to meet Mother, and he was most well behaved. He walked up to her bedside in quite a dignified manner and placed his head where she could easily touch it. He seemed so apologetic for the intrusion, and I could have sworn that his little grunts were a "good day, ma'am." Mother smiled and tried to stroke his ears, and I was so pleased. She seems a little better. I read to her from Victor Hugo's letters, and she held my hand while I read.

It is awful to remember it, but Auntie says that we are lucky Mother did not die; I was not allowed to go near her at first, and it almost killed me. Auntie A. was afraid to let me see her, for the seizure was quite disfiguring at first. But Tad sat with her every day for hours.

I remember rushing away from St. Ed's, my clothes all a jumble in my trunk, and then taking the train to Owen Sound the day after the telegram summoned me home because she might be dying. I held it all the way in my hand, crushing it and telling myself that it could not be true. And then I could not see her—not really see her—for weeks!

And now she is so silent. The woman who has been my teacher and companion my whole life, unable to speak even simple words. Even at the college, I felt her with me: it is because she has always been so patient, always guiding and nurturing me. It is she who really understands me—who understands the true nature of choices. Yet even without words, somehow Mother and I communicate; ever do I feel her love, as if some invisible thread connects us forever.

Her Christian name is Fabienne, and I love to hear Tad speak it: he says it in such a tender way that time seems to stop. I know he loves her dearly—my rough Tad. She was supposed to marry…a man of a different class, I suppose. Tad went to school, but she—she was very well educated. It seems not to have made a difference between them, and sometimes I have wondered about this. Could I ever care for a man who was not educated? I know that there is a difference between ignorance and an education. I could never bear the former! Auntie A. said Mother's family was very rich, but I am certain this is an exaggeration. Mother once told me that her father's plans to marry her were thwarted when a young soldier rescued her from her carriage. It had overturned in the street because one of the wheels had broken. She was not injured, but that is all I know of how they met—except that in Montreal I have a grandfather who seems very angry with Tad. And there is Mother's sister, my Aunt Louise, who prays fervently for a family reconciliation. It seems all so remote and unreal from here. I have never met either of them, though Aunt Louise writes us faithfully.

Could I ever be so hard as to disown my own

child for marrying the man she loved? I cannot imagine doing such a cold and heartless thing; it seems a tyranny that only humans are capable of. For though we call animals dumb beasts without the discernment of good and evil, is it not worse to possess a soul that can love deeply and then betray it because of our own prejudices?

August 28

Miss Ferguson has persuaded Mrs. Stewart to forgo the annual picnic she always holds at the Lodge for the holiday families, and instead to sail to Collingwood aboard a pleasure boat. I am surprised at her suggestion after what has happened—it seems so thoughtless, especially as she included Dr. McTavish in her invitations. Allan says that Caroline finds the Basin "quaint," but that she pines for more "interesting" amusements. I have managed to avoid her for most of the summer, and indeed I do not know how she spends her time. I do know that she is with Effie and Mrs. Stewart constantly, and that I have been remiss in my attentions to them, though Dr. McTavish has kept me very busy and my excuse is an honest one.

Allan is my only source of information on the inner life of the Lodge, and there are times when I wish that my curiosity were not…such that it is. From him I gather that George and Miss Ferguson are quite intimate and that they hold long conversations upon intellectual and philosophical topics. I sometimes wonder if Allan is quite telling me the truth about them, since

I catch him out on inconsistencies now and then, but he is quick to query my interest, and then I must drop the subject.

It seems that Miss Ferguson's father will meet the party in Collingwood and that he is coming to visit Effie and his grandchild and to be introduced to George as a possible sponsor of his work. I know that old Mr. Stewart is quite pleased with Miss Ferguson's attentions to his stepson, but I am not so sure about Mrs. Stewart. I walked past the Lodge at noontime yesterday, and I saw her sitting alone on the front veranda. She beckoned for me to come over and join her, so I advanced and took a chair beside her.

I noticed with some dismay that her cheeks were moist, as if she had been weeping, but I gave no indication of it. She seemed old and frail all of a sudden, so I rose to fetch a shawl, and I wrapped it gently around her shoulders. As I bent over her, she grasped my hand and almost clutched at it, as if she were afraid to be there alone. I returned her grip firmly, and then I began to tell her about my drawings for Dr. McTavish and about the birds we had netted, keeping my voice low and soothing.

Mrs. Stewart gave no sign that she heard me, and her eyes seemed vacant, as if her thoughts were elsewhere. At length I stopped, and the silence deepened around us. The she turned to me and said, "How is your mother?"

I told her that she had seemed a little better of late and that we were hopeful.

"Your mother and I were friends at one time," she said. "When we were young girls."

I looked at her in surprise, for I had no such knowledge of their acquaintance. Then Mrs. Stewart turned her face toward me and uttered rather strange words.

"We both swore to one another that we would marry for love—and we did." She hesitated. "And then he died, and I forgot my promise."

I could see two large tears forming in her eyes. They spilled over onto her lashes and hung there so eloquently. I knew, then, that her heart was breaking and that she was a terribly unhappy woman.

I pressed her hand, saying nothing. The door from the house swung open suddenly, and she turned to me and whispered hoarsely, "Don't you forget such a promise."

Old Mr. Stewart appeared with George, and I could feel her body stiffen instantly; the teardrops disappeared. I know not how, but it was as if they had evaporated and her features settled into their usual expression. In that moment I saw that she was still a very beautiful woman, but her face expressed nothing but the icy exquisiteness of its own form.

Mr. Stewart scowled at me rather ferociously, and George took my elbow as if to draw me back and away from a bitter exchange about to take place. On an impulse, I bent over and kissed Mrs. Stewart's cheek and her beautiful lips curved in gracious forgiveness of my impetuosity—but I knew that she was already gone and that some other entity had returned to endure her husband.

I walked with George through the garden, and he deposited me silently at Dr. McTavish's gate but would go no farther. I searched his face, and I saw a great sadness cross his features—it was such that my own eyes filled with tears.

I felt I had no right to intrude upon his pain, and so I lowered my eyes and walked away from him without a word.

September 1

I shall never remark upon Claude's lethargy again! Indeed, I had no idea of his power and swiftness until this evening, and I will ever be grateful to Mr. Samuels for sending him to us. I shiver even now to recollect the experience. There is no doubt in my mind that Captain Howarth is an evil man and that he is a disgrace to his uniform.

I have not told Tad or Uncle Gilbert of what happened, and perhaps I will not have to, for I am afraid of what course of action they might pursue. Surely it is best to leave events as they have unfolded. But I am quite certain that Captain Howarth will no longer molest me with his presence lest he risk a repeat of Claude's ferocity. I fear also that Claude has left him disfigured, but surely it is only as he deserves!

This evening I had to return a small boy—a child who had wandered into our garden—back to the fishing camp. It was just after supper, and the poor fellow had been crying profusely. He was sure that he would be severely punished if ever he were to find his mother again. Auntie and I tried to soothe him. We gave him a ginger cookie and some milk, and this seemed to make his travails all the more worthwhile, for he soon became quite cheery and between mouthfuls told us all about his family and their adventures at the camp. He seemed to have so many brothers and sisters that I was not certain that he had even been missed. I proposed to escort him home, and Auntie A. assented as long as Claude accompanied me.

At first Jeffie—for that was the little boy's name—was quite intimidated by Claude's enormousness and hid behind my skirts, afraid that his massive jaws would swallow him up in a single gulp. By and by, I coaxed the boy forward, and I placed him on Claude's back as we took the path down to the camp. Jeffie started out by insisting he hold on to my sleeve, but by the time we reached his tent, he was riding like a wrangler and urging him onward with his heels. Claude, however, had had quite enough of his passenger—for it was a good half-hour walk—and he unceremoniously dumped Jeffie at his mother's feet and left her standing, speechless with fear, at the entrance to their cooking quarters.

I was quite amused by all this, but soon repented because the poor woman had been quite frantic as to the whereabouts of her littlest one, and it was only with some effort that I quieted her shrieks. But it seems that I was not quick enough, for before long several women appeared banging pots and pans and asking with some urgency where was the bear. I must say that Claude showed remarkable foresight in disappearing into the bush, and it was Jeffie who was left to explain that he had ridden on a great beast that was a dog and a bear all at once.

The women were distant to me, and I could not

blame them, for I had enjoyed this little bit of mischief—though I was to regret it only minutes later! I whistled to Claude, and I heard a great creaking and crackling of dry sticks in the woods, and then I set off back up the path assuming that he was behind me in the growing darkness.

It was a cool, clear evening, and the wind had risen so that the trees tossed around me in a stormy, surging sea. I had my back to the water and was but ten minutes or so away from the camp, when an intense shaft of light lit up my path and I turned expecting to see someone with a lantern. It was the moon appearing from behind the clouds, and it cast its full and brilliant light on the path before me. I stopped to admire it, and it was then that Captain Howarth stepped out of the woods and stood impeding my way forward.

I gasped and froze. I thought perhaps that he had seen me earlier, though I had not discerned him, and that this was no chance encounter. He waited for a few minutes, eyeing me ominously, and there was a strange tension in the man's form, as if he were a steel coil wound tightly and ready to spring. I looked about for Claude, but I could not see him.

At last he said, "Good evening, Miss Brice."

I did not like his tone, for it seemed faintly mocking to me, but I swallowed and nodded, my heart pounding and a strange, unfamiliar fear freezing my limbs.

"I shall walk a ways with you," he said, and took my arm roughly.

I mustered my wits and withdrew my arm fiercely and turned upon him a look of what I wished to be utter disdain. He laughed a low, unpleasant laugh, and then, after glancing around as if to assure himself of our isolation, he faced me and placed his hands upon my shoulders, working them slowly up to my neck. Then he put his thumbs on my throat, just below my chin, and applied a slight, almost caressing pressure. I felt the man's raw strength in his hands, and he seemed to be intent on provoking some reaction in me. I felt that if I screamed he would strangle me on the spot.

I became very still.

"Yes, just stay quiet, just as you are," he muttered, his breath coming in short, shallow bursts like an animal panting. Then, with his hands still around my neck, he moved his face close to mine, and I could feel his breath upon my face. I closed my eyes, not knowing what to do, thinking that once his hands were released from my neck, I might try to escape.

I have no doubt of what ill he intended for me, but it was Claude who saved me. With a low growl, he leapt suddenly out of the woods and tackled Captain Howarth with all the force of his big body, knocking him down onto the path, and there he tore into his neck and shoulder with his great jaws. The man writhed beneath Claude's huge form, but he could not lift the dog off him. I turned and ran up the path as swiftly as my legs could carry me, and then I heard Captain Howarth's screams behind me. I was sure the dog was going to kill him, and so I called to Claude frantically. He reluctantly backed away but continued to snarl at Captain Howarth, whose face was wet and covered in dirt. He lifted his arm to his mouth and wiped blood from it, his form prostrate and breathing heavily.

"Call him off, call him off," he shrieked at me, and Claude crouched as if to resume his attack.

I called Claude's name again and again and whistled urgently. Finally he came to me. I ran all the way back to the cottage with Claude at my heels, leaving Captain Howarth bleeding in the pathway: but I made sure to turn back at the hilltop, unsure as to what to do if he were indeed dying. I saw him rise and then lean heavily against a tree stump. I did not linger, but made my way home with as much haste as I could muster.

At least he is not dead…

I will have to tell Tad. I see now that I must. Might he not bring harm to another? I will just bathe my eyes and tidy my hair; and I must give Claude a drink of water and clean his face for I am sure that Captain Howarth's blood must be upon him!

September 2

It has rained and rained for the past two days, and the wind has been fierce. I have stayed inside and have made much progress with Dr. McTavish's papers. They are now carefully organized, and I have gently extracted from the doctor a description of what he envisions for his book. I believe now that I can help him complete it, and I have even been so bold as to suggest an outline of chapters for the text. I believe that my training in composition will be of some assistance, for Dr. McTavish has bits and pieces of all kinds of fascinating facts and observations, but he seems to lack a sense of the overall organization of his book. I have discovered that it is not that he is untidy; indeed, he seems to know where everything is. And how he remembers what he has worked on from year to year is quite a miracle, yet he does! No, I have decided that it is more like going into a room that looks cluttered but really just reflects the sensibilities of an eccentric. I must help him make "his room" look like a book, and I believe that I can be of service to him in this respect. I suspect, too, that he likes the fact that I do not scold him for his disorder, though sometimes I grow exasperated and think longingly of the efficiency that an Auntie Alis would bring to his library.

I am also enjoying my drawing very much. Dr. McTavish has already taught me a great deal, and he has urged me to take up sketching just to train my fingers and, as he says, to turn my thinking to visual forms. He is most pleased with my progress, and I have learned a great deal about mixing colors and the differences among all the various types of brushes and how they can be used. The work Dr. McTavish does is very different from George's painting, for his birds are quite lifelike and he is extremely diligent as to the detailing of the plumage and color.

I saw George today from the doctor's window; he was standing out at the Point, looking at the waves in the rain. He seemed quite meditative, and so I watched him for a little while, wondering what he was thinking. Then, on an impulse, I took up a pencil and tried to sketch his form amidst the intermittent sheets of rain with the wind tugging at his coat. I had barely started when a figure in white, whom I took to be Miss Ferguson, joined him and seemed to entreat him to turn about and come back to the house. At first George seemed not to heed her, and then I thought that I saw him put his arm around her waist and go with her back to the Lodge.

September 4

This afternoon, Tad drew me aside after he had arisen. Auntie Alis looked to Mother while I made the tea, and he told me that Captain Howarth is no longer stationed in our area.

I hardly dared to look at him, for I did not wish to show him my relief. Still, the image of Captain Howarth shrieking under Claude's attack disturbed me, and so I asked after his injuries. Tad gave me a stern look and said that it was none of our affair, and so I did not pursue further conversation with him.

Auntie A. asked me what had made Father's countenance so black, and I told her everything—more than I had told Father. I cried a little as I told her, but it did me good. But then she became Auntie again and set forth all her arguments about why a woman needed a husband. I only half listened, but I did not object as I usually do, for if I am truthful, there is something in me that is drawn to the idea of a husband. If a man truly loved me, then I think I would find the grace to accept his tender care, but I could never acquiesce to any authority masquerading as protection.

September 6

First the rain, and now three days of the most dreadful heat with barely a respite in the evening. It has tried everyone, even those with the best of tempers, and we all seem to be at sixes and sevens with one another. Allan told me that I have been quite cross with him, and so to make it up, I announced that we would abandon our work and take a long hike up the shore.

This hike is a bit of an annual event, for each summer we walk just a little farther than the previous year's trek. Both of us are convinced that the shore will eventually lead us to some extraordinary site, but it just repeats itself in a seemingly endless series of points. We always pretend that we have come to the last one, only to reach it and see the same pattern appear beyond.

I packed a hearty lunch with all of Allan's favorite treats: Auntie's gingerbread, jam and bread, and a thick wedge of ham. We set off well after breakfast—Tad was still asleep when I left—and we took Claude, who seems to be the only one unruffled by this hateful heat. The flies have been dreadful, and so we did not take Dewi, who is tormented so awfully by their sharp bites. Claude rolls himself in the mud by the pond, and though we will not allow him in the house because of this acquired filth, I must admit that it seems to keep him free of flies. Poor Dewi—I don't think we could ever convince him to give up his coveted place on Mother's bed, and so he shall just have to suffer through this torpid weather with flies and all.

Allan and I must have walked for two hours when we stopped exhausted, both covered in perspiration but feeling so much better for our activity. Allan was soaked through, and my skirt was quite wet also, for there are several spots where one has to climb around pieces of the escarpment that jut out into the Bay in order to make one's way to the next inlet. But the heat was such that it was not long before we were dry enough to make our picnic.

It turned out that Allan had been sampling our lunch for quite some time—indeed, I had seen him out of the corner of my eye—and that our gingerbread supplies, in particular, were severely diminished. I pretended to be cross, but no one was fooled except Claude, who came and licked my hand with a great series of mollifying sighs and whimperings. We both laughed and laughed and then teased Claude for being such a big, foolish creature.

Allan went for a swim while I packed up our lunch, and then, while he rested in the sun and I reclined in the shade, we watched the waves and a lovely sense of idleness came over us.

It was then that Allan sat up and said, "Margie—there, you're coughing again!"

I had not noticed it, but it was true. I had almost grown accustomed to the dry, hacking cough that has assailed me since the evening I spent in the cemetery when the fog caught me unawares. Allan insisted that I move into the sunlight, and so I wrapped one of the napkins around my hat and stretched out in the sun. The warmth was undeniably healing, and I closed my eyes only to open them and find Allan eyeing me rather intently.

"What is it, Allan?" I asked.

"Do you know," he said, cocking his head to one side, "you've not been well this summer…rather sickly in fact."

"What do you mean?" I sat up indignantly. I hardly liked to think of myself as weak and frail, and I deeply resented the imputation.

"You hurt your ankle, remember, in George's studio? And then your hand was all bandaged up for days, and now you are coughing all the time. Really, Margie, I am quite worried about you."

I was most taken aback, and I could not tell if Allan were joking and teasing me in his usual fashion. But I thought upon it for a moment and what he had recounted was true, though I had not attributed any special significance to my mishaps. Indeed, I am rarely without bruises or bumps and scrapes at the light station—though to be sure, it is not the same as living in a city.

"And," continued Allan, "now you have a great gash across your face."

My hand flew to my forehead. I had indeed acquired a scratch in my scuffle with Mr. Howarth, but had quite forgotten about it since it was not a serious injury by any means.

Allan turned gloomy and sighed.

"Allan, whatever is the matter?" I asked.

I will not recount in detail the discussion that ensued, but we talked for over an hour and it seems that Allan is being exposed to some—I regret that it does sound judgmental but I know no other fitting word—*nonsense* about something called spiritualism by Miss Ferguson.

Indeed I had heard of it at the college, for there was a girl whose aunt took us to a lecture by a woman who communicated with spirits. I was rather unnerved by her, and I did not like at all what she had to say, though the lady who took us was quite enthusiastic.

Allan, it appears, is convinced that I am at some great risk, for he feels that there is a black cloud hanging over me and that I must do something to dispel it else my fate will be a dark one indeed. Allan is rather confused in his description of spiritualism, but he thinks that my "accidents" are an indication that I am not in proper connection to the world around me, and that I perhaps require some guidance from the spirit world.

I was most alarmed by his discourse, though I showed none of my dismay. To do so would only be taken as encouragement to a boy like Allan, and so I kept my visage calm and noncommittal. I did, however, ask him how he had heard of all this, and he explained that Miss Ferguson, and her father in particular, were zealous spiritualists. In New York, they had held a gathering where a woman—a medium he called her—had tried to contact Caroline's mother and strange things had happened. There had been rappings on the table in answer to questions, and Caroline was convinced that her mother had returned from the grave.

I asked Allan if Miss Ferguson had told him all this—because I could not imagine her taking such an interest in a young boy—and he rather sheepishly explained that he had overheard her talking with George and Dr. McTavish. The doctor, it seems, is quite skeptical, but Allan thinks he may be convinced to try to contact Mrs. McTavish through such means.

It was with some effort that I got Allan on to other subjects, and I assured him that I was not suffering from a series of portentous accidents, but rather was troubled only by a regular round of little mishaps, such as one might expect living where I did. He seemed doubtful, but he did not resume his talk of spiritualism.

And now I am quite at a loss. Is George interested in such things? I can see that Dr. McTavish, in his extreme grief for his wife, might bend an ear to such talk, but I cannot imagine that George would take it seriously. Perhaps I have not thought of it enough. I do admit I know little about it, but there is something in me that resists it.

September 10

They have all left for Collingwood, and it could not have been a more beautiful day for their departure. They will be gone for four days, and I wish that my heart were more generous toward this excursion, but I must admit that I am more than a little resentful about my exclusion. I made nothing of it, though, for Allan, I think, felt divided in his loyalties and uneasy at the absence of an invitation for me. I am afraid that these ideas about spirits have taken root in his fertile imagination and that Miss Ferguson may be developing—perhaps—an unsought but nevertheless significant influence over his thoughts. He is still ever with Tad and Uncle Gil, though, and I take great comfort in this, for I cannot think of better company for a young, impressionable boy.

September 11

Yet again I must turn to this diary to discover my true thoughts—for this has been a strange day. I don't know why, but I think I am pleased with it, though I sense that he might have had something further that he wished to say to me.

I awoke this morning fretful. I do think the pleasure party to Collingwood irked me more than I liked to acknowledge, and I suffered from a peculiar depression. As I brushed my hair before the glass, I grew so dissatisfied with my appearance that I scowled at myself.

I don't know why, but I could not stand the thought of remaining at home, and so I resolved to go out riding for the whole day and return after supper. I announced this to Auntie, who eyed me sternly but was wise enough not to gainsay me. Perhaps she was not unrelieved to have me gone for a few hours, for I do think I have tried her patience these past two days.

I made sure Uncle Gil had no need for Flore and then saddled her up, packing my lunch and paper and some pencils Dr. McTavish had given me. It is not the first time I have disappeared for a stretch of hours in this way, but Uncle Gil instructed me to take along Claude, and I knew by his tone that there was to be no contradiction.

Claude is quite an agile creature despite his massive size, and with his long legs, he is able to keep pace with Flore for a good distance. So we bore away, following the old Mill Road and then striking off into the bush for a short space, finally coming to a path that I had never seen before. Its aspect was rugged, and

Flore shied away from it, for the roots of the cedars had crisscrossed its surface and they looked quite like snakes. I got down, took her reins, and then the three of us proceeded forward, going deeper into the woods and following the path without knowing where we were going.

To be sure I was not truly lost, but I felt just a little lost, and to my surprise the sensation this produced in me was one of tranquillity. The temperature was cool, and the earth smelt fresh with fermenting needles. I breathed in the verdant perfume of the cedars, and I felt myself growing calm and quiet. With each step I took, I felt my dissatisfaction and restiveness diminish, and I was no longer plagued by that awful sensation of looking at myself in the mirror, disliking what I saw, and then hating the mirror for its silent acquiescence.

I do not know how, but the forest took away all of my ill-feelings, and I followed the trail with a deep, abiding serenity, though I did not know where I was going, and yet I trusted it and took a secret delight in its quiet mystery. I felt as if I walked in a dream, yet I was aware that I was dreaming, and so I knew the dream was fleeting.

We came to a clearing, and the forest broke suddenly, for the Bay showed itself not thirty paces away. I was about to step forward onto the uneven sheets of rock when Claude growled low in his throat as he does when he detects a stranger's presence. I hushed him and held him by the collar, but his ears pricked up and his tail began to wag. I peered through a spray of branches and saw George precariously perched on a ledge and standing before his easel. I drew back startled. I had thought he had left with all the others for Collingwood, but here he was before me! I doubted my eyes, and so I took another look. It was indeed George, and from my hidden bower, I watched him, noting his expression and movements almost as a bird might be studied unawares. So intrigued was I that I inadvertently loosened my grip upon Claude, and before I could stop him, he had bounded, forward barking joyously and interrupting George in his work.

I stayed back, embarrassed at intruding upon his privacy and foolishly hoping that George might send Claude away and simply resume his work.

"Where's your mistress?" I heard him say in response to Claude's animated communications, and then the silly creature came leaping back to me, giving away my hiding spot without a second's hesitation. Indeed, Claude looked as if he expected some reward for being so clever in finding George for me!

I came forward tentatively and waved as if to indicate that we were just passing by. It must have looked a little ridiculous, as it was quite a secluded spot, and if anything, George must have suspected that I had followed him to it. I was positively mortified at the thought, and so I held back awkwardly. But he smiled so broadly and beckoned me forward. I tied Flore to a tree and then stepped out onto the rock, the bright sunlight blinding me for a moment.

"Marged," George exclaimed. "You've come to my rescue. I've forgotten my lunch, and I'm famished! Do you have a few morsels of food you could spare a starving artist?"

I could not help smiling. His tone was friendly, and

he did not seem at all displeased to see me. I was suddenly glad that I had taken so much trouble that morning with my provisions, and I ran back to get them. George folded up his easel and tucked his canvas and box of paints carefully behind an outcropping.

I felt my old shyness of him descend upon me, but he seemed not to notice and chatted quite gaily about his good fortune and the prodigious contents of what he called my equestrian pantry. He seemed like a man so much in his element, so much at ease out on the rocks and amidst the wind and water. It was as if he were in his own castle surrounded by familiar things and confident in his ownership of them.

I so liked to see him thus, and it must have seemed as if I were staring, but I finally found my tongue and told him how we had discovered the path and of my desire for a day of quiet meandering in the woods. I dared not ask him about why he had not joined the party to Collingwood, though my curiosity was strong.

We talked much on idle matters—I refused to eat until he was settled with a piece of bread and a slice of cheese, and then he said he would not take a bite until I prepared my repast. So I cut myself some cheese with his pocketknife, and he asked me about the birds I had seen in the woods, and we talked of the dearth of holiday boaters in the Basin this year. His brow darkened only once, when I mentioned the fishermen's camp, but he quickly moved on to another topic. I think he did this to put me at my ease, and before long I felt quite comfortable, though we were sitting on rough rocks and the wind kept blowing my hair into my eyes.

I asked him about his canvas, and he told me it was a

painting of the two buoys that flanked the entrance to the Basin, and that he had come out to this location because he wished to paint them against a rougher backdrop of water. I remembered what Allan had told me and asked him if this were the painting he was going to call *Good and Evil*. He laughed and said that he gathered Allan had been spying on him. Then he turned suddenly serious and asked me what I thought of the title.

I was quiet for a moment, for to be truthful, I had not liked it, and yet I did not know why.

"Well," I began, "one buoy is for starboard and the other is for port. I do not see how one can be good and the other evil, for both are guides and the one is necessary to the other."

"Precisely," said George. "But do you not think that good and evil have meaning for us only when they are in tension—when they are together, the one contingent upon the other?"

I nodded, for I understood what he meant. After a few seconds, I turned to him and said, "But do you not think that we can—that man has the capacity to truly discern the one from the other? If you are right, then all that we can hope for is passage between them and nothing else."

He looked at me curiously, and then he asked me the most peculiar question.

"Which are you, then, Marged, starboard or port?" His eyes were looking intently into mine, and I could see the golden flecks shimmering in them.

I was silent again and sat looking out over the water, struggling to find the right words. Then I got up, and dusting off my skirt, I answered him.

"I think that I am neither, for I am more inclined to the waves that move around and through the buoys. The buoys are tied and pull constantly at their leashes. They are captive to man's desires; they are his tools of navigation. I could only find but a passing reference in them, not a true course. For that, I would head for the open sea. Isn't that what one really wishes for when one is sailing? It is the open water that is the best part of being on a boat; when the wind takes you where you are going, and for a moment it seems as if the boat and the wind are one and the same. That's the true course."

I do not know what possessed me to say such things to him, but in my way I think it was a gesture of my friendship, for I had answered his question with my real thoughts and had not twisted them in deference to any polite convention.

He did not answer, but he held my gaze for a few seconds, saying nothing but looking at me quite thoughtfully.

"Then where are good and evil?" he asked.

"Why, both are in ourselves," I exclaimed, bending over to gather up the remaining food.

He placed his hand on my arm, arresting my movement.

"You know," he said slowly, "Dr. McTavish thinks that you are quite…that you are a girl of great intelligence."

I flushed and moved away, though I was pleased to hear this.

I think he might have wished to say more to me, but his face grew closed, as if the image of someone or something passed before his eyes, and he withdrew. I took his hand and gently pried open his fingers and placed two of Auntie's ginger cookies in his palm, then closed his fingers around them one by one.

Then I smiled at him and wished him a good afternoon and whistled for Claude.

I am not at all sure what to make of this encounter, except that I feel it was a lovely, lovely day. It is as if a small ball of fire is alight in my heart, and sometimes I am aglow with happiness. Yet in the next instance, I feel a terrible ache and I grow afraid.

September 14

It has been a wild and windy day, and Dr. McTavish said that there would be no netting of birds today, for these gusts might bring them injury. Sometimes I cannot fathom how the trees withstand the wind, as they seem to bend right over and the wind shakes them so furiously. Perhaps it is a game between the two of them, a contest of wills and strength. I do not sense that the wind is patronizing these trees, but is in true earnest as it seizes them anew with fresh gusts and unrelenting power.

Allan has told me all about the trip to Collingwood and seems a bit disappointed that the activities were dominated by the wishes of the adults. He brought me back a stick of peppermint, and I took this to be a gesture of great regard, for I am sure that Allan would not forgo a sweet without great sacrifice!

Mr. Ferguson—Caroline's father—has come to the Lodge for a few days, and I met him yesterday morning as I walked back from the Point. Though in his sixties, I should think, he is still quite a handsome man, with thick silver hair and a well-groomed beard. His manners are most gracious, and he kindly acknowledged that he had heard of me from Allan who has told him that I am "jolly" and quite "sporting." For some reason, I did not mind that he should tease me in so gentle a fashion though we have not met before, and I smiled thinking of Allan's description of me.

I saw him for a second time in the afternoon, for Mrs. Stewart invited Dr. McTavish and myself for tea—and Mr. Thompson of course. Miss Ferguson is attentive to her father, though I perceive a coldness between them, and he talked much of his other daughter, Ruth, who is, I gather, an accomplished musician.

Miss Ferguson barely acknowledged me when I entered the drawing room and seemed quite preoccupied. George was there, too, and I tried to catch his eye but soon gave up, as he took no notice of me, and then he was absent from the room when I took my departure.

I found the conversation stilted and uncomfortable, and Miss Ferguson kept directing it back to a discussion of George's art show in New York. She spoke as if it were a confirmed event, and as George did not contradict her—though he was strangely silent on the matter—I assumed it to be true.

I took my leave soon after for I did not wish to prolong my stay among such uncomfortable company: everyone appeared so constrained and Mr. Thompson spilled his tea, twice, and knocked over a small plate of cakes. To my surprise Miss Ferguson accompanied me to the door, and as I thanked her for the tea, she became suddenly animated and, grasping my arm, she said how pleased we must all be for George, for this was to be the beginning of his career as a great artist. Her eyes blazed with such strange lights, and she said that they were to be very busy in the next few weeks making arrangements and that she hoped that nothing would interfere with these preparations.

I gazed at her silently, wondering at her. For my part, hers was an unsolicited volubility. I discerned that they were to leave shortly—the Fergusons and Stewarts, and of course George.

I could feel her fingernails pressing disagreeably through the fabric of my sleeve, and I gently but firmly removed her hand from my arm. She seemed taken aback, and she surveyed my face as if to read its reaction, though I kept my features impassive. I thought I saw in her manner a strange…desperation! And then I felt a sudden pity for her. Perhaps I conveyed some of this in my face, for she stepped away haughtily and eyed me with what struck me as a look of sheer poison.

Well, I, too, have had my share of winds today that seem to test my mettle. To be sure I have stood my ground, but I must observe my trees more closely, for they seem to retain their equanimity better under such sieges and I—I seem to have lost a good deal of mine!

September 16

I am extremely busy these days—trying to get all the

doctor's papers in order before he leaves. I am so tired at night that once or twice I have fallen asleep without fully undressing.

George came over to Dr. McTavish's today, and they were closeted in the library for quite a time. I thought he might stop to speak with me, but he left without a word, though I know he was aware I was in the study at the drawing board. Perhaps he is thinking of all his preparations. I am saddened that they are leaving in just a few weeks.

September 25

I can no longer mistake George's avoidance of me. I have no right to expect any particular attention, but his behavior is so queerly distant, and certainly he seems to evade any exchange with me beyond a mere greeting. And these are so constrained. He will not even look me in the eyes, and I am puzzled and not a little hurt by all of this.

September 27

I now avoid going near the Stewart's Lodge altogether, for it gives me a strange depression to know that George eschews my presence—or that it gives him some displeasure for reasons that are unknown to me. Perhaps I offended him when I spoke of his painting, but truly he gave no indication of it at the time.

September 29

My cough has grown more troublesome, and Dr. McTavish walked home with me and instructed Auntie A. to put me to bed. He spent a long time in the kitchen with her, supervising the brewing of a tea that he has had sent up to me, and I am to drink it three times a day.

Allan came, and he kept me amused with his caricatures of the fishermen while I sat in the window, bundled up as if it were the deep of December though it is but a few days from the beginning of October. There is already a tinge of winter in the air, and I felt quite drowsy as I watched the leaves drift gracefully to the ground. Such vivid costumes of red and orange for such a short flight! Even nature has her vanities…

October 1

Dr. McTavish's tea is quite foul-tasting, but I have been drinking it faithfully, though it seems to do me little good. I have only a meager appetite for food, and a strange languor possesses me. Each movement costs me such great exertion, and my chest feels as if it is burning all the time. Dr. Clowes has been to see me and says that I have a cold and that I must rest and only rest. Auntie A. says Mother misses me, and so we have devised a little scheme whereby Claude is our messenger, and I attach little notes to his collar, and he brings them to her room. Tad reads them to her—they are not lengthy—but even writing these seems to tire me so.

October 3

I awoke feeling better today, and so I rose and convinced Auntie to let me sit by the stove in the kitchen. I grow lonely in my room, and so I was quite content to watch her ministrations for supper.

I learned that Dr. McTavish has come practically every day to inquire after me and has scrupulously supervised Auntie A.'s production of that awful tea. The tears came to my eyes thinking of his kind attention, and I realized then how fond I have grown of him. How greatly do I miss his company and the stimulation of his knowledge and instruction!

Allan has been a bit of beast. He insists on relating how Miss Ferguson's intimacy with George is advancing—but it is all through suggestion and insinuation. Indeed he tortures me with his allusions to them, and yet I cannot tell him to cease his chatterings, for in truth, they have nothing to do with me. Auntie sent him away today, and I think it is the first time I have ever heard her speak harshly to him.

October 6

I am afraid that Auntie has offended Allan—for he has not been here. Now I am so remorseful, for what if I should lose his company!

October 8

Dr. Clowes has forbidden me to leave my bed, and I am now taking a medicine that leaves me drowsy and disoriented. The wind shrieks so and will wake me up…I am so very tired all the time.

October 15

I am much better today. Allan came to visit me, and I was so pleased to see him. I insisted on leaving my bed, though Auntie A. begged me not to, and went to my chair by the window. I was shocked to see how bare the trees are.

Allan brought his regards from his mother and from Effie (who would have visited, he said, except that she fears contagion). He did not mention George at all, and I thought it hard that George would not even send his regards.

And then a strange thought crossed my mind.

"Allan," I said. "Does George know that I am ill?"

He fidgeted awfully and would not look at me.

"He is going away soon, isn't he?"

Allan scowled and kicked at the rug.

"You *are* getting better, aren't you?" he demanded. He said it as a small child might, asserting his will despite adverse indications.

"Of course." I meant to reassure him, but a fit of coughing overcame me.

And then Allan was gone—as if the wind had taken him.

October 16

George came to visit me this morning, and I must admit I was glad to see him. I was feeling poorly, for I have been hot and fretful, and it is only now that I hear Tad coming to get Uncle Gilbert for his turn at the watch that I feel my fever subsiding a little.

How is it that around George I seem to think better—that I am not afraid to face my thoughts?

This morning I was awakened by the sound of Auntie Alis speaking to George downstairs and then their footsteps softly coming up toward me from the front stairs.

"She is not to be moved," Auntie was saying. "Dr. Clowes says that we are to get him if she worsens."

I grew agitated at the thought of seeing George, and I could feel my face growing hot and flushed. What should I say to him? I thought of his imminent departure and Caroline and her father, and yet, in all honesty, I was not happy for him.

George entered my room, and he held his hat awkwardly, as if to indicate his reluctance to intrude upon my sickroom and signal the brevity of his visit. He paused and looked to me from the doorway, and then, in a startled fashion, he strode over to my bedside. His eyes searched my face with no small degree of dismay, and I shrank a little under his inspection. He turned and flashed an angry expression toward Auntie.

He put his hat down upon my desk and pulled a chair up close to me, and then he took my hand with lines of worry creasing his forehead.

"Marged!" he said softly. He held my hand gently

between his own, and they felt so cool and pleasant to me. "Marged—I did not know you were this ill!"

I said nothing but looked into his eyes and my heart was suddenly filled with a deep and overwhelming sorrow. A great and ponderous unhappiness pervaded me, and it seemed as if I were already dead and gone and that I looked out at him as if from my grave. No doubt it was my fever distorting all that I felt.

"Marged! Will you not speak to me?"

My eyes started to water. I felt it was so stupid and childish of me, but I knew my fever to be returning and I could not help it.

"George—Allan says that you will be selling all your paintings at a show in New York, and I am so afraid…"

He looked at me with such a puzzled expression that I could not bear to face him as I spoke, so I turned my head away and addressed the wall. "I know you must, and of course you will be a great artist, and Miss Ferguson, her father—will be your—sponsor—but—"

Then it burst from me: "Oh, I am afraid that you will sell that painting—the one of the cedar chapel!"

It came out as a rush of words, all jumbled and confused, not at all the way I had intended to express myself. I pressed my hands to my temples in an agony of frustration. I did not know how to speak to him! I sounded like such a fool!

He drew back, a little surprised. "What the devil has Allan been telling you?" he exclaimed.

"George," I said, sighing, and then suddenly sitting upright, I grasped his hand and pressed it with agitation. "Please, please do not sell that painting!" I pleaded with him.

My voice must have alarmed him and perhaps the feverish glitter of my eyes, for his expression grew more worried. Auntie Alis came to me and stood by us, wringing her hands nervously.

"She is not herself, Mr. Stewart," she murmured. "Her mind wanders in her fever, and she takes a fancy to…"

The effort drained me of all energy, and I sank back against my pillow exhausted. I think I wished I might die, though the thought that my illness was a truly serious one had not occurred to me. In that moment it seemed to me George had been gone a long time and that he was going away again, perhaps forever, and that the painting, too, would disappear and with it would go a piece of my own soul.

My breath became labored, and I pulled at my collar, for it seemed to choke me, and my chest felt hot and tight and burning.

"Mrs. Barclay," George said quietly, "I want you to fetch Dr. Clowes right away."

Auntie Alis ran from the room, and I grew fretful again and started to toss and turn, pulling at my coverlet. I could not still my hands; they seemed to travel to my face and hair, and then they rested on George's sleeve and flew away as if burnt by hot fire.

He took one of my hands in his own, stilling it, and then he said, "Marged, I will never sell the painting of the trees. It will always be with you, wherever you are."

"Never?" I said. My voice sounded so peevish, so querulous!

"Never," he repeated, and I felt a soft reassurance steal over me.

And then I must have fallen asleep, and I was dreaming. And some of my dreams were so sweet. I dreamed that George stayed beside me, holding my hand, and he whispered, "My heart, my heart," into my ear, but ever so softly—like an owl's wings sweeping across a midnight sky.

I do not know what day it is. Dr. Clowes says I have been very ill but that I am over the worst of it. He says that I must not exert myself and that I must rest and stay quiet. But I feel myself growing well—each day I am much stronger.

Sometime earlier George brought over his picture of the cedar grove, and Tad has put it up where I can see it from my bed. And even now, as the light is changing, I can watch the trees and know them to be outside and close by.

I feel a strange sadness, for I know that I must separate from my trees for a time. Tad has told me that once I am strong enough, Mother and I will be going with Dr. McTavish to his home in Toronto for the rest of the winter. He has not decided whether he will go with us or stay with Uncle Gil and Auntie. He says there is a doctor there who can help Mother and that Aunt Louise will come and that it would be best for me to accompany her.

George and Dr. McTavish have not left the Basin yet, though they are making preparations and wish to leave before the winter storms commence. All the others are gone.

I am looking at George's painting—at my sylvan chapel. In my heart I believe these trees will bless us and protect us during our journeys. I know that they will wait for me through the cold, gray winter—bending with the wind as it blows across them unseen—my trees. Ever graceful, ever prayerful…ever faithful to God's wild breath.

And I, trusting to my return.

Nine

"Are you sure that's enough light?" I asked, walking toward her.

"I prefer natural light." Miss Brice hastily removed a pair of reading glasses and tucked them into her pocket. "I've never liked gas or electric light. Especially electric light. It's much too bright, and it hurts my eyes."

I could tell by her tone that she was pleased to see me. "Did you read my diaries?" Her voice quavered slightly.

"Of course," I thought. "She must be apprehensive about my reaction."

I told her I'd read them and then placed the journals in her lap. "In fact, I couldn't put them down. I stayed up two entire nights reading them. They're remarkable diaries. Needless to say, I was particularly surprised to find that the entries also featured two very famous Canadians."

"Oh, you mean George and Dr. McTavish. But let's not talk about all of *that*."

"Pardon me?" I tried to suppress my surprise and disappointment. "Would you mind telling me why?"

"Because"—she hesitated—"I'm aware that as a historian, you're probably much more interested in George Stewart, but Perdita is really the reason why I've had you read my diaries."

"Perdita? You mean the name you gave to the child buried in that cemetery?"

She began to pluck absently at her housecoat. "No, I don't mean *that* little girl. But before we go any further, there's something we should get out of the way."

"What's that?"

She sighed deeply, and I could tell she was making an effort to keep her voice calm. "You probably don't believe that they are my diaries. You probably think they couldn't be mine—isn't that so?"

I waited for a few seconds before replying. "Marged," I began gently, "you know, if you were the person who wrote those diaries—well, that would make you very old, wouldn't it?"

"Yes." She nodded firmly. "Yes, but I happen to *be* very, very old."

"Some people might find that hard to believe. I mean, hard to believe that someone could actually live for that long."

She turned to stare at me. "Do you? Do you find it hard to believe?"

I cleared my throat. "Yes, frankly, I do. You see, if you wrote those diaries, then in a little over three months you'll be turning one hundred and thirty-five." Again she nodded. "Marged, that's not—let's just say, not very likely. The oldest verified person on record is a woman who lived to one hundred and twenty-two years old. So a one-hundred-and-thirty-five-year-old person would break all the records instantly."

There was a long silence.

"Yes, I know it's not likely," she said at last, echoing my words. "But it's the truth." She gave me one of her penetrating looks. "What would make someone like you believe me?"

I explained that as a historian, I would look for something called empirical continuous documentation: a set of documents with dates that would connect her to the person's name on them.

"But Ava's lawyers took away all those things! I could only hide my birth certificate. Isn't that good enough?"

I shook my head. "That birth certificate could have belonged to someone else. Another female relative in your family, maybe an aunt—maybe even your mother." I looked at her out of the corner of my eye as I said "your mother," but she didn't flinch. "Are you sure you're not mistaken?" I asked softly. "Sometimes, as we age, we can get confused about things."

"I don't have dementia!" she exclaimed, her eyes blazing, and then she quickly took another deep breath, calming herself. "I know you have to ask me these things. It's just that I'm getting so tired of it all. I went over it again and again with the lawyers." She looked out the window moodily. "I don't suppose you could arrange to take a piece of me? Then you could date me like those archaeologists do. How I wish I could give you a chip of bone, and then you could set your mind at rest about my age."

"Marged," I insisted quietly, "believe me, I don't mean to offend you, but if you are the same Marged Brice as the woman listed on the birth certificate, then there would have to be some way to prove it."

"Has anyone ever asked you to prove who you are?"

I shook my head, instantly chastened by her question.

"Are you sure you don't have other documents?" I asked. "Say tax records or health cards or a passport. Do you have a driver's license? Even an expired one would be helpful."

"A driver's license! But that's not what you asked me. Don't you remember?"

I looked at her quizzically.

"You asked me, 'Who is Perdita?' That was your question." She leaned over and placed one of her hands on mine. "And then you said you would help me," she whispered hoarsely.

"Yes, I know I did. I've done a bit of research. I found out that there's a Perdita in one of Shakespeare's play—"

"Oh, no, Garth, she's much older than that. Perdita goes back much further than Shakespeare. Oh, we *will* have to do it the other way! But I'm warning you, it won't have anything to do with tax records or driver's licenses or that kind of thing."

"I'm open to whatever you have in mind."

"But it might—it might change you—change the way you think about things." She was studying my face again. "It's funny, isn't it? How our thinking can change. So suddenly sometimes. Things we never imagined. They can come upon us, like a bolt of lightning, can't they?"

Without waiting for my reply, she reached into the drawer and pulled out another leather-bound book. "I want you to keep reading, Professor Hellyer, just for a little while longer. You see, I'm trying to be very careful this time." She handed me the journal. "I just wish I knew how to prepare you."

"Prepare me for what?"

"Don't ask me, Garth. Please don't ask me—at least, not yet."

Toronto—January 20, 1898

Dear Auntie Alis,

I am writing this very quickly, for this letter will go with Tad, as he has agreed not to be present when Grandpere arrives. This morning he told me that he will go home to be with you until Mother's treatment is finished, and although I begged him not to, he insists upon it. Grandpere has made Tad's absence a condition of *his* visit, and I feel so keenly the injustice of such a demand! But Mother's confinement cannot be too much longer, I feel.

I will not dwell upon this, since there is much I wish to write of—too much, I fear, for the time I have in hand, and I am sure I will forget something important and scold myself for it after Tad has left. Tad is packing up his belongings as I write and says that I must be quick—indeed he fears the roads may not be passable beyond Owen Sound, but he is determined to reach home nevertheless.

I am sorry that I have not written you a proper letter since coming here, but the weeks have gone by so quickly, and I am very surprised to find that it is nearly two months that we have been here. I miss both you and Uncle Gil very much, and a day does not go by when my heart does not ache for home—though between the hospital and Dr. McT.'s bird drawings, I am kept very busy, and so you must not think that I am neglected and left idle to wallow in self-pity.

Mother is generally well; she continues to respond to the treatment, and I usually spend the afternoons with her. She is especially content and peaceful after she has received her "manipulation," as the nurses call it. Tad will explain, but this is a kind of slow, pushing movement of the hands over her limbs, and the doctors believe that these ministrations will assist in reversing the effects of the apoplexy. We have been wrong to keep Mother so still and quiet—or so her physician, Dr. Reid, has informed me. Here the nurses encourage her efforts to sit up by herself and to speak.

Sometimes they seem a little too forceful, and I must hold myself in check lest I interfere with them. But I cannot, in truth, argue with their methods, for Mother can hold a spoon quite securely in her right hand, and I do not think it will be long before she has the strength to bring it to her lips. It is just her speech that remains unimproved; the low gurgling sounds she makes are still perplexing, and sometimes I cannot discern whether she is expressing sadness, discomfort, or perhaps gratitude to us. I think this must tire Mother excessively, but she sleeps so pleasantly afterward, and I bring my books to her room and continue some of my studies as she rests.

I cannot even begin to tell you how many books Dr. McTavish has and the size of his library!

Tad and I are always the first ones Mother sees upon waking in the afternoon, and she seems quite content to find us there by her side. She often presses my hand while I sit with her, as if to reassure me that she is getting well and that we may have confidence in her convalescence.

I am not sure if Tad informed you of this in his last

letter, but Aunt Louise is now here, too; she is staying with us in Dr. McTavish's house and perhaps came to prepare the way for Grandpere. Tad will tell you that she is shy and a little nervous in her disposition—but perhaps it is because she must speak English among us and ever does she seem confused as to how to end her sentences. The result is a queer, rambling sort of speech, but I have grown quite used to it. Dr. McTavish has nicknamed her "mourning dove," for she is very loving and gentle (and quite plump!). She and Tad have had many tête-à-têtes, and though I have not been privy to their discussions, I am sure that they have come to an understanding about Grandpere's unseemly behavior.

Aunt Louise has certainly taken a fancy to me: she has procured almost a whole new wardrobe for me, as well as all the accoutrements of a fine lady. I am almost afraid that one day I will come to dinner in my undergarments, mistaking them for a fine gown—so elegant are some of these! She says that I must always wear a hat when I go outdoors—even if it is for a walk by myself about the grounds, and is not pleased with my habit of throwing a shawl over my hair. The hats Aunt Louise prefers for me are much too fancy, and already Tad teases me about my supposed fondness for couture.

I must say at least a little about Dr. McTavish's house, for I know Tad will not do justice to it. It is quite an enormous and beautiful home; the floors and walls are all of a dark wood that Ethel, the housemaid, seems to spend endless hours polishing. The house is full of light—almost excessively so—as almost every room can be lit with gas even on days when the sky is overcast and gray. To me it seems to be at least three houses in one, for it has two very large wings and immense gardens at the back, and along one side there is a funny little courtyard, and also a stable where the doctor's two horses, Guy and Fawkes, are housed. Of all the rooms, I am drawn most to the dining room. It is a round room—the first I have ever seen—and the chairs and the table are of a heavy wood, most elaborately carved and upholstered in a deep damask fabric that shimmers in such a way that I am reminded of blackbirds. There are heavy curtains on all of the windows, and Mrs. Evans, the housekeeper, loops these up with gold cords during the day so that the room might be brightened for our meals. Unlike the other rooms, this does convey a somber aspect, but it is so interesting that I am ever enchanted by its rich colors and all its ornaments.

My own bedroom on the second floor is of a lighter spirit, but it is very cozy. I have my very own fire, which Ethel lights for me in the morning before I have risen; and when I am gone in the afternoons, it is swept clean and a new one laid.

Dr. McTavish's house is set back from the crest of a very steep hill, and from my window I can see the Lake in the distance, though it is too far away for me to hear its movements. The street on which he lives is named Spadina, and has other grand mansions upon it, but the road itself is a very long one and extends down the hill, where there is a denser collection of smaller houses and buildings. I am told the street ends right at the Lake, and Dr. McTavish says that its name is an Indian word, though there is some disagreement over what it means.

Tad has spent very little time in the house, his hours consumed by his visits to the hospital—for such is what Mother's residence is called, though it also was once a private home. Now it is a hospital for patients with various illnesses, and there are several doctors there who have an expertise in the kind of ailment that has afflicted Mother. It is not far from here, and I can easily walk there, even in all the snow, for men have been hired to keep the roads and walkways cleared; indeed, they seem to always be about this work. They are strange, roughly dressed men of all ages, and some appear to be mere boys, but I am told that this kind of employment falls to those who are newly come to the city and that most of them speak only foreign languages. Yet thanks to their constant labors, I have had little difficulty in getting about and have discovered many pleasant walkways. I am quite strong again, and Aunt Louise is sometimes taken aback at my insistence on vigorous exercise; she seems to think my health delicate, but I think this is her general impression of all women.

Tad will be able to tell you more about Mother's progress—except here I will assuage any fears you may have about the hospital's cleanliness. The building is not large, I am told, as far as such institutions go, and though it sits on a considerable property of woods and garden, I do not think a wandering speck of dust or errant flake of dirt would last seconds indoors, so clean and tidy is it kept! Mother's room is small but quite comfortable, and she has a large window that looks out upon what is now an old and neglected orchard.

Nearby, but beyond the hospital grounds, are some lovely cottages—or so they are called, but to me they are quite large buildings in comparison to our own dwelling of that appellation. These belong to a group of artists, many of whom are friends of George Stewart. They have formed a kind of artists' community and have meetings and discussions about a variety of intellectual topics. Dr. McTavish is a member of this group and has hosted several of their gatherings. I find these occasions very interesting. The Stewarts have decided to winter in their Toronto home and so attend these gatherings as well; and I have been able to see Allan quite frequently as a result.

Tad says I must finish with my letter. Please forgive me if it seems scattered, for I have had no time to compose my words and arrange my thoughts in a proper order.

This separation is very hard on Tad! Even Mother seems to bear it better—though it was clear to me she was loath to have him leave her. Dear Auntie, I know you will be kind and tender to him. I fear I will meet my grandfather with a great anger in my heart. His request is so cruel—and Tad so generous to him!

Please give my love to Uncle Gilbert and tell him that I miss him so very much.

May God bless you all and keep you safe, and may we all be together again very soon.

Your loving niece,
Marged

Postscript. Tad is to give you a little sketch of a sparrow that has taken a fancy to my windowsill. Please tell Claude I miss him, too. And Dewi and Agnes and Flore. Kisses and hugs, my own Auntie Alis.

MARGED BRICE
Toronto—1898

January 22

I am glad to have remembered to bring my journal with me this afternoon—for it is in these quiet hours, when Mother sleeps so peacefully, that I am left with my thoughts and I sometimes grow restless trying to arrange my impressions. As ever, if I commit them to paper, it is as if I express myself to a trusted friend and my mind clears of some of its confusion. To be sure, our sojourn here—thus far—has brought me many solitary hours. Yet I feel that I am not overly lonely.

I must not think of these hours as heavy and monotonous, but rather fruitful spaces for thinking. Perhaps this diary is, in some ways, my mind's manner of drawing; these words begin as rough strokes as I strive to recount my experiences, and then, as I grow more confident, my thoughts become more subtle and nuanced. What an unusual and yet delightful image!

Perhaps it is being indoors so much that makes me restless sometimes. I watch the orchard fill up with snow almost as a bird might, looking out at the world through the bars of her cage. Why is it that the most interesting things seem to happen when I am outdoors, as if Nature tugs at my hand and pulls me headlong to share in some discovery. Such was the case with my stumbling upon the fountain yesterday—and of my meeting with Dr. Reid, the physician in charge of Mother's care.

At first introduction, he seems a somewhat rough

and disapproving man, and yet, as I grow accustomed to his direct and almost provoking manner, I find I like him. He is obviously a gifted doctor and is extraordinarily gentle with Mother. She trusts him; I can see it in her eyes as she looks at him and tries to follow his commands without any protestation. Tad, I think, was not a little angry with Dr. Reid for his abrupt and detailed inquiries into our habits and the foods Mother has been accustomed to eat—including some peculiar insinuations about her consumption of wine. But I was asked to leave the room for the remainder of that interview, and I fear he was even more probing. I am sure it offended Tad, for when he emerged from the doctor's office, his brow was black indeed.

I have since obtained a somewhat better sense of the man. He must be in his late thirties, or perhaps a little older, and would be a handsome man if he did not wear a habitual frown upon his face. Except around his patients, his visage seems to communicate disapproval of the human race and its proclivity to disease and illness. Yet, I have misjudged him, I am sure; perhaps he glowers to hide other emotions. To be sure, as a physician, he has attended to much suffering and even untimely death.

Yesterday, the nurses were delayed in coming to bathe Mother and then, when they did arrive, they requested that I leave them to their task for an hour or so. I was secretly glad, for it was a beautiful afternoon; the temperature was almost warm, the sun was shining so brilliantly, and the sky was a bold, fresh blue. I stepped downstairs with a lighter heart, and I was filled with a sudden and peaceful gratitude for the caring hands that surround Mother, and I felt as if I might take a respite from my watch.

I looked about for Aunt Louise but could not find her, so I got my coat and then, once outdoors, I wandered alone down one of the hospital ground's pathways until I came to a glade of very tall white pines. They towered above me like great, gentle giants, and I rested my hands against one of them, listening to the sound of their boughs moving softly. And then, because I did not move and waited with no expectation, I heard the whole forest sigh. It was such a beautiful sound—the wind moving from one end to the other and all the trees stirring as it moved past them so that, all together, they emitted a long, soft, fragrant breath. My eyes filled with tears, for I felt that somehow my pines at home were there with me in that gentle sigh, and that these trees were friends.

The snow was not deep under the forest's canopy, and so I ventured off the path and into its dark coolness—but I grew chill without the sun, and so I soon stepped out into a modest clearing that bore the faint tracks of some small animal in the melting snow. I quickly discerned that I was in a sort of walled garden, and at its center was what I took to be a fountain containing a statue that was disproportionately large in relation to its basin. There were still remnants of snow on three rather weatherworn forms, and a chickadee sat atop the foremost figure eyeing me saucily.

My first thought was that here were the Graces, for the three human forms were certainly Grecian in their aspect, and I thought I discerned Thalia languidly holding a spray of flowers in her upraised hand. But on closer inspection, I realized that the object she was grasping was a pair of shears, and instantly I knew that here was Atropos readying herself to sever the thread of life spun by her sister Clotho. I brushed off more of the snow and discovered Lachesis between the other two Fates, and suddenly I grew pensive. It is she who assigns each man his portion of time. I wondered what had brought me there, face-to-face with them, and I grew uneasy thinking of Mother.

"It's a peculiar statue for a hospital's grounds, isn't it?" a voice said, and I whirled around to see Dr. Reid standing not ten paces from me. He had on a dark coat, but no hat, and he held one hand to his forehead to shade his eyes from the bright light. "Not very cheery," he added in his gruff way. "Do you know who they are?"

I nodded silently.

"It belonged to the family who lived here before. I should probably have it removed, though I rather like it."

There was a long silence between us, and I hardly knew what to say to him; it seemed almost disrespectful to pursue a course of idle chatter in front of the three Fates.

As if reading my thoughts, he approached me, and taking my arm firmly, he led me back to the pathway, but instead of directing our steps toward the hospital, he turned us toward one of the cottages at the far end of the property and seemed content to lead me toward it without any explanation. I shivered involuntarily, and then breathed a sigh of relief as the sun reappeared and shone with bright intensity upon us.

"Are you chilled?" he asked, and drew my arm closer to his. He pulled the cuff of my sleeve down over my glove as he did so—just as a father might to a daughter—but I felt strangely shy of him. Still I said nothing, and it is a wonder that he did not find me rude, but I was keenly aware of his form and uncomfortable at this sudden and unasked-for proximity.

"There. That's better," he finally remarked, patting my hand. "Now you are back among the living where you belong and not among those morbid Greeks!" And then, much to my astonishment, his face broke into an almost mischievous smile.

I could not help myself, so surprised was I at the appearance of such an expression on *his* face, that I laughed.

"Dr. Reid," I said, finally finding my tongue, "even the gods must bow to the will of the Fates; surely medicine must do the same."

"No doubt. No doubt," he replied affably. "But we medical men make that third one—the lady with her scissors—we make her earn her keep. There are as many times as not when she has had her shears readied and we have managed to delay her task."

I think perhaps he said this to assuage my fears about Mother, for he must have guessed the direction of my thoughts; therefore, I tried to be light in my rejoinder.

"Well," I said, "then do not remove the statue, but commission an addition and place a doctor there among the sisters."

Dr. Reid smiled wryly at that, seeming to find amusement in the image that my words had conjured.

"Would such a grouping give my patients comfort—and perhaps more confidence in my abilities?" he bantered, smiling broadly now and arresting my steps.

I paused and could not help but smile, thinking of the rather serious and even sternly scientific doctors whom I had seen in attendance at the hospital. I tilted my head slightly and replied, "Your patients perhaps—though I am doubtful as to your esteemed colleagues." It was my turn to grin a little impishly at him.

Now it was his laugh that filled the air around us. "Well, Miss Brice..." he said, and he peered into my face as if inspecting a new patient and within his rights to do so. No, that wasn't it—I think he scrutinized me more as a subject that had surprised him a little, a man who had inured himself to the unexpected.

I remained calm under his inspection, and in meeting his eyes, I took my own measure of him. Perhaps it was this that seemed to startle him, for he betrayed more of his own self in that inquisitive stare. I sensed a deep current of restlessness in him, moving below the austere outlines of his face—and then I thought I saw in his expression the eyes of a creature whose practice perhaps suited his proclivities but not his imagination. There was something more he wanted; it was as if a shadow flitted unexpectedly below a glass surface, appearing and then disappearing with equal rapidity. I stepped back and lowered my eyes, as if I feared to intrude upon the privacy of this inner world I had inadvertently glimpsed.

Again, he must have caught my thoughts, for it seemed that he grew a little abashed. "Do you? Are you—an admirer of the classics?" He asked it awkwardly—the doctor who had fired his questions at poor Tad with the skill of a marksman and sympathies of an assassin!

"Oh, yes," I said. "And my mother, too," I quickly added. "She is a most accomplished Latinist and knows the Greek poets quite well." I felt myself becoming awkward, and I longed to go back to the hospital.

"Do you read to her?" he asked somewhat brusquely. And I explained that I had not of late, for she mostly slept in the afternoons. He encouraged me to do so and to select her favorite works—the mental stimulation would be most beneficial, he explained.

I was indeed grateful for this counsel and thanked him. Then he became the doctor again and I—I was the patient's daughter. His professional demeanor returned and settled upon his shoulders like the great, heavy coat he was wearing. He offered to accompany me back to the hospital, but I politely declined and made my way alone. I was determined not to look back, but I could not help myself from turning at the bottom of the stairs. He was still standing where I had left him, staring after me. He moved abruptly away and so did I.

An unaccountable experience! But I am firmer in my regard for him as a result. This morning I brought a copy of Hesiod from the library, with Dr. McTavish's permission of course, and I read Mother a few passages from *Works and Days*. I also procured *Alcestis* and *Prometheus Bound* from Dr. McT.'s collection—though Mother loves these two plays, they are perhaps not well suited to our circumstances, and I am fearful that they may depress her spirits. Dr. Reid, however, nodded approvingly when I showed him these volumes and even stayed for a few minutes while I read to her.

Mother's eyes lit up as I began. "'Pierian Muses, bringers of fame: come…'"

To be sure he is both a perceptive man and a good doctor!

January 24

I am feeling quite desolate without Tad. I do my best to keep my spirits up, but I feel a strange hollowness in my body and my heart aches for his company. I sometimes find myself so restless here, as if I am incomplete somehow and fearful that I have forgotten something. I am ever drawing in my skirts close around me, and there is nothing I like so much as to wrap myself up in a throw and sit before the fire quietly listening to Dr. McT.'s stories just as if we were back at his lodge. I think Dr. McTavish intuits my distress, and he has been so kind and attentive; he is determined to keep me busy so that I won't mope. He claims that he has grown fiercely attached to my smile and is determined to see it several times a day—at the very least.

It is strange, but I am *uneasy* that I am beginning to feel more *at my ease* in the city: I suppose I really mean Dr. McTavish's household. To be sure I am still quite a stranger to having my soup served first—and then to have it placed before me by Peter, a man thrice my age! Dr. McTavish's servants address me as Miss Brice, but I am ever at a loss as to how I should address them. Leah is the little girl who sweeps and cleans my fireplace, and she is the only one whose name I utter with any ease—though I have taken care to show her, poor thing, to cover her mouth with her apron to prevent her from breathing in the dust from the ashes. I think she holds me quite in awe; how surprised she would be to know that I have performed the same task myself many a time!

This morning Dr. McTavish and I visited one of his old friends—a Mrs. Ross. She is a well-to-do elderly lady whose husband was a parliamentarian, and it seems he was also fond of taxidermy. She lives in what I am told is a fashionable area of the city; there is a beautiful boulevard of trees in the center of the street, and in this, the winter season, their boughs are snow-covered and they seem so stately. It was a chilly morning, and so we took the smaller carriage, and on the way Dr. McTavish showed me the mansions of some of his friends. I can remember only a few of their names—the Masseys and Jarvises, I think, and Flavelles.

The properties are impressive and the homes massive, but I find them sinister and grim, almost too proper in their dispositions. Even today in the damp and chill, there were many street sweepers busy at their work while the houses frowned upon them. I think I am fond of the cottages near the hospital most of all; these other grand front yards and gardens seem so well behaved and almost too beautiful to enjoy. I am not quite sure what I mean by this, except that I know I am meant to look at them and admire them; I can't imagine ever belonging to such places, and they seem to condescend to agree with me.

Hazelborn—the name of Mrs. Ross's property—is filled with the strangest assortment of stuffed creatures. They are all so lifelike and yet so lifeless. Mrs.

Ross complains vociferously—in a very heavy Scottish accent—about having the "horrid things" about her all the time, and desires that Dr. McTavish take charge of all the birds in her collection. They seem innumerable, but he is to take them off her hands a few at a time. We returned in the carriage with an osprey (*Pandion haliaetus*), a somewhat moldy sora (*Porzana carolina*)—Dr. McTavish quite startled Mrs. Ross with his extraordinary rendition of this bird's strange whinny—and a large and magnificent raven (*Corvus corax*), whom I have put on my dressing table. I have named him Edgar in honor of Poe, and I hung the strand of pearls that Aunt Louise gave me around his neck, which I am sure pleases him to no end.

Dr. McTavish says that not all birds lend themselves equally to taxidermy, but he admits that he has used several of Mrs. Ross's subjects as models for his drawings. When I asked him why Mrs. Ross does not rid herself of all the birds at one time, he observed rather wryly that if she did, he would have no reason to visit her. Given the current state of her reserves, Dr. McT. estimates that he must pay her at least seventy-five more visits at a rate of two or three birds per house call. He did have me laughing at that—and seemed so pleased.

January 26

I have long sensed that Aunt Louise has wished to speak to me alone and about my grandfather, but I am almost sure she hardly knows where to begin. This morning I decided to take matters into my own hands. When she came into the studio, I continued at my task but greeted her in French. She insists upon discoursing in English with me, but I am convinced that this contributes to her unease. And so I told her that I must practice my French lest I forget it and asked her to tell me about Mother as a girl and how they were as children together.

I have so longed to speak to her on this subject!

Aunt Louise flitted about the room at first, but then she settled on the chair beside me and stayed for over two hours; she would have gone on longer, I am convinced, were we not interrupted by Peter's announcement of luncheon. I am beginning to realize how much she adores Mother; she refers to her by her middle name, Alphonse. In her eyes, she is both beautiful and accomplished, and as I listened, I wondered that she felt no jealousy of her sister. Aunt Louise describes herself as fat and clumsy—as the ugly one. It was useless to contradict her, for I think her quite pretty and I could hardly tell her that Dr. McT. finds her the "quintessence of pleasingly plump," as he puts it. But it also became evident to me that Aunt Louise is her papa's favorite, and that there were many arguments *entre* Maman *et* Grandpere.

This remains a mystery to me, for it appears that Grandpere was very pleased with her intellectual abilities and did not spare any expense for her education. Aunt Louise explained that he believes very strongly that women should be properly educated, for Grandpere's grandmother was the celebrated hostess of a popular salon in Paris during the great revolution. My heart thrilled as Aunt Louise told me that this ancestress purportedly entertained Monsieur Benjamin Franklin (as she calls him)—though I rather suspect my aunt of adding her own embellishments. Aunt Louise whispered that even some of the more notorious Jacobins frequented the family home, and then she crossed herself devoutly. I could barely suppress a smile, she did it so earnestly. And Grandpere's own mother was a well-known satirist, writing under the initials S. A., and assumed to be a man because of her erudition. And then the story of a relative who served in the household guards under Napoleon III but was killed in the aftermath of a terrible battle—and then Aunt Louise whispered that she had heard it rumored it was a suicide for shame at the emperor's surrender. And then another story about a cousin who was mistaken for a Communard and shot by the Versailles army during the great fire in Paris—all because he wished to see the Tuileries burning instead of staying at home as his wife had urged him. This was all a jumble, coming from Aunt Louise's voluble lips, but I listened attentively, secretly delighted by her descriptions, and yet somehow I felt disloyal to Tad in succumbing to my excitement. I do feel so ignorant about all this history—and my family's role in it.

At length, Aunt Louise came to a pause, and I could not prevent myself from asking her about herself. Was she not educated? Did not Grandpere have great aspirations for her?

"*Mais non,*" she exclaimed. "*Je suis très bête!*" And then she added, "*Comme ma mère.*"

I was a little shocked to hear her describe herself as stupid—and also my grandmother, for that matter. But surely my grandfather loved his wife; Aunt Louise describes them as quite a devoted couple, and Grandpere was heartbroken at her death when Aunt Louise was still a little girl.

And so today I have learned something of my mother's early life—but remain quite in the dark as to her feelings for her father and the tensions that seem to have so divided them.

January 29

Allan came today and we spent the whole morning together. I am newly shocked each time I see him; truly he is a boy no longer! It seems as if overnight he has grown six inches and everything about him—his hands and arms, his neck and the span of his shoulders—are now a man's. And yet his spirits are still those of a boy—I am sure! He still teases incessantly, and he has found a new devotee in Aunt Louise.

Dr. McTavish is quite fond of Allan, too. I am coming to appreciate how extraordinarily perceptive a man he is. I wonder if it is his experience with birds, for he approaches people sometimes almost as if they *were* birds. I mean by this that he sees them as creatures with their own, unique characteristics. Not immoral qualities or inclinations necessarily, but just ways about them that are part of who they are. I am astounded by how many of his friends simply talk to him about themselves. To be sure, he takes copious mental notes, and I am often the beneficiary of his cogitations about all his strange acquaintances, but they do come to him, almost as birds to an outstretched hand.

Once he said to me that a truly wild bird will never come to a human. I asked him why and he grew thoughtful. I remember that we were sitting by the fire at his lodge, both of us staring idly into its glowing embers.

"I do not fully know," he said at last. "But that is how I can tell that a bird is truly wild. The ones who will not come; they are the wild ones. You may stand quietly near them, if they permit you—but even in such proximity, there is no illusion about who is the stranger and who is not. Perhaps that is why I come to this cabin year after year…to be in the company of wild things."

He said it in such a way that I marked his words, and then I remember noting the distance between our chairs, and I began to ponder our own proximity to each other in that cozy room, the wind howling outside—me with my shawl across my shoulders and ready to depart into the growing darkness with Claude at my heels. I wondered if I were like a domesticated bird partaking of his gentle kindness—or were I the wild bird grown accustomed to his presence in my own environs?

He did not look up at me, and the moment passed.

January 31

There is a steep hill at the far boundary of Dr. McTavish's property and a precipitous footpath that winds its way down to the road below. A little farther, there is a terminus for the streetcar where often a fresh horse is exchanged for the poor creature that has just pulled its heavy load up the street. This footpath is used, I believe, mostly by tradesmen and the day servants who come to these houses early every morning and then depart often long past the dinner hour. I have watched them sometimes, disappearing down this pathway, heading farther south, and then descending into worlds that are unknown to me.

Dr. McTavish has told me that this hill marks the old edge of the Great Lake, and that long ago, as the massive slabs of ice melted, the waters withdrew and left behind the long stretch of flat land that so appealed to the city's first settlers. I do not know why, but I am very drawn to this ledge. I will ever take this route on my walk to the hospital, for there is a copse I like to visit—where I like to pause and look down at the city and think of the waters that once covered it and the waves that once must have crashed and played where my feet now stand. The place is somehow both an edge and a dividing line; here I feel caught between the city and the open country that sits atop the large estates behind me. I must admit I possess a peculiar affinity to this place and its echoes of the Great Lake that stretches out like a gray ribbon near the horizon. Although my own Bay is many miles away, this Lake seems even more remote—almost lost, as if wounded, or imprisoned perhaps. I do not know! But I am troubled by its elusive presence. It is an odd thought, but I think that it is at this threshold, this edge between the old and the current Lake, that one might truly hear its movements—neither closer, nor farther away, but here at this juncture of land and spectral waters.

Earlier this afternoon, I was in my usual place, stopping for a moment to watch the trees as they gently divested themselves of snow and straining my ears to catch sounds of the ancient Lake. I must have been so intent upon this that I did not at first notice a man walking up the pathway near me; as he drew nearer, I assumed it was a tradesman or one of the groundskeepers. It was George, however, wearing a dark, heavy coat and a thick scarf tucked in at his throat. He did not see me, as he was careful to observe his footing on the treacherous path, and it crossed my mind to let him pass by me unobserved, for he has been so strangely distant—as if uneasy around me, and it pains me so to see him thus. I had once thought that we might be—better friends—or so it seemed given his attentions to me during my illness. I wonder if he has forgotten giving me his painting? I would, of course, return it if he requested it, but I think my heart might break. I have taken to avoiding George because I sense somehow that it displeases him to see me. Perhaps I am too proud, but sometimes I find myself even a little displeased with *him*. What kind of a man is he really? I am so drawn to his paintings, and yet does their beauty truly belong to the man who makes them?

I watched him reach the top of the hill, and I thought him so changed: his face so haggard and drawn that it frightened me to see him so wretched. I called out his name as he passed by the copse—my voice now ever tentative and shy around him, but this time I felt fear in it. He did not hear me—his hat was pulled close about his ears and he passed not five paces in front of me. I caught a closer glimpse of his face as he trudged forward—so hard and unhappy, oblivious to the crest of the hill and the movement of the trees as they dropped clumps of snow onto his hat. Oblivious to me. I hesitated and thought to call out his name again, but he was soon too far away. I walked to the hospital saddened and troubled—thinking of the Lake that no one seems to take heed of and feeling my own inconsequence.

This evening, Dr. Reid accompanied me home after my visit to the hospital and stayed to dine with us. We had a pleasant walk together, for Dr. Reid was in high spirits and full of amusing conversation, and he was scrupulously attentive to me as we traversed icy patches of road, taking my arm firmly to guide me, and I was quite content in those moments to receive these solicitous attentions. I entered the house warm with animation and eager to take off my coat, for I felt flushed by our conversation and the brisk pace that our trek through the snow had taken.

I was surprised to find George with Dr. McT. in the vestibule, and more so because for the first time in weeks he seemed genuinely pleased to see me. He greeted me warmly, and I think my heart was in a flutter as he shook my hand. I withdrew it rather quickly—and then I was annoyed with myself, for Dr. Reid was observing me closely and I knew that those sharp eyes of his miss little. Indeed, I caught him looking at me several times throughout the evening, and though I do not find his gaze unpleasant or ominous in the least, I feel somewhat transparent under his inspection. He knows too much of human nature, and I feel that I might betray myself too easily to him!

I took extra care in my dress for dinner—and with my hair, too—and I held swift and pointed counsel with Edgar, who looked on all my careful ministrations with his usual reserve. It is true that he is but a common raven, but I have cleaned him up and elevated him to the status of "keeper of the pearls"—which pleases him immensely—and he has become my confidant. No doubt Mrs. Ross would disapprove of this usage of him, and he is still rather shabby on one side, but I have grown quite fond of him. I justified my preening to him with dispatch and then flew down the stairs, pausing at the bottom to collect my wits.

I was a little aggravated with myself for seeming to be so pleased with George's sudden friendliness, and so I stilled my features and tried to look composed—but I will admit my heart was beating so loudly that I was afraid that Dr. Reid might notice.

We had a lovely dinner in the round room, and though I am still unused to having dinner served in such a formal manner, I felt more at my ease than ever before. Dr. Reid told George and Dr. McTavish about accosting me at the fountain and of his determination to replace the statue of the three Fates with something "much more medical and less pagan," lest his patients think his methods to be some form of quackery. Dr. McT. teased me, accusing me of producing unsettling effects on modern science, and I pretended to be nettled—but it was all in good fun and no one seemed to mind Aunt Louise's breathless and bewildering sentences in English. I do believe that at times she reminds me of Flora in *Little Dorrit*, and Dr. McTavish positively tortures me with his little grin and seems to dare me to laugh out loud at her labyrinthine expressions. I pray that the angels prevent me, for I would be mortified to hurt her feelings and cause her even the slightest embarrassment!

When she and I joined the men afterward in the front drawing room, they were well into a discussion of a Dr. Stone. She—for Dr. Stone is a woman—is a colleague of Dr. Reid's. She strikes me as a formidably accomplished person. She is among the first women to practice medicine here and is a great advocate for women in all the professions. Dr. McTavish expressed some reservations about her: apparently he was once the object of her wrath for speaking publicly against admitting women to the university, and although he has since modified his views, she has never quite forgiven him. This, it seems, is much to Dr. McT.'s amusement, and he continues to invite her to the various literary colloquies he convenes in his home, but she has yet to attend one. I was most surprised to learn that she is a neighbor of sorts and that she resides near the Spadina Crescent.

Dr. Reid defended her warmly, praising her skills as a physician as well as her courage in a profession deeply prejudiced against women. I wondered if there might be romantic sentiments hidden beneath his admiration—yet I sensed a certain hesitancy in him as he spoke of her, and perhaps a touch of overexertion in his praises. Dr. McTavish then turned to me and asked me playfully if I thought women should vote in elections. "Of course," I responded stoutly, but I was alert to his next volley and refused to be trapped into defending the merits of my entire sex. I knew too well to fall for such a snare—and besides, I had watched him tease his friend Mrs. Ross on exactly the same subject and knew precisely his technique of feint and thrust.

I don't know how we quite came upon the topic, but Dr. Reid then began to tell us about his interest in diseases of the mind, and especially the ill effects of melancholia and its destructive course if left unchecked. He described the sufferings of some of his patients, and to be sure there were terrible cases among them: a man who was forced to have his hands tied at his sides to prevent himself from savagely biting his own fingers. Oh, and even more dreadful, a woman who tore out her hair a fistful at a time, seemingly unaware that she had done it, and though it left her bleeding and in great pain, she was unable to resist the urge to do so again.

But then he told a story of a woman whose little girl had died of a sudden illness and that this had left her heartbroken. Her husband tried for many months to turn her thoughts away from the tragic event, but with little success, and he began to grow very worried as his wife's melancholy deepened. It seems that each day she would rise, dress, and then walk to a distant corner of their garden where the child had played, and stand for hours in silence in that location, seemingly lost in thought and with a vacant, sorrowful expression on her face. There was naught that could deter her from this daily activity, not even inclement weather, and eventually the husband was forced to place her in a sanatorium where Dr. Reid now attends her.

I grew very silent as he told this tale. I don't know why, but I could almost see the woman in my mind's eye and her silent and solitary form…and then I recalled my own self standing at the crest of the hill, brooding and straining to hear—something! Some voice perhaps. I know that it is there, but I cannot hear it, or rather I cannot discern it, though I feel so intimately connected to it. It is a feeling quite unlike any I experience elsewhere—different even than my response to Mother's strange efforts at speech, for those sounds I know to be semblances of words. This other voice I seek out is something quite unlike regular human speech. I thought perhaps this grieving woman felt something of the same.

"Marged, why are you so silent?" George asked quietly from his place by the fire, and I looked up at him. I realized that he had been studying me closely for several minutes and that I had been aware of it—though I was too preoccupied to become self conscious.

I shook myself a little, feeling as if I had drifted out of the room and back to the edge of the hill. Dr. Reid was now studying George silently. I rose and moved closer to Dr. McTavish, and then I asked Dr. Reid if he had ever been to the place in the garden where the grieving woman had stood and was astonished when he grew abrupt and even impatient with me. He said no, that he never had been there and would not be inclined to go there for that matter. What could he possibly expect to find there? It was as if he seemed intent upon finding fault with me, and I grew a little distressed.

I don't know why, but then I asked him somewhat timidly if there were trees in the garden, perhaps? Tall and old pines like the kind near the hill—but I regretted the words as soon as I had uttered them.

"Trees?" he exclaimed. And then more mockingly, "I suppose there might be trees in a garden. Trees are usually to be found in gardens. But what could they have to do with this poor woman's affliction?" He seemed annoyed with me, but somehow also fretful.

Then we were all silent. I felt horribly awkward. I did not answer him, and I placed my hand on Dr. McT.'s shoulder, I think seeking a steadying presence in what I felt had become a sea of strangely shifting currents. He wore a thoughtful expression upon his face and patted my hand reassuringly, for I feared that I had somehow offended Dr. Reid. George leaned forward as if to say something, but Dr. McTavish motioned him to be silent. Dr. Reid frowned, looked directly at George, and then got up, abruptly announcing his departure. This of course broke up our colloquy.

But perhaps Dr. Reid was not really affronted—for before he left, he managed to take my hand and mutter that he hoped that he had not spoken in a way to discomfort me. I tried to withdraw my hand, but he would not let me, and so I assured him that he had not. He explained that he was more accustomed to argumentation with Dr. Stone and sometimes forgot himself in the presence of other kinds of ladies. I cannot imagine what Dr. Reid means by this—except perhaps he sees me as being made of weaker stuff and hence more susceptible to bruising!

Then I was aggravated, for George and Dr. McTavish had moved into the library, and though I wished to bid him good night, I dared not disturb them.

And now it is quite late and I am so tired. No doubt I have made no sense at all. I shall ask Edgar to give me a good, sensible scolding in the morning—a request to which he will acquiesce, I am sure, with great pleasure.

February 4

At last I have met the celebrated Dr. Stone. But perhaps more to the point, I found myself admiring her almost immediately. It was quite by accident, and I am so glad that she has decided to forgive Dr. McTavish and will come to the theatrical he has planned for next month.

I quite esteem her, and I feel that we have a kindred curiosity about each other. She is a strongly built woman, and her face, though pleasantly feminine, is quite square, and her expression kind but unyieldingly practical. She must be at least ten years my senior and has soft brown eyes and almost masculine lips, but her expression is frank and direct, and there is a kind of firm gentleness about her that I am drawn to. She is like looking into a clear pool of water, and though it is not deep, one is unaccountably reassured to see the bottom.

I learned that Dr. Stone has dedicated herself to administering medicine to working women—for such is how she refers to them—and by this I understand she means principally poor women who are employed in the factories not far from where she lives. She lately had a great triumph at one such place. Until quite recently, the women had no separate washing areas and were forced to share facilities with men, but she succeeded in getting the women their own washroom. She also trains nurses to visit the homes and teach the women about sanitation and other such matters. I quite admire her, but I could not help thinking of Auntie and of how she might respond to a visit from Dr. Stone and her nurses. In fact, as I think of it, I should be rather worried for Dr. Stone!

February 7

My grandfather arrived today—he is two days early! My heart is still pounding as I think of our rather frosty meeting in the library. He, too, insists on speaking English, and I am so grateful to Dr. McT. for being there and helping me through that awful encounter. After a brief greeting, he watched me silently for a full minute, and I would not lower my eyes from his piercing stare. Finally he muttered that I was quite like my mother, and I, a little defiant, thanked him for the compliment.

I am undoubtedly a little wary of him, for I cannot forget that it was he who insisted that Tad depart before he would come to see his daughter. But truly, I do not know how to conduct myself toward him. He spent some time with Dr. McTavish while I went to dress, and then when I appeared with my cloak, he announced that he would be going with Aunt Louise to visit Mother; it was clear that I was not to accompany them for this first meeting.

All day Dr. McTavish has been so kind and has tried to distract me. He has read to me from Mr. Thompson's letter and of his adventures in Italy, where he is sojourning for the winter. Mr. Thompson is quite an engaging writer, and usually I would have been an eager listener, but today I am too distracted. I shall just have to trust to Dr. Reid. Oh, I am anxious for their return!

It was as if he knew of my distress!

Dr. Reid came back to the house with Aunt Louise and Grandpere and held a private discussion with me while the others dressed for dinner. I am sure that he deliberately sought me out to assuage my fears, for he came to find me and I could tell from his concerned expression that I had ill-disguised my anxiety. But he told me all about the meeting between Grandpere and Mother and assured me that Mother took the presence of her father calmly and that he, Grandpere, was very tender with her and even grew misty-eyed as he held her hand and spoke to her.

I think I must have been under a terrible strain, for I found myself sobbing in Dr. Reid's presence, and though it was great relief to me, I felt a bit of a fool. But he took it all in stride and handed me a linen (though I had my own) and patted my arm. I don't know quite how it happened, and I am sure that he must be quite used to it as a doctor, but I found myself crying against his shoulder while he held me gently. Then Dr. McTavish came in, and I flew to him and had a good cry against his shoulder, too—and now I am not a little ashamed of my behavior!

But I do feel so much better—and I am resolved to give my grandfather a fair reception. I am equally determined that he will find no deficit of kindness or respect in me and that I shall do my utmost—for Mother's sake—to esteem him.

February 11

It was most surprising, but George came unexpectedly for luncheon today, and afterward, as we began our preparations to depart, he offered to walk with me to the hospital. Dr. McTavish said he thought this a capital idea, as I sorely needed some exercise. Truly I do miss my walking, for Grandpere always takes the carriage—the *equipage*, as he calls it—and I have been accompanying him. I cannot fault him, for he is at the hospital morning and afternoon. Yesterday I left him for a few moments while he read Hugo to Mother, and when I stole back, he had placed the book facedown on the coverlet and was holding Mother's hand so tenderly and speaking softly to her. I thought that my walking to the hospital might afford Grandpere a little solitude, for Aunt Louise is always with him in the mornings.

Though I felt a little awkward, I thanked George and accepted his offer. My grandfather looked at him with great attention and seemed about to interfere, but hesitated and then prepared to depart by himself without further words.

George gave me his arm as we left the house, and I think that this is the first time that we have walked thus. I rather liked that I could be so near him, and that

I could turn my face either toward or away from him, and yet not appear unnatural. Still, I was not entirely at my ease, and I sensed that he knew this. He is so very handsome in my eyes—not devilishly handsome, of course—but I do so like his features. And there is not a drop of vanity about him.

There has been an unusual thaw for this time of year, and the air grew thick with fog as we walked toward Davenport, and George was most solicitous that I should not slip, though there was little to fear, as the path was quite soft and even soggy in parts.

I let him set the pace, and he kept our gait quite slow—so slow that I began to suspect that Dr. McTavish had spoken to George about my nervousness and that George was overly anxious for my tranquillity.

Finally, I could stand it no longer and I exclaimed, "George! You are treating me as if I were a frail old lady!"

I am glad I said it, for it broke the ice between us. He smiled a little sheepishly and replied that he was under strict orders from Dr. McTavish to be careful with me, for Dr. McT. felt I needed fresh air but intimated that my spirits were a little raw. I admitted as much and recounted how I had burst out crying—though I did not tell him about my crying on Dr. Reid's shoulder.

He was sympathetic and assured me that the strain of meeting my relatives for the first time was bound to take a toll on my emotions. Then he asked about Tad and then Auntie A. and Uncle Gilbert, and before many minutes had passed, I felt more at my ease with him. I told him that I thought his mother and mine knew each other in Montreal, and he nodded in assent though he offered no further information. Then I asked him about Allan, and he smiled ruefully, calling him a rapscallion, but I could see his great affection for Allan in the curve of his lips.

Then I told George some of the things that Aunt Louise had told me about my family, and he listened with great interest. Before I knew it, I was telling him about my grandfather's antipathy for Tad and how difficult it was to know how to conduct myself toward him. George, I think, knew intimately of what I spoke, and it wasn't until later that I realized that I might have been describing aspects of his own relations with his stepfather.

George asked me if I might like to go to Paris and see for myself some of the places that my aunt had described—and perhaps visit the homes of my ancestors. I told him of Mr. Thompson's amusing letter and of the colony of wild cats that he had discovered at the Colosseum, musing that perhaps I might choose Rome over Paris if I had but one choice in the matter. And then he related some of his own impressions of Italy and of his time in Paris as a student of art.

I was almost saddened to come to the hospital entrance, as it put an end to our discussion. George deposited me in the vestibule, understanding that Mother could have no visitors other than her family. Dr. Reid met us there and seemed to be in quite an ill temper. I feared that something terrible had happened, and he quickly had to reassure me that it was not so. He was quite curt to George, and it struck me that perhaps the two men do not take to one another; they are indeed quite different in some respects.

But now—it is most aggravating! Grandpere eyes me strangely, as if he suspects something afoot between myself and George, and on our ride back from the hospital he positively interrogated me about the Stewarts.

Surely he must see that I am nothing to George—only a mere acquaintance—and that I would never see him if it were not for his deep friendship with Dr. McTavish.

February 15

My heart is still racing from this evening's events; it is impossible to think of sleeping, and yet I do not know if I can bring myself to write about what has taken place. I long for Tad, and my own dear room—and Claude would bring calm, I know, to my throbbing temples.

Oh, why did I agree to join them? I see now that I should have left as soon as they began! Did I remain to protect Allan or to sate my own curiosity? There is a knock at my door—it is Aunt Louise. Oh, I shall welcome her presence this night!

February 16

I am more composed now; the daylight has produced a calmness in me, and I am able to think more clearly. I almost dare not recount the evening's experience, for I still feel so unsettled.

Perhaps if I had been prepared for it—I believe I would have refused to join them. Yesterday I had felt unusually fatigued and so had gone to my room before dinner to lie down. Indeed I fell asleep and so was absent for some hours; perhaps Dr. McTavish learned of their intended visit during this interval.

At any rate, when I came downstairs refreshed, well after the hour at which we usually dine, the hallway was crowded with guests: Caroline Ferguson and her father, George and Allan, Dr. Reid, two other gentlemen I did not recognize as well as their wives, and a very plump, dark-haired lady who was emerging from a swirl of abundant and luxurious fur. Beside her was a slight and somewhat sickly looking young boy. At first I thought he must have been ten years old or younger, but later learned that he and Allan are the same age. The boy, I almost immediately divined, was blind, for he stretched out his hands for his mother, the dark-haired lady, and, once finding her sleeve, hung on to her with a ferocious grip. For her part, she did not seem to mind this and swept him along with her as if he were but part of her frock trailing behind her.

I gave my greetings to all, and Caroline, though distant, was cordial. She was very beautiful in a gown of deep red, and there was a trimming of Spanish lace at her wrists and throat. I was rather dismayed that I was wearing only a simple dress of navy silk, though I thought it became me. Mr. Ferguson's salutation was warm, and he introduced me to a Mr. and Mrs. Claremont, as well as the other couple, Mr. and Mrs. Poole. Madame Gzowski (for that was the dark-haired lady's name) I did not meet until we were all assembled in the drawing room, where her son, Ivan, did the most peculiar thing. He transferred his grip from his mama to me, begged that I give him a tour of the room, and insisted I describe its most interesting objects. I caught George looking toward me, his eyebrows raised in some surprise and amusement, but at my quizzical expression, he gave a slight nod as if to say, go ahead, the fellow is quite harmless.

I was happy to comply, for Caroline was next to George, talking in an animated way, and she frequently pulled on his sleeve, giving me the impression that there was an intimacy between them. Perhaps I was still a little sleepy, but it made me very cross to see them thus, and I was glad of some task that would draw my attention elsewhere. Dr. Reid had struck me as somewhat subdued when he greeted me, but he kindly moved some chairs away and created a path for Ivan and me to circle the room. While all of this was happening, Ivan's mother never ceased speaking and she was deep in conference with Dr. McTavish, who, I surmised, was already well acquainted with the lady. I looked about for Allan, but he was standing with George and Caroline, and I was reluctant to appear to notice their colloquy by drawing away Allan's attention.

Ivan was a very queer boy with a high squeaky voice and restless hands. He soon stopped our perambulations and insisted upon running his fingers all over my face and hair. I gave him license to do so, as he was thoroughly blind, but his slender fingers felt like mice running across my features, and I held very still, almost in an agony until he might stop. Again Dr. Reid was so kind; he stayed quite close by me, and I flashed a grateful smile at him. It was not that I was uncomfortable around children—just that Ivan was so unusual a boy!

"Are you pretty?" Ivan piped at me. I was surprised

at his boldness and did not know what to say, and my eyebrows lifted of their own accord.

His fingers caught the movement, and he quipped, "Ah, I have surprised you. You must be pretty, and I think that you are not haughty; your eyebrows are too quick and light-footed." Then, feeling beneath my chin, "And your skin does not sag like my mama's." Dr. Reid coughed and said quite sternly that Miss Brice was very pretty: fair of both face and form. I blushed a little at his compliment—but there were Ivan's fingers on my cheeks again, feeling them go warm, and a devilish smile on his lips! And then his fingers were tapping and tugging at my hair. "Your hair is very soft, and your ears are pointed like a fairy's." I smiled at that and queried how *he* could be so sure that a fairy's ears were pointed.

"You are treating me like a child!" He pouted and withdrew his hands immediately.

"Are you not a child?" I exclaimed.

"No," Ivan answered. "I am fourteen, though Mama says that I am small for my age and sickly."

I was silenced by his comment, and perhaps he felt my mood, for he said, "Do not pity me! I have special gifts, and even Mama is sometimes disconcerted by my powers."

I led him toward the bookcases and then guided his fingers to the sora and barn owl that we had recently placed upon one of the shelves and cautioned him to be gentle. He took a greedy interest in both objects, and I was amazed at how quickly his fingers moved across them in exploration. From behind us I could hear an animated conversation, and then I distinguished Caroline's voice urging George to agree to some proposal. There was the sudden sound of clapping and laughter, and then I saw Allan beginning to push away the sofa and pull back the chairs to clear a space in front of the fire.

I looked over my shoulder at Dr. Reid inquisitively and stepped away from Ivan. He explained in a low voice that Caroline had brought Madame Gzowski—a celebrated medium—with the express purpose of inducing Dr. McTavish to hold a séance. My expression must have betrayed my misgivings, for he looked rather gravely at me.

"But surely," I said, "not with Allan and Ivan present?"

"I am perhaps of the same opinion as you, Miss Brice," Dr. Reid replied. "For I have no enthusiasm for the Fergusons' experimentation with spiritualism. You remember my opinions regarding melancholia. I am convinced that this comes of a morbid sentimentality toward Caroline's mother and a refusal to accept the fact of her death."

I murmured my agreement with his reservations, but it was Allan's impressionability that troubled me, and I felt my old fears from the previous summer returning.

By this time they had decided that the dining room would serve their purposes best, and Dr. McTavish gave instructions to have the fire stoked. We all moved toward the round room, and Mr. Claremont began to draw the heavy curtains while his wife extinguished all the lights, except a heavy candelabrum, which she placed upon the mantel.

"Ivan," I said, turning to the boy, "perhaps you and I and Allan might find amusement elsewhere."

"Oh, no," he retorted. "Mama will never communicate with the spirits without me!"

I turned to Dr. Reid, aghast. Could it be that this woman used her own son in her…theatrics? I could think of no other word, for I had no confidence in any of these proceedings.

"Perhaps, Miss Brice, you might wish to forgo the séance. It has absolutely no effect upon me, but you…" he muttered.

I did not know what to say, for Ivan was already drawing me toward their voices and hence to the table, where all were taking their places, including Allan. Dr. McTavish was wearing an expression I could not fathom. I was relieved that Aunt Louise and Grandpere had retired early, for Aunt Louise in particular—a most pious Catholic—would have vehemently opposed such an activity, and perhaps even abandoned the household if her admonitions went ignored. Almost instinctively my hand went to my throat and the small silver cross that she had given me. Though I was certain I was not superstitious, still I felt disturbed.

Dr. Reid, I think, was amused by it all—at least at first.

Two chairs at one end of the table were reserved for Madame Gzowski and Ivan. The rest of us took our places, and I found myself between Allan and Dr. Reid. I looked closely at Madame Gzowski as she arranged the folds of her dress and drew a dark scarf over her hair, heightening my impression of her as a Gypsy. She instructed us to close our eyes and join our hands together. I was reassured by Dr. Reid's firm grip to my right and the gentle pressure with which he held my hand. Yet I could almost feel Allan's uncontainable excitement on my left, and through my lashes, I kept my vision surreptitiously trained upon the medium.

She remained in a deep silence for several minutes—so much so that some of the company started to become restless and Mrs. Poole began to whisper to her husband.

"Silence, if you please," Madame Gzowski intoned, and then after several more seconds, "We are not arranged in an optimal sequence, and I request that some of you change your places." She then proceeded to separate the Pooles, and she instructed Caroline and me to exchange our chairs. I left Allan reluctantly and found myself with George on my left and Ivan on my right. The boy's hand was moist and cold, and I shrank from his touch. In George's hand my fingers trembled against my will, and I desperately tried to calm my agitation. I resolved to keep my eyes shut no matter what occurred and determined to think of other things no matter how Madame Gzowski might direct our thoughts.

By and by the silence deepened, and I could hear Ivan breathing loudly beside me as if he were falling asleep. Then he began to murmur—strange disconnected words. I felt this to be extremely uncomfortable, and so I decided to do my best to ignore him and to train my thoughts elsewhere. I imagined the Bay, thinking of its snow-covered shoreline and of its silence at this time of year. Before long I felt myself drifting there, and in my mind's eye, I was standing below the lighthouse watching the moon light up great drifts of snow and shimmer across frozen sheets of ice. Ivan's breaths grew faint and insignificant.

At first I felt an idle pleasure in thinking of my home—but then, all of a sudden, it seemed as if I were really there! My body drifted up toward the cottage, and then, gazing through the window, I saw Tad and Auntie Alis and Uncle Gil at the kitchen table, a solitary candle lit and Tad reading to both of them as Auntie bent over her darning, ever working. I wanted to go to them and draw my chair to the table and listen to Tad's deep voice as he read to us. And then before long I was out behind the kitchen door and there was snow everywhere—deep and lustrous in the moonlight. But I felt none of the cold, and the stinging wind swept past without molesting me. My body drifted down the familiar pathway, through the deep woods, and then—oh, it was *so* real—I stood at the edge of the Basin where it lay frozen and blanketed in snow.

"Marged."

There was a voice calling my name from somewhere deep below the snow and ice—and yet I knew that I must not step upon its surface, though my heart yearned to follow the voice. I stayed suspended there for a few moments, and then the clouds extinguished the moon and I knew that I was back in the dining room. Ivan's hand was limp in mine, and he was slumped back in his chair, sleeping peacefully, or so it seemed to me. I gently released his hand, but as I did so, he sat bolt upright and whispered, "You are the one who fetched her—not I!"

I opened my eyes immediately—for all that I had imagined thus far had occurred with my eyes closed. I heard Madame Gzowski softly admonishing us to keep our eyes closed no matter what might happen.

My own traveled unhurriedly across the features of the Claremonts, Caroline's furrowed forehead, and then Allan's strained visage. Madame Gzowski's voice intoned strange words, and I felt my limbs grow terribly heavy—so heavy that I could barely cling to George's hand, nor could I turn my head toward him. With great effort, I cast a glance toward Dr. McTavish, and without any warning, he opened his eyes and stared straight into mine.

It was then that I saw her behind him—oh, I am afraid to recount it! She rose up behind him: a young woman in a light-colored gown that seemed to be in constant movement around her. Against my will, I felt myself float up from the table and drift toward her. As I came closer, and to my horror, I perceived that her dress was a sheet of living spiders—scurrying madly across her body with long, shimmering filaments trailing from their bodies. The woman wore an expression of extreme anguish upon her face, and she carried a pair of silver scissors. These she brought to her forehead in great distress, and she seemed bewildered as to what she should do. She looked at me—and beyond me—and my heart was filled with a great and overwhelming anxiety for her. I strained to take the scissors from her hands, but my own limbs were so heavy that I could not make them heed my commands. And then, casting a look of utter despair at me, the woman took a deep breath and, holding the scissors, she began to rend her dress, tearing at the fabric indiscriminately and sending the spiders flying in all directions. Some of them scattered upon the table, and I wished to call out a warning, but my voice was locked in my chest, just as the woman seemed to hold her own breath captive.

In a matter of seconds, her dress was in shreds and the remaining spiders had collected at her bosom. With one last frenzied movement, she clutched the scissors to her breast and tore at the front of her gown. At this, the spiders fled in earnest, and I saw them leap back away from her and into the air. And then I seemed to feel them fall upon my face and in my hair, and I screamed!

George was standing beside me, calling my name, and I was gripping his hand so tightly that my nails must have pierced his flesh.

And then Dr. Reid was there on the other side of me, his strong arms drawing me away from the table and then lowering me into another chair. Dr. McTavish was pressing a glass of water to my lips. I sat down in a daze.

"What did you see? Tell us what you saw!" It was Caroline's feverish voice, and I could see her eyes glittering at me with a strange intensity. Madame Gzowski was equally intent upon drawing from me what I had witnessed, and she urged me in her deep voice to tell all while my impressions were still fresh.

We moved back into the drawing room, Dr. Reid taking my arm and leading me to the sofa. I was shaking uncontrollably, but I felt somewhat reassured by the room's cheery fire. Dr. McTavish called for Mrs. Evans and asked her to take me up to my room, and I heard George's worried voice affirm the wisdom of this arrangement.

It was Dr. Reid, however, who said that it would be better for me to relieve myself of my impressions before I retired for the evening, lest they become more monstrous under the workings of my imagination. Then in a gentle voice, he asked me to describe what had startled me.

I took a deep breath, and, as well as I could, I told them of the woman and her frantic efforts to destroy her dress, and then the confusion of the spiders and their bewildered dispersal. I did not tell them about my visit to the Bay and the voice that I had heard. I do not know why, but I did not tell them.

Then I heard Dr. Reid ask me quietly if I could describe the woman. I recounted her features and dress as best I could. To my astonishment, Ivan chimed in, adding his own details to my description—yet how had he seen her?

Dr. Reid drew a short, sharp breath when I had finished. "What is it, Dr. Reid?" I heard George ask.

"Nothing," he said. "Only that Miss Brice—and Ivan—have described with a strange accuracy the woman whom I told you about the other evening, the one who was under my care for melancholia regarding the death of her child." He paused. "I am sorry to report that she—she took her own life this very afternoon. She did so with a pair of scissors that one of the nurses carelessly left in her room."

And then the room began to swim before me—oh, I must stop else I find myself in a swoon again.

I will pray for her. I will kneel by my bedside and say a prayer for her—for this poor woman. For what else is there for me to do? I do not believe that God could be so cruel as to prolong her separation from her child. Her husband, poor man, did not understand the nature of her connection. Nor could he fathom that what she sought in her garden was consolation and knowledge that her dear child was safe and cared for—and that it was her trees who provided this communication!

February 17

George came to see me today, but I could not see him. I shall be myself in a day or two, but I just could not bring myself to see him.

February 18

I have had another restless night, and Dr. McTavish has grown worried about the dark shadows beneath my eyes, as well as my loss of appetite. He thoroughly regrets the events of the other evening and is most anxious that I feel settled again. I have tried to assure him that this state of nervous agitation is passing and that I shall be my own self again before long. I made an extra effort to eat at breakfast, and then I indicated that I might like to go to the studio. I think I am most at peace when I am in this small, dear room just off his library—most content when Dr. McT. is in his library working on his papers and I, just a stone's throw away, intent upon my own tasks. He seemed pleased at this suggestion, and though I did not mention it, I thought that I might go out in the afternoon, as I was anxious to visit Mother. Aunt Louise was most indignant upon hearing about the séance, but Grandpere—who

I am gathering is quite a *philosophe*—dismissed it as nonsense.

February 21

George visited me unexpectedly this morning while I was still in the studio. Dr. McTavish was nowhere to be found, and so I was quite surprised to look up and find George standing over my shoulder and looking down upon my work.

He smiled and bent closer to see my handiwork. I was a little abashed, for I had had no time to prepare for this inspection!

"Oh, George," I blurted out with some exasperation. "Why do you come to visit me just when I am so wretched-looking?"

"Marged," he replied, "you must never wear any masks for me. I depend upon you not to."

I turned away—to be honest, so exhausted did I feel that had I looked like one of the Graiae, I should not have been able to lift a finger to improve my appearance.

"Besides, you are as lovely as ever," he said, and I turned to eye him rather severely for his compliment, for I am no coquette and do not care for empty flattery.

George, however, was not to be deterred by my severity.

"Is it so displeasing to you," he said, "to have a man pay you a compliment?"

"You must not tease me today," I said, "for I am still all at sixes and sevens with myself."

"Are you still disturbed by the other evening?" he

asked, bringing a chair up to sit by my side. Then I told him about the first part of my experience: of going to the Bay and seeing Tad and Auntie and Uncle Gil at the table. And then of the voice and how real it had all seemed. George listened and was silent while I talked, but I felt no ill judgment directed at me, and his demeanor was one of sympathy.

I asked him if he thought she were real—the woman whom I had seen—or if he felt that my imagination, suffering under the impressions created in me by Ivan and his mother, had merely generated her. Such had been Dr. Reid's conclusion—though he had no answer as to why I described his patient, whom I had never met, with what he had admitted was a disturbing accuracy. George shook his head and said that there were always things that we could not explain and that trying to do so sometimes created greater strain upon ourselves and that it might be best if I just set the experience aside.

We both stood up, and I felt quite grateful to him, for his words gave me much needed assurance, and I resolved to follow his advice. I placed my hand on his arm, wishing to communicate my thanks for his solicitousness.

I must have looked very forlorn indeed, for George suddenly turned to me and unexpectedly took me in his arms, pressing me closely to his chest. I was startled at first—a sea of emotions washing over me—my head reaching to just beneath his chin, so that our faces were hidden from each other.

I am not sure how long he held me; it must have been a few seconds at most, for Dr. McTavish was again in the library, and George released me.

And now my thoughts are all in a tumult again! What does his behavior mean? Perhaps his affections toward me are only brotherly, and I should feel so foolish if he discerned that mine were of a different order. I have heard nothing further about his relations with Caroline, but neither have I heard anything to contradict what I have already surmised. Am I to give him some sign? And why do I so savor the sensation of his arms around me? I am almost ashamed to admit how wonderful it was. If only I knew what course to take—for I am without buoys in these open waters!

February 25

I think I must write of tonight's inspiring experience—though it is very late, just a little after midnight I believe—for my mind is far too stimulated by the evening's events to seek immediate repose. Yet I am so tired, almost too weary to undress! I think my fatigue is owing to my lifting all the babies, and then I had to carry a good number of the toddlers, too, coaxing them to stop their crying so that their mothers might hear Dr. Stone's instructions.

Yet I am so glad that I attended the Baby Clinic, for such is it called. It has been just the right thing to stir me out of a strange lethargy, and I am determined to go again since it is held every Wednesday evening. I do believe there must have been thirty or more women there tonight, all with their babies and numerous other small children. Dr. Stone had two nurses with her—women of my age—and everything seemed a jumble of caps and mittens! One could not turn around without coming upon a child crawling across the floor, and I had to be so careful in my movements lest I inadvertently step upon small fingers or toes. I was given the task of placing the babies upon the scale and making sure they did not fall off; there was only one such instrument, and we had to weigh each baby while one of the nurses recorded its weight in a book. Oh my—how they all cried! There was only one among them all who was silent: a little boy with soft dark eyes. He looked so surprised at finding himself quite naked and placed upon a chilly metal basin; he kept staring up at me in such wide-eyed astonishment throughout the whole procedure that finally we all had to laugh.

Many of the women did not speak English—or only in bits and pieces—and Dr. Stone repeated her instructions regarding pasteurization in at least three different languages. I discerned German, as well as a strange dialect of it—I later learned it was Yiddish—though it is all a blur given that I had to be attentive to the wailing children, and one little fellow, barely able to stand, somehow got himself out of the window and halfway out onto the ledge before I stopped him!

I so admired the intelligence and animation of the women who attended the clinic. They were of all ages, and they seemed so eager to learn. On the way back to Dr. McTavish's house, Dr. Stone explained that she holds these clinics in the evenings because most of the women work long hours at factories during the day, the majority of them in garment industries. She complained of the deplorable working conditions and castigated the factory owners with great vehemence for not providing more suitable and sanitary working conditions.

Once I heard Dr. McTavish ask Dr. Reid about Dr. Stone's *politics*, and it seemed to me that he evaded giving an answer. For my part, I am drawn to her direct manner of speaking, and clearly the women respect her, for she is very knowledgeable and even a bit stern with them. I don't know quite why, but I am inclined to admire Dr. Stone; perhaps it is her firmness of purpose and the seeming freedom of her thoughts and movements. As I watched her tonight, I was reminded of myself back at home, picking my way along the shoreline without a thought as to how others might regard me—in my own element, so to speak, and unafraid of censure. Such is Dr. Stone in *her* clinic.

I am burning with curiosity, however, to know if Dr. Reid has some romantic connection with her. He is almost reverential when he speaks of her and grows quite prickly if Dr. McT. suggests, even in the mildest way, some criticism. And yet he seems somehow not entirely pleased with her.

This evening when Dr. Stone and I returned, he was with Dr. McTavish in the library and they seemed to be engaged in quite an animated conversation when we came upon them. I was quite surprised when Dr. McT. offered Dr. Stone a glass of his prized brandy, and even more so when she requested whiskey instead—I have ever regarded this as a man's libation. Dr. Reid seemed quite displeased at this, but Dr. Stone, for her part, appeared to sip from her glass defiantly despite his obvious disapproval. I cannot say that I felt strongly one way or the other about her behavior. Auntie A.'s unyielding censure of all spirits has perhaps engendered an opposite tolerance in me. I think I took it much more in stride and minded not at all to see her drinking such a potent liquor. Perhaps it was witnessing firsthand Dr. Stone's extraordinary competence at the clinic. Surely she is a woman who knows what she is about.

Oh, but Dr. McTavish was in one of his horribly mischievous moods! He offered *me* some of the drink, too!—knowing full well that I could only refuse, for I have no inclination for the stuff, and indeed, I do not think Tad would give his approval for such a thing. But what was I to do? I knew very well that Dr. McT. did so to reveal some kind of contrast between Dr. Stone and me, but I was quite on Dr. Stone's side. I think I must have looked quite severely at Dr. McT., for he seemed to relent, and he asked Peter to bring me a glass of sherry—which I took as a gesture of peacemaking on his part.

Dr. Stone was soon engrossed in a heated discussion with Dr. McTavish, and Dr. Reid turned his attentions to me. He inquired about my impressions of the clinic, and soon we were both laughing at my description of all the children and the wailing mayhem that prevailed all evening. I was free and animated in expressing my admiration for Dr. Stone, and Dr. Reid grew so quiet and thoughtful looking at me that soon I relapsed into silence, knowing full well that he was in one of his studying moods and I the object of his meditations. Finally I looked at him quite boldly, meeting his gaze unabashedly with my own, and then he uttered the most incongruous thing.

"Miss Brice," he murmured, "your eyes are quite the most extraordinary blue I have ever seen."

I was speechless, and then I became aware of a silence at the other end of the room and grew a little flustered, for I was not sure if Dr. Reid's strange comment had been heard by them.

Dr. Stone rose and asked if Dr. Reid would see her home—and he of course assented immediately.

We saw them to the door, and as she departed, Dr. Stone inquired if I might like to accompany her on one of her weekly visits to the factory homes, and I indicated that I would be most eager to join her. We settled on next Thursday; I shall have to curtail an afternoon with Mother, but I will attend to her earlier in the morning.

I am so eager to tell Mother of my adventures this evening! But I must stop as my eyes are barely able to stay open, and I will fall asleep at my table if I do not hasten to bed.

February 26

In a few days, Grandpere and Aunt Louise will return to Montreal—but only briefly. They have asked me to accompany them. Of course I refused—oh, I do hope that Aunt Louise is not offended!—but I said that I could not leave Mother, and in this I spoke the truth. Aunt Louise promises that they will return shortly, for I do believe she saw me growing teary at the prospect of her departure. I have grown so fond of her.

Yesterday Mother sat up in her chair for over an

hour, and then, at teatime, Dr. Reid carried her downstairs and she sat briefly in the solarium. I am certain that the warmth and sunshine did her much good, for she seemed content and peaceful. Dr. Reid is very solicitous—and his attentions are never condescending, but so gentle and mildly teasing at the same time. Such suits Mother well; though she cannot speak, her quick, roving eyes indicate that she understands all that is said around her, and Dr. Reid's manner assumes that she does so.

I am deeply grateful to him, for Mother is improving tremendously under his care. He told me yesterday that he is doubtful that her speech will ever return. He was very gentle about it, but nevertheless direct. I feel as if I can trust him, for he is honest with me and yet there is an unaccountable tenderness in him—or so it seems to me. Perhaps it is my imagination, or perhaps it is his skill as a doctor, but I find myself depending upon his advice and he—he seems so adept and manly about taking charge of his patients that I cannot but admire him for it.

Allan visited while I was out at the hospital, and I was disappointed to miss him. Indeed I seem to see so little of him despite our proximity. Dr. McTavish told me that he is full of George's art show that is to be held in a few weeks; this is not the grand affair that Caroline has planned for him in New York, but a smaller one to be held at a distinguished gallery near us (whose name I now forget). Nevertheless, there are to be art critics in attendance, and the show will be an important event for George.

It seems that we shall be kept busy over these next

weeks, for in a few days, Dr. McTavish is hosting one of his colloquies—this time quite a large one, he says—and so the house will be filled with "artist types," as he calls them. And then the following week, he will be giving one of his famous bird performances, but here at his own home and for a small gathering of friends. So far, "small" has meant sixty-two invitations, and he keeps adding more to the list! I am very excited about this performance, as I have heard a great deal about the doctor's performances but have never witnessed one. And then, after that we will attend George's Toronto art show.

Dr. McT. says we are to be very fancy in our attire. He has asked Aunt Louise to take me to the dressmaker before she leaves, and I am to have a gown of black velvet for his performance—for Dr. McT. says that he has a hankering to see me in such a dress. I am quite delighted by this: I love the thought of wearing velvet skirts as I come down his great staircase. In some unaccountable way I feel that they will swish just as the meadow grass near his lodge does when the wind stirs it.

I was a little puzzled by Dr. McT. this evening—though we are grown so used to each other, and after Tad I believe that he is the dearest man, but sometimes I do not know what to make of his remarks. He implied that this showing of George's work was very significant, and I asked him why. He looked at me strangely and said that it might decide George's future: not just his future as an artist but his future as a happy man. I cannot imagine what he means by this, and now I am almost fearful to attend the event!

February 29

My dress is perfectly lovely. I had my first fitting today, and Aunt Louise actually cried when she saw me in it. She says I look like Mother—and yet so like Tad, too. I smiled to see her caught in one of her delightful and not infrequent contradictions. She has become like a second mother to me, or sister perhaps. Sometimes I cannot tell who takes care of whom—for she is wont to caress me and even to slip her arms around my waist as if I am a little girl, and yet to me she seems like a bird nestling up close.

I told Dr. McT. after dinner this evening that he must wait until his performance to see me in my dress, and he seems quite content with what no doubt is a sudden abundance of feminine activity in his house. At times, I find myself thinking of his poor wife. I have learned from Mrs. Evans that Mrs. McTavish was attentive to her dress and Dr. McTavish took much pleasure in this. I should like to please him, too, on this account, for he has been so kind and generous. And yet—there was one of Aunt Louise's priests admonishing women for their vanity last Sunday. I wonder how many women went home afterward with remorse in their hearts; yet home to husbands who encouraged their sartorial sins and preening with tender glances and even approbation!

I do not think that I should care so much for my wonderful velvet gown if Dr. McT. had not seemed so gratified at my desire to surprise and please him. This evening after dinner, he left me alone in his library for a short time and then reappeared carrying a small box.

"Marged," he said somewhat awkwardly, "at one time, I thought that I might give these to…a daughter. And as you have become such to me, I do believe that these are rightfully yours."

I was surprised, but I opened the box with a quiet dignity that I felt suited the occasion. Inside the box was a necklace of sapphires. I gasped when I saw it, for I found the stones to be quite beautiful. He fastened it around my neck and drew me to the mirror above the mantel—and though the glass is somewhat mottled, I could see the stones shimmering against my throat. I threw my arms about him, and I felt that I might give him some measure of comfort for the terrible loss of his wife.

What a dear, dear man he is—never speaking of his own sorrow and yet so attentive to others. I am chastened to think of my seeming indifference to what must be a great, great grief—and yet, perhaps in me, he finds a channel for his great capacities of affection.

March 1

This evening we hosted the colloquy, and I dearly hope that I have not disgraced myself—though Dr. McT. has assured me I have not and that he wishes more young women had the courage to give Mr. Michael Sparke "the shove"!

I do not quite know what he means, except that it all happened as a result of his hosting such a large number of distinguished art patrons in the house, in addition to many unusual and rather strange-looking artists. Poor Peter seemed almost offended by the latter, disapproving of their ill-fitting coats and certainly dismayed that many of the men had no hats. Some of the women wore their hair loosened, and a few had bands of beads and feathers. I must admit that I do not care for this style of adornment, for I think that the feathers remind me too much of Mrs. Ross's moldy birds.

Toward the end of the evening, I met a woman—one of the artists, I am certain—who was also ill disposed toward these feathers. She discoursed with me at length about them, and it became evident that she was vehemently opposed to the usage of animals for female ornamentation. She spoke against furs and the cruelty of eating animal flesh—quite eloquently I might add—so much so that I shall have to think further upon her arguments, for many of her points seemed quite sound. But she was so peculiar, and I could hardly countenance the strange hissing sounds she made when one of the "feathered maidens" passed close to us.

By and by, I was able to take leave of her, and suddenly I grew tired, as if the stimulation of so many stylish and clever people in conversation with one another taxed me. And so, a little mind-weary, I sought repose in a quiet corner of the room—in a large chair that had been placed against the wall and next to the bookshelf. From there I was almost hidden, but still I could observe the activities of the room. I looked at Dr. McT.'s guests at my leisure and perhaps felt as the books on the shelf did watching a strange and noisy species chattering at—though it appeared rarely listening to—each other.

I was not left long to enjoy my solitude, for a middle-aged man with a closely cropped beard and cold, gray eyes caught sight of me and directly came over to my nook as if he wished to speak to me. I had exchanged a brief greeting with him earlier in the evening as the guests were arriving, but I had thought nothing of it, and certainly had not sought his attention. He bowed slightly before me and introduced himself so quickly that I did not hear his name or occupation, though I gathered that he was not one of the artists. We remained thus in silence for a few moments, as for some reason I found his company disagreeable, and I did not wish to encourage its prolongation by holding conversation with him. He took this to be some sign of favor, for he soon launched into a withering review of the artists present. I thought perhaps that he had mistaken me for someone else, but I was quite trapped, and it did not seem to make a bit of difference to him that I uttered not a word—for he continued, growing more harsh in his choice of words. I am almost certain that he mistook my silence for approbation, for he grew ever bolder and more animated.

For a good quarter of an hour, he went on in this manner, and I of course had no idea of whom he was speaking—until he came to "George Stewart." I am sure that he positively sneered when he uttered George's name, and then he referred to some of his paintings in the most insulting manner. I will not repeat what he said except that he accused George of "prostituting himself to bourgeois tastes," and at this—though I hardly knew what he meant by it—I was deeply offended. I stood up wishing to divest myself of his presence and barely able to contain my anger, but he would not move away.

"Sir," I said, fixing my eyes upon him and doing my best to appear imperious, "would you step away?" But he ignored me, and even had the audacity to push me back into my chair!

He grew intolerable. I am sure that somehow he sensed my discomfort at his critique of George's work, and so he grew bolder and more disrespectful in his discourse. I tried to close my ears to him, but he seemed determined to bait me, and then he insinuated such terrible things about George and the Fergusons that I could not bear it.

"Will you not stop?" I cried. Again I stood up, and without thinking I thrust him away from me. To be sure, I did not intend to do so with such force, for he reeled back, his face registering great astonishment, and then he fell against a table, overturning it and pulling everything on it down to the floor in a great clatter. The room grew utterly silent, and I was horrified at what I had done! I rushed to assist him, but he shrank back as if I might do him greater harm. George came swiftly from across the room and stopped me.

"Steady, Marged," he said under his breath, drawing me away. "What the devil has Sparke done now?"

I hastily explained, without telling him precisely what the man had said, but George smiled when I recounted my indignation and refusal to be forced to listen to him.

"Bravo, Marged!" he exclaimed. "There's more than one person present who'd like to give Sparke a good kick, but dare not do it."

I asked George who Mr. Sparke was, and my heart sank when he told me that the man was an important art critic who was courted by all the painters. I told George that I should not be seen standing with him, but he laughed at that and said no harm could come of it because Mr. Sparke already thoroughly detested his paintings and had published quite unflattering things about them. I could not regard the man's behavior in so light a manner, and George seemed amused at this. I am sure that my eyes were still flashing irritation and that I bristled with indignation for the rest of the evening.

As he was departing, George teased me and asked me if I would commit battery against a few of the critics who were bound to attend his show—he would point them out beforehand, of course. I think he wished to assuage my fears that I have done him some irreparable harm, and though my cheeks are burning now, I do not think that I regret pushing that man—though of course I am sure that I wish him no real injury.

March 4

Earlier today I accompanied Dr. Stone on one of her "house visits," and truly I did not care for it—I much prefer the clinic. I suppose it might be the small rooms we saw, and so many children. Where they all might sleep I cannot imagine. Yet Dr. Stone seems unperturbed in the presence of such poverty; impervious to the resentment that I detected, though she brings medicines and I am almost positive that the money she sometimes gives is from her own reserves. I left the few coins that I possessed on the windowsill of one family.

I could barely look at the children, for they seemed so cold and hungry, and one little girl had terrible bruises upon her arms and neck, as if she were not infrequently beaten. To be sure, some of the families were cheerful and welcoming, but it is remembrance of the poorest ones that stays with me.

As we left the last of the boardinghouses, we walked along Spadina and came to a large market that was bustling with activity despite the frigid temperature and the late hour. I felt my spirits lift in the open air—though it was very cold and our breaths showed each time we spoke. As we traversed the sidewalk, I noticed great heaps of clothing placed upon the ground and clusters of women at each pile, lifting out garments and examining them. I asked Mary—one of the nurses—what the women were doing, and she explained that every month there was an "old clothes market" and that this was where many of the working families came to purchase their clothing. She said the piles were organized by cost and that the prices corresponded to the quality of the clothing, for everything had been worn before and then discarded. Mary stopped before a foul-smelling mass and explained that this pile was among the cheapest, for the clothing was worn almost to shreds, but that the poorest had no choice but to purchase their garments here.

I watched a woman draw out piece after piece from the pile while a vendor looked on, his coat open, a watch chain hanging below his vest, and a large mustache hiding his expression. The woman turned frequently to protest his prices, but he watched her silently nevertheless. I expressed my dismay to Mary, and she nodded, quietly remarking that the woman most likely worked as a seamstress but was unable to afford decent clothing for her own family.

Such sights have depressed my spirits tonight. As I write, I have an image of Auntie A. in my mind, sitting near the stove, the window open behind her and some piece of sewing in her lap. I thought of her staying up to make my gray silk dress—for she has made practically everything that I have ever worn, except what I have acquired in Dr. McT.'s household. Indeed, I take great delight in my new dresses and especially my cape—for it is lined with fur and so warm!—and yet it is strange to think of that woman's hands perhaps stitching such garments, and then her fingers searching through that foul heap of unwashed clothing.

Auntie—it is almost as if she stands at my elbow while I sit here and write. I am certain that she would not care for this house, or for the city, for that matter, yet I find myself seeing her in my mind's eye, ever in her apron. Sometimes she has come to me in my dreams, smelling of bread and candles—and I am always comforted.

March 8

At last I have finished my horned grebe (*Podiceps auritus*). I suppose I may be quite pleased with it, for Dr. McTavish has been almost lavish in his praise. The gray tints across the plumage gave me no end of trouble. I think that this is the very first piece of work in which I feel that my abilities have met with his expectations. I think *I* am even a little astounded at the progression of my skills.

Yet, I don't know why, it recalls to my mind the time when we first let Dewi off his leash and I was so surprised to see him return when I called him, despite his still being a puppy and his obvious enjoyment of a newfound liberty. I feel an unusual restlessness in finishing this piece, as if my training has given me both a sense of obligation and freedom all at the same time. Now, perhaps like Dewi, I shall wander off a bit—but shall I also always return when commanded so that I might practice the skills which I seem finally to have mastered?

March 14

It is only two days more until Dr. McT.'s performance, and we have practiced and practiced until I feel as if the house were full of birds! I am sure that I will fall asleep to the sound of a sora (*Porzana carolina*), for Dr. McT. has insisted that he perfect it, and today he must have repeated it a hundred times. Or perhaps it will be a snipe (*Gallinago delicata*) that will keep me awake tonight—truly I do not know how he imitates the strange courtship sounds it makes! It shall be a wonderful event, I am sure. Dr. McTavish says I am to be his "queen" for the evening, for then he will not dare to disappoint, though how he could possibly anticipate anything other than resounding success I cannot imagine. Aunt Louise and Grandpere return tomorrow, and I am so pleased that

Aunt Louise shall be here for the debut of my gown. I am quite like a child, for every day I pull it out from my closet and stand admiring it before the mirror.

March 15

Today Dr. McT. had me clean and polish all his whistles and the funny bits of metal that he places in his mouth as he performs his birdcalls, and he teased both Allan and me terribly by pretending to swallow one! We soon caught on, for after he collapsed into his chair and sated himself on the expressions on our anxious faces, he began choking like a pomarine jaeger (*Stercorarius* …?), and then he started wheezing like a Caspian tern (*Sterna caspia*), and finally swooned into his chair like a tufted puffin (*Fratercula cirrhata*). We could barely stop laughing, it was all so ridiculous, and when we both scolded him most furiously for fooling us, he merely turned coolly to us and hooted *Strix varia*, the barred owl, and started us all over again. We had to beg him to stop, for our sides were hurting so.

Stercorarius pomarinus—I think I am very close to having mastered almost all the Latinates. Dr. McTavish insists upon it and now has me learning even the binomials of trees, though I still think of them just as *my trees*.

March 16

Truly I did feel as a queen this evening, though I am perhaps a little silly in admitting it. A good queen, mind you—and though there were many very beautiful women present (far more lovely than I shall ever be!), still I felt a strange and yet exquisite sense of holding court. Dr. McTavish was quite distinguished in his evening clothes—he wore a plum-colored waistcoat that I had never seen before, but it suited him perfectly. He was most gracious to his guests and kept me close to his side, introducing me to a rather large number of young men, and yet he would not let any of them take me off his arm. Indeed, I felt a little like a bird perched on his shoulder, and at times it seemed as if his visitors came close to peer at the curious creature he had tamed to stay by his side.

Yet he had an almost unfriendly encounter with George—Dr. McT. was almost derisive in his tone toward him.

"Marged belongs with me," he said to him. George said nothing, and Dr. McTavish continued, "A rare bird is ever to be forfeited by those who choose not to see her," and then he moved us briskly away, I looking up to observe George's expression and finding him grinning in a cynical fashion. It was a most disagreeable sight! I think I must have shivered and shrunk away, for his expression changed in a flash as he looked at me, and it was as if a mask had been removed for an instant and the actor behind it revealed.

But I had little time to dwell upon this, for Dr. McT., unbeknownst to me, had placed a chair close to his own, and to my surprise, I was to sit next to him throughout his performance, housekeeper to the silver case in which he keeps his whistles. I was a little flustered at first, planning to slip away when he turned his back, but it was as if he anticipated my thoughts, and he caught me twice and replaced me in my chair: the audience amused and enjoying all of this impromptu comedy. At last I succumbed, and just before Dr. McT. began his birdcalls in earnest, I caught Allan beaming upon me from the front row of chairs, and the rascal even gave me a wink.

I do not think there was one among us who was not spellbound by the performance. I cannot explain, even to myself, how Dr. McT. does it—for he is a large man, white-haired and whiskered, and his beard is full and streaked with a lustrous sort of gray and not at all like any bird I can imagine. But still, he makes us see birds, not just hear them. It is in his eyes and the movements of his head and body, not just in the sounds he makes. We all found ourselves becoming very quiet and leaning toward him, watching intently and holding our breaths as if he might fly off at any second.

Dr. McT.'s owls were most remarkable, especially his vocalizations of the screech owl (*Megascops asio*), as he uses no aids in reproducing the sounds for this bird. I held my breath while he performed this one, for he told me that it is really quite a difficult call to master. For the male trill, he must tilt his head back and hold just the smallest amount of saliva behind his front teeth and on his upper palate to produce a slightly gurgling sound, and yet whistle through his pursed lips at the same time.

Undoubtedly, though, the audience was the most enthralled with his ivory-billed woodpecker (*Campephilus principalis*), which Dr. McT. says he always saves for the end. He had the audience come upon it after trekking through a swampy woods, our boots wet and muddy, our spirits flagging just a little and yet determined to see it, though the gnats and mosquitoes buzzed about us voraciously. (I am almost sure I saw Effie swat at one near her hair, so convincing was his description!) And then, at last we saw it, high upon a branch, stripping the bark and searching greedily—and many of us no doubt thought gruesomely—for larvae. Dr. McT. rapped the wood loudly with his "bill," and then he turned his head toward the audience, the bird suddenly catching a roomful of people looking at him. No one dared move, and then, after what seemed like eons, he gave its peculiar *kent* call. Everyone gasped after he had finished it, and Allan cried "encore"—and then as Dr. McT. performed it again (it is the most unusual and bizarre series of sounds!), the room erupted into laughter.

There was a great burst of applause, and we all broke up after that. Dr. McTavish was instantly swarmed by enthusiastic ladies who showered him with profuse admiration. I found myself with Allan and Dr. Reid: Allan was almost giddy with excitement, and Dr. Reid sent Allan on a mission to secure us "something edible" from among the throng at the tables. My grandpere came to us, and he seemed very pleased; he spoke little, but he eyed the rooms and the congestion of people in them approvingly, and I wondered if he perhaps was recalling pleasures of his own past. Aunt Louise was among the crowd around Dr. McT., quite unable to reach him and speaking French rapidly to her immediate neighbors, who, I rather suspect, knew not a word of what she was saying, but they humored her most graciously. Dr. McT. caught my eye and how his own sparkled—I had a sudden image of Claude turning over on his back and offering up his belly for a good rub!

At one point, Grandpere turned to Dr. Reid and, speaking to him in French, asked him if he had enjoyed the performance, and much to my surprise, for he has never done so before, at least in my presence, Dr. Reid responded in the same tongue. He spoke it most beautifully, and I think I must have shown both my amazement and my admiration, for he looked at me with an impish grin—not unlike the one I had seen on his visage the first time I had met him at the Fates. He seemed pleased with me this evening; his eyes glowed appreciation so openly that I, like the royal bird I was for the evening, found myself preening just a little under his gaze.

The house was very crowded, but still across the room, I could see George with Mr. and Mrs. Stewart, as well as Caroline and her father—and Allan, perhaps forgetting us, was being divested of the two plates he was carrying. But I was determined not to care. I cannot explain it, but somehow I felt that my grandpere stood square to Mr. Ferguson, bishop to bishop… and I wondered that I, a lightkeeper's daughter, could feel herself a queen.

And Caroline—is she a queen as well?

Tad once told me that there is only one true queen on a chessboard. I remember asking him which one it was, and he asked me what I thought in return. I hazarded that she was always the one that won the game, and he shook his head slowly.

"No, child," he said. "A queen may lose the game at hand, but ever is she a queen."

Now, what has put that memory into my mind tonight?

March 21

Cold and gray—and so dreary! Five days of this unending bleak cold—and everyone wishes to stay indoors. I went for a long walk by myself, and even the forests behind the house seem dispirited and rather low that a stubborn cold snap has come upon them so late in the season. We are all waiting for signs of change—of earth thawing and snows melting. I find myself wishing so fervently to be home.

I try so hard not to think of it! Indeed, I have even forbidden myself to write of it, but I do not know what has become of George—or the Fergusons. There is a great silence on this subject, and somehow I dare not ask Dr. McT. about it.

March 23

Mr. Thompson arrived today and he is quite—inexplicably changed! Not in his appearance so much, though he is quite tanned as a result of his exposure to the sun, but he is certainly changed in his demeanor. I am not at all sure that Dr. McTavish is pleased with it.

I recall him being so reticent and quiet in his manner; though we did get a glimpse of his theatrical talents one evening when he gave us the most extraordinary recitation. Perhaps it is these gifts that have been loosened in him, for he has acquired a deportment that is most definitely thespian. For one thing, he has adopted Italian expressions and sprinkles them quite liberally throughout his speech, and he also kisses his fingers most expressively. Moreover, he seems to have lost all his timidity around Dr. McTavish, and—how shall I describe it?—he has become most colorful in his dress. This evening before dinner, Dr. McT. asked him where he had acquired such an "execrable" suit of clothes, and this set in motion a long and seemingly inexhaustible address on "the fashion." Grandpere positively disdains to be in the same room with Mr. Thompson, but Aunt Louise is fascinated and encourages discussion particularly on this subject. I am not at all sure what results this may produce.

March 25

Mr. Thompson has refused to accompany us to the lodge, and Dr. McT. is furious with him. For my part, I suppose I am rather relieved that the storm has broken and now we may at least return to some semblance of normalcy.

Oh—but Aunt Louise is inadvertently to blame! She has invited Mr. Thompson to visit Montreal, and I am sure that Grandpere is not pleased, though he is too well bred to counter his daughter's invitation. But it afforded Mr. Thompson an opportunity to decline what he termed Dr. McTavish's "invitation to accompany him in the pursuit of ornithographic trivia." Such a statement hardly sat well with the doctor, but I must say that he took it in stride and largely ignored him. Oh—but then Mr. Thompson proposed that we build an aviary at the top of the house and instead have the birds delivered to save the Doctor and his poor assistants the bother of trudging off to "the edges of civilization," as he called it. I heard Dr. McTavish mutter, "*Risum teneatis, amici,*" but in the most unfriendly way, and so I tried to introduce another topic. Mr. Thompson, however, would not cease and began to ridicule the "northern climate" and its beastly insects and explained to Aunt Louise that men in such locales were required to grow their hair as thick and as uncomely as a bear's.

I think Aunt Louise and I both heard Dr. McT.'s warning growl, for we joined forces and both rushed Mr. Thompson from the room on some pretense. Good heavens—does a voyage to Europe always produce such spirited effects in hitherto retiring and diffident young men?

March 26

We are to go home April 15—not long after George's show. Dr. McT. has told me, and I immediately wrote Tad to tell him of our intended return. The journey will probably take at least two days, and we must be very careful not to overtax Mother's energies, but she seemed so pleased when we told her.

Dr. Reid thinks that she will continue to improve as long as we do not "mollycoddle" her, and I am to be especially vigilant in explaining all this to Auntie Alis. I do not think that Dr. Reid entirely approves of our departure, for he was quite gloomy during our consultation and has insisted that I receive extra instruction from the nurses who have attended her—almost as if he doubts my abilities.

I am a little ashamed that I feel such excitement at the prospect of going home. I must be very careful not to inadvertently injure the warm hearts that have taken such good care of us. Dr. McT. said that Mother may come back next winter if she wishes, but I secretly hope that she will not want to return, or that her health will be such that she does not require further convalescence.

March 28

I fear that I have not done justice to Dr. Reid, for I have not fully appreciated either his character or the depth of feelings that he seems to conceal so carefully behind his doctor's face. And now I must examine my own self and the nature of my feelings toward him. Have I evaded such investigations? For some inexplicable reason, I wish to avoid this introspection; it is true that I am both very happy at the prospect of going home, and yet unhappy at the prospect of leaving him, for I now see him almost every day and can hardly imagine what it would be like not to have Dr. Reid with us.

But now he has, to some degree, forced the issue. As we walked back from the hospital this afternoon, he asked me—oh, for once I cannot recall the words exactly! I am sure it was something to the effect of "did I think I could ever feel toward him more than the regard with which I now honor him?" Truly I did not know what to say! For once I wished that I might have a veil to hide my face, but even so, I think my heart thrilled a little. We continued to walk, I striving to make my steps calm, and I did not remove my hand from his arm even as he tightened his grip upon me.

"Miss Brice—Marged, you are not angry with me?" he said, and I, of course, shook my head. I said that there was no reason to feel anything but gratitude to him, given all he had done for Mother—but he interrupted me. He said that I was speaking to him as to a doctor, but that his question to me had come from himself as a man.

I looked at him directly at that—and again I caught the restless movement of something in his face. I do so like his face; I have grown to watch its expressions and to depend upon its gentle candor, so that to me he is a very handsome man, though I do not doubt many women might find him a little austere and even grim at times.

He asked me if I would think upon it, and I assented, and then he said, speaking in uneven tones, that it grieved him to think that a time might come when my presence—when I—would no longer form a part of his day. I listened, and somehow I also felt a bit of the same. I realized that in the joy of going home, I had not thought of what I might leave behind.

He—I have often heard Dr. McT. call him Andrew—did not directly declare his feelings for me, in words at least, but I can hardly doubt the purport of his expression. But in this I believe he intended that I might silence him immediately if I wished and not be agitated by attentions repugnant to me.

Yet I did not find his question in the least repugnant, and as much as told him so. In this I was at least honest—but still, I do not know what I might feel for him! Could I love him? I think it safe to say that I have a deep regard for him, and an affection certainly, and though I am extremely sad at the thought of not seeing him each day, still, this does not quell my desire to go home.

March 29

[Moisture damage for three paragraphs.]

...and Caroline seemed almost feverish and even a little exultant as we greeted her. Mr. Ferguson was more subdued, and he remained quite aloof, watching the crowd with a critical appraisal, or so it seemed to me—as if George's paintings were now upon the scale, and some unseen hand were moving the weights to secure and then record their value.

I looked at all of George's paintings—but I was drawn most to the rear room, where he had hung his landscapes, and so I returned there to take more time with them. I had noted at the outset that Mr. Sparke was among the thick throng of visitors and had resolved to avoid him at all costs. I was therefore not a little startled to find him at my side as I perused the landscapes—he bowing once again and mumbling some pleasantry about the evening and how pleasurable it was to find himself among "beautiful things." I was tongue-tied—of course remembering the violence of my previous encounter with him—and I hardly knew what to say, though I think I uttered some response. He then took my arm in a most cordial fashion and said that I must see the "only really good piece" in the whole exhibit.

I could hardly refuse, for he seemed quite friendly (and I assumed forgiving), and so we went toward a corner where he drew my attention to a painting set within in an ornate gold frame and executed in dark tones against a vivid and changing background of blue and gray. At my first reconnoiter with the picture, I had recognized the Basin's west shore, just after the sun had set and with the light hovering on the water as the horizon disappeared. At Mr. Sparke's prompting, I moved closer to inspect it—for of course I recognized the scene—and then discerned that there was a darker form, barely perceptible, blended into the shoreline. It was undeniably a female figure; her features were all in shadow except that a careful observer could make out the faint crest on her forehead. All of a sudden I felt self-conscious—for here was the suggestion of my own form—and I wondered if George had drawn me thus, turning away from the Bay to head back home. It was as if he had caught me—in the movement of light and shadow he had caught my form!

Mr. Sparke was studying me closely, and then he said, "Is this not your portrait, Miss Brice? This one is titled *Eidos*."

I shook my head, pretending not to understand.

"This is at once a landscape and a portrait—the figure

of the woman blending and moving with the natural elements behind, as if she, too, were in constant motion. I like it far better than the other portraits," he added, "though Stewart did render Miss Ferguson's formidable but rather static beauty well, wouldn't you agree?"

Still I was silent, for Caroline's portrait had in truth depressed my spirits, though undoubtedly it was well painted and certainly she was quite beautiful in it.

I must have remained silent for some moments, and I looked up to find Mr. Sparke staring at me curiously.

"Tell me," he continued, undiscouraged by my taciturnity. "You are from these parts, are you not? What do you make of these landscapes?" He indicated with a sweep of his hand the rest of the room. "Do they capture something of this place?"

I think it must have been his choice of words, for when he uttered "capture," I felt my back stiffen. I frowned and looked away from him. I do not know why, but I felt irritated by his question.

"Tell me what you think, Miss Brice," he urged. "Do not spare me in your choice of words."

I shook my head again, frustrated because I did not know how to express myself—and he whispered, "Please."

Then I paused, choosing my words carefully as my thoughts formed.

"These paintings do not 'capture,'" I said.

"Like those others," he interjected, pointing toward the front room, and I nodded in spite of myself.

"Then why do you like these paintings?" he asked me. "Do they not remind you of these places and scenes?"

"Oh, yes," I said quickly. "That is precisely it. I know that George has been to these places and that"—how I struggled to express myself!—"and that he did not paint them to take them away somewhere else, but to paint them *as* and *where* they are."

I shook my head, feeling that I had expressed myself poorly.

"Isn't that capturing the spirit of the place, then?"

I shuddered as he said it—and stepped back as if offended at the thought.

"No," I exclaimed. "George's paintings never do that—as if to cage a wild creature. They are not just 'beautiful things' that give a passing pleasure. *You* do not like these pictures because they are not tame!"

"You are mistaken," he answered. "I like these ones very much!"

I was silent, surprised at this confession, and Mr. Sparke stared moodily at *Eidos* for a few moments. Then he turned to look at me, and I grew a little uncomfortable under his scrutiny.

After some further moments, he said, "Do you not think it is a portrait—even of the Bay?"

I shook my head and smiled, for I suddenly understood my own thought, and I responded, "The Bay is never still enough to be a portrait. On the calmest of days, there is too much movement even in its repose. I think George understands this somehow. I see it in his paintings."

"In *all* his paintings?" he persisted.

"No," I whispered, for I wished to be truthful, but I felt a little sad in saying so.

I don't quite know why, but I felt more kindly

disposed toward Mr. Sparke, and even understood a little of why he railed against George, and thought that he perhaps even wished to help him.

Then, as if discerning my thoughts, he said, "Ah, Miss Brice, now you see that I am not the enemy that you have supposed."

Before I could reply, George appeared in the doorway and, seeing us, came up to us, his face composed, though I felt rather than saw an undercurrent of tension in him as he approached Mr. Sparke.

Mr. Sparke's visage assumed a slightly caustic expression, and he quipped, "I have just been discussing your paintings with someone who seems to know far more about them than even you do, Stewart. Miss Brice and I seem to agree that these landscapes represent your best work—"

"George," I said interrupting him, and perhaps too precipitously. "That is hardly the case…" But he stopped me and seemed even pleased at Mr. Sparke's inference.

"Now, about this portrait—" began Mr. Sparke, but I could not bear to remain to hear them discuss the painting, and so I moved quickly away, no doubt appearing rude, but truly I could not help it.

George followed me, but the room had become so congested that I was forced to pause and wait until a path to the front room cleared. He stopped behind me and, bending quite close, whispered into my ear, "Well, and did you like your portrait, Marged?"

I pretended not to hear, but we were pressed by the crowd and he came even closer—so close that I thought I felt his lips against my ear.

"Marged," he said, keeping his voice low. "You must tell me."

I nodded, leaning back against him ever so slightly, and I felt him take my hand and hold it, hidden in the folds of my black velvet gown—there in the midst of all those people, and yet the gesture was invisible to all of them! Then, as the crowd dispersed and I moved to go forward, he released my hand, and I felt dizzy, as if I had been placed in water and a brisk current had taken me up. I turned, wishing to ask him why he had titled the painting *Eidos*—but a man approached him and drew his attention elsewhere. And then I was gone, taken into the swirl of the room, coming to rest, at last, upon Dr. McTavish's arm, and there I remained for the rest of the evening.

March 30

Aunt Louise and Grandpere will leave in a week—and then only another will pass before Dr. McT., Mother, and I depart.

Grandpere has given me a considerable sum of money, given under the trust of Dr. McTavish until I am twenty-eight years of age. I have asked Dr. McT. not to mention this to anyone, not even Tad, for I fear it will nettle him, and in truth I do not think we quite feel the sting of poverty that Grandpere attributes to us. Indeed, we have always had Mother's money, though Auntie says that it is a modest amount; still we have never suffered for want of funds, and those terrible weeks of deprivation last year were owing to the ice and not to penury. I tried to explain all this to my Grandpere, and he smiled sadly and asked me if I were determined to dissuade him. He asked this of me in such an unusual manner, and I did not wish to appear ungrateful. Then he explained, his back to me and facing the fire, that there were many things that he might have liked to do for me, his only granddaughter, but that a foolish perversity had prevented him—and now there were but few things that he might do and this was one.

"Beware of perversity, Marged," he said, turning back to me, and his eyes were full of sorrow. "It is something that your great grandmother had, though she was a great woman and of a gifted intellect. You have a touch of it, I think. I have seen it on occasion in your flashing eyes."

Though he spoke a little sternly, as is his habit, I sensed affection in his words, and on impulse I embraced him. He stroked my hair so tenderly that I was glad I had hidden my anger from him, for never have I spoken disrespectfully to him, though at times my heart has held bitter feelings toward him on account of his treatment of Tad.

Aunt Louise wishes me to visit her in Montreal, and I have promised that I will do so—though when I could not say with any certainty. I am so glad to have met her and to think of my connection to her across so many miles. I feel as if I now have family that I might visit, for though Tad says I have many cousins on his side, they live an ocean's crossing away from us.

Dr. Reid seemed anxious today; though he forbears

to express it in my presence, I know that it unsettles him to hear us talk of our departure.

I think I must close this. I am so tired from the day's events and desire only a deep and peaceful night's rest. I will think more on this, but nevertheless I must tell Tad of it in my own time.

—

[Moisture damage for half a page.]

We sat by the fire in a small parlor—there was a desk at one end, piled high with a confusion of papers and books, and more of these were stacked in a corner behind it. The room struck me as untidy in a mannish sort of way, for I was reminded of Dr. McTavish's library, and though it is dusted faithfully by Ethel, still it refuses a housekeeper's touch.

Dr. Stone drew down a bottle from a cabinet as Mary poured our tea, and she alone drank from it, for none of us—neither Mary nor myself nor the other nurse, Miss Graves—were offered any of its contents, though I knew it to be some form of liquor, for I recognized its amber color and then its odor: whiskey.

At first I was not alarmed, for Dr. Stone is not like other women and certainly I sometimes think of her as a man, though she is pleasing in form and I find her features quite beautiful. She sat in a leather armchair placed close to the fire while we, her guests, perched on cane chairs opposite her, and she began to discourse upon the disease of the baby that we had seen. Dr. Stone said it was a very rare disease—and told us its name, though I do not remember it—but it lies partially dormant in the bones and gradually corrupts the body as the child grows. Then she began to describe it, quite without emotion, detailing its characteristics and the progression of its deforming effects quite calmly. I felt myself flinching under the stinging precision of her explication, for it was a horror to think of what the child would grow to become and of its sufferings; and ever did I have the image of its mother's eyes before me, so luminous and pleading, that it almost broke my heart to think of it—but I kept silent, listening quietly, as did Mary and the other nurse.

At length she poured herself a third glass, drank it down quickly, and then poured a fourth, spilling some of the whiskey on the table as she did so. A heavy silence came upon us; I could hear only the soft roar of the coals burning in the fire, and then it struck me that I had no way of getting home and that I had expected that Dr. Stone would oversee my return passage, for such has been the arrangement during my previous visits to the clinic.

Dr. Stone brooded for some moments in silence, and as we three grew increasingly restless to depart, she began to provoke her nurses—for both of them are missionaries of some sort and pious women—Mary in particular. Dr. Stone began by mocking them—for what kind of God would create such a disease, she asked. An affliction that grew infinitesimally worse each day, just as the creature infinitesimally gained consciousness of the effects of the malady. And the parents, too; they would begin with a seemingly perfect babe—beloved and cherished—only to watch the disease transform their angel into a horror. They would be spared nothing, she said, the disease would linger, the child's suffering returning each day as a Promethean agony—death many months, even years, away.

It was dreadful to hear her speak so! A devil, she said—only a devil could devise such a disease and then inflict it upon the perfect form of a child! A devil or a vengeful god, Dr. Stone muttered, and then she eyed me most strangely. During all of this, Mary and Miss Graves slowly collected their wraps and then departed, almost as if they were accustomed to this kind of denouement to the evening's activities—leaving me, however, alone with Dr. Stone and the bottle of whiskey, now half gone, upon the table.

It is true that I was a little afraid, but it felt not unlike a time when I was twelve and Tad and I came suddenly upon a bear, and he motioned for me to stand still and be silent. I knew that I must not move, though all my senses urged me to run, for the bear was large and it gave off a fearful smell.

Dr. Stone drank in a leisurely way from her glass, looking at me with what seemed to be an undisguised hostility. Gone was the doctor and her impenetrable visage—gone were the pale gray eyes that took in much but gave little indication of what thoughts or emotions beset its keeper. She poured herself another glass, and it appeared to me that the bottle was almost empty—and then, drinking it down quickly, she turned to me, and I felt the full weight of her livid, malevolent stare.

"You are stealing Andrew from me," she said. And then she laughed in a hideous fashion. "I do not care for thieves," she added. "And yet you are such a pretty thief! Such a young and pretty thief. Like that little baby, you seem such an angel. Yet it is I who suffer and not you!" She smote her hand against her breast in a dramatic fashion and then paused, seeming to fight something in herself. Then she drew her hand across her forehead and then to her mouth, as if to silence what lay there, as yet unspoken.

Yet she could not contain her words, and the whiskey by now had the upper hand. "Each day—how I suffer!" she continued. "Each day you steal just a little more of him from me. And I hate him for it! I retire at night filled with hatred for him, and then rise each morning full of love for him again!"

I stayed perfectly still, focusing all my efforts on doing so, remembering—no, almost hearing!—Tad beside me whispering, "Steady, Marged. Do not move, daughter. Our lives may depend upon it."

She tried to rise but could not—and she fell back into her chair, frustrated and furious at her own impotence to reach me. Her face contracted, and I saw sheer hatred contort her features. I knew that had the means been at her disposal, she would have killed me without remorse. I knew her to be dangerous—but also drunk and like a wild thing.

Dr. Stone then began to call me terrible names, but I knew by then that the bear was retreating and my danger was lessening, for to be truthful, she was by this time too inebriated to stand, and the alcohol that had liberated her tongue had turned traitor and robbed her of locomotion. I thought of how I might find my way back to Dr. McTavish's house. I heard the bell from the streetcar outside the window and thought that this might be my best means of transport, for I had little money with me and had no sense of how I might procure a cab at such a late hour.

Dr. Stone began accusing me of practicing vile artifices toward Dr. Reid. They were of such a debased nature that I could hardly believe she was capable of forming such thoughts! She cast in my face the inferiority of my position and implied all manner of immoral conduct from my upbringing—yet I sat, as if made of stone, under her torrent of insults. All of a sudden, I felt myself before Miss Crabbage once again, and I was recalled to that other horrible scene and her poisonous insinuations about my regard for Professor Latham.

I do not know how I endured it!

Dr. Stone pursued this course for some minutes and then sank back into her chair as if she had exhausted some foul reserve of venom. She motioned for me to come closer to her as if she might like to touch me or even embrace me. I kept my distance and would not approach her, and this seemed only to frustrate her and rekindle her anger.

Then, just as I had resolved to leave, the door opened and Dr. Reid entered.

She did not at first see him and continued her vicious attack against me. I saw his expression change into one of disgust and then revulsion.

"Emily!" he cried. "Stop it!"

She ceased instantly and began to weep, her glass falling from her hand and its contents spilling onto the carpet. She cried out to him in the most beseeching manner—it still chills my heart to think of it! "Andrew, you do not love me! You do not love your wife!"

I was astounded, but I was careful to betray no emotion on my face, and quietly I got up to collect my things.

Dr. Reid turned to me, his expression grim and unfathomable, and asked me if I would wait for him in the vestibule, and though I did not assent to this, I was glad to leave them. Indeed, I thought that I might walk alone, out into the night air, and escape that fulsome scene and the perturbing turn that the evening's activities had taken. Without waiting for him, I began to walk up toward the hill, moving swiftly and silently. I knew that I should not do so, for I have been told that the streets are full of dangers for women walking alone, and no doubt this is true, but I stayed in the shadows, once passing two men who stared hard at me, but I paid them no attention and moved on.

I was glad that it was terribly cold, for the streets were empty of people, and though my face soon became numb, I continued apace. At length I heard Dr. Reid calling my name behind me, but I did not slow my steps, for I was quite close to the edge of the hill by now, and I knew my way even in the darkness. He caught up to me, but I would not stop walking though he took my arm and tried to still me.

"Marged," he said, "listen to me! She spoke under the influence of drink. It is not as she claims. Good God, she is not my wife!"

"Dr. Reid," I rejoined, as quietly as I could and stepping away. "I only wish to be—home. This evening has taken a most unpleasant turn, and I am a little shaken by it."

In this I was at least honest, for I was by now too cold to know the nature of my own thoughts or to converse with him about the scene that had taken place and the words that Dr. Stone had uttered. In truth, all I wished was to be in my own room and alone. He seemed to collect himself and then asked if he might take my arm, and I did not refuse him. We mounted the hill in silence, and my senses were strangely alive to the nighttime; I could hear each of our footsteps with extraordinary precision and the quiet of the trees and the sheer and utter silence of the city. It was very dark, and yet I felt sure of my footing, though the pathway was icy and at points became quite treacherous.

As we reached the crest of the hill and my copse of trees, I shook his arm off, feeling—oh, what was it? Was it some perversity in me? Or anger at him perhaps?

I felt as if I were truly at home, stepping sure-footed along the shore. I thought of Tad, and of when I wrested him from the Bay—or perhaps it was the Bay that gave him back to me and I caught him! I saw myself not as some feeble ward to be walked along pathways and directed safely into doorways, but as a woman who had seen the suddenness of death and the ineffable resilience of life.

Who was I to sit demurely and receive a lashing from one who was so basely intoxicated and be forced to bear the sting of her lascivious imagination? Who was Dr. Stone to rant to *me* about disease and the world's capricious cruelty? Who was Dr. Reid to bring me safely home?

I felt myself changed in that moment. I do not

know if I can describe it. Somehow this night, at the crest of the hill, I felt myself changed.

"Marged," he murmured, "have I lost you? Tell me that it is not so."

I left him, running on ahead. Peter let me in, expecting me and no doubt thinking that I had come home in a cab.

April 2

Dr. Reid came early today and asked if he might speak with me alone. Dr. McTavish was silent, leaving me to give my own answer, and though I was still agitated by what had occurred at Dr. Stone's home, I assented. We were closeted alone together for some minutes in the studio. I spoke little, but I am glad that he came as he did, and thus did not leave me to brood over Dr. Stone's words and develop a suspicion of some unseemly behavior on his part.

He began by expressing his regret that I had witnessed Dr. Stone in such a state—and then he explained, choosing his words carefully, that she had developed a proclivity for alcohol as a medical student and that it had become worse in subsequent years. He said that Dr. Stone might go for weeks without any apparent craving for liquor, but inevitably an episode would occur. These, he said, were always wretched and ugly scenes—and they had eventually forced him to break off his engagement with her. He told me that this had happened ten years ago and that in spite of this rupture, they had remained colleagues with mutual regard for the other.

He paused, and I think I must have drawn in my breath, for it struck me unpleasantly to think of them as once betrothed—though as I consider it now, I did suspect some romantic entanglement from the beginning. But still, it did not please me to hear of it, and I felt my heart grow cold toward him.

"Marged," he said, "Miss Brice…I hope that you will allow me to tell you of this…period of my life, though it pains me very much to recollect it."

I said that I was confused, for she had referred to herself as his wife.

He interrupted me.

"We were never married! It is essential that you understand this—that I have no previous marriage, though it is true that we were at one time engaged."

He was very grave as he said this, and I remained silent, for though I dearly wished to hear more of his engagement, I did not feel that it was my right to press him and open what was for him an old and awful wound.

He looked terribly uncomfortable, as if old sufferings were washing over him anew, and at length I could hardly bear to see him thus, and so I said, "Dr. Reid, please do not speak of this if it is too painful. I do not expect it!"

There was a long silence. "Are you sending me away, then?" He asked it of me so bitterly that I felt my heart fill with pity for him.

"No!" I cried, and I ran to him. I placed my hand on his arm and tried to see his face, for he had turned it away from me.

"She has never really accepted that I will never marry her," he muttered. "And though I have a great respect for her as a physician, the tender regard that I once held for her is over—forever." He said this almost harshly, as if spitting out words that were still dreadfully distasteful to him.

Still he did not look at me.

"No doubt you will think me a shallow and heartless man. She certainly accuses me of such when alcohol has loosened her tongue!"

"Dr. Reid," I exclaimed, "I could never think anything of the sort about *you*."

He turned abruptly and moved his arms as if he wished to embrace me, but I stepped quickly away, clasping my hands in front of me, for truly I was not certain of my own feelings—and if I am honest, I must admit that in my mind I thought of the time that George had embraced me, almost in the spot where I was now standing, and it was *his* arms and not Dr. Reid's that I suddenly wished were about me.

Our interview ended awkwardly, for Dr. McTavish appeared in the doorway. I discerned considerable curiosity in his countenance and wondered if he had overheard my conversation with Dr. Reid, though we had discoursed in low tones. I knew that further discussion with him about what had transpired between Dr. Reid and myself was inevitable, and indeed I was correct in this—for after lunch we had a long and private talk about it, and Dr. McT. told me a few of the details regarding Dr. Reid's engagement. His perspective on the matter is that Dr. Reid admired the doctor in Dr. Stone, but not the woman—and that this, perhaps, at least in part, may have been what drove her to drink.

I find Dr. McTavish a little cryptic about this; no doubt he intends it. Is he suggesting to me that I might love the doctor but not the man? Yet now I know the explanation for Dr. Reid's strange deportment toward Emily Stone—that mixture of admiration and dissatisfaction that has baffled me from the beginning.

April 3

I have had a letter from Tad, and he will attempt to meet us at the train station; he says that the ice has mostly receded, for it has been unseasonably warm, and so we should expect a smooth journey to the Cape as long as the weather holds. I am to tell this to Mother to calm any fears she may have, and he has given me no end of instructions as to her comfort for the train. Indeed, his letter is one long series of underscores in relation to these directions! Dear, dear man—how I long to see my Tad!

April 4

Mother was quite agitated today, and it was such a struggle to settle her. Dr. Reid said that Grandpere and Aunt Louise's leave-taking has taxed her and that it would be best if I left her to rest quietly for a day or two.

I am so very tired from packing, though Aunt Louise has been remarkable. They leave tomorrow.

April 5

Aunt Louise and Grandpere are gone; the house seems so quiet without them! Dr. McT. has had me running about, doing all kinds of errands, so much so that I have not had time to dwell upon their departure. He says that he has a surprise for me tomorrow and has commanded me not to stay up late writing in my diary, but to go to bed and get a good night's rest. Edgar has relented and granted me five minutes for writing—but now his black eyes are sparkling and must be telling me that my time is up.

April 6

I have seen the Lake—this was my surprise, for Dr. McTavish has known of my great desire to see it. Yet it was not as I expected it to be, for the roads were poorly cleared and we had to pick our way through seemingly endless yards filled with lumber and all manner of warehouses. I suppose it was because I asked if we might follow Spadina to its terminus—though Dr. McT. said that there were other more picturesque routes and vantages that we might have taken. Yet I was insistent to follow Spadina; I think because I have so often seen the Lake from my copse of trees, and I had my heart set upon following the great, long road to the water's edge. But it was so ugly! As we came closer and closer to the shore, the buildings became rough-looking, and the yards were full of mud and debris. It reminded me of the dockyards at Owen Sound, and I almost had no desire to leave our carriage, for there was a thick fog adding to my impression of its filth and despoliation, and the water lay still and very silent.

But that was not the worst of it!

Dr. Reid joined us at the last minute, and so he made us a foursome along with Allan, Dr. McT., and myself. He was very solicitous in handing me into the carriage and in arranging the blankets about me, and for my part, I smiled as cheerily as I could, for I did not wish him to think that I held any ill feelings or thoughts in regard to him. His mood lightened in turn, and Dr. McTavish soon had us all laughing at his ridiculous and, I may add, implausible stories. He told us a long and colorful yarn about being stranded on a boat in the Arctic for days and days so that his eyelids froze and he could not sleep—though none of us believed a word of it, except perhaps Allan.

I suppose I must have grown quieter as we neared the Lake and my face disclosed its dismay, for Dr. McT. remarked that he had predicted my disappointment and warned me again that our passage along this route would only grow more unsightly as we neared the Lake. At length Spadina ended, and we were forced to follow Brock Street to the water's edge. The mud was thick and gruesome, and poor Guy and Fawkes struggled in their harnesses and strained to pull the carriage forward. We were eventually compelled to turn our course toward a pier that Dr. McT. said was named Queen's Wharf.

I could see gray patches of water through the fog; all around us were men, busy with hoisting crates into heavy nets and then pulling them upward by means of pulleys. Many of them stopped to stare at us as we stepped out upon the dirty planks that formed a kind of boardwalk. Dr. McT. stayed to talk with one of the foremen, and so Allan, Dr. Reid, and I walked out toward the end of the pier, passing smaller boats and great piles of empty crates and rotting wood.

Toward the end of the pier, we stopped and were able to look out across the Great Lake, but it was still and silent, as if wounded and wary of our approach. I was disheartened and therefore eager to return, and so we began our walk back—Allan in the lead, quite cheerfully interested in all the bustle around him. Dr. Reid stayed with me, and we did not speak, though the silence between us was not an uncompanionable one. The fog grew thicker, and soon we lost sight of Allan, and I became worried that he might stumble and injure himself. I asked Dr. Reid if we should make haste to find him. He placed me in a small enclosure behind a stack of crates and told me to wait for him, promising to come back in a few minutes if he were not successful.

I stood there alone, watching the fog drift in, sometimes lifting so that I could see the men moving about, and I heard several of them swear and curse it. I was concealed behind a makeshift wall of crates and skids, but to my right, not ten yards away, a group of men were deep in conversation. They were not dressed like dock men, but seemed to be of a military aspect, and I grew a little curious as to who they were and what business made their conversation so animated. I stepped out a little to take a closer look at them, and just then a heavy blanket of fog enveloped us, not unlike a great avalanche of snow. I heard the men exclaim at its density, and then the fog began to move about them in an uncanny fashion.

At first it dissipated slightly, disclosing some of their heads, and these heads continued to converse atop bodies that remained hidden in the fog, so that they seemed to waft upon the air. Then, while these heads hovered, the fog would stir again and yet another man's shoulders or legs would appear, and so their body parts seemed all to be floating, and no man had a single form. I was rather intrigued by this effect, and I again stepped forward to observe it, but stopped when I felt rather than saw that one of the men in their grouping had come closer to me. I drew up the collar of my coat, suddenly feeling a sense of danger. I stared out into the fog, trying to discern the man's movements, and saw only the upper part of a man moving closer to me—a man with one of his arms in a sling. The partial form stopped, and the mist stirred slowly about him until I could see the other arm, both his legs, and a lower portion of his face. I felt as if in a strange dream—and then, without warning, the fog drew back from his face and Captain Howarth appeared not twenty paces away from me, his black eyes staring intently at me and a frightful scowl upon his face.

I gasped, horror-struck at the unexpected sight of him!

He said nothing but continued to stare ominously at me. I could see a deep and nasty scar across one side of his face. But for this, he looked the same.

I was paralyzed with fear and stood rooted to the ground, barely able to breathe, so frightened was I. The fog had conjured him up so suddenly, and I seemed to feel his hands about my throat once again, and felt myself powerless in his grip.

He moved slowly toward me with an evil smile on his lips but—oh, I must bless my guardian angel!—just then Dr. Reid returned, and though he did not immediately see me, he called out my name with some urgency. Captain Howarth turned to eye him and then the two men stopped—with perhaps thirty or so paces between them—each one facing the other, while I stood almost equidistant from both. Great waves of fog, white and swirling, drifted between the two men as if moved by some unseen current.

They looked intently at each other across the boardwalk without speaking for some seconds. I felt my fear ebbing from me, and I do not know how it came to me—perhaps it was the strange effect of the fog—but George's painting of the buoys seemed to float before me, and in my mind's eye the two men stood to each other as if they had become the markers for starboard and port.

I knew Captain Howarth to be a man most certainly of an evil cast—but it was Dr. Reid whom the fog made me see with better clarity. I saw him as one of George's buoys, standing sentinel in the gloomy vapor—and it came to me that though his moorings have been tested by capricious waters, yet I knew him to be good, so very good a man!

I ran to him and clung to him, as if to save myself from the evil of the other man. Captain Howarth glowered silently at us both, and then he faded away into the fog, and I shivered in Dr. Reid's arms.

I told Dr. Reid after dinner why I had been so

frightened; we were sitting alone by the fire, and Dr. McTavish was off in the library for a few moments. Dr. Reid looked very grim and said that it had been wrong of him to leave me there by myself, and though I protested that such was not the case, still he remained somber and thoughtful.

He had taken my hand while I was speaking, and I had felt his hold tightening as I spoke. I thought that he might be unaware of what he was doing, but even after I had finished, he did not relinquish my hand, and when Dr. McT. returned, he still had it in his own.

I got up abruptly—a little flustered to be found with him thus—but he only shifted his hand to my waist and said to McT., "Marged has been telling me of this Captain Howarth."

The two men looked at each other across the room, and I sensed that some unspoken words were being exchanged between them. I excused myself, thanking Dr. McT. for arranging the excursion, but saying that I found myself fatigued after the day's adventures.

And now that I am alone and readying myself for bed, I am thinking of George's painting again—of the two buoys. Yet I do not think that he included it in his show. I keep trying to remember if I had seen it among those pictures exhibited—but I am almost sure that it was not. Perhaps he has not finished it.

April 7

I do not know what to make of George! Should I feel offended, or have I become too sensitive after Dr.

Stone's attack upon my deportment? Do I attribute thoughts and motivations to him that are not there?

Yet I know that I did not seek him out, nor did I plot to hold any secret conference with him.

When I came back from the hospital this afternoon, the house was quiet, and upon my inquiry, Peter indicated that Dr. McT. was in the library. I made my way there expecting to find him behind his untidy desk and amidst his even more untidy papers. The door was open, and I paused before entering, hearing movement within and assuming that it was he. I looked past the door and saw George—alone and sitting in the doctor's chair next to a brisk fire. He looked rather pensive, and there was a decanter of Dr. McT.'s brandy on the table at his elbow and a glassful of the substance in his hand. I hesitated, for he seemed to be staring moodily at the carpet in front of him and I was reluctant to disturb him. I was about to beat a silent retreat when he looked up and saw me backing quietly away. Instantly he was upon his feet.

"Marged!" he exclaimed. "Is that you, or have I only conjured you up from out of my thoughts?" He rubbed one of his hands across his face and grimaced, as if fighting down a powerful and yet inescapable emotion.

"George," I said as calmly as I could, for my heart was beating so. "It is I, Marged. I do not wish to disturb you…"

He beckoned for me to come in with a rough motion and then waited behind his chair, indicating that I should take it. I did so with some reluctance, for I felt unsure of him, or at least of which parts of him might still be just George and which under the influence of Dr. McTavish's brandy. I sat there quite primly, my back very straight and my face no doubt betraying my anxiety, for he turned to me and his features seemed to soften at the sight of my discomfort.

He looked at me pointedly for several moments, as if turning something over in his mind.

"Marged," he said finally, "I've got a beastly decision to make."

Suddenly I feared that something had gone wrong with his show, and strange emotions swept over me—both of relief and great anxiety. My voice trembling, I asked him, "It is not the reviews, is it, George? Did not the critics praise your work?"

He smiled ruefully and shook his head. "Oh, no," he said. "They liked my paintings well enough. The reviews have been good—tolerably good. Good enough..." He paused. "Good enough for me to be introduced to New York society." He grimaced again and took a deep gulp of the brandy.

My heart seemed to stop. I knew it was Caroline's father of whom he was speaking, and of course, also Caroline.

I felt myself sinking as if into a deep hole, yet somehow I whispered, "Congratulations, George. I suppose this is what you have always wanted."

"Is it?" he asked me almost savagely, and then he threw his glass angrily into the fire.

The crash of it breaking startled me, and in a second I lost all of my composure. I cried out, resenting that he should keep me there in thralldom to his ill temper and to the violence of his own emotions. I covered my face and began to sob. I was so ashamed of myself! But I could do nothing to assuage the sense of desolation that came over me, and like a child, I gave in to my despair. Then he was at my feet, gently trying to pull my hands away from my face and begging me not to cry. I barely heeded him, for I felt as if my very soul was expiring in that moment. All that I could think was that he was going away and that it would be forever this time.

"Marged." He said my name as if pleading with me. "Would you come away with me—to Florence perhaps? Or we could go to Paris—or Rome. Then I wouldn't give a damn what they say."

I looked up at him in astonishment. "George," I said, arresting the flow of his words. "What is it that you are asking of me?" He drew back, and I saw a flush suffuse his face. I let out a small exclamation of dismay for I thought—

"No, Marged," he said. "Do not mistake me—" but he left his sentence unfinished. Then he walked to the chair opposite mine and sat down, pressing his hands to his temples and leaning forward onto his elbows. I was at such a loss; he seemed so agitated that it quite distressed me to see him in such a state. I rose and went over to him, and then I placed my hand timidly on his shoulder.

"George," I whispered, "I wish that your heart weren't so twisted up inside you! Does it not offer you counsel?" He took my hand and pressed it to his lips as if to prevent himself from speech. I do not know how long I stood there next to him with my hand thus, but I felt a soft tranquillity steal over me, and I was loath to move. It was George who finally stirred and then got up. He turned away from me, asking me somewhat awkwardly to forgive him, and then muttering that he was not quite himself and that I shouldn't pay any heed to what he had said. I waited silently for a few seconds, and we both could hear the wind howling down the chimney and the soft humming of the embers below.

At last Dr. McTavish came in and broke the silence. He was frowning at George and pressed me to leave them and ready myself for dinner. George bid me good evening in a husky voice, and I sensed that he would not be joining us for supper.

I could barely speak—what words had I to say to him? I turned and left him standing with his back to me. I do not think that I shall ever forget that image of him. I still see it before me now; even as my eyes fill with tears, I see it still.

April 9

I miss Aunt Louise so terribly—and am more than ever grateful for her assistance in helping me pack up our belongings. And yet there is so much left to do! Dr. McT. is a dreadful responsibility—he will even unpack the boxes that I have readied. I am sure now that Mr. Thompson must have been a saint to undertake all these preparations, for I am almost at my wit's end.

And George—will I see him again before we go? The Stewarts, I know, are coming to the Lodge toward the beginning of May, but I do not know if he will be among their company. Surely he will come to see me before I leave!

April 10

Dr. Reid has reassured me that I have acted under some great strain and a depression of spirits, but I must admit that I did not tell him everything.

Very late last night, I felt an inexplicable and urgent desire to get outside. I woke up hot and fretful, my chest constricted as if I could not breathe, and though I rose and lit a candle, still I could not shake my unease.

And then, seemingly acting on impulse, I wrapped myself up in my green shawl and descended the stairs. The house was dark and silent, but still I managed to find my boots in the vestibule, and I drew out my cloak from the front closet. I do not know why, but I felt strongly impelled to go outside. I opened the front door carefully and left it slightly ajar; the cold instantly penetrated my wrappings, but still I did not yield to mental arguments urging me to return to my bed. I stepped out onto the pathway and into a sheer and utter darkness—there was a strange surfeit of some forceful emotion moving through me that I could not for the world explain, and yet I felt it so powerfully drawing me out into the frigid night air and toward my copse of trees at the far end of the doctor's property, near the edge of the old Lake. I thought I heard Dr. Reid's disapproving voice, informing me once again that of course one might expect trees to be in a garden, but I did not heed him.

I followed the path toward the gate and then pushed on through it. The temperature was so cold it hurt my throat to breathe, and I could feel the wind pushing against my back, driving me toward the ledge and the tall forms of the pines. I stopped before them and looked up to see the trees in such a terrible tumult—twisting and turning in the wind, bending and groaning as if they might break. I felt as if I were in some horrible nightmare and that the forest was being felled by an invisible swarm of devils and that at any second I would hear the fearful sound of axes cutting into the flesh of their trunks and the pines would begin to fall. I longed to cry out, but my voice was dry and frozen in my throat, and so I stood before them, watching their perilous motion and yet powerless to stop the terrifying storm that swept through the glade and seemed to force the trees to breaking point.

I do not know how he found me or why he came, but Dr. McTavish was suddenly beside me, drawing me away from the trees; he was still dressed in his evening clothes and without a coat. He called my name and attempted to pull me back toward the house, but I resisted him.

"What is happening?" I cried, pointing to the trees. "What is it that is trying to destroy them?"

"Marged," he shouted next to my ear. I could barely hear him, for the sound of the boughs tossing was overwhelming. "Let him go! You must let him go!"

"What do you mean?" I cried. It seemed as if the whole forest was about to collapse upon us. The trees were moving with such wild agitation!

"Let him go," he insisted, this time as if beseeching me, and then somehow I knew he meant George, and I sank down as if some livid cord of fire had been extinguished in me. Then the trees quieted, and I knew they were out of danger—and though their boughs continued to move with a lingering restlessness, I knew them to be safe.

Dr. McTavish led me back to the house and saw me safely into bed, covering me up as he would a small child and staying with me to see that I was settled. As he departed, he asked me if I wished him to leave the candle burning, but I told him that I wanted only darkness.

April 11 [?] (One page missing.)

…My eyes filled, and I turned away from him. Again, what was he asking me? I was not sure, but he grew so quiet and anxious. He took my hand and held it for a few moments, almost in a mournful manner. Then he just left—without saying a word. I am glad that he did not say good-bye. Somehow I am glad.

I think I must be in love with George—or in love with the part of him that paints such beautiful pictures.

April 15

We are arrived at Owen Sound and will spend the evening in this hotel. I had hoped to see Tad, but he has not as yet arrived, for we were told that the water was quite rough yesterday and this may have delayed him.

I am sure that I have been a wretched companion for Dr. McTavish; honestly, I do not know what possessed me to be so peevish with him! And he has been so kind and patient that I doubly feel remorse for my conduct.

I think it was that he insisted upon interrogating me as to what birds I recognized as we stopped in each station, and then I must also name the trees that we saw through the window as the train moved northward. I was so enthralled to see the forests as they appeared and then grew suddenly frustrated at having to name the species for him, including, of course, all their Latinates. I am sure that Dr. McT. did this to distract me, for I have been most anxious about the trip and how Mother might take it. She, however, has done beautifully and seems quite content...but I grew aggravated, for I felt that I knew my trees quite well enough, though I do not possess his naturalist's eye.

I tried to explain that I do *see* them—not as he does, but I see the trees in their movement or form, as they stand together. Was it not enough that I should see them so?

He said that I was now trained to see things differently—to develop new powers of observation—for such was how I could paint his illustrations and provide the detail that he desires for them. I grew peevish and declared my dissatisfaction with my painting of the grebe. I exclaimed that though it took so much care to render each of its feathers, yet to me it looks nothing like a real grebe! In my mind's eye, I said, I see the bird as a shadow moving on the water—the outline of a head—and then I hear it calling and know it to be a grebe. I cannot see it without the sky and water...

My thinking no doubt was all in a tumult—for I know Dr. McT. to be correct in teaching me to know the trees individually and to learn the habits of different birds so that I might identify them. Mr. Muir does the same, urging us to love nature as a teacher. Dr. McTavish said that if what one saw was "just trees," then they belonged to no one, and that is why the timber companies cut them down and destroyed the forests without thought to preserving parts of them. He said that the naturalist must appreciate the trees and study their attributes, for in so doing, we show them to be the homes of birds and other animals.

I responded that I did not disagree, but that it was not what I meant at all when I said that I saw them whole—to me their great beauty is in their *collection,* in the way they seem to tumble into each other. Dr. McT. shook his head and said that a forest is no "tumble" but rather a "system" that naturalists understood best. I suppose that he is right, but I was stubborn and closed up my lips, and would not speak further on it. And now I am truly sorry for my ill temper.

Tad has come to meet us! I can hear his voice below!

April 17

Home! At last, I am home! Even now, Claude thrusts his great, lovely head into my lap, demanding *all* of my attention.

April 18

Beautiful and alive—there are a thousand things that I might write of and yet I cannot. I want to see everything at once—be everywhere at once. Auntie's hairbrush always placed to one side of her dresser, the sound of distant waves stirring in the morning—the smell of Tad's rags for cleaning his gun and the new grass as it whispers near the Basin. They are all exquisite to me, defying any order or description that I might give them in my journal. For once I am not drawn to writing, but only do so from a reluctance to abandon my habit.

April 19

Uncle Gil says that I have become quite a lady! He will not let me do my chores as I have done before, but instead takes the water pail and will carry it for me and will not allow me to carry the wood. Yesterday he lifted me onto Flore, but not at my request, for I have mounted her by myself many a time.

Have I changed so?

It is true that I wear my hair a little differently, and that my clothes are finer than before, but I am not changed. Each day I seem to find more and more of myself!

April 20

I am so happy to be here—and yet there is a restlessness in me that exists alongside a deep contentedness. It is George, of course: I think I am waiting for him to come with the boaters, and though I keep reminding myself that he will not, still I go to the Basin almost every evening to watch for him.

April 21

Tonight I walked the long way round to the Basin—away from the fishing camp, for already there are quite a number of the families there, and I can smell the smoke from their fires. I came to the clearing and saw two schooners and knew that the season was starting again—a season with all its familiarities and routines, its constants and continuities. But even so, I feel a hollowness—though my heart devours each blessing and each returning part.

Claude followed me out to the Point and stayed close by my side as if to offer me his sympathy for a mood he discerned but did not understand. I looked at the Lodge thinking of George, and though the Stewarts will come and Allan is so dear to me, still it will be lifeless without him. I grew anxious, for I wondered if I might ever be happy here without George. As if George and this place were one and the same, and in denying me his heart, he had absconded with part of my soul and I should never be whole.

I was angry with myself for such thoughts, and so I walked back along the coastline, and it did me good to walk across the stones and choose my footing carefully. I felt the quick alliance between foot and eye as I stepped briskly from rock to rock, and no jagged outcropping stopped me, for I mounted these and made my way across them undeterred.

It did me much good, for the water was rough and restless, out of sympathy with the shore and dissatisfied with itself. Perhaps I was a fitting companion, for I am also out of sorts with myself.

Yet even so, I think that I am perversely pleased that I might brew a storm for no apparent reason. I'd swig my storm down—like Dr. Stone and her whiskey! Perhaps that is why she drinks—not to quell but to nourish some inner storm that has no impassive shoreline and weathered rocks to endure it.

April 22

I am sending a letter to George—am I foolish to do so? Will it only pain him…or perhaps he will treat it as the foolish fancy of a young girl. And yet I *must* write to him. I am wrong to think of us as day and night! Perhaps George did try to cross the threshold—and it was I who withdrew.

But do I possess the courage to send it to him?

April 22, 1898

Dear George,

The last time we saw each other, you asked me if I might go away—with a man like yourself, you said, and travel all the world. I did not answer your question but instead evaded you.

I am sorry for this. It was unworthy of you. I do not

know your thoughts, and much of the time you seem to avoid me—and then you are there again, saying things I cannot fully fathom.

Dr. McTavish has told me that you will be leaving soon, and I fear that I shall not see you for a long time. I cannot think that it will be forever; surely there will be a time when our paths might cross again.

I am afraid that you might think that my regard for you is…so much less than it truly is. Perhaps this is my fault, for ever do I seem contrary in your presence. And yet, I do not mean to be so! I do not know how you mix your paints or indeed how you know to place your brush in such a way that the strokes convey the spirit of this place; it is only a part, but it is such that I can see the Bay in your canvases, living and real! I can see the trees, and I hear them moving, though your canvas is silent. I do not know how you do this, and it is a wondrous thing to me because I can do nothing like it. I can only be here—as a part of this place.

Somehow I feel that everything about myself—all my strivings and even my stubborn perversities, but certainly all that is truly good in me—has been, is already here, out in the Bay. All that is myself has already been formed in the Bay, and it hardly matters what moment it is in which I breathe and live and die. I feel as if…I have already happened. I am already an echo of myself. I have already been lonely, restless, tranquil by these waters. They know me before I know myself.

I think people come here sometimes—the boaters perhaps—and find a fragment of themselves. They do strange, incongruous things because it is only a piece, but nevertheless a piece of themselves. I cannot do this! I find everything here. All of me! There is nothing left behind, no other place that has a claim to me. Here my heart breaks whole. Here my soul is filled. Here my hate and anger are true storms—and here my love fills all the heavens and all the earth.

Dearest George, may God bless you always.

Yours,
Marged

April 30

George has left for New York. Dr. McTavish told me as I unpacked my paints and arranged them. It is almost as if he has told me that George will marry Caroline Ferguson.

I think he told me so that I might be busy and not have to show my face to him. The Stewarts will be here next week, but I cannot expect that George will be among them.

I do not think that what I feel is jealousy, but my heart feels as if it were full of sharp knives and that, as I walk about, they shift and pierce me anew. It is not just that I feel he will not be happy. What I feel—what I sense—is something more! As if some cold-blooded thing were pushing him forward and I am powerless to release him from it. Surely he must know that it is wrong—so wrong! I cannot believe that he might love her…

I am crying and I must not let the others see my red eyes. Now I am left to wonder if he received my letter before he departed. Perhaps I will never know.

May 2

Dr. McTavish says that I have become terribly brooding and that if I don't smile at him at least once soon, he shall cast himself into the Bay.

He is anxious for me—of this I am aware, but I am not quite sure that he fully understands my temperament, and this causes him some unrest. I asked him if he ever had something that he wished for, but knew that he could not have. He answered promptly with a firm yes! I was surprised and asked him if he could tell me what it was.

"An ostrich," he said. "I have always wished to perform an ostrich, but I am far too stout and could never pull it off." He looked so solemn as he said this that I burst out laughing—and then I think I was crying. And then he said, "You see—I do not dwell on the dark things as you do, Marged. I hoped for a smile, but have been granted your laughter."

May 5

Mother was asleep in her chair downstairs, and I came upon Auntie, though she did not hear me enter the room behind her. For once her hands were not busy, and she sat staring out the window and I could see that her thoughts were far away.

I came up to her and put my arms around her, and in a slight, oh so slight movement, she rested her head against my arm. Somehow I knew she was thinking of Luke, of her little boy, so beloved, and whom she will not see again until her journey to the next life—and even in this, we are never spared all uncertainty.

Of all of them—Mother and Tad and Uncle Gil—I think Auntie Alis would truly understand my sentiments. Though she hardly ever speaks of her own feelings, and her spoken words are often harsh and uncompromising—she would understand.

May 7

Tad has had a talk with me. I am glad, for I feel as if my own thoughts have become a torment to me, and there is so little that he does not see and perceive about me.

He asked me outright. We took a walk down to the gate to see if the beavers were causing a flood again, and he said, taking his pipe from his mouth and in his quiet way, "Marged, is your heart set upon George Stewart then?"

I started to cry, and we stood looking at the gate—I with my arm in his—and he waited patiently until I might finish and compose myself.

"He's a fine man," Tad said finally, "but he knows not how to be content with being master of himself, but instead he wishes to rule all the world around him."

"Whatever do you mean, Tad?" I cried, for I found him to be so enigmatic, too!

He pulled on his pipe a bit, and then, as I quieted,

he said, "My own father always told me that 'tis the man as is the master, but 'tis the woman who rules. I never knew what he meant by it until I married your mother. George will find it out soon enough, Marged, but it's a lesson no woman can teach him, nor any man either."

We were silent some moments, and then he asked me if I might leave off my writing for a bit and not let my thoughts sit so hard with me, but to let them come and go as they might.

I was not so sure, but I have agreed to his request.

Ten

"Garth!"

I jumped—it was Edna hurrying up the stairs behind me.

"I'm sorry, but you can't see Marged. She's not up to a visit today."

I let her catch her breath. "Is everything all right?" I asked anxiously.

"She's been complaining about an owl hooting in the backyard and keeping her up nights, so we gave her a sleeping pill. She's very eager to see you, though."

Edna leaned against me heavily as I helped her back down the stairs. "I'm glad I caught you, Garth. I've been so busy, but I wanted to ask you how it's been going with that birth certificate."

"I'm still working on it."

"What do you think? Could she be the same Marged Brice?"

"I'm certainly not saying she is," I replied evasively.

"I know, I know," she grumbled. "But you're not saying she *absolutely isn't*, are you?"

I said nothing.

"Good!" Edna exclaimed. "Then we're still in the game as far as the Longevity Project is concerned." She paused on the bottom step. "Wait a minute. Take this before I forget."

She handed me a large manila envelope, then eyed me curiously, trying to peek inside as I opened it. "What is it?" she asked.

"Just something Miss Brice wants me to take a look at."

"Oh? I wonder what it could be?"

I hesitated for a split second. "Actually, it's one of Marged's diaries. She's asked me to read some of them."

Edna gave me a shrewd look. "Marged mentioned she'd given you her journals. In fact, it was sort of my idea."

I reminded myself never to try to deceive Edna.

"By the way—" She stopped me as I opened the front door. "Since you're already here, would you mind saying hello to Walter Graham? We're having a bit of a crisis today."

"What's he been up to?" Walt happened to be my favorite veteran at the Clarkson.

"He's been upsetting the residents with some nonsense about a ghost in the home," she said disapprovingly.

"A *what*!"

Edna laughed. "Believe me, this isn't the first one he's seen!"

I found Walt dozing in a lawn chair out under the trees by the front porch. I coughed a few times and then waited patiently for him to wake up. After a minute or so, I stepped closer and gently shook him.

A breeze suddenly pushed a branch forward, and it grazed the back of my shoulder, making me wince as its needles pierced through my shirt and pressed uncomfortably against my scar.

"Perfessor, is that you?" Walt sat up and blinked at me from behind an enormous pair of sunglasses. "Where the heck you been? I've been waitin' to finish that story about Perugia."

I apologized, saying that I had been busy doing something for Edna.

Walt took off his glasses and rubbed his chin. "She sent you to read me the Riot Act, didn't she?"

I smiled. "What's all this about a ghost?"

"Is it my fault we got a new ghost?"

"A new ghost?"

"Yep. I been here eight years, but this one—it's a doozy!"

I tried to keep a straight face. "Tell me about it."

Walt looked at me hard. "Yer not pullin' my leg, are you?"

"No, Walt. I want to hear about it."

"Well, this one I never see, but I hear her. It's a little kid. She pats my face. Tells me I'm still alive, first thing in the mornin'."

"First thing in the morning?"

"That's what I said. She pats my cheek jest like this. Jest soft like this. *Walter—alive!* That's what she says."

I looked at him and grinned. "Come on now, Walt!"

"I'm not kiddin'," he protested. "And I'm not complainin' neither. It's a nice way to wake up. I'm probably jest as surprised as she is that I'm still breathin'." He sank back into his chair. "And I'm not the only one who's heard her. No, sir. Don't let that Edna say I'm the only one makin' all the trouble."

"Who else has heard this…ghost?"

Walt ignored my question. "Some of us are thinkin' that the new lady up on the third floor—maybe she's got somethin' to do with it."

"Why's that?"

He cleared his throat. "Somebody said somethin' about her being pretty darn old. Like too old to be alive."

"Walt, listen. I've met her. Believe me, she's not a ghost. Her name is Marged Brice."

"Brice?" He gave me a sharp look.

"Yes. Did you know the Brices? Hugh Brice the lightkeeper? You used to live up near Cape Prius, didn't you?"

"I didn't know 'em, but I had a girlfriend—Esther—she worked for the daughter, for Miss Brice. In that big place of hers, off Dyer Bay."

"Do you remember the address? Or anything about the house?"

"Nope. Can't say I do. It was a long time ago, Perfessor." Walt closed his eyes.

"Think back, Walt. Did your girlfriend ever talk to you about Miss Brice?"

"Lemme think. Esther said she was a real nice lady. But—" He lowered his voice. "We all knew about her. We knew about her havin' a baby by the doctor. Back in those days, that was thought to be pretty bad. Not like today, eh?" He looked at me rakishly.

"What doctor?" I was careful to sound casual.

"You musta heard a' him. Yer a perfessor, I'm sure you heard a' him."

"Do you mean a Dr. Reid?"

Walt shook his head. "Doc Reid? I knew him. He lived over in Griffon. I almost married the doc's housekeeper. Angela's her name. A real good-lookin' girl! But she chose Tom Phelps over me. Ha—he's dead and I'm still livin'!"

"Was Dr. Reid the father of Miss Brice's child?" I asked.

"Come to think of it—nope—I think it was the painter fella. But the baby died, and she went a little crazy. She kept on like it was still alive. Miss Brice kinda had a reputation as bein' a bit of a wild one." He yawned and slumped back into his chair. "She's long dead, though," he added, dropping his sunglasses. "Went to her funeral," he muttered.

"You went to her funeral?" I repeated quickly. "When was that?"

"Poor Esther." Now Walt could barely keep his eyes open. "It was in the wintertime. She died of the cancer. Couldn't get her in right away because the ground was froze hard…"

Just then I heard the sound of frenzied barking.

I picked up Walt's glasses, carefully placing them in his lap, and then quickly went to fetch Farley.

He was standing near a flower bed at the back of the house, his body quivering and his eyes riveted on one of the upper windows.

"Farley," I called, but he wouldn't move.

I marched over to get him. "Farley! Come!"

I looked up to see what had caught his attention. My eyes roved across the side of the house until they came to rest at Marged Brice's window.

I stared—there seemed to be a small figure standing at her

window, looking down at me. The form of a very small child with one hand raised and its forehead pressed against the glass.

A sharp stab of pain shot through my left shoulder. I blinked and shook my head.

And then the figure was gone.

Eleven

A LOW ROLL OF thunder came off the Bay as we sat out on the deck, watching a storm gathering on the horizon. I was handing Clare a glass of wine while Doug rummaged through my father's tackle box.

"Did you see Miss Brice today?" she asked.

I told her that Marged hadn't been up to it, but that she'd left me another diary.

"I'm getting pretty hooked," I confessed. "The last one left off with George Stewart going off to get married—and not to Marged Brice."

"Not to Marged Brice? What do you mean?"

I shrugged and kept my expression neutral. "Marged had a rival: an American heiress named Caroline Ferguson. So far I haven't found any marriage record, so I don't know that he actually did marry her. But didn't you mention something about a secret marriage?"

Farley darted past me, and Clare bent down to scoop him up. "Yes, but I've been hoping that Marged Brice was the bride."

Farley started producing one of his sputtering motor sounds.

"You'd never be tempted by one of those nasty heiresses, would you?" she cooed at him. "You're far too sensible to do something like that." Mars instantly came over and sat down at her feet, fastening his eyes on Farley. "Or you, Mars," she added, reaching down to stroke his ears. "Of course you wouldn't be dazzled by all that money, either."

A deafening clap of thunder rent the sky above us.

"Hey, Garth, what's this?" Doug held up a silver fishing lure with a dark feather dangling off the end.

"That's one of my father's creations," I said, still watching Clare. Now she was cradling Farley in her arms and stroking his belly. I reached over and put my hand firmly on Mars's collar. "My dad claimed there wasn't a fish on the Peninsula that could resist it."

Clare glanced up at me, startled. "Your father's creation?" She quickly put Farley down. "But it couldn't be!"

We waited, both of us surprised at her outburst.

"What I meant was—it must be the same lure I used to catch that enormous whitefish. The one in the photograph I knocked off your wall, Garth."

Doug stared at me. "What photograph?" he began, and then stopped abruptly. "Oh, never mind. Can I borrow it? I'm thinking of taking the boat out early tomorrow." He turned his attention back to the tackle box. "Do you want to join me, Garth?" he asked, not looking up.

"Sure," I said vaguely.

"Aren't you going to open your delivery?" Clare gestured toward the package she had placed on the table. "I'm surprised the driver let me sign for it. It has 'confidential' and 'express' and all kinds of urgent markings all over it."

Doug grunted. "Ha! That's a good one. As if he stood a chance! You probably—" He stopped himself midsentence.

"Oh, I managed to resist steaming it open," she said mildly. "But I'll confess to reading the return address. Who's Muriel Hampstead?"

I picked up the package and turned it over, explaining that Muriel was a classics professor who had taught with my father. "She's an expert on Greek and Roman mythology, and my father collaborated with her on several projects."

"Ah, you think she can help explain who Miss Brice's Perdita is!" Clare's expression brightened.

I nodded. "That's the idea. I called her up a few days ago. She wasn't up to talking long, but she told me that she and my father were working on a paper about a myth involving a Perdita."

We both got up as the first drops of rain hit the awning above us. Clare shivered slightly and reached for the shawl she had brought with her.

"We'd better get inside," I said, taking her arm. "Why don't you go ahead and open Muriel's package and I'll lay a fire. Then I'll see if I have anything edible to offer you two."

Clare sat down in my father's chair while I started to rip up some newspaper and carefully arrange the kindling. Doug followed with the tackle box and noisily dumped it on the dining room table. "Mind if I help myself?" he asked, eyeing the bottle of scotch I'd left there.

I heard the rustle of pages as Clare thumbed through the manuscript. After a few minutes, she raised her head. "The paper Muriel wrote with your father looks murderous! It seems to be all about Aeolian dialects and one of Hesiod's works, the *Theogony*. But she's also included a letter addressed to you, Garth—a rather longish letter."

"Hesiod?" Doug muttered. "Am I supposed to recognize the name?"

Clare got up and placed the package on my desk. "Douglas, must you always play the cretin?" She walked over to him and gently laid her head against his shoulder. "You know perfectly well Hesiod was a Greek poet, writing about the time of Homer," she added.

"Of course!" Doug quipped, putting an arm around her. "How could I possibly forget! And who's Homer, by the way?"

"Hopeless." She sighed as he gave her shoulders a squeeze. "Just hopeless!"

Out of the corner of my eye, I saw Doug silently hand Clare the silver lure.

She took it from him hesitantly, holding it up to the light and watching it slowly twirl at the end of her fingers. Suddenly she released it, and the lure dropped silently back into the tackle box. Doug gave her a quick look and fished it out again, but she'd already turned away.

"Garth, do you know if your father kept any of Hesiod's works in his library?" she asked.

"Check the shelf to the left—way up at the top," I answered, returning my attention to the kindling. I placed two logs in readiness to one side, and then I turned around.

I froze, my eyes on Clare.

She had paused in front of the bookcase, her expression slightly pensive as she looked back at Doug, his attention still focused on the fishing gear. She was pushing her hair away from her face—almost exactly as she had done in the photograph—the shadow of a frown playing across her features.

Our eyes suddenly met.

"I don't think I can reach it; I'm not tall enough," she said, just a shade unsteadily. "I'm afraid I'll have to ask Douglas to get it."

I got up quickly and went over, reaching past her and pulling down the volume.

"Clare," I said quietly, then I raised my voice. "And, Doug. I think you'll both have to stay for dinner." There was another crash of thunder, and this time a sizzling stroke of lightning. "It seems to be the will of the gods. You can't go back out into that storm."

"Sure we'll stay," Doug said easily. "I'm getting desperate. Practically all I've eaten since I got here is chicken potpie."

Clare glanced up at me, her expression curious but her eyes twinkling. "Well, it's not fair to expect Garth to eat it all, is it?"

I laughed and took Clare's hand. "Would you take a look at Muriel's letter for me?" I asked, keeping my voice low.

She searched my face, a little surprised. "Of course."

"Bring it into the kitchen, then." I released her hand as Doug looked up. "And why don't you read it out loud. That way I can get started with some whitefish and listen at the same time."

"Actually—you know, I think I'll pass on dinner," Doug announced. "I want to turn in early. Feel free to join me bright and early—if you're up."

"But, Douglas, the lightning!" Clare warned.

"I'll be fine. Believe me, the odds are on my side."

"It's probably because you're cooking fish," Clare whispered. "Douglas is funny. He likes to catch them, but he absolutely hates to eat them."

"I'm sure I could have found him something else," I muttered, secretly pleased at Doug's sudden exit.

"I guess it means more Georgian Bay whitefish for us." Clare pulled a stool up close to the counter. "All right, are you ready?"

"Please don't feel obliged to read it all the way through." I watched her tie back her hair while she glanced rapidly over the first page.

"Dear Garth," Clare began, putting down her wineglass.

Twelve

Dear Garth,

How pleasant it was to speak with you last week, even if only briefly. I meant to put something in the mail days ago, but I have delayed fulfilling my promise. Please excuse this belated package, but needless to say, I'm very glad that you came to me with your questions about Perdita.

Most people associate Perdita with Robert Greene's *Pandosto* or Shakespeare's *The Winter's Tale,* but she has much deeper roots in the ancient world and Greek cosmology. I am one of perhaps only a handful of scholars who know this—your father was another. He deeply shared my interest in Perdita. We had great debates about her: wonderful arguments and disagreements that surely would have continued had he not slipped away from us in so untimely a manner. I hope that I do not reopen old sorrows by mentioning this, but there is not a day that goes by that I do not miss my dear friend, esteemed colleague, and generous mentor.

Now—if I may state my position succinctly—Perdita has been my passion for almost forty years. I am convinced that she plays a vital role in the cosmology of the ancient Greeks and is critical to how they understood destiny and fate. But she is also a terribly elusive figure, even more neglected by classical scholars than Iacchos, one of your father's favorites.

I first came across a reference to Perdita during one of my stints at the Vatican Library. In fact, I believe that you had just been born, for I seem to remember hearing the news while I was in Rome. Though there were many troubled years that came later, I know you were a source of great joy to your father. I can attest to that firsthand, though I must admit he never complained of the severe trials that ensued as a result of your mother's health.

My research at the Vatican was on Aeolian dialects in the works of Hesiod, a Greek poet who lived in the eighth century BC. I am sure you must know of his major work—the *Theogony*—and its account of how the world was created.

Of course it goes without saying that there's no *true original* of the *Theogony*; we classicists have had to depend on various copies that have been preserved and passed on over the centuries. Much of my research has focused on copies that were made by a Roman poet named Lumenius (c. 100–160 AD). Although Lumenius is not well known among classicists, his poetry is quite important for Hesiod scholars, namely because he had one strange (and for me very lucky) idiosyncrasy: Lumenius frequently inserted lines composed by his favorite writers into his own poems. Sometimes he even reproduced complete stanzas. Again, luckily for me, Lumenius was very fond of Hesiod and frequently inserted lines from the *Theogony* into his own poetry.

You may wonder at Lumenius's method, but let

me clarify that he was no plagiarizer. He was always very careful to distinguish between his own work and that of other authors. He had several different ways of doing this, but in the case of the *Theogony*, his method was to write his own verses in Latin and insert the copied Hesiod excerpts in Greek. This is a most important point to remember. It was this technique that led me to the discovery that Lumenius was working off a version of the *Theogony* that I had never seen. To make a long story short, after reading the Hesiod excerpts reproduced in Lumenius's poetry, I began to suspect there must be a longer version of the *Theogony*, containing pieces of unknown text: a very exciting idea for a classicist!

It has taken me almost forty years of research, but I am now fully convinced that at one time there was a very different and much longer version of Hesiod's *Theogony*. By piecing together several of Lumenius's excerpts, I discovered fifty-one lines that do not appear in standard versions of the work. More to the point, the missing fifty-one lines relate to the segment where Prometheus steals fire and woman is created—and it is here we find Perdita.

Now, to use an expression that your father always used with his students: *time to fasten our seat belts and turn to the text*.

Let us begin with standard versions of the *Theogony*, meaning the kind you can buy in any bookstore. Hesiod's poem recounts Prometheus's many transgressions against Zeus, including how he steals fire from the gods and gives it as a "gift" to mankind. Furious at Prometheus for giving mankind fire, Zeus decides to give a different kind of "gift." He commands his son, the blacksmith Hephaestus, to fashion a beautiful but wasteful and deceitful maiden: this is none other than Pandora. Once manufactured, the maiden is sent off to Epimetheus—Prometheus's brother—with a "box" as her dowry. Yet, unable to quell her curiosity, Pandora opens up the "box." Zeus, however, has stocked it with nasty spirits, and thus Pandora carelessly unleashes sickness, pestilence, and misfortunes on mankind. (Note: it is actually not a box but more a clay "vessel" or "jar," but we can thank Erasmus for the confusion.)

Now, as mentioned, the above myths of Prometheus's theft of fire and Pandora's creation are included in standard versions of the *Theogony,* but in the fragment I reconstructed, not only does the sequence of events change, but also the substance of the myth itself.

In the extra fifty-one lines, Hephaestus unexpectedly falls in love with Pandora as he is making her. At first the blacksmith feels affection and friendship (*philia*) for Pandora, then passion (*eros*), and eventually unconditional love (*agape*). Day after day, Zeus comes to see if the maiden is finished and ready to be sent off to Epimetheus, but Hephaestus puts him off, always saying that he has more work to do.

Hephaestus eventually lies with Pandora, and they have a child. Hephaestus names his child Emmenona: a variation of *emme/mona,* a Greek term meaning "to be lost in a passion." (It is the poet Lumenius who later translates Emmenona into Perdita, from the Latin for "lost," i.e., *perditus.*)

Hephaestus and Pandora's connubial happiness

soon ends. Zeus sends a messenger announcing that the maiden must be ready by the next day. Deeply attached to Pandora but fearful of Zeus's disapproval, Hephaestus hatches a plan. He tells Pandora that they must part, but he promises that it will only be a temporary separation, for Hephaestus plans to secretly abduct her and put the blame for her disappearance on mankind. As a precaution, he convinces Pandora to preserve their three loves—*philia, eros,* and *agape*—by tying them up in a bundle and giving them to their child, Emmenona/Perdita, whom he hides away in his forge. Hephaestus, however (and unbeknownst to Pandora), adds a fourth love to Perdita's bundle: *biophilia.*

The missing fragment tells us that *biophilia* is a powerful but secret form of love that connects all living things. It is rather risky for Hephaestus to hide it with Perdita, because it is a love that is known only to the gods. Yet Hephaestus plans to give *biophilia* to Pandora once he is reunited with her because he believes that it will complete their love and render it eternal. Hephaestus then hides Perdita in his forge. Zeus arrives and the beautiful but object-like Pandora (now bereft of *agape, eros,* and *philia*) is taken away from him.

Pandora, however, is tricked by Zeus and unwittingly tells him of Perdita's existence. Zeus wrathfully claims that the child is his rightful possession and demands that she be handed over to him. Fortunately, Hephaestus gets wind of Zeus's outrage and quickly takes Perdita out of his forge and tries to hide her.

The blacksmith goes to the first of the three Fates,

Clotho—the sister who spins the thread of life—and begs her to take Perdita. Clotho promptly consults with her two sister Fates: Lachesis, who gives each man a portion of the thread (a destiny), and Atropos, who, with her shears, severs the thread at death. The sisters agree to take Perdita, for it seems that in exchange for sanctuary she can perform the Fates a service.

We now come to a section in the extra fifty-one lines that deeply fascinates me. The fragment describes the Fates as sisters who do not always perform their tasks in an orderly fashion. Sometimes Clotho spins the thread of life too quickly or too slowly, thus creating both an excess or a dearth of thread. Atropos at times wearies of holding her heavy shears, and so she fails to sever the thread properly, and sometimes she even cuts it in the wrong place. Thus it is poor Lachesis, the sister in charge of allotments, who is left to deal with all these "mistakes of fate," or what in contemporary terms might be called "loose ends."

The three sister Fates hide Perdita among these "extra threads," and she is given the task of concealing them under Lachesis's robe. The excess threads, however, eventually become so voluminous that they begin to push out from under the edges of Lachesis's robe, and the sisters decide they must hide Perdita elsewhere. The Fates appeal to their mother, Themis, and she wisely advises them to give both Perdita and the extra threads to Prometheus. Prometheus consents, announcing his plan to steal fire from the gods and promising to reunite Perdita with Pandora (thus reconstituting woman as a "vessel" of love). This is probably the original meaning of Pandora and her box: obviously her role in classical mythology was drastically changed after Hesiod, but I will leave that argument to another time.

Prometheus cleverly conceals Perdita in the folds of his cloak and procures a fiery coal. He gives the forbidden ember to mortals, but also places Perdita under their care. Yet mankind, seeing fire as a useful tool, but not the least interested in the child Perdita, quickly abandons her by the sea. Fortunately, Perdita is rescued by the Okeanides—water nymphs—and is adopted by them.

In the last four lines of the missing fragment, Zeus furiously demands that the water nymphs hand all the extra threads of fate (as well as Perdita) over to him. The Okeanides, however, are one step ahead. They have already bundled the threads into a succession of forms (child nymphs) and distributed them throughout the seas, oceans, and freshwaters, so that Zeus might never possess all of them at one time. Themis, mother to the Fates, tells Zeus that he can only have the child "reassembled thread by thread" through acts of clemency.

At this point, the fragment abruptly ends. It is not clear if Pandora ever returns to Hephaestus, and we do not learn what becomes of Perdita and her threads. I think it must have been longer, but I have only been able to piece fifty-one lines together thus far.

As you can see, it is an extraordinary fragment of text. At some point, virtually all of it must have been excised from the *Theogony*—why and by whom remains a great mystery! But we certainly owe a debt to Lumenius for preserving Perdita. (Had I not stuck it out with his torturous prose writing, she might have been lost to us forever!)

Moreover, Lumenius gives us an interesting interpretation of how Perdita fits into classical mythology. He describes the child as "the keeper" of the "lost threads" (*fila perdita*) that connect all living things. He suggests that the *fila perdita* of love relationships—more than any other kind—are Perdita's special province. (Lumenius might have had personal motives for doing this, as there is evidence to suggest he had a passionate but unrequited love for a married woman.)

I should mention there is only one other scholar who has written on Hesiod's missing fragment. He is the Canadian-born scholar Victor Latham, who taught at St. Edmund's College in Toronto and then later at Trinity College until his death in 1935. (If you like, I can send you what I have on him, but I warn you, it's pretty thin.)

Now for a confession. I have kept my discoveries about Hesiod's *Theogony* and Perdita largely to myself—sharing them only with your father. A few years before his death, I convinced Edward to coauthor a manuscript exploring the cosmological significance of Perdita, but it is now an unfinished and perhaps unfinishable work without him.

As you can imagine, Perdita was a source of much discussion between us. Your father and I attempted through lexical proofs to establish that the fifty-one extra lines do indeed belong to Hesiod and that the missing fragment represents a foundational aspect of the ancients' understanding of fate, the nature of love, and the connections among all living things. Edward contested every argument I made; he died before I could fully convince him to go to press—though I still feel in my heart that his reservations were not of an intellectual cast, but related more to deep ambivalences within himself.

So here, ultimately, is my loose end—and perhaps his. Nevertheless, Perdita is someone who belonged to the two of us. I believe she links us to one another, but there it is: an unaccountable thread.

I hope you will pardon me, Garth, if I have gone on too long here. I am almost inclined to tear up this letter! I cannot justify to myself why I might send you this strange epistle; and yet I feel that at seventy-five years of age, some allowance might be made for my verbosity and candor. Perhaps I am sending this because you and I, though barely known to each other, share a thread in your wonderful and beloved father.

Warm regards,
Muriel Hampstead

Thirteen

"WELL!" CLARE RAISED A glass of water to her lips. "That was quite the letter."

"Did Muriel say Victor Latham?" I asked.

"Yes, here it is: 'the Canadian-born scholar Victor Latham, who taught at St. Edmund's College in Toronto and then later at Trinity College until his death in 1935.' Why do you ask?"

"I believe he was Marged Brice's classics professor, but I'll have to double-check."

I placed a grilled fillet of whitefish on her plate. "What did you mean by 'quite the letter'?" I asked.

She smiled mysteriously and sliced the fish in half, transferring the larger piece to my plate. "I only meant that it's *quite* an amazing discovery. I can see how the Perdita myth must have influenced Shakespeare, can't you? But what's really amazing is how it changes the Prometheus myth."

I must have looked a little puzzled.

"Prometheus doesn't bring just fire to humankind—you know, just technology, so to speak. Through Perdita he also brings love," she explained.

"Why is that so significant?"

"For one thing, it represents a completely different take on the idea of Prometheus as the bringer of fire and technology to humankind."

"I think I see. You mean because Prometheus also brings Perdita along with the four loves she carries?"

"Exactly! And that fourth kind of love in Perdita's bundle—*biophilia*—isn't it rather intriguing? You know there's a Harvard scientist who's written about it. He thinks that all living things have an instinctive orientation toward one another. *Biophilia* is supposed to be deep in our biological makeup. But if Muriel's right, the Ancient Greeks thought of it more as a kind of love."

Clare looked out toward the Bay, her expression growing thoughtful. "You know, Garth, Muriel's discovery could be something quite important. I mean, in terms of the history of ideas."

I smiled ruefully. "I don't know, it all seems pretty speculative. Even my father seems to have had his reservations."

"What do you think his reservations were about?" she asked quietly.

I stood up. "Shall we continue this out on the deck? I think the storm is pretty much over, and we should be fine out under the awning."

Clare managed our plates while I fetched a towel and wiped off two deck chairs.

The air was fresh and cool, and every few minutes we could hear the wind swishing through the treetops. Clare ducked back inside for a few minutes and reemerged carrying my father's *Collected Works of Hesiod.*

"I'm just checking, Garth, but it looks like those extra fifty-one lines aren't here."

I let her read for a few moments. "Clare, you still haven't told me what you meant by it being quite the letter."

She put Hesiod down and looked over at me. "But I've already told you."

"Come on, out with it," I said firmly. "That stuff about Prometheus and *biophilia* wasn't really it. Not entirely anyway. Am I right?"

"Partly right. I was thinking of something else." She was watching me carefully. "But first I want to know a bit more about Muriel."

I shrugged my shoulders. "She was one of my father's graduate students—a star student. Very brilliant. She often came over to the house when I was little. And then later, she became a colleague in his department."

"Did you see much of her when you were older? As an adult, I mean?"

"No, not much. I lost track of her when I was at university. My visits home were much less frequent by that time. I guess I saw her most recently at my father's funeral. I remember because she was so distraught, I had to take her home myself."

"And your mother, did *she* like Muriel?"

"Hmm…now that you mention it, she definitely wasn't keen about Muriel being around."

"What's Muriel like?"

"Muriel is—in a word—*eccentric*. She used to wear one of those dead foxes around her neck: you know, with a big bushy tail and the eyes sewn shut. I was pretty fascinated by it as a kid." I began to uncork a bottle of wine. "Now, for the third time: quite the letter?"

"Well, this is totally reading between the lines, but…" She hesitated. "I'm just going to say it. I think Muriel might have been in love with your father."

I stared at her. "How did you get *that* from her letter?"

"I'm sorry if I'm shocking you, Garth." I could see a faint smile playing about the corners of her mouth.

"My father was pretty liberal, but when it came to marriage…" I began. "I can't imagine that—"

"Oh, no," Clare interrupted. "I don't mean *that*. It obviously was an unrequited love." She held her glass while I poured. "I hope you won't take this the wrong way," she said after a pause. "But for Muriel's sake, I hope your father might have returned her affections, even just a little."

"Why?"

"Well, it would be very terrible to be deeply in love with someone who *didn't* love you back. Don't you think it would be easier to accept that the person just *couldn't* love you back: that circumstances prevented it. His marriage, for example."

"I'm not sure I understand you." I was a bit bewildered about where she was heading.

"I knew your father wasn't happily married, and I used to wonder if he might have had a long-lost sweetheart or something along those lines."

"If he did, it was a well-kept secret. That's all I can say."

"Well of course it would be! And then Muriel might take some comfort in knowing that he—owing to circumstances beyond his control—just couldn't return her affections. Not explicitly anyway. It would be a sort of unrequited romance or what the Victorians used to call an *unlawful passion*."

The wind sent a few drops of water splattering across the awning above me.

"I can't speculate on the secrets of my father's heart," I said lightly, "but from his end of things, unrequited love for someone like Muriel didn't appear to be his biggest problem."

"Oh?" She took a sip of wine, looking up at me over the rim of her glass.

"No. To put it bluntly, I think my father's love troubles fell well within the bounds of a lawful passion. He simply fell out of love with my mother. I suppose it happened gradually, but the experience left him pretty washed up. He married as an older man, and I really don't know that there was much left in him for Muriel."

"Hmm—one never knows the full story, though."

I went inside to pour myself a scotch. "Well, if my father harbored a secret passion for Muriel," I called out through the screen, "I'd probably be the last person to see it. But I certainly had a front-row seat for his disillusionment with my mother."

Clare's eyes followed me as I returned to my chair. "I wonder if those kinds of love are part of Perdita's bundle?" she mused. "Of course some of her threads must be those wonderful and beautiful kinds of love. But I suppose they might also include the terrible kinds, too. You know: Lumenius's unrequited love and your father's disillusioned love." Then she laughed. "In a way, Perdita is a bundle of love."

"'Bundle of love'? Isn't that a Motown hit?"

She grimaced. "I know it sounds sappy. But even so, I think that's what Muriel was trying to get at in her letter."

Both of us sat quietly looking at the stars begin to pierce through the night sky, a cool breeze stirring the cedars above us.

"I'm glad Muriel's Perdita keeps those threads," Clare murmured softly, as if speaking her thoughts out loud. "I think I might feel something like *biophilia* for this place. Don't you, Garth? I suppose I'm an incorrigible romantic, but I'm drawn to the whole idea."

I liked her term—*incorrigible romantic.* It suited her. "What idea?"

"The idea that it's love in all its varieties that really connects living things. Perdita offers us the possibility of understanding our connections, including our broken or ill-fated connections." She reached down for her shawl and drew it up over her shoulders. "Maybe she even represents the chance to pick up a lost thread. What did Muriel call them: *fila perdita*?"

We were both silent after that.

I took a sip of scotch. "Clare," I said suddenly. "Why didn't you ever tell me it was you who caught that fish?"

"Fish? What fish?"

"The one in the photograph: the big whitefish you gave me for my birthday."

She looked away, laughing. "Oh, Garth, it can hardly matter now."

"Well, you've put me in a very bad light, you know."

"What do you mean?"

"All these years and I've never thanked you for my birthday present."

She smiled. "You're forgiven."

"You're sure?" I was surprised at how serious I sounded.

"Of course, Garth. Completely forgiven."

"And forgiven for the photograph? The one of—of all of us…?"

She gave me a puzzled look. "But you didn't have anything to do with that. And besides, now I'm freed from captivity, aren't I? Or at least I'm freed from the anonymity of being placed off frame."

"You were right, you know. I couldn't find you in any of the photographs my mother put up. I'd like to believe it was just a coincidence."

"Oh, indeed! Just a coincidence," she replied a little drily.

"Have you ever taken a look at how Davey Sullivan is eyeing you in that photograph?"

"No. Why do you ask?"

"Whatever happened to him?" I continued. "Did you keep up with him? Doug and I never did."

"I always thought he was sweet on Evienne," she said a little evasively. "I mean, wasn't everyone?"

I took another slow sip of scotch. "Clare, I've probably no right to ask you, but you never liked Evi, did you?"

"Not very much. I know it sounds like a cliché, but I don't like to speak ill of the dead."

"You know Evienne was—she was very prone to jealousy," I ventured cautiously. "Especially around other beautiful women."

Clare got up and walked restlessly to the edge of the deck.

"I always thought Evienne was such an unusual name," she said after a few moments. "Did you know—well, do you know about that name?"

I shook my head. "Is there something special about it?"

"I suppose it's a bit obscure, but Evienne is a derivation of

Nimue: the Lady of the Lake. Nimue is the enchantress who beguiles Merlin and puts him to sleep."

I was surprised. "Did you ever tell Evi that?"

"Oh, no—of course not. It was your father who told me. It was after you and Evienne announced your engagement."

"How long does Merlin sleep?" I asked, watching her closely.

She turned and fastened her blue eyes on mine. "A long time—a very long time. In most accounts, he sleeps forever, but your father told me that in a very few versions, he awakens."

I laughed awkwardly. "It's been quite a literary evening, hasn't it? We've covered Hesiod, Shakespeare, and now we're getting into the Knights of the Round Table."

The wind was picking up, and Clare pulled her shawl tightly around her body, shivering slightly. I jumped up, exclaiming that she must be getting chilly, and asked if she wanted to go in by the fire. But she turned away slowly and called to Mars, saying that she had better get back to Douglas.

I followed her down the stairs to the beach and found myself thinking that she would have to go back in the dark, across all those stones and then up the embankment.

I asked her if she was all right to go back by herself.

"Of course, I've got the stars to light my way." And then she was gone, with Mars following at her heels.

A few seconds later, it was only her voice floating back to me from out of the darkness.

"Thanks so much for dinner, Garth. You'll probably be up all night reading that next diary, won't you?"

"Yes," I called back out into the darkness. "Yes—I probably will."

MARGED BRICE
Cape Prius—1898

September 5

I feel that I must break a long silence—for George has come back. Unaccountably, suddenly, he has returned.

He arrived alone and has been here two days already, and I have yet to see him face-to-face. Dr. McTavish, I think, conspires to keep me from meeting him, and I do not dare to visit the Lodge, although Dr. McT. has been over there several times since yesterday and never once has asked me to accompany him.

I can hardly bear this! Surely someone will tell me why he is here and what these long months away have yielded for him.

September 6

I saw him at the Point this evening—just as the light was fading and he was only a black outline against the sky, but I knew that it was he.

He was smoking and had his back turned to me. I went as close as I dared, right to the edge of the forest, and stood behind the trees watching him.

Like an animal in the darkness, I watched him—without his seeing me.

September 15

At last George and I have met, but I am afraid that it was ill-timed.

I came across him standing in the grove of cedars; he was smoking again, and I did not like the acrid smell of his cigar in a place that is to me so sacred, and so I think I must have frowned at him when I saw him standing there and showed my displeasure. Perhaps it is my fault, then, that our meeting took such an inauspicious turn.

He extinguished his cigar immediately, and we stood silently for some seconds without looking directly at each other.

"Well, Marged," he finally said. "I am back again. Are you surprised to see me?"

I said that I had heard he had gone to New York—and then I stopped, for I was unsure how to proceed with him, and yet I hated the false constraint that seemed to catch at both of us and hold us there so awkwardly in each other's presence.

At last I could not bear it, and so I said, "George, no one has told me anything, and indeed I have no desire to intrude upon your privacy…but I hope that you are well, and that all is well with you."

He seemed relieved by my candor, and he came closer to me, searching my face for some sign of my estimation of him. I felt my own eyes grow teary, and he gently took my arm, and we started to walk back along the path, coming to a clearing at the edge of the Basin. I was keenly aware of his form beside me—as if after a terrible thirst, I had finally been granted a drink of water. We stopped there, to watch a boat come in and lay anchor to the windward. At length, George sat down upon a fallen log and began throwing stones into the water while I stood beside him, though not close to him.

"I'm not going back to New York, Marged. I couldn't now even if I wanted to, but I do not want to." He hurled a succession of stones into the Basin with some violence, and I discerned that something troubled him excessively.

"What has happened, George?" I said it quietly and with a calm that surprised even myself. I took a place on the log a little distance away from him, and tucking my skirts up around me, I looked away from him so that he did not feel any scrutiny.

"I've done a very miserable and dishonorable thing." He said it savagely. "She didn't deserve it; of that I am certain."

"What did you do, George?" I exclaimed. And then, for I could not restrain myself, I whispered, "Did you marry Caroline?"

He got up and moved a few paces away, shaking his head.

"No," he said, frowning at the horizon, his jaw clenched so tightly that I could see the muscles straining in his neck. "I did worse than that," he said, and he kicked at the log contemptuously. "I practically left the bride standing at the altar. I couldn't go through with it, Marged. There were five hundred people invited. It must have been horrible for her!"

I said nothing. How could I? I was ashamed that I felt somehow so jubilant, and yet I was mortified to think of Caroline.

At last, I said, "What will you do now, George?"

"I am going to stay up here—and paint." He said

it quietly, still frowning at the horizon. "Any career I might have had in America is most certainly over. Caroline's father will see to that, I am sure." He said it so bitterly. "McTavish is going to help me. He has a property not far from here, and I will set up there."

I don't know what made me think of it or what foolishness prompted me to utter it—but I thought of the money that Grandpere had given me, and I said to him that he could have it, if he wished.

He turned to look at me then and said not a little scornfully, or so it seemed to me, "You wear your heart too much upon your sleeve, Marged."

I leapt up, as if struck by lightning! Shame washed over me and then changed quickly into hot anger. For what had he thought I was proposing? In a flash and without thinking, I flew at him and struck him with all my might across his face—and then drew back, aghast at what I had done. He did not flinch, but stood there staring at me while my teeth began to chatter at the violence of my actions, and I felt that I might be sick there in front of him.

"You wished for me to do that, did you not?" I cried. "Did you not wish for me to strike you? Have you not baited me?"

I ran from him—as fast as I could, never stopping once to look back, and sobbing that he should use me so grossly for his own expiation.

September 16

I am filled with remorse. I must find some way to make an apology to George. He came today and hovered about Dr. McTavish's rooms, but I would not leave my studio, though I heard him asking if I were about.

And now I am so sorry, so very sorry that I struck him; had I been a little older and wiser, I might have foreseen the imprudence of my offer and how it might wound him. I think I must write him and tell him how sorry I am. I will say no more, and then there can be no misunderstanding.

September 17

George came to me today. I was in the shed brushing Claude and removing the thick carpet of burs that he has managed to accumulate since yesterday. George thanked me for my note and said that it had been unnecessary, for the error had been all his own and he apologized to me. His tone was kind and gentle, and it reminded me so much of the old George that I felt a little of my own contrariness returning as he assumed his self-possession. I think I must have communicated this to Claude, for he yelped suddenly. George took the brush from me and began to comb him, and I moved off to one side while we conversed.

I was more than a little agitated at first, but he seemed to wish to put me at my ease. He remarked upon Mother's wonderful progress, and soon I was telling him how she had fared during the journey home and then of my own reflections upon my time in the city. At length, he finished with Claude and moved away as if to leave, and all of a sudden, I asked him if he had received the letter that I had sent to him before he left for New York. He shook his head and said that he had not, and then he asked me what had been its contents.

"It was of no consequence," I replied, but my heart was in my throat as I said it.

George asked me if I had kept a copy, but I looked away to avoid answering him, and then he said that he would very much like to have my letter and asked if I would give him it. I said nothing, neither agreeing nor disagreeing to his proposal.

I think perhaps Grandpere may be correct, for sometimes I feel that I do indeed have a streak of perversity, for I am not sure if I quite like smooth sailing—and such a courteous and affable George. I don't know why, but somehow I feel as if I prefer the stormy weather.

September 20

I had tea with the Stewarts today. I was almost afraid to do so, for Allan had warned me that his stepfather has been in a terrible mood and has been an absolute bear to George. But though he was distant, his manner was polite, and Dr. McTavish had a pleasant conversation with George about his plans to paint. Old Mr. Stewart did look black indeed during this portion of the afternoon, but thankfully he left, and the rest of our time there was quite pleasant. George and Allan came back with me to the cottage and stayed to visit—Allan eating almost all of Auntie's cookies, and she scolding him for it, but nevertheless pleased.

As they were getting ready to depart, George took

me aside and asked me again for my letter. Indeed, I had already prepared a copy, though I was still undecided about giving it to him. He pressed me gently for it—and I gave it to him! I hope that I shall not regret it; my cheeks are almost burning as I think of it, and yet I did not change a word.

Perhaps after all I do like the quiet weather, for it is so agreeable to have George and Allan with us. Sometimes my time in the city seems as if it were a dream and all the places and people there seem as characters in a book that I read long ago and they have left only impressions upon me.

At times I am a little sad thinking of Dr. Reid, but it is a quiet kind of sorrow. Dr. McT. has told me that he has gone to Montreal to visit a colleague for several weeks. There has been no communication between us. I am surprised by this. I wonder if he has forgotten about me. I think that I must write to him—lest he think me ungrateful for all his kind attentions.

September 26

Beautiful night! This morning Uncle Gil said that he felt a storm in the air, but I do not care, for this is the most beautiful of all nights! And yet an ordinary night, too, for it began as any evening might.

Allan and George came to visit us after supper, and we were seated so cozily around the fire, except Uncle Gil, who had the watch. I was playing a game of chess with Tad, and our match had gone on for almost an hour when they arrived. I was not a little pleased to think that I had kept Tad at bay. Truly it was difficult to know which of us had the upper hand, for both queens and our bishops were still in play—though he had taken both my rooks and I both his knights. Still, I thought that I might beat him, and so I took my turns cautiously and resolved to take no risks.

Tad conversed with George and Allan as he played, but at length he grew exasperated with my caution, took his pipe from his mouth, and said, "What has happened to your game, child! Though you ponder each turn like a theologian, can you not see your next move?"

Allan and George laughed heartily, and I looked up at Tad quizzically, for I had been keeping a careful eye upon his bishops and knew them to be the most wily of his players; too often have one or the other of them stolen a victory from me that I had thought secure.

"Your queen, Marged!" he exclaimed finally. "Ever do you neglect your queen and stay her in a corner as if she were some precious piece and not your most powerful player. Look to her now. Can you not see it?"

Allan and George came closer to inspect the board as I studied it carefully. At last I cried out—for I saw it all of a sudden and checkmated Tad with dispatch.

"Well," he grunted, "if you were blind, daughter, you could not have played a poorer game." He said it in good humor, though there was but the slightest edge to his tone.

"Why don't you play your queen, Marged?" Allan asked of me.

"I don't know," I replied. "Perhaps I am too afraid to lose her—"

"No, Marged," Tad interrupted, "you must not be afraid. She may forfeit a game now and then, but ever is her heart a stout one, and strong. Her master, the king, knows this." And pointing to the board, he said, "Tomorrow she will take up her place faithfully and play the game with *all* her courage, but only if you will let her."

I looked up and met George's eyes.

Tad was looking aside at Mother as she sat by the fire, and Auntie Alis had her head bent upon her sewing. Allan was moving the pieces on the board, checking to see if we had overlooked some escape for Tad's king.

"It's checkmate all right," he said gloomily, no doubt taking Tad's part in the match.

Still George held my gaze.

Tad rose and said that we would see them both to the gate, and fetching my shawl, he said for me to go ahead with Allan and wait for them, for first he would go to the Light with George to check upon Uncle Gil. Auntie rose, protesting that she might do so, but Tad silenced her with a look and took George's arm.

Allan and I walked out toward the gate; we both shivered for the night had become cool, but the stars were out and we played an old game of ours and quizzed each other on the constellations. By and by, George came to us, but without Tad, and the three of us stood there, our heads thrown back, watching for shooting stars. All of a sudden, Allan saw a great horned owl glide across the night sky—an enormous bird, or so it seemed from the shadow that it cast upon us. He ran out into the night, chasing after it and urging us to follow.

I stayed behind, just inside the gate with George. We both smiled a little, listening to Allan's cacophonous attempts to hail the owl—and then George turned to me and, taking my hand, told me quietly that he had read my letter. I nodded, but would not look at him, keeping my eyes upon the night sky. He asked me if I regretted giving it to him, and I shook my head and said that I would never regret writing that letter, for it belonged to him and was written—I wanted to say by my very soul, but I stopped, for I was overwhelmed with such strong emotion. George drew my hand to his lips, and we stood in silence for a few moments, just as we had done once before by Dr. McTavish's fire.

Then he turned to me, and holding my face between his hands, he said that he loved me—that he had always loved me. But that there had been something in him—an obstacle in himself—that had prevented him from acknowledging it. He said that he had come to know it—fully know it—as soon as he had read my letter.

"Could you ever forgive me, Marged?"

Again I nodded, but still I could not meet his eyes.

Then he asked me if I would marry him.

I felt my heart grow very still. And then a peaceful sort of joy came over me as if I stood in a wave of it. I looked up at him, and I think my whole face must have expressed my love for him—for with my whole soul I said yes to him! And then George kissed me—and oh, it was such bliss! In all the heavens and all the earth, this first true kiss of ours was bliss!

And how am I to sleep? As if I could ever sleep this night! Somehow my Tad has done this—I don't know how, but I just know it.

September 28

There has been a terrible argument, and George is furious at his stepfather for keeping my letter from him. Mr. Stewart is dismayed at our engagement and has said the family will leave immediately, though Mrs. Stewart, I am told, has refused such a hasty proposal. George says that I am not to take any heed of what Mr. Stewart says—though I know that he is very, very angry with his stepfather and I heard him apologizing to Tad while I ran to fetch my shawl.

Tonight we walked down to the Basin together, and he made me promise that I would always love him. I do not know how many kisses he made me give him on this account, but he teased me, insisting that it would be a promise I must daily renew.

We watched the sky growing dark together, and I felt as if we—George and I together—I felt as if we were taking up a place in all the wild beauty around us. As if our love were now part of *all* creation and belonged as much to the sky and forest, to the wind and the Bay, as it did to ourselves.

I feel it so when I am in his arms! All the world seems to be there with us. There is no other place that draws me away, and I can only tremble in the ardor of his kisses, like a field of grass stirred by the wind…

September 30

Uncle Gil's storm has finally come—and now we fear for some of the fishermen, for its appearance was sudden and now it is almost pitch-black, though it is only late afternoon, and the sky is a menacing dark gray. There are two large vessels on the horizon, though I think most of the smaller boats have come in. Tad says that the two schooners will have to make much haste to reach the safety of the Basin.

The little girl is gone—it is inexplicable! I cannot find her anywhere! Auntie says that there were no children among the survivors, but she must be mistaken, for I brought the child in with me. Most assuredly I placed her with Mother for a short time while I ran to find some article of clothing to cover her, for the poor thing's garments had been torn away by the storm. Then I left her sleeping in my bed, but now I cannot find her anywhere.

I must search again. She must have awakened and felt frightened without her mother, and so has gone and hidden herself in some small space. If only I knew her name that I might call her.

Now she is back again. I awoke and there she was beside me! She has taken off the chemise I gave her and is quite naked. She opened her eyes sleepily as I tucked her under my blanket—such a sweet and darling little creature. I shall just doze in my chair and so will be alert when she awakens.

I cannot imagine where she hid herself. To be sure the poor thing must be hungry…

October 1

Gone again! This morning George and I looked everywhere, but we were forced to give up. He is still almost dead with exhaustion after the storm, and I urged him to go back to the Lodge and get some rest. I even made Auntie A. look everywhere with me, but to no avail. I appealed to Mother, but, alas, she can offer no words to confirm that the girl was here; now Auntie looks at me strangely, and she made me take a cup of tea and watched me drink it down. If only Mother could speak! For she saw her—the little girl that George and I rescued from the storm. I do not know where she goes. Surely there is some hiding place that she has found. Now Auntie is talking to Tad in low tones, and I am growing vexed. Was it all a dream? But then, George saw her, too.

October 2

I did not see the girl last night at all, but late this evening, she came back and was sleeping in my bed, just as she did upon the first night. I went immediately to get Auntie A. to come and see her, but as soon as I returned, she was gone!

Am I dreaming again? But it cannot be so, for George saw her, too, though he is very ill and I shall say nothing to disturb his rest. Dr. McTavish says that he shall be fine in a day or two, but still I did not like to see him so feverish. I have been with him all day and much of the night, for he seems to be calmer when I am by his side.

I must get some sleep so that I can arise early and go to him; I shall just have to set this mystery aside until George is well again.

October 4

George was so much better today. He was sitting up in bed, and he seemed pleasantly amused with all my fussing over him. Perhaps I shouldn't have done so, but I crawled in next to him and put my arms around him, nestling up against his chest and kissing his cheeks. There was no one about to disturb us... George said such sweet things to me, but after a few minutes he bade me to return to my chair, saying that though he was ill, he was still a man and I the woman he loved.

I have been so very, very worried about George. I know that I could never bear to lose him!

I told him of my strange experiences with the little girl, and he listened, holding my hand and covering it with kisses so often that I soon became distracted. He said that he has had strange dreams in which the child comes to him and awakens him by placing her hand lightly upon his face, and then she runs away laughing.

George does not know what to make of this, but he thinks that we must hold our tongues—though I can see that he, too, is shaken and has no ready explanation.

Who is she? And why has no one else but Mother seen her?

October 5

Again, I awaken to find the child sleeping next to me. If she is a ghost, I seem to feel no fear of her. I can feel the warmth of her body next to my own, and my hand strokes the softest of tresses as I write this. Her hair is of so unusual a color, turning a dark auburn at the ends—and if I listen carefully I can hear her breathing. I have placed the candle above us so that I can look upon her. I fear that she may be ill, for she looks to have a bit of the jaundice.

She stirs—yes, she must be real!

Was it all a dream—that night upon the shore and the men rushing to the boats to save the passengers? Perhaps I did imagine it; perhaps both George and I experienced some strange hallucination. And yet my memory of it is so clear.

I remember that I followed Tad down to the boathouse—and George was there, too, and I experienced the fear I always feel when there is a storm and those I love must brave it.

The Bay was in an awful rage, and our men could not get their boats out beyond a few yards before the waves pushed them back against the rocks. Above the surge, we could hear the distant cries of men in the lifeboats, and Tad said that all we could do was to try to seize the boats as they came closer and attempt to guide them to the dock. So the men waited with their hooks and ropes readied, but it seemed so futile a plan, for the waves were savage and unrelenting.

We had some success with one of the smaller boats, but it was dreadful for me to think that there might be terrible death occurring all around us, out in the darkness. The rain became even more intense and—I cannot explain why—I grew angry at it, and I felt a wild defiance take hold of me. I seemed to scorn the shrieking wind and the fierce sheets of rain that made the rocks so treacherous. It was a perversity in me, I am sure, to feel thus—for it was madness for anyone to be out in a storm like that, seeking to steal its fire and risk its awful fury.

What a tumult the Bay was in that night! I had never seen it so furious before. Here was no Dionysian cry of savage power but something deeper—more of a mother's fury, as if its rage were drawn from Demeter's anguish at having the darling of her heart stolen from her.

I remember moving away from the men and stepping deeper into the darkness. Again I do not know what rebelliousness drove me forward, but I walked to an outcropping of rocks near the Point, just where the wind seemed wildest. There I was on the shore, the sharp face of the cliff close behind me and pressing into my back, and I seemed to taunt the waves, for I was but a hair's breath away from where they were crashing and I defied them to touch me.

I felt my own fury mounting—and then we were facing each other in a furious storm of anger. I felt its terrible frustration and then its overwhelming anguish.

"Marged!"

"Who is calling me?" I cried out.

I looked up, suddenly afraid at my own terrible yearning to go out into it—to step into the Bay's wild embrace! It was then that I thought I saw it. No—I am sure that I did! There rising before me from the water and gasping for air…was a woman! Her face was a ghastly white, and her hair was strewn about her features, and through the darkness I could discern her strange, liquid eyes, staring at me with an intensity that seemed to pierce right through me. I tried to step back, petrified, but the cliff prevented me. And then, to my horror, she raised the limp form of a small child in her arms and extended it toward me. My heart cried out—for I felt myself back among all the babies at the clinic, and almost of an instinct, I reached forward to grasp it and prevent its fall. So, too, the drowning woman leaned toward me, stretching her arms out with the child, and I knew that I must step into the waves to catch it, knowing that my peril would be great.

I felt the water catch greedily at my skirts and pull me forward—and then I felt George's rough face against my cheek. I did not know how he had come to be there, except that perhaps he had seen me, or that someone had noted my absence and he had come after me. He seemed almost to be sobbing as he held me—or perhaps I was holding him. I do not know! Still, I could not give him my full attention, though my whole heart cleaved to him, so preoccupied was I with the chilling vision of the woman I had just seen and the tiny child that she held slipping from her arms.

The wind rose in an angry pitch around us and seemed to try to drag us back out into the Bay. George put his arms around me and pressed my face close to his chest and pulled us both back against the cliff. We stood thus for several seconds waiting for the wind to subside: George sheltering me with his body against the furious onslaught of rain and surf. It was then I felt it—a stiffening of my dress and then an urgent tugging as if some weight had attached itself to the hem of my skirt. I looked down and saw the child's head and her wet locks pasted to her skull.

"George," I cried, "she is on my skirt! Can you reach her?"

He looked down, and we both saw the form of a naked child, twisted into the folds of my dress and gripping the wet fabric with an almost superhuman strength. George bent down, taking me with him, and we both lifted her up as she transferred her tiny arms to my neck with a ferocity equal to the wind's howling madness.

I cried out in pain, so violent was her grip, and I recalled Tad's stories of rescuing drowning men and his caution to never get into the water with one of them without a rope—for, so terrified of drowning, they will cling to their rescuer and drag both to their deaths.

"Marged!" I could not tell who was calling me.

George must have seen how precarious our position was upon the shore. He shouted out to move toward a broken ledge of cliff face that had fallen out onto the rocks and which had a cavity behind it. This was all that offered us any chance of refuge from the wild wind.

Little by little we edged back from the crashing water, and then George, still pressing me close to him and the child clinging to me, lifted us all up until we were behind the wall of rock. We both were panting heavily from our exertions, and the child's lips were blue with cold. It had burrowed its head against my heart, and I felt as if all of us, George, myself, the ghostly pale child—the great cliff of rock—we had all merged together as part of the shore, flesh and blood, rock and stone, wave and water…

October 7

I must keep reminding myself that George and Mother have seen her, though Auntie thinks that I have hit my head and imagined it all.

Fourteen

"Why don't you tell me about what happened to the little girl mentioned in the diary," I asked, breaking the silence. "The child rescued from the storm. Did she survive?"

Marged stared at me.

"But, Garth!" she exclaimed impatiently. "Of course she survived. *That* is Perdita!"

"The little girl in that—account—of the storm? That's Perdita?"

"Of course! That's the whole reason why I've had you read my diaries. Now you know. You know all the circumstances that brought her to me—my engagement to George, and the storm, and—" She stopped suddenly, eyeing me anxiously.

"Yes," I acknowledged. "I've read about all of that. But I couldn't help noticing there were some pages torn out at the end of the last diary."

Marged said nothing.

"Did you tear them out?"

"Yes."

"Was it because you didn't want me to read them?"

"No—not exactly."

"I'm pretty curious to know what happened between Marged and George Stewart."

"I'm sorry, Garth, but I don't wish to discuss George with you. Not today anyway." She pursed her lips and turned her face away abruptly.

I got up restlessly, a little surprised at my reaction. The story about the little girl and the storm had been intriguing, but it was far less interesting to me than the outcome of Marged Brice's relationship with one of Canada's most famous painters.

"Please come back and sit down." Her expression softened as I returned to the chair across from her. "I'll tell you what," she said in a more conciliatory tone. "First we'll focus on Perdita; then we can—we can discuss those other things. Does that sound fair?"

"All right, Marged."

"Now, first of all, you must be absolutely frank with me," she continued briskly. "There's to be no beating around the bush. You think Perdita is a hallucination, or something like that, don't you?"

"I don't think she's a hallucination. Are you sure you want to hear what I think?"

"Yes! *Please* tell me."

I hesitated. "I don't want to upset you, Marged, so you've got to promise that you'll let me know if you want me to stop."

She swallowed and then nodded.

"In longevity research, there's something called psycho-intertextuality—PIT," I began.

"Please!" she interrupted. "Just tell me in plain English."

"Straight out?"

"Yes!"

"Well—I think there's a strong possibility that you might be Marged Brice's daughter."

I waited, but she showed no signs of unease or irritation.

"You may continue, Garth. I'm listening."

"Let's just think about it calmly for a moment. What do we know from the diaries so far?" I was extra careful to keep my voice calm. "It's clear that Marged Brice had a romantic relationship with the painter George Stewart. It's also clear they were going to be married."

"Oh, yes. It was very difficult for us at first. But I don't understand. What does all this have to do with Perdita—and the woman giving her to me?"

"My sense is that the Marged Brice of the diaries must have—probably—imagined that story about the storm."

"You mean I made her up?"

"No, not exactly. But there's a theme that runs through those diaries—a sort of thread that connects several events."

"A thread?" She smiled wryly.

"What you might call an *imaginative* thread. Think about it: first, there's the grave of the child in the cemetery that Marged calls Perdita. Then there's a discovery of a corpse with a dead baby. Later on during a séance, she sees a ghostly woman mourning the loss of yet another child—and then, after all these events, comes the storm and the rescue of still another child. Do you see what I mean?"

"I saw that awful corpse on Lonely Island before the incident with Flore in the graveyard," she muttered.

"At any rate, you can see where I'm going, can't you?"

"No, I cannot," she answered coldly. "Once I did see a drowned woman with her infant, and once I did take a fancy to a child's grave in the old cemetery. But those children—they aren't the Perdita I'm talking about!"

"Okay," I said. "Maybe we should think of it this way. Suppose Marged Brice and George Stewart couldn't be married for some reason. And…" I hesitated; she had fixed her blue eyes on me intently. "Suppose a child was born," I said gently.

Her eyes widened—and then quickly narrowed.

"Needless to say," I added hastily, "none of that business about being born out of wedlock would have any relevance today. There would be no need for that child to feel shame or to hide her original identity."

Marged let my words sink in.

"Ah," she whispered. "I understand! You think Perdita is an assumed identity. You think my mother gave me this identity because I was an illegitimate child. Then Perdita became…an alter ego—a part of myself that I couldn't let go of, except by actually *becoming* my mother. Do you mean something along those lines?"

I looked at her surprised. She had guessed the gist of my thoughts with extraordinary swiftness. "Yes, something like that."

She was silent for a few minutes. "That's very original, Garth," she said gently, and then more firmly, "I don't wish to offend you, but I'm afraid you're mistaken."

"Marged," I replied, also becoming firmer in my tone. "Why can't we just agree that you're probably among the world's oldest living persons. But my explanation would put your age more in the range of one hundred and ten years, not off the charts at one hundred and thirty-four. I'm sure that if I went to your family, I could find someone who would help clear up this whole business."

"No! You mustn't do that!" A wild look came into her eyes. "They'll come and take everything from me. My diaries—everything! And then I shall be as one erased from the walls of the pyramids. You don't understand. Ava doesn't want anyone to know who I am. Promise me you won't go to them!"

I assured her that I would do nothing without her permission.

Marged took several deep breaths. "I suppose what you suggest is possible, and I don't blame you for…thinking it." Her lips quivered. "But please let me clarify that Perdita is not the result of an unsanctioned union. I did not invent her. She was not created to cover up something I was ashamed of."

She swallowed, calming herself, and then she motioned for me to pull my chair closer. "But all that is irrelevant. You seem to think that I might be Perdita, but I couldn't possibly be her."

"Why not?"

She looked straight at me, her manner becoming almost

businesslike. "I could not possibly be Perdita, simply because she has been with me all these years."

"With you? She's here in the home with you then? One of the residents maybe?"

Marged began to chuckle. "Now you really are humoring me. But no—you don't understand. She's still the same little girl—a sweet, dear little girl. Perdita hasn't aged at all. She's the same as when she came to me, quite a scamp at times. Very playful. She loves to slide down that banister, and I've had a terrible time trying to stop her."

She looked at me searchingly and then sighed. "Ah, now you're changing your mind. Now you think I've made her up, that Perdita is some sort of imaginary person."

"I've told you what I think. But even so—maybe she has become an imaginary friend. Sometimes people do things like that, especially if they live in isolated settings."

She frowned and shook her head. "Yes, children do that sometimes, but I wasn't a child when Perdita came to me." She smiled sadly. "It was my classics professor, Victor Latham, who gave me the idea for her name. I used to meet with him after our classes. Some of the other instructors thought that it was improper, but there was nothing like that involved. Dr. Latham was the one who introduced me to Perdita."

"Yes, I almost forgot," I said slowly. "Latham also knew about the missing Hesiod fragment."

Marged started. "But how do you know about it? Dr. Latham said I must never tell anyone about the fragment."

I explained that my father had been a classicist and that he had had a friend—a colleague—who had discovered it, too.

"So you know all about Hephaestus and Pandora's illicit creation," she said softly. "About Perdita as she came to be called in the beautiful poems of Lumenius. The Greeks called her Emmenona, but I much prefer Perdita."

"Yes, I know about the extra fifty-one lines."

"Fifty-one lines?" she said sharply. "It was much longer than that."

"My father's colleague mentioned that the fragment might be longer, but she's only pieced together fifty-one lines."

"Only fifty-one?" Marged eyed me thoughtfully. "George painted Perdita, you know. He did several portraits of her. I gave one to Professor Latham, but I loved George's sketches the most. I made him keep those." Then she sat quietly, again looking out the window for a few moments.

After several minutes, she turned back to face me, the blue of her eyes growing more intense. "I'm finding that I grow tired very quickly these days," she murmured. "And there's been a great horned owl in the garden. It's been hooting at night, and sometimes it keeps me awake."

I immediately got up, saying that I would come back when she was feeling more energetic.

"Wait." She held up her hand. "I want you to take charge of something." She pointed to a large, flat package, wrapped in brown paper and sitting on her trunk. "I want you to take that parcel with you. It's made me very anxious to have it here. I keep thinking that Ava or her lawyers are going to show up and claim it as part of Gregory's estate. I know it will be safer with you."

I walked over to her trunk and picked it up.

"Please be very careful!" she said urgently. "It's very, very precious to me! I want you to open it, but not now. Not here. When you open it, you'll see what I mean.

"Garth," she called out faintly as I moved away. "Wait. Here are the pages I tore out. They're rather private, you see—but I said I would trust you, didn't I?"

I came back, and she slowly reached into her drawer. "You must also read these letters," she said quietly, handing me a small packet. "Otherwise you won't understand those—those other pages."

She looked up at me searchingly as I took the letters. "But Garth, I want you to open that package. Then if you *still* don't believe I am the Marged Brice of those diaries…"

She hesitated.

"Can you come back tomorrow?" she whispered hoarsely. "No, come back in a few days. Make sure you get a good rest. I want you to be well rested."

"Ycs, I'll come back in a few days."

I stopped in the doorway to look back at her.

She no longer seemed aware of my presence. The sun was streaming in through the window, throwing her face into shadow and giving her an ethereal aspect. All of a sudden, it looked as if the bones of her body were barely able to support the weight of her flesh. She raised her hands up in front of her—as if she were caressing something on her lap—and then sank back down into her chair.

Fifteen

"You put it in the trunk of your car?"

Clare was looking at me astounded.

"It was perfectly safe there."

"It might be one of George Stewart's canvases," she continued. "You must be aware of how valuable his paintings are!"

I looked away, beginning to chafe slightly at her tone.

"Garth, I'm sorry." Her voice softened, and she dropped her eyes. "That was just the curator in me speaking! Shall we take a look at it together?"

She began to clear off the dining room table.

By the time I brought the package over, she was standing like a surgeon, ready with a pair of scissors and a couple of clean cloths.

I placed it on the center of the table and stepped back.

Clare carefully cut the twine and then, even more carefully, started to peel off the paper tape at the back. I stood watching her, taking the bits of tape and paper from her as she removed them and setting them to one side.

It took us a good ten minutes to remove the exterior wrapping. Clare was extraordinarily thorough, peeling back each layer of paper one sheet at a time and very, very gently.

Underneath the exterior packaging were several additional layers of a light brown paper. I glanced up at Clare, but she had a look of deep concentration on her face and had already started to detach the first sheet. After what seemed to be countless strips of the light brown paper, we encountered a thick swaddling of heavy white fabric, then straw, and at last a layer of soft cloth.

Clare cautiously lifted the cloth away—and the back of a framed canvas appeared before us.

"It's definitely a painting," she said, looking up at me. Then she stepped away from the table. "You—you'll have to turn it over. I'm shaking too much."

I took a deep breath, not trusting my hands to lift it out.

I waited for a few seconds, then I gingerly lifted the frame out of the remaining paper and turned it over.

I gently blew off bits of straw from its surface, but even before they were completely cleared away, I recognized the canvas.

I was thunderstruck. "Isn't this—isn't this *Sylvan Chapel*?"

Clare placed her hand on my arm, gripping my wrist. "Yes!" she gasped. "That's Stewart's most famous painting!"

I could hear her swallow, and then she moved up closer to me, hugging my arm as if to support herself.

"But," she whispered weakly, "it *must* be a copy—some sort of reproduction!"

But even I knew—at a glance—that it was not.

I shook my head. "No, the one in the National Gallery, the one that thousands of schoolchildren come to see each year—that's the copy."

We both looked up from the canvas at the same instant and stood staring deep into each other's eyes.

She waited for me to speak.

"George Stewart must have painted a second *Sylvan Chapel*," I said slowly. "But evidently he kept his word to Marged Brice. The original stayed with her."

October 10, 1898

Dear Marged,

I am just returned from Montreal and have opened your letter awaiting me; alas, only to read of your engagement to George Stewart. I will be frank. It has distressed me almost beyond measure. You know the nature of my feelings toward you. I am sure that you can appreciate my disappointment in knowing that you do not, and feel that you cannot, return my affection.

Yet I do not mean to criticize you for this, Marged, for your letter is so gentle and considerate, and I only wish that I could be satisfied with your gratitude and esteem for me as a doctor and as your friend, but I cannot.

My feelings for you remain unchanged, and I wish you to know that I hope you will always regard me as someone who holds your welfare far above his own desires, and indeed, his disappointments. For this reason, I am urging you to take no rash action toward any marriage, at least until I might have had a chance to speak with you. I do not wish to intrude in your affairs, but as you know, my regard for you is of no ordinary order.

I have become aware of a report that relates to George Stewart, and I am positive that you must know nothing of it. I have thought a great deal about this and feel quite strongly that you must be made aware of it before you take any further steps in regard to Mr. Stewart. I cannot, however, communicate this information to you in a letter and feel most strongly that I must speak with you directly. I have therefore written to Dr. McTavish and requested that he arrange for us to meet. I have received his consent and have booked a ticket for Monday next.

Please know, Marged, that I have no desire to interfere with your happiness. You are far too dear to me for that to ever happen, and should you send me away forever, I would go with the best grace that I could muster, though with a heavy heart.

Forgive me if this letter causes you any anxiety, but this matter is of such a serious nature that I cannot and will not remain silent.

Yours always and faithfully,
Andrew Reid

October 23, 1898—Toronto/Davenport Station/6:00 a.m.

Dearest Marged,

I am writing this in haste as I wait for my train.

By now you will have heard of my departure from McTavish and he will have fulfilled his promise to give you this letter before expressing his own views on a matter that I must tell you of.

Yet you must believe me when I say that I knew nothing of these circumstances. Had I even the slightest suspicion of them, you must believe that I would have exercised much greater forbearance—that I would have loved you remains unchanged.

Yesterday, I met with Andrew Reid as you desired

and told him of your wish that he communicate his reservations regarding our marriage directly to myself.

He did so—quite candidly.

McTavish was there, too. I cannot tell whether I am glad or not, but I do know that he always has your best interests at heart and fiercely protects them, and for this I am at least grateful.

Marged—I was married once. When I was twenty-two and studying to become a painter in Paris, I made a foolish and reckless choice. Against the counsel of my closest friends, I married a woman—an art student like myself—who also was studying under Frank McCauly, my former mentor.

I knew it to be a terrible mistake after the first two months. I have not the time to relate the events that led me to this conclusion, but I dearly regretted my precipitous marriage, as did she, and it was not long before we agreed to part.

I fulfilled my financial obligations to her generously, and we lived independent lives. We both agreed to leave the question of a more formal separation stand for the time being, and shortly afterward I left the Continent.

Sixteen months after our separation, I received news that she had been killed in a fire. I went back to Paris, and we buried what we believed to be her remains. McCauly—who was also injured in the fire and who himself only lived for a few months after it—verified that she had been killed. At that point, I thought that this chapter in my life was closed forever.

But yesterday Reid destroyed that hope.

It seems she was not killed—that somehow Lydia managed to escape the fire but was badly injured. She wandered alone and confused for several days until she was found by a physician who was in Paris on holiday. She ended up under his care—that is, under the care of a Dr. David Petersen, an associate of Andrew Reid.

Apparently Petersen fell in love with her and eventually married her. She, too, it seems, genuinely returned his affections but deceived him about her former marriage. She claimed that I had died in the fire and that she was now a widow. Eventually she even convinced herself that such was the case.

Shortly after their marriage, Petersen moved with her to London and then to Halifax, and they have lived there together and apparently quite happily for the past thirteen years, now with two sons. Reid went on at length about what fine and good boys they are.

Reid found out about this by sheer accident—or so he claims. He met with Dr. Petersen during a recent visit to Montreal—Dr. Petersen having taken his wife to a hospital there. I have learned that Lydia—Mrs. Petersen—suffers from a degenerative disease that has gradually destroyed her lungs and that the disease is likely to take her life in what may be only a few months. Apparently she has religious qualms about her duplicity to her husband and told Reid her secret while he was there. Dr. Petersen still does not know about her deception.

Marged, I will write to you again and at length about this. I will be in Montreal for a few days, where

I am to confirm the identity of my former wife. There is a very faint possibility that all this is a mistake, but I have prepared myself for the worst.

My immediate reaction to this news is a determination to legally separate from her—yet Reid insists that I consider what consequences this would bring to her family, and especially to her sons.

It goes against my instincts to write to you in this way, but I have little choice at the moment. I feel that I must go to Montreal and settle this whole affair quickly. Clearly there are many futures at stake now, including those of Dr. Petersen and his children.

McTavish, however, insists that I immediately release you from our engagement.

I cannot bring myself to do this, but my conscience as well as my recognition of your young age force me to acknowledge the validity of McTavish's position. Please believe that this and only this is what has prompted me—no, forced me!—to write this letter. That you would live to regret your promise to me…I am capable of selfishness, but not of that kind!

Marged, I believe that we will find a way to be together.

Let us both trust in each other, then. Let us both look to the moon each night—when we can—and know that the other is gazing on the same orb though hundreds of miles separate us.

My own Marged! My darling—now we are both in those open waters of yours. Let us both look to our hearts to guide us through them!

I will write as soon as I can from Montreal.

You have all my heart,
George

October 27, 1898

Dearest George,

At last I know! Dr. McT. has given me your letter, and I have read it yet again.

Your letter sits there on my desk: three seemingly innocent sheets of paper covered in your handwriting. Yet still it comforts me to know that our hands can somehow meet over these pages. Though it ends these terrible days of anxiety and waiting, it is still a devastating revelation to me.

George—how can it be that you are still married?

I am looking out at the moon, hovering in the sky outside my window. Why does it seem so fragile to me tonight? As if it might drop from the sky and disappear forever, and yet I know that it could not be so!

Oh, George, what have they said to you? How could it ever be a question of releasing you? They do not know it, but we *are* married! No one could convince me otherwise. In my heart, in my soul, in all of my limbs—in all of me, George, you are my husband.

Do you not remember?

It was just after dusk, and through the trees I could see you heading back from the shore; you seemed so carefree and happy, your good humor spilling out and filling up all the air. It seemed to me that the forest leaned toward you, as if all of them—the cedars, the pines, the aspen—all were curious about the joyful man in their midst.

We watched you, the trees and I—your form moving so gracefully along the path and the muscles of your chest and arms rippling in the waning light; your skin still wet and glistening from your swim in the Bay, a towel wrapped around your waist.

I had come to fetch you, just as we had planned—yet the Bay was rough, and I had to drop anchor beyond the Point and then come to you overland. You thought that I had changed my mind and would come in the morning, but of course I came just as I said I would.

And you were so beautiful! You saw it in my face, in my eyes, did you not? That I thought you so beautiful...

And was that not our true wedding night?

Though you brought me back to the cottage—don't you remember the stars that night?

Were they not our nuptial guests?

And did not this very moon witness our vows—and the forest sanction our love?

Yours—wholly yours,
Marged

October 28, 1898—Montreal

My Own Marged,

Again I am writing in haste—forgive my brevity. This has been as a nightmare to me!

By now you know through McTavish that I am still legally married. But the doctors expect Lydia to live only a few months. It is for this reason alone that I am reluctant to bring a storm of shame and destruction into the lives of her husband and sons.

The solicitor who is now acting as my counsel has advised me to remain in Montreal, and so I shall be here at least for several weeks.

Marged—I know that I ask much of you—but can you come to me?

Reid has told me of his plans to join McTavish at his lodge until your family departs for the winter. He has been above board regarding his intentions toward you and has conveyed to me that, should you encourage him, he will renew his proposal.

I am not a man given to jealousy, but surely you can understand how much this has aggravated me, and yet I am powerless to stop him, as he has McTavish's consent to stay with him.

For this reason, I feel that you must come to me here, since I cannot come to you.

Marged, it is the only way! I am confident that all will end well—that I will be free to marry you in a matter of weeks and that Lydia's husband and boys will remain innocent of her deception.

Again—will you come to me? Will you trust in the future?

Marged, you must come to me!

I love you with all my heart.

George

Sixteen

"Are you sure this is the right address?" Clare whispered. "I saw a 'T. Phelps' on the mailbox."

I gave the door another loud knock.

"Yes, I'm sure," I whispered back. "This was Andrew Reid's home. Edna told me that his housekeeper, Angela, lives here now. Tom was her husband."

"Andrew Reid is the one who tried to prevent Marged Brice from marrying George?"

"Yes, I'll fill you in on the details later, but that's what I've gathered from the letters Miss Brice gave me."

"Oh, I see. But why are we whispering?" Clare slipped her arm conspiratorially in mine.

The door inched open, and we both straightened up. The pungent smell of something burning in Mrs. Phelps's oven wafted toward us.

"I think it might be lasagna," Clare warned, keeping her voice low as we followed Mrs. Phelps back to a spare and spotless kitchen.

Eight minutes later, a thick and very crispy wedge of the stuff was sitting on a plate before me, and Mrs. Phelps was eyeing me anxiously. "It's very good," I told her, avoiding Clare's doubtful glances and taking up another forkful. "Really, it's very tasty."

Mrs. Phelps smiled broadly and turned to Clare. "Now, what was it you wanted, dearie?"

Clare explained our errand while I did battle with the lasagna.

Angela Phelps didn't remember any family by the name of Brice, but she seemed very interested in the Longevity Project. "I'm only in my eighties," she confessed. "Still a youngster, I guess, for your group. But Dr. Reid—why, he lived to one hundred and ten."

"And you were Andrew Reid's housekeeper for how many years?" I asked, wiping my mouth and politely refusing another helping.

"Fifty-five years," she answered proudly. "My husband's mother was housekeeper first and then me. Between the two of us, we took care of the doctor's home for fifty-five years." She went on to explain that it had been such a shock. "I mean, Doc Reid leaving me his house in his will."

"The doctor practiced medicine till he was about ninety-five," Mrs. Phelps continued.

"Then it was on and off for him till he died. He never really declined," she said, smiling fondly. "He was walkin' around—a little slower, mind you—but still an independent man right up till the end. It took us all by surprise—his passin' away, I mean. There was no sign of it coming. Why, I think we all sort of believed that he might live forever."

"Was he ever married?" Clare asked nonchalantly.

"No, but he had a—" Mrs. Phelps lowered her voice and turned to Clare confidentially. "He had a passion—you know, for a woman. I think Emily was her name. I never seen her or met her, but me and Tom—that was my husband, he's deceased—we knew about her. For a while there, once a month the doctor would go to Owen Sound, like he was goin' to visit patients, you know. And then he'd slip away and take the train down to Toronto. Tom told me about it—his gettin' on the train. He saw him do it a couple of times, but he kept quiet about it. We never tried to find out about her. We figured the doctor had a right to his privacy."

Clare wondered out loud if Dr. Reid might have married this mystery woman in Toronto. I just sat back, admiring her technique.

"Well," Mrs. Phelps continued, not missing a beat, "not to our knowledge, certainly. But then, who's to say? He was a very good-looking man." She gave me a quick glance and then turned back to Clare. "I'm sure you'd find him good-looking, too, dearie. All the women liked him; they liked to come to him with their troubles. The men liked him, too; they knew he was a good doctor and an honorable man, even if their wives were a bit sweet on him. There was no harm in it."

Mrs. Phelps got up and left us for a few minutes. Clare smiled brightly at me. "Aren't you glad you brought me along?" she asked, nodding toward the other room. "I thought it would help to have a woman present."

Mrs. Phelps returned carrying a heavy photo album, and Clare sat down beside me. I began to flip through page after page of photographs, Clare making me stop at a formal portrait of the doctor.

"He must have been fortyish here," I thought, "around my age." Andrew Reid looked to be slightly shorter than George Stewart, but he had powerful-looking shoulders and arms…dark-haired, with a close-cropped beard and an intense, intelligent gaze.

"Doesn't he have lovely eyes," Clare cooed, and then she looked over at me. "You know, Garth, you look a little like him."

"That's what I thought the minute I saw you." Mrs. Phelps beamed. "You're almost the spittin' image of him."

We looked through what seemed to be endless pictures of Dr. Reid at professional meetings, then photos of him at town functions, and then a handful of shots showing him in his garden as a very elderly man. As I turned the last page, Clare looked at me quizzically. I shook my head; I hadn't seen anyone who I thought might be Marged Brice. Disappointed, I gave the album back to Mrs. Phelps, when a piece of paper slipped out and fell onto the floor. Clare swiftly bent down to pick it up.

It was one of those photograph postcards that were popular in the last decades of the nineteenth century, all yellowed at the edges.

"Oh dear," said Mrs. Phelps, "I guess the glue is gettin' old. I'll have to fix that."

Clare handed me the postcard, and I felt a chill run down my spine.

A young woman was standing in front of the Cape Prius lighthouse, her figure slightly willowy and her face strikingly pretty. She was gazing out at the Bay, her long white skirts sweeping out as the wind caught at them. Standing next to her was Andrew Reid. She had her arm entwined in his, and a bouquet of white roses rested limply in the crook of her other arm. Her expression was hard to fathom, but it struck me as—wistful?

"Who's this?" I asked, careful to keep my voice casual.

Mrs. Phelps took the photograph. "Oh, that's an old picture of his cousin. I never met her, but the doctor was very fond of her. She suffered from some terrible ailment—of the mind, I mean. He often visited her over on Dyer Bay. I always said she should come and live with us, but the doctor said it wouldn't suit her. She always had to be near the water. It was a bit hard on him. Poor man, but we all loved him so."

"She has a widow's peak, doesn't she?" Clare murmured, picking up the postcard gently. "You know, if you ask me, this looks a little like a wedding photograph."

This time Mrs. Phelps put her glasses on and peered closely at it. "Well," she said slowly, "I suppose so. But back in those days, all the women liked to have flowers when they got their pictures taken. And I'm sure that's the doctor's cousin—Deborah Jane."

"Oh," Clare said, still not looking at me. "Are you sure that was her name?" Mrs. Phelps turned over the photograph and showed us the inscription on the back. There in tiny letters, bottom left, were *AR to DEJ*.

"That's Andrew Reid to Deborah Jane," Mrs. Phelps explained.

"You mean Andrew Reid to dark-eyed junco," I muttered under my breath: so it *was* Marged Brice in the photograph.

"Poor George Stewart," I heard Clare murmur softly behind me.

"What was that, dearie?" Mrs. Phelps asked as she took up the album and headed toward the other room.

"Oh, nothing," Clare called out and then placed her hand lightly on my shoulder.

Seventeen

"I WONDER IF MARGED Brice really did choose Dr. Reid over George Stewart?"

I opened my eyes a crack. Clare's cheeks were flushed from our brisk hike over to the lighthouse, and she was busily spreading out the contents of her knapsack. She looked up as I shifted and caught me admiring her.

"It seems that Dr. Reid was very smitten with her," she continued. "I mean, he moved up here, didn't he, to be near her?"

"There's no record of him marrying her—"

"But didn't you discover there was a fire? And that some records were destroyed?"

"Yes, in 1910, the county courthouse caught fire and some documents were lost. But I'd put my money on George Stewart coming back for Marged Brice. Either that or Marged went to him. You—we might be reading too much into that photograph with the white roses."

Clare reached over and removed a piece of grass from my hair. "Hmm. I'm not so sure, Garth."

I rolled over onto my side; a light breeze was rippling across Georgian Bay, and from our position high up on the escarpment, we could see a massive shadow spreading westward as the sun sank toward the horizon.

"You'll have to tell me if you discover anything new as soon as you've read those extra pages. Remember, you promised!"

"I remember," I said, laughing.

Clare smiled back at me and then turned her gaze toward the Bay. "Look," she exclaimed, pointing. "Isn't that a boat way out there? I certainly hope it makes it in before dark!"

I nodded absently, but it wasn't the sky or the water that I was watching.

"Garth," she said after a few moments, still looking out toward the horizon. "There's something I've been wanting to say to you. I keep thinking I'll find the right moment, but—"

"You don't have to worry about 'right moments' with me, Clare," I said, sitting up.

"It's about Douglas. I don't think he broke his promise, but he told me what happened. He told me about the accident."

"Oh." I sank back, strangely relieved. "Yes, I know. Right before he left, he let me know he'd told you."

"It was a very honorable thing to do," she continued quickly. "What you did. Especially in light of the…the circumstances."

"Was it? Sometimes I've asked myself whether it was."

"It's a miracle you weren't seriously injured or even killed!"

"Believe me, I know. I've a scar on my back that won't let me forget how lucky I was."

"Yes. That night I saw you on the beach—I thought it must be from the accident."

We were both silent for a few seconds.

"Garth, there's something else. I don't quite know how to put this, but it was a bit of a shock, what Douglas told me. You see, I got such a different picture from your mother."

"What did she say to you?" Even to my own ears, my voice sounded a little sharp.

Clare looked away. "I'm sorry. I shouldn't be bringing all this up."

"No," I said, reaching for her hand. "I'm glad you are. Please go on."

"Of course I couldn't really talk to you at the funeral, but I did talk to your father."

"Yes?"

"He—and Douglas—they were like a pair of clams! Neither of them would discuss the accident. Now I think I understand why: that whole business about Evienne being the driver and not you. But that left me only your mother to talk to and, well, she told me a very different story."

"What did she say?"

"She told me Evienne was the love of your life." Clare took a deep breath before continuing. "And that you'd never get over her death. I kept asking how you were doing, but she made it very clear that she didn't want me to get in touch with you. In fact, she became extremely angry with me and accused me of interfering—"

She stopped, and I knew she was waiting for me to say something.

"That's not entirely surprising," I said slowly. "I can't say I fully understand my mother's motives, but I do know that she took Evi's death very hard. Even before the accident, she was furious with me for calling off the wedding."

"Why? Didn't she know about—what had been going on?"

"She knew. But that wasn't it."

"Surely she didn't want you to be unhappy."

"It wasn't about me or what was good or bad for me."

"Then—why?" Clare whispered, her eyes searching my face anxiously.

There was no reason not to tell her. "Evi was my mother's drinking buddy. It was as simple as that."

Clare shuddered slightly and looked away. "Was Evienne an alcoholic, too, Garth?"

"Sadly, yes. Of course I had no idea—not at first. I was just happy that my mother liked the girl I brought home. You know how awful she could be to my friends."

"You always protected us from all that. Your father did, too."

"My father also tried to protect me from a lot of stuff. He even tried to warn me about Evi, but I was very determined to lead my own life."

"That must have been very hard for him, to see you—" She hesitated.

"Make the same mistake he did?" I finished for her.

She started to shake her head.

"It's hard to explain, Clare, but I was…sort of caught in a net with Evi. I'd started to make my way out of it, and then the accident happened, and it really threw me for a loop."

"Of course it would! But it makes a world of difference that you weren't the driver."

I looked at her, waiting for her to explain.

"Garth, you weren't any more responsible for Evienne's drinking than you were for your mother's! And that includes the consequences of their drinking."

I smiled wryly. "Yes, but it's taken me almost four years to reach the same conclusion."

"I'm so glad you have. So glad for *you*. That makes it all worthwhile—"

"Maybe so." I let go of her hand. "But do you mind me asking why you believed my mother? You knew about her drinking."

"I guess I didn't believe her, not fully anyway. I knew—I sensed—something. But Douglas never said anything. He never contradicted her. And, well, Douglas has always been my ambassador when it comes to you."

"Maybe he should stop being your ambassador," I said quietly. "When it comes to me."

"All right." This time she reached for my hand, her eyes glittering. "I'll say it myself. I'm so sorry—so sorry about the accident—about everything. I'm so mad at myself for not just calling you up. Truly I am."

"Thanks, Clare." I returned the pressure of her fingers. "You don't have to—"

"I didn't know, you see." She was growing a little weepy. "I feel terrible, but I just didn't know. It's no excuse, but I would have at least tried to call you. How awful it's been for you!"

"Clare, really, I'm fine—just fine."

She smiled faintly and began wiping her cheeks with the palm of her hand. "This is silly, isn't it? I mean, your comforting *me* like this."

"No, it's not silly at all," I said, and moved a little closer. She was being careful to keep her face averted.

I put my arm around her, and then, after a few seconds, I felt her rest her head gently against my shoulder.

A cool wind was blowing off the Bay, but neither of us moved.

Clare was the first to speak. "I'm sorry, I don't mean to ruin our picnic, but I'm glad to get that off my—" She stood up and then took a step backward.

"Watch out!" I leapt up, quickly pulling her back. "That edge is closer than you think!"

"You should take better care of that pretty wife of yours, mister," a man's voice said behind us.

We both looked around, startled.

An elderly volunteer lightkeeper was eyeing us inquisitively. "It's almost a sheer drop."

"Yes, I know." I kept my arms around Clare and made her take a few steps forward.

"I came over to see if you'd like a candlelight tour of the lighthouse," the man said, leaning heavily on his cane. "We like to do the tour just after sunset so you visitors can get a feel for what it was like up here a hundred years ago."

We both hesitated.

"It'll be my last tour until next year," he added mournfully. "I'm headed back to the city tomorrow."

"I'll go," Clare whispered. "Farley and Mars could do with a bit of exercise, don't you think?"

Mars was ecstatic at the prospect of a walk, and Farley looked on patiently as I snapped on his leash. The three of us ambled down toward the Point and then over to the dock at Drake's Basin. The sky was rapidly becoming dark, and I saw a beam of white light streak out from the light tower and sweep out across the Bay.

Mars pulled me along to the far end of the pier, and then we paused in front of a weather-beaten plaque nailed to the railing. My thoughts were on Clare as I absently read off the list of shipwrecks:

The Dorset—wrecked November 11, 1880.

The Fairweather—lost November 1, 1881.

Douce Mer—wrecked October 14, 1882.

The Mary Jane—wrecked July 3, 1897.

The light was rapidly fading, but suddenly I peered closer.

The Mystic—wrecked September 30, 1898.

It was the date in the diary: the date when Marged Brice had recorded a woman rising from Georgian Bay's stormy depths and handing her a small child, a little girl she later named Perdita.

I watched the shadows as they lengthened on the water, Farley and Mars resting quietly at my feet. Twilight was thickening, and in the distance a cormorant stood sentinel on a large stone outcropping. I stared moodily toward the ruins of the Stewart Lodge, the remains of its front porch protruding from the forest and facing the Bay.

George Stewart couldn't have been such a fool, such a stupid fool to lose her!

Suddenly I thought of Clare coming back all those summers and her words to Doug about me not *seeing* her—not *really seeing* her.

The cormorant shifted its position and took off in soundless flight, and I watched its graceful form disappear from sight, half wondering if Marged Brice had ever stood there, perhaps in the very same spot.

She might have wrapped her shawl tightly around her as she watched the boats in the Basin—Marged—waiting for the Stewarts' boat to arrive. I could almost see her slim form and sweeping skirts silhouetted against the deepening hues of the night sky.

Then Marged Brice would have become a dusky shadow as the nighttime enveloped the Basin.

Marged—becoming indistinguishable from the darkening forms of trees blending into darker rock, and then black rock melting into the still blacker water.

MARGED BRICE
Cape Prius—1898

November 3

Andrew Reid is here.

How he came, I do not know, but he arrived at Dr. McTavish's lodge late last evening.

I have been terribly distraught; the news of George having a wife still living has left me numb, almost to the point of making me feel horribly ill if I think of it. And now this—I did not expect it! I am truly shocked by Dr. Reid's sudden appearance here at the Cape.

This afternoon, he stayed with Mother for almost two hours, but I remained in my room for the duration of his visit. As he was departing, I heard him ask Tad to tell me that he requests an interview. But I have refused to see him. Auntie A. was just here, chastising me vigorously, but I began to cry and so Tad took her away.

I am sure that George would be furious to know that Dr. Reid has come here—but Tad must stay until the Bay freezes, and even now, as I look out my window, I can see another ship on the horizon.

Why has the Bay remained so warm this year, as if to confound our plans to depart with Dr. McTavish?

And Dr. McT.—why does he remain for so long this year? The Stewarts left last week, and yet he refused their kind offer of passage with them.

How I miss Allan! Surely he would be able to distract me from all this brooding and worry.

November 4

Shall I hate Andrew Reid?

Oh, how he has made me suffer!

Shall I unleash my fury upon him just as the Bay does in one of its wild storms?

Yet I cannot hate him! I cannot! He has not done this to wound me.

Even now, my strange perversity is such that I wish that I could go to Dr. Reid and seek his counsel—that he might help me to know what to do. Such is the depth of my trust in him.

Yet I should be reluctant to tell him about the little girl: she still comes to me at night, and for reasons I cannot explain, I take such comfort from the sensation of her warm body nestling next to mine.

November 5

I have had a second letter from George. He asks that I go to him.

But how could I go to him at present?

I am sure that I could stay with Aunt Louise and Grandpere, but Tad is very, very angry that George has even suggested that I go to him. And Dr. McTavish is equally disapproving.

"It does not do you honor, Marged," he said to me, and then he took my hand and begged me not to consider it, not even for a moment.

Tad is firm that I wait. He is very worried for me, but he is very stern on this point. He insists that I do not go to Montreal and that George must come back to me: married or no, he must return to us.

What kind of life would I lead with George there? Tad asked me, and truly I did not know what to say to him. George wishes us to stay together—waiting until the disease takes its natural course—and then to marry me.

But Dr. McTavish says that it might be months or even years before she dies, though undoubtedly the disease will claim her.

Could I live there quietly, anticipating his wife's expiration and all the while carrying on a secret liaison with George? I am ashamed to think of it—and yet, I think I could do it!

There is a part of me that does not care. If it were not for Tad and Mother, I think that I would fly to him.

Yet how could our love bloom in such rancorous and ill-natured conditions? How could any love deepen? Would George not end up despising me? Dr. McTavish suggests as much.

November 7

I have been crying in my sleep, and the little girl has tried to soothe me. I woke up and felt her stroking my hair.

I have finally named her. I have called her Perdita.

I have just written George, telling him of my choice. I wish to have his consent because in my heart of hearts I know that she belongs to both of us. Who she is or what she is, I do not know—except that she belongs to George and myself. Just as I am connected to the Bay and the sky and the trees, so Perdita links George's life to mine.

I cannot explain any of this to anyone, just as I cannot make Tad or Uncle Gil, or even Auntie, see Perdita.

Even if George chooses to forget her, even if he insists that she is just a dream…even though he may be angry that I cannot come to him, it is Perdita who will not forsake my connection to him—or his to me.

November 10

A third letter from George, but this one so harsh and so cruel in its tone! George has made me weep. He is breaking my heart with his recriminations! He cannot have received my letter. Dr. Clowes warned me that it might take days to reach him but promised to do his best.

Does George not understand this? He accuses me of a silence that he believes is a condemnation of him.

I will burn this letter. I know that he could not mean what he says—only that he must have written it in great distress!

November 12

Dr. Clowes has confirmed that my letter was indeed posted to George, and this has made me so happy! Surely once he receives it, he will rest assured of my love for him.

I told Dr. Clowes that his news was like a gift for my birthday, for he was very curious as to what Auntie Alis was baking in the oven and I explained that it was a kind of cake with currants that I have loved since I was very little. I begged Auntie to give him a slice, and though she said *I* must wait until tomorrow, she did as I requested.

I will be twenty this year.

Dr. McTavish has tried to boost my spirits by teasing me about getting old and says I am to take "an old maid's luncheon" with him at his lodge, but I told him that he could not expect me to be very spritely, for my heart was still breaking over George. He embraced me so tenderly after that.

"What I wouldn't give to see you happy, Marged," he whispered, his voice cracking. "And what wouldn't I give for it to be so?"

I returned his embrace warmly, and I am sure he knew what was in my heart, though I did not say it in words—that he is as a second father to me.

November 14

I have just discovered that Aunt Louise has written to Tad, asking him if we might come to Montreal—just Mother and myself.

I have urged Tad to consider it, but he has remained tight-lipped. I think he prefers that we go with Dr. McT. and would like that Mother's treatment resume. I heard him talking to Dr. Reid at length about her recovery, and though I could tell that Dr.

Reid was cautious, he gave Father reason to hope for further improvement.

There was no other letter from George. But surely our correspondence will become easier once I am in the city. Dr. Clowes came by again and said that there will likely be no more mail until after the spring if we stay much longer.

I try not to let myself think about how much I miss George or worry for his peace of mind. Surely he has my letter by now; and surely he has written me retracting all the terrible things he wrote in his last letter.

November 15

Tad thinks that Mother and I will leave in a week's time, for the weather has taken a turn, and he does not wish us to travel during the first of the winter storms. He says that Auntie A. and Uncle Gil will winter at the light station and that he will join us in Toronto in December.

Mother and I are to go with Dr. McTavish, as Tad has arranged for a boat to pick us up and then take us to Owen Sound. Of course Andrew Reid will be returning with us, too. I am beginning to realize that I cannot possibly continue to avoid him in this way.

This morning Tad gently urged me to at least give him a greeting and not to run away and lock myself in my room whenever he is present.

And so, when Dr. Reid came to the door this afternoon, I stayed to open it for him. He seemed very startled to see me, and I hardly dared to look him in the face. Yet I could not ignore his outstretched hand, and so I gave him mine. His fingers were trembling, and I felt a strange shiver take possession of me as he held my hand, not releasing it but saying nothing.

I could not help it. After a few moments of standing in such an uncomfortable silence, I looked up into his eyes. I do not understand myself—but it was as if my heart stopped for a few seconds at the sight of his face.

"Marged," he whispered, for we could both hear Auntie moving about behind me, "do you forgive me? You know that I did not do this to hurt you."

"Yes," I whispered back, wiping my eyes. But that was all that I could say, though of course I felt that there was nothing to forgive him for.

November 16

At last I saw Dr. Reid alone. It was early this evening, just after I left Dr. McT.'s lodge, and I was in a hurry to get back before dark.

I must have been distracted—or too deeply buried in my wraps now that the cold has truly come upon us—because I did not see him until I looked up, and then there he was, just a few paces away from me.

My face must have expressed my anxiety and confusion, for his own became very grave as he looked at me.

Then he called out my name softly. His voice seemed strained, and I felt rather than saw him attempt to retain command over a wave of strong emotions.

"Marged, you seemed so thin and pale yesterday..." he said softly, coming up to me and then taking my arm.

Again I looked up into his eyes but remained speechless, yet this time I drew back a little, for he did not mask his thoughts but let his eyes peer openly into mine.

I had never seen him so bold before, and then it slowly dawned on me that he wanted me to know.

I gasped, suddenly feeling myself beginning to sink into his gaze, my knees and then my arms starting to become soft and pliant. He came closer and put his arms around me, and I could feel the roughness of his beard against my cheek—

I stopped him, needing to draw a breath, and then I ran from him.

But I do not think that it was out of anger that I fled.

Was it fear that made me run from him? Fear of what my own heart holds for him?

How can this be? Am I fickle and wanton?

How it is that I am wretched without George, and yet my heart wavered as I looked up into Andrew Reid's dark eyes, burning deeply into my own?

November 17

Dr. Clowes has brought what he says will be the very last of the mail until next April—and no letter from George!

Why does he not write me?

And I have not seen Perdita for two days. Now even I am beginning to wonder if I have imagined her.

November 18

We were to leave today, but there was a bad storm last night that left the Bay quite rough, and both Dr. McTavish and Tad agreed that it was senseless to risk passage on it.

I am so reluctant to leave my Bay; in some ways I would much prefer to stay over the winter, but not with Dr. Reid here. I am almost urgent that he should leave—and yet the thought of his absence makes my heart ache. I do not know what to make of myself!

November 19

I think I must have fancied her. Perdita must have been a figment of my imagination.

And yet—I am sure that she was real!

Is there something wrong with me?

Would Dr. Reid tell me that I am suffering from some disorder of the mind, some illness that has been born of my anxiety and distress for George?

November 20

In one moment I am absolutely wretched and despairing of myself, and yet—in the next—I am lost to the memory of how his arms felt around me.

I accuse myself of all manner of ill qualities, yet I know in my heart that none of it is true of me!

Is it what Grandpere called my perversity? How he warned me against it!

I know that I did not intend for any of it to happen. I had deliberately avoided Andrew Reid after our last encounter, not fully trusting myself to be alone with him.

I had gone to the Point—not to seek out another interview with him, but to find Perdita.

I had thought that I might ask the Bay—somehow I thought it might know.

I strained my ears to hear the Bay, but I felt the wind push angrily against me. It did not want me to hear the Bay, but kept lashing at me with frigid gusts that stung my face and fingers until I could hardly bear it.

"Why will you not let me speak with the Bay?" I cried out to it, but it only howled and shrieked as if to frighten me away. And then—it was so strange—but I felt its jealousy—a furious jealousy. But of what or whom I could not tell. Did it hate me for my affinity to the Bay? Or was it angry at the Bay for its inclination toward me?

The wind grew even more incensed, as if it discerned my thoughts, and then it threw the trees into a fierce commotion until there was a riotous cacophony. I could not tell which was the voice of my Bay: even the trees seemed to protest against the wind's perverse willfulness, but they were forced to bend and humor its terrible temper.

I watched the wind dance in all that tumult of sound, and then I grew very quiet, deciding to play a sullen audience to its wild mood. This only angered it, for then it began to pull at my cloak, as if to steal it from me and then run off. I bent over, clutching at my wrappings—and felt as if I were in some fierce contest of wills with the wind.

Ever have I tried to befriend the wind. Ever has it evaded me!

The sky grew dark with clouds, and I began to shiver, for the wind suddenly blew very, very cold, and my teeth began to chatter. I felt that it was punishing me for some transgression, but still I would not succumb to its lashings.

Then I felt someone wrapping a heavy coat around me and pulling me back from the shore.

It was Dr. Reid!

"No!" I cried, trying to draw away from him. "You must keep your coat. It is far too cold!"

Truly I was afraid for him—for he did not know the wind and what it might do to him!

He tightened his arms around me, and together we began to move toward the sheltered outcropping where George had rescued me from the storm and where Perdita first came to me. But the wind was so violent; it howled even louder and seemed determined to prevent my escape until its fury was satiated.

When at last we reached shelter, Dr. Reid pulled me behind the rocks—both of us catching our breath, both of us now protected from the furious wind.

His arms stayed around me, and he did not loosen his hold—and I rested my head against his chest, relieved to be out of the thrashing wind and its incomprehensible violence.

I looked up into his eyes. Again I saw him looking at me with such a deliberate intensity, as if he were laying some claim to me now that the wind had forced this sudden proximity upon us. Then I felt a strange uneasiness descend upon me as Andrew Reid—the man Andrew Reid and not the doctor—began to fill up the hidden cavern as if he were a great tide washing in from the Bay.

He said nothing, but taking my face between his hands—just as George had done—he began to kiss me.

I felt my heart quicken, and then it seemed to me as if the wind were laughing—cackling from somewhere up high and outside the rocks, as if it were pleased with its work.

Again and again he kissed me.

I closed my eyes, and then I felt myself drift out into the Bay, away from the wind out into the open water—way out beyond the buoys and their markings of safe harbor. Even the lighthouse was lost from my sight, and the Bay seemed to be stretching out in all directions around me in one enormous undulating current of George and Andrew—Andrew and George.

Eighteen

"It's time, Garth," Marged said. She seemed very restive. Her face was flushed and her pupils dilated. She took several deep breaths, seemingly struggling with something.

"Time for what?" I asked.

"I suppose it's only fair to warn you." She turned her face toward me and subjected me yet again to one of her piercing blue stares.

"Dr. McTavish—" she began. Then she seemed at a loss for words.

I waited quietly for her to continue.

"Dr. McTavish always blamed himself for his wife's death. He thought that Perdita might be able to connect him to her." She looked at me with great appeal in her eyes, almost as if she were begging me to understand and forgive her for…something. "I didn't know that it would be so hard on him. He was quite elderly at the time." Marged looked away, and I caught the dim glimmer of tears in her eyes.

I asked her to please explain.

She was silent for a few seconds. Then she whispered, "It killed him."

I drew back in surprise.

"I brought Perdita to him. But it was too hard for him. He died almost instantly. Andrew said it wasn't my fault, but I was so sorry. So very sorry!" She began to cry softly.

I immediately went over to her. "Marged," I said kindly, "if

Perdita will come to me, I'll take the chance. I'm pretty sure it won't kill me."

"You're humoring me again." She was practically sobbing, anguished at the thought of bringing me harm.

"I promise that I'm not humoring you. I will take the chance."

"Then would you—would you do it now? Would you *now*?"

I sat down and gave her a minute to compose herself.

"There is a risk, you see." She cleared her throat. "It's important that you understand me."

"I've told you, I take full responsibility." I was absolutely determined that this time we would get past this business of Perdita. "If you feel this will help clear up all the things we've been talking about, then by all means, let's go ahead with it."

She still seemed indecisive. "I'm sure she will come to you. Perhaps—perhaps you might even know what to do with her."

"Yes, well, let's just take this one step at a time. Now, what do you want me to do?"

She seemed confused. "What are you asking me?"

"I mean am I supposed to do anything to make her come to me?"

She shook her head. "You can't exactly make her—oh, but I see what you mean. No, there's nothing you should do. Just stay where you are."

"Just stay sitting here?"

"Yes, you see, she's been here the whole time."

"She's been *here*?"

"Oh, yes," Marged said softly. "She's been in my lap, but she's coming down."

Nineteen

THE FIRST THING I heard after Marged said "she's coming down" was a humming sound.

Then I felt a hand on my shoulder.

It rested lightly on my shirt for a few seconds, and then it slowly moved up toward my collar. Then it touched my neck.

Every hair on my body seemed to be standing on end.

The hand began to stroke the side of my face, very gently, and I could feel soft, cool fingers. Then it began to pat me on my cheek, just below my ear.

I felt a deep, paralyzing fear wash over me.

"She doesn't want you to be afraid," I heard Marged say.

"Who is it?" I whispered, barely able to speak.

"You must turn to see her."

A stinging pain washed over me as I started to slowly move my head. The thought that I might be having some kind of heart attack suddenly flashed across my mind as I felt my pulse beginning to race. Marged became a blur before me, but I gritted my teeth and forced myself to turn my head toward the hand.

There was a little girl between one and two years old standing beside me. She was completely naked and smiling shyly, sucking on her thumb.

As soon as I saw her, the pain stopped.

The girl searched my face, clapped her hands together once, and then clambered up onto my knees, using my shirt collar to steady herself. Then she turned and settled herself on my lap, so that we were both facing Marged.

I remained completely immobile, dumbstruck, and yet profoundly relieved that the awful pain was gone. Then she took each of my arms and brought them down across her tiny body so that she could nestle her back against my chest.

"Isn't she lovely?" I could see Marged's eyes tearing from where I was sitting. "You're the first person she has ever come to—since George. Andrew so wanted to meet her, but he just couldn't bring himself to it."

I swallowed once or twice, trying to collect my wits. "This—this could be a little girl—a little girl visiting the home." As soon as I said it, I felt the edge of the pain returning.

Marged leaned forward quickly. "No, Perdita! Patience—remember? You've promised me. You will have to do a trick. It's the only way. Remember—with George, we had to do a trick, too."

The little girl squirmed and then laughed; her voice was like a bird's. "Show him your doll," Marged instructed.

The child turned around in my lap and stood up on my knees, this time steadying herself by holding on to my shoulders. She placed her fingers on my cheeks, tweaking my nose and pulling on my lower lip, as if my face were a toy.

It was then that I got a better look at her.

At first she seemed to be a mass of soft, dark hair, hair that fell down her back in a long wave, turning a deep red at the ends. Her skin was flawlessly smooth, but it seemed to have a strange, almost greenish tinge to it. Then she looked up into my face. Her eyes—like Marged's—were of a blue so intense that I almost had to look away.

"Marged," I whispered. "Who—what is this?"

She ignored my question.

"Show him your doll," Marged urged again.

The child reached behind her, sticking out her belly to balance herself, and then she drew out a little bundle. She rocked it in her arms as if it were a baby and then beckoned for me to look closer.

At first it seemed to be made of rags, but as I looked, the bundle grew luminous. I could see strands of a viscous material that seemed to be quivering. The girl took one of my hands and placed her doll in it, and I could feel it moving, alive with the motion of a thousand tiny parts.

"*Piders*," she announced dramatically, dropping the *s*, and then she shook her head back and forth in a cocky fashion, as if thoroughly pleased with herself and her "trick."

The bundle began to vibrate, and I could hear a faint humming sound that began to grow louder and louder. At first it was like the buzzing of bees…

Marged was watching me, her face suffused with happiness. "Now listen—listen carefully."

I strained my ears.

"Don't you hear it?" Marged whispered. "Don't you hear the waves moving and now the pines bending in the wind?"

"*That Marged*." The little girl laughed. "*Now Garth*."

All of a sudden I heard Farley barking—then there was Clare's laugh. The sounds seemed to surface and then fade as others replaced them. I heard a blue jay's jeer announcing dawn at my cottage—then my father striking a match against one of the hearthstones. I heard my mother sobbing as she turned in her sleep—then a tremendous crack of lightning and rain beating against the roof.

The girl pressed the doll against my chest, and I seemed to hear my own heartbeat.

The cacophony swelled until I couldn't stand it. "You may have it back," I gasped, hastily thrusting the bundle into the little girl's hands and feeling a sticky substance remain on my own.

She looked at me sternly and said, "*Welcome*," before jumping down from my knees and running back to Marged.

Then she climbed up on her lap and turned to face me.

"You see, Garth; she *is* real. This is Perdita."

I sat there, unable to utter a sound, and then the little girl disappeared before my very eyes. It was not that she vanished—no. She disappeared gradually, taking a minute or so. She just…faded, and then was gone from Marged's lap.

I stood up abruptly.

From behind me, I heard a laugh and I swung around. She was at the door and darted quickly away, running off down the hallway.

"*Now* do you believe me?" Marged asked.

But for the life of me, I could not answer her.

Twenty

I REMEMBERED NOTHING OF the drive back.

As soon as I arrived, I got out of the car and immediately headed down to the beach, stripping down by the boathouse and plunging into the Bay.

I must have had thoughts. I must have made rational conjectures about what I had just seen, but all that remained with me was the sensation of the little girl sitting in my lap, the warmth of her body pressing against my chest.

She had seemed so real…

I stayed in the Bay for over an hour, holding my ground against the waves and sinking down beneath them. I made myself focus on a single, simple task—diving down and keeping myself underwater for as long as I could, and then coming up to feel the cold spray burst over me.

At first I just let the waves wash over me, but at last my head began to clear.

Maybe Doug was right. I grasped at the thought as soon as it surfaced.

"Not so much your body," he had said. "That's in great shape. It's your head—that brilliant mind of yours—it needs a real rest."

Was that it? Was some part of myself playing along with Marged Brice's fantasy?

Who was that little girl?

Now the phone was ringing.

I found myself back inside the cottage, and I answered it automatically.

"Garth, are you there?"

I took a deep breath, trying to concentrate. "Yes! Yes, Clare, I'm sorry. What were you saying?"

"I've got to go back to the city. It looks like for a few days. I don't want to go, but I have to."

She sounded upset, and I asked her if there was anything that I could do.

"Could you take Mars? It would be best if he didn't come with me."

I told her I'd be happy to take Mars.

"Could I come over now? Have you—have you finished your swim?"

"Yes—yes, I'm finished."

I managed to have a shirt and shorts on when she arrived.

She froze when she saw me. "What on earth has happened?"

Clare came up close to me and put her hands on my arms, her eyes searching my face worriedly. Without warning, I grasped her shoulders and then hugged her to me very tightly, closing my eyes.

I immediately felt calmer.

After a few moments, Clare gently lifted up my arms and made me sit down. She brought me a glass of water, and I could see that she was growing alarmed at my silence.

"Garth, I think you should see a doctor."

I looked up at her, my face still ashen. "No. I'm okay. Something happened at the home today, but I can't talk about it right now." My voice became unsteady.

She bit her lip. "Of course, but I'm worried about you. Won't you please let me take you to a doctor?"

"No!" I said it much more forcefully than I intended, and she drew back in surprise.

"I'm sorry. But really, Clare, I'm beginning to feel much better."

"Well, I'm going to stay. Can I at least stay until your…normal color comes back?"

Clare made me promise that I would immediately call a neighbor if I felt any worse.

"Are you sure you wouldn't like me to stay?" she asked again, lowering the window and looking at me anxiously.

I took her hand. "Will you call me when you get in?"

"I'll call you as soon as I've arrived."

"You didn't say…" I began. "Why are you leaving so suddenly?"

She looked away.

"Oh—it's Stuart Bretford. I think I told you about him. He's flown in from London, and I've got to meet him."

I dropped her hand. "Will you be coming back up?"

"Yes, I'm sure I'll be back in a few days."

I watched her car as it disappeared down the driveway.

I went back inside and put two bowls of food out for Farley and Mars and then went straight to bed.

Clare's call woke me just after midnight. I told her that I was feeling much better, and she brightened, telling me that I had given her quite a scare.

The next afternoon I called Edna to let her know that I wouldn't be coming down to the home for a few days.

She was sorry to hear that I was under the weather. "Marged keeps asking about you."

"Please let her know I'm fine. And, Edna—it's very important that she not be concerned about me. You can tell her I'm planning to be back after the weekend."

"Yes, yes. You just get some rest," she said soothingly. "And don't worry about Marged. I'll let her know you're on the mend."

I hung up, relieved that at least I wouldn't have to worry about Marged. Now I could—

What was I going to do about Clare?

Twenty-One

"Are you feeling better?"

It was Clare on the phone.

I told her that I was fine—fully recovered.

"You're sure? Absolutely sure?"

"Yes, I'm perfectly fine. I just needed a day's rest."

"I'm so glad!" She sounded very relieved. "I didn't like leaving you like that! But listen, I haven't got much time. Do you feel well enough to drive to Toronto for tonight?"

"Why tonight?" I asked, not telling her that I had already resolved to drive down and put in an appearance while Stuart was in town.

"I'm going to a party tonight, and my host is an art collector. Apparently he's just acquired two of George Stewart's paintings, and he said he'd be happy to show them to me."

"That would be interesting but—"

"He told me one of the paintings is titled *Perdita.*"

There was the sound of voices growing louder in the background, and I lost her for a few seconds.

"Garth, can you hear me?"

"Barely, but yes—I'll drive down this afternoon."

"You'll have to go black tie. The limo will be at your house at nine fifteen on the dot."

"A limo?" I repeated, surprised.

"Yes, that's not my choice. Mr. Sparke insists on it, and I've already told him that I'll be bringing a guest."

"Sparke!" I exclaimed. "Clare, did you say Sparke?"

"Yes, but I've got to run! See you tonight."

Clare was punctual. I opened the door at 9:15 p.m. and stood, taken aback for a few seconds. My expression must have shown how beautiful she looked.

She paused in the hallway, evidently very pleased with my reaction, and did a full turn for me. "Do you like my dress?" She smiled at me playfully. "It's sort of modeled after a piece from our Elizabethan collection. I adore these long draping sleeves."

"What color is that?" I asked, looking down at her while she adjusted my tie, secretly charmed by her evident delight in seeing me.

"Aubergine." She gently smoothed my collar and let her hands drift down over my jacket, straightening the sleeves. "It's an aubergine silk."

"Aubergine? That sounds like a color an incorrigible romantic would choose."

"I wore this color for that Queen Hermione role I told you about," she replied, smiling broadly. "And I've been addicted to it ever since."

Now we were in the limo, and she continued to scrutinize me. "I quite like you in black tie, Professor Hellyer. I suppose I don't have to warn you that there will be lots of actresses and models at this event. And lots of unfulfilled wives of very rich men. You know, absolute barracudas."

I laughed, telling her that I thought I could take care of myself.

"Just don't tell them you're single. You'll be eaten alive if you do."

She was obviously in very high spirits. Wisps of hair kept falling into her face, and she brushed them back, her eyes shining. I smiled, thinking how pretty it made her.

"Actually, I don't think it will matter, you'll be eaten alive anyway." She was still inspecting me.

"What about you?" I asked. "Should I assume that you can take care of yourself?"

"I've long learned that there are few principled men in my line of work. Art collectors are all about possession."

"Does that include your trustee—your baron?" I made an effort to keep my tone light.

Clare looked at me. "Oh, I shouldn't have said that so glibly. But how—how did you know he's a baron?"

"When did he arrive?"

"Stuart just flew in from the UK. Didn't I tell you? It was all unexpected."

I wanted to ask her more, but the limo had pulled up at an enormous iron gate. We passed through without stopping, our chauffeur nodding breezily to the armed security guard.

"I haven't told Stuart anything about Marged Brice or—all that," Clare whispered as I opened the door. "I've just told him you're an old friend."

Baron Bretford was there at the entranceway: an athletic, good-looking man, slightly gray around the temples and a good fifteen years older than Clare, I guessed. I met his outstretched hand firmly and found myself fighting a strong desire to dislike him, realizing only half a second later that the feeling was mutual.

Stuart stepped hurriedly in front of me to take Clare by the arm and usher her into the house—she turning to give me an encouraging smile over her shoulder. Once we were inside, Clare deftly slipped her arm out of his and stepped back. Stuart was instantly seized by a throng of people and vanished from sight.

She smiled at me brightly. "I'll start off with you, but it's a foregone conclusion that we'll be separated, probably in seconds. I'll try to find you..."

A tall man in white tails grabbed Clare around the waist and gave her a lingering kiss on the neck. She pushed him back. "Gary," she said smoothly, "whatever are you doing here?"

Gary disappeared without a word, and she looked over at me.

"My, what friendly friends you have," I said mildly.

Clare laughed mischievously. "*Ciao, bello,*" she whispered, her eyes sparkling, and then an extremely thin woman in a silver cocktail dress took her arm, and she disappeared into the crowd.

At around midnight, I found a corner and stood watching the room, a bit exhausted from all the small talk and wondering how and when I might get a glimpse of the Stewart paintings.

"Garth!" It was Clare at my side. "*Where* have you been?"

"What do you mean? I've been right here in this room. Chatting with all these…people!"

"I couldn't find you. It's packed, isn't it? Have you been eaten alive yet?"

I smiled. "I'd say several times."

"Do you want to be rescued?" she asked archly.

"Only by you."

"The perfect answer, Professor Hellyer," she teased, "so here's your reward. I've asked Mr. Sparke if we can see the paintings, and he said to go get you. He's waiting for us in his gallery."

A man in a dark suit appeared and silently led us up a short stairway, sweeping us past a cordon of security guards as we moved deeper into the house. "Mr. Sparke comes from a long line of distinguished art collectors," Clare explained as we followed the man. "His grandfather was a famous art critic and knew George Stewart quite well. Apparently the current dauphin is much friendlier than his predecessor, but perhaps a tad less brilliant."

"Was his grandfather's name Michael?"

"Why yes! But how did you know?"

Before I could answer, we were taken into a small vestibule, and without a word, another security guard appeared. He did a quick pat down of me, merely nodding to Clare. Then he opened a door, and we walked into a long, windowless room, a thick, dark carpet covering its floor and paintings hung across every inch of its walls.

"Over here," a deep, pleasant voice called out.

Clare took my arm, and we walked toward an elderly, hale-looking man who was playing with the ends of a well-groomed mustache. She introduced me to Mr. Clement Sparke.

"I've just procured two of Stewart's works," Mr. Sparke announced and proudly led us toward a far corner of the room. "They're very rare and wonderful pieces. Very unlike his other work because these have human subjects."

He stopped and pointed to an oil painting hung in an ornate golden frame. "This one is titled *Eidos.*"

I inhaled sharply. "Marged's portrait," I murmured involuntarily.

Mr. Sparke turned to look at me curiously. "I beg your pardon. Do you know this painting?"

"No," I replied hastily. "It just reminded me of something—something I'd read somewhere."

"It's gorgeous," Clare purred. "Absolutely gorgeous."

Mr. Sparke smiled at her warmly.

"I can see the outline of a woman," she continued. "Doesn't it look like she's walking on a shoreline? Or at least somewhere there's water and sky behind her?"

"Take a good look at her, Clare," I said quietly. "Can you see—can you see a widow's peak?"

Clare swallowed, looking once at me, and then peered closer. "Yes, I think you're right. She might have a widow's peak."

Mr. Sparke bent closer to his painting. "How remarkable. I've not noticed that."

Clare smiled demurely. "This is a real treat for Professor Hellyer and me. We're so grateful! Didn't you say that you had another painting by George Stewart?"

"Yes, but not a painting; it's a sketch. This one is *most* unusual."

He flicked on a switch, and a soft light went on over a smaller picture.

I stepped toward it and began to inspect a charcoal drawing.

"This one is titled *Perdita*," Mr. Sparke was saying. "My agent told me that it's a sketch of a woman who's been rescued from a shipwreck. There were quite a few of those near the old Stewart property on Georgian Bay."

"Do you know why it's called *Perdita*?" Clare let go of my arm and drew Mr. Sparke's attention away from the picture.

"All I know is that Stewart named this one himself," I heard him say. "That's his writing at the bottom, on the left. I was very lucky to get these, my dear. In fact, it's a small miracle that I have them. The bulk of Stewart's work has gone to the National Gallery, and virtually nothing ever goes for private sale."

"Really?" Clare murmured. "And why is that?"

"The Stewart family is very protective of his collection. But for some reason, they were willing to let go of these two pieces."

Their voices seemed to fade away as I stared at the sketch.

The picture was a mass of dark grays: everything blended and fused in George Stewart's signature style. He had done the sketch in quick, rough strokes, skillfully obscuring the boundaries between objects and forms. After a few seconds of intense staring, I was able to make out the body of a woman, lying on her side and covered in a blanket—a quilt of some sort—her hair strewn across a pillow.

I stepped closer.

It was almost impossible to see it—but it seemed to me that there was a shadow next to the woman. It looked like the dark shape of a child curled up against her back, a child with one arm outstretched, her fingers touching the woman's face as she slept. The child appeared to be uncovered and naked, and Stewart had made her long, tousled hair a deeper shade at the ends.

Was it just my imagination? I bent closer, searching for Stewart's writing.

"Mr. Sparke?"

Both Clare and the collector looked over at me.

"This sketch isn't titled *Perdita*," I announced quietly.

"Oh, but it is," Mr. Sparke countered politely. "Don't you see Stewart's handwriting there at the bottom? That's where he titled it."

"Yes, I see it. But George Stewart has written *Marged and Perdita*."

He came closer to take a look and then stepped back.

"I believe you're right," he muttered. "I must have missed that. It looks to me as if someone or something has smudged the writing. I must say, you've got good eyes!"

I could feel Clare's hand on my arm.

"Now, I wonder who *Marged* might be?" Mr. Sparke mused out loud. "I should have my agent ask the family."

"Garth—what time is it?" We paused on the steps. The party was still in full swing, and someone had started playing the piano. Soon the rest of the hired band joined in.

I looked at my watch. "Just before one." I must have seemed strangely quiet to her. Clare yawned and leaned against me. I put my arm round her and looked out across the dance floor, drawing her close. I would tell her everything, I thought. Tomorrow I would tell her about Perdita.

Or would it be better to tell Doug first?

I stared at the dancers moodily. "I should never have listened to Edna," I muttered.

"What?" Clare asked sleepily. She looked up at me, pushing her hair back from her face, and suddenly my heart gave a sharp twist.

Out of the corner of my eye, I saw Stuart Bretford making his way toward us, and the sight of him deeply irritated me.

"Clare, I'm going to head back to the cottage," I announced abruptly. "Don't worry about that limo getting me home; I can make my way alone."

"What?" She peered up at me, her expression bewildered. "I thought we'd leave together. I'm planning to head back up, too."

I dropped my arm, and she drew away, her expression puzzled.

"I think Bretford's looking for you," I said tersely.

She flushed. "What are you trying to say?"

"Well, he is your fiancé, isn't he?" I was still strangely agitated by Stewart's sketch—and I knew I wasn't behaving very well.

"No, he isn't, Garth," she said quietly, stepping away. "I told him this morning that I couldn't ever marry him."

"Clare," I began, instantly penitent, "I'm—"

But she was gone, swallowed up by the party.

I stood at the top of the steps for a few seconds, grimly watching the baron continue his stoic search for her. Then I stepped down, determined to go after her when I felt my phone ringing.

Twenty-Two

I MADE THE DRIVE back up to the Clarkson in just under four hours.

Edna met me in the foyer.

"I'm sorry to call you in the middle of the night, Garth. But I'm so glad you made it. This afternoon she took a turn for the worse and has been asking for you ever since."

Marged was in bed, her head slightly raised. A nurse was there, dozing in a chair beside her, and an oxygen tank sat ready at her bedside. She opened her eyes as I approached.

"Edna," she said, her voice weak. "May I have a few minutes alone with Professor Hellyer—with Garth."

They left us, the nurse emptying a container in the bathroom on her way out.

Marged smiled at me. "Garth..." she began.

I pulled my chair up close.

"You mustn't look so glum," she said gently. "I know it sounds odd, but you can't imagine how—how happy I am to be dying. *Finally dying.*"

I tried to smile, telling her that she was indeed the first person I had ever met who was so...enthusiastic about dying.

"You're familiar with this, then, this dying?"

"Oh yes. Remember, I'm a war historian. I've heard a great deal about dying."

"Then this can be one of your happy dying stories," Marged whispered, her voice growing faint. "Don't think I'm morbid, but truly, I am happy that this is finally coming to me."

I felt my eyes growing moist.

"They were worried I might die before you got here, but I knew that I wouldn't. You see—there's still Perdita. She's there, at the end of the bed. Do you see her?"

I started and then looked. I saw the little girl, squatting on Marged's bed and cooing to her white bundle, her doll.

"Do you feel any pain?"

I paused—then shook my head.

Marged sighed. "That's good. That's what I wanted to tell you. Perdita is going to go with you."

"What?" I was suddenly alarmed.

Marged grinned. "I was right, you see. I told the trees; I asked them to send me someone. I just couldn't go on like this, Garth! But now I want to be with him. Truly be with him!"

"Yes—but—" I stammered. "Why is she coming to me?"

"I've wanted to tell you, but I'm afraid I might not have the time to tell you. You see, I'm very close."

"But surely you can't expect me to believe that she's—one of the immortals or…"

"You'll have to sort that all out for yourself, Garth. But I must tell you something, while I can."

"Yes?"

"The missing fragment from Hesiod. It's much longer, just as your friend suspected. She knows only the first part, but there is more." Marged took a few quick breaths. "Pandora doesn't go back to Hephaestus and become immortal. She falls in love with a man."

"Marged, please don't exert yourself." I could hardly believe that she had postponed her death in order to give me a lesson in Greek mythology.

She shook her head. "Listen carefully. Tell your friend: Pandora takes the three loves from Perdita and shares them with her lover.

But Pandora doesn't know about the fourth one. You remember—Hephaestus secretly added it to Perdita's bundle."

"I remember," I said, deciding that it would be best to humor her. "You mean *biophilia*?"

"Yes." She pressed my fingers firmly. "Perdita tries to give *biophilia* to Pandora, but she is *unsuccessful.* It is Lumenius who puts it so beautifully. Perdita's fate is to always seek a mortal who will draw out this fourth thread from her bundle."

I felt the little girl touching my arm and then her fingers stroking my cheek.

"There must some other explanation," I insisted. "You must—"

But Marged was no longer looking at me. She had closed her eyes.

"Humankind," she continued almost breathlessly. "Over and over again, Perdita comes to mankind but he abandons her. So she returns to the water nymphs. But she is destined to come back, always seeking a protector. That's the fragment, Garth. That's basically the rest of it. You must tell your friend."

I held her hand silently, watching her face, anxiously listening for the return of each breath as the intervals between them lengthened.

"Garth?" Marged said after a few moments, opening her eyes.

"Yes, I'm still here."

"I wouldn't be abandoning Perdita—not if there's another thread, would I? Not if there's someone else who will take the fourth love from her, someone who will risk a great love."

I didn't say anything. The little girl was pushing up against my legs as if she wanted to come up into my lap, and I was focusing my efforts on staying very still.

"There must be another thread. That must be why Perdita will go with you. She's coming to you so that I can go. So you must have a thread…"

I remained silent, but I lifted up the little girl and let her crawl into my lap.

"Ah, so you won't tell me," Marged murmured. "Well, I've had my secrets, too, haven't I? You've wanted to know about George and Andrew. Isn't that so?" She turned and looked straight into my eyes. "Whom do you think I chose? No—wait. If you were me, whom would you have chosen?"

"George," I said without hesitation.

She looked at me with one of her piercing stares and then laughed; it was such a soft, haunting laugh. "That's because you're from the Georgian Bay side. Andrew was Lake Huron."

She was quiet for a moment. Then she said, "I'm from the Bay side, too. For a long time, I loved them both. Indeed, I still do. But only a peninsula can hold two bodies of water in perfect balance, and I made the mistake of thinking that I might be a peninsula. But I came to know…"

I waited, practically holding my breath.

She raised herself off the pillows a little. "I came to know that the people one loves—it's all mixed up. Like Perdita's bundle. She saves them, you see, all those connections. We always want to get rid of them, but she saves them." She took another deep breath and then turned her head toward the window. "But it was this beautiful Peninsula that helped me to my choice. You remember your Latin, don't you? *Paene*—for almost. *Insula*—for island. *Peninsula*. Almost an island." She pronounced the words carefully, again as if she were giving me a lesson, and then began to cough.

"Garth," she whispered after a long pause. "I'm sorry, but…"

I bent closer.

"I want you to take my diaries. They're over there in that box on the night table. You must take them. I don't want anyone else to have them."

She looked up at me anxiously. "And I've made you the executor for my painting—George's *Sylvan Chapel*. You are to do something for the Clarkson Home with it. Please make sure that it is safe. I know you will, won't you?"

I nodded, pressing her hand.

"Now," she said, "you've wanted to know—about George and Andrew."

"Yes, Marged. I very much want to know."

She closed her eyes, her face becoming extraordinarily beautiful as she approached her death—like limestone under water, I thought.

"What would you have done, Garth, if you were George?" she asked.

I hesitated. I could feel Marged gently stroking my fingers. "I loved George with all my heart—with all that I was and all that I am," she said softly. "I loved him with all the loves that are given us. Even the fourth love, because Perdita brought it to us. But he wanted me to come to him, and so he could not see it. Not at first—"

"What couldn't he see?"

"The thread!" she exclaimed, the blue of her eyes now blazing into my own. "He was blind to the nature of his own connection to me. As if our love could be…anything other than what it was. He had made mistakes, but there was a part of him that was afraid. You see, he wanted me to be there for him—but a thread—well, that is not the nature of a thread."

"But, Marged, what did George do? Did he come back to you?"

"Oh, Garth." She sighed. "That's not your question! I've just given you your question!" She grew very calm and then after a few seconds, she closed her eyes. "I have so wished for this. Would you stay with me until…?" She could barely utter the words as she grasped my fingers.

And then—it was terrible.

Suddenly I was in the emergency room and it was Evienne before me. Evi—dying. I was dazed and bruised, but I had her hand in mine, and my eyes were filled with tears. I felt that I should hate her, but my heart was broken—breaking for what we could never be to each other. Evi was conscious, but they couldn't stop the bleeding, and I knew that there were only seconds left.

She was grasping my hand and looking at me—in the midst of all those tubes and that awful smell, she was looking at me as her life's blood left her. She was swearing horribly and then—"Garth," she moaned, "what happened?"

I remembered that I bent over and kissed her as she died.

I was back at Marged's bedside, bending over her, holding her hand in mine and gripping it hard, as if to fasten her life onto mine. Perdita was standing beside me, patting my face just below my ear.

There was a scratching sound at the window and a flicker of light, and I turned my head to see the sweep of an owl's wings—and then I heard it hooting.

Perdita moved away from me and went over to the window. She stood on tiptoe looking out, struggling to lift up the heavy sash. Then she turned to me, beckoning for me to come and open it.

I slowly rose and went over to the window and then opened it a few inches.

There was a rush of air, and I knew that Marged Brice was gone.

Twenty-Three

I WOKE UP TO the sound of Perdita's whimpering.

It was pitch-black outside. I stumbled out of bed, bleary-eyed and disoriented, at first thinking that it was my mother calling out in her sleep and wondering why my father wasn't quieting her.

The little girl was in the chair by the fireplace, fast asleep and cuddled up with Farley, Mars stretched out on the floor below them. She had her doll nestled in her arms, and I stared at her, desperately trying to disbelieve what I was seeing.

Farley looked up at me, and our eyes met for a few seconds. Then he yawned, gave one of her knees a lick, and tucked his head back down under her arm.

I stood there for several minutes watching the three of them sleeping—deeply troubled. Then I staggered back to bed.

Perdita woke me up at dawn by patting my cheek just below my ear.

"*Where Marged? Where Marged?*" she moaned fretfully, and then she disappeared and I saw nothing of her until nightfall, when I heard her crawling into my father's chair and calling out for Farley and Mars.

The next morning, I heard Perdita singing to herself. There was a soft thud, Farley gave a few quick barks...then silence.

I lay in bed, watching the room slowly grow brighter.

Where was Clare?

I had called the number she'd given me several times, but no one answered. The phone rang and rang and then cut me off abruptly. Worse still, there seemed to be no way of leaving a message.

Doug wasn't around to help me out either. His receptionist had told me that he was off on holiday in the north of Scotland, wandering around the moors.

"Is it an emergency?" she'd asked. I had paused and then said I'd call back in a few days.

~

I sat out on the deck late into the evening, moodily watching a thick fog roll in. I kept listening for the sound of Clare's car on the road.

Surely her mother—surely Donna would help me get a message through to her?

Suddenly I felt a little hand tug at my fingers.

"*Garth. Come with you.*"

Perdita led me down to the dock, and we both waited quietly for a few minutes, watching a massive wall of fog engulf everything around us.

"*Come with you,*" she repeated, and nimbly climbed into the rowboat, motioning for me to follow her. I hesitated, watching her as she took a life jacket and made a cushion for herself on one of the seats.

"*I show you.*"

I cast off reluctantly and took the oars. I couldn't see more than three feet in front of me. Perdita crept up close and planted herself between my legs as I started rowing, and then she began to hang on to my arms as I bent forward and pulled back.

"*Row, row, row,*" she crowed gleefully.

After several minutes I stopped and lifted the oars. The fog above us had parted momentarily, and I looked up and saw stars.

"*Big dippa? Marged show me.*" Perdita started to pull on my ears.

"Perdita." For the first time, I addressed her directly.

She stopped. "*I go?*" she asked, pinching my cheeks with her fingers.

"Well, yes. That would be best."

"*Why?*"

"I think—I think your sisters want you to come back. For now anyway."

"*George,*" she squealed, suddenly finding me very funny. "*Garth like George!*"

"Am I?"

"*Marged all gone?*" Now she was whimpering a little.

"No, she's not all gone. You have her doll. Remember? You can take it with you."

"*Garth come, too?*"

I shook my head. "Only you this time."

"*Take your doll?*" She was thrusting her bundle toward me, her expression anxious.

"Would you keep it for me?"

"*I keep! I keep Garth's doll.*" She grinned delightedly.

Then I closed my eyes and felt her little fingers softly stroking the side of my face. She patted my cheek a few more times and then stepped away. I felt a slight, almost imperceptible movement of the boat. It wobbled unsteadily for a fraction of a second, and I heard a soft splash.

Suddenly it seemed as if a huge school of fish were beneath me, shaking and rocking the boat as they rushed forward. I felt myself rise, as if on the back of an enormous whale…

I clutched at the gunwales to steady myself and felt a sharp twinge in my chest, instantly recognizing the terrible pain that I had experienced in Marged's room. A ghastly fear washed over me. I knew that I wouldn't survive its full force a second time.

I concentrated all my efforts on breathing. The water seemed to be trembling with the movement of thousands of water creatures below me. Then I heard Perdita begin to laugh. The air was instantly filled with the sound of other children joining in her laughter.

It lasted only a few seconds. Then a heavy silence descended, and the water became glassy calm.

Twenty-Four

I COLLAPSED INTO A deck chair and closed my eyes. The pain in my chest was gone, but I felt utterly drained and horribly nauseous.

I must have drifted into a deep sleep…

Clare.

We were out in the boat, under the stars. She had the oars, and I was leaning forward trying to take them from her, but she shook her head, laughing.

Clare was trying to say something to me, but I couldn't hear her—and then the boat started to stretch and expand. I knew it was impossible, but she was being carried farther and farther away from me, her body becoming blurred and distorted.

I woke up with a jolt, startled to find myself outside in the darkness.

I felt myself begin to shiver violently. Then the first pellets of rain hit my face.

I knew that I had to get myself inside, but I must have fallen asleep again, because I woke up to hear Clare calling my name.

"Garth, wake up," she was saying softly. "It's going to rain…"

I looked up and saw her face all in shadow. She was bending over me, her hair falling forward and brushing against my cheek, her hand lightly touching my arm. I could see the dark curve of her body as she leaned toward me.

"Clare," I whispered back. I reached up and took her face between my hands and began to kiss her—very gently at first—and then I started to pull her toward me.

I felt myself being hauled upward, almost as if through water; swiftly rising up toward the surface and then breaking through, my lungs sucking in the cool air.

I sat up gasping. The telephone had just stopped ringing.

I got up unsteadily and stumbled into the cottage, almost falling over as I reached for the phone.

There was no one on the other end. I quickly accessed my messages.

It was Clare's voice.

"I'm just calling to say good-bye, Garth. I'm flying back to the UK tonight, and I didn't want to leave without saying good-bye."

She took a breath and cleared her throat.

"I hope that you have a wonderful summer…and that you get your book done. Oh…and of course, I hope you find out who Miss Brice really is." I thought I heard her swallow. "And I'm sure…I'm sure our paths will cross again. Stay well, Garth…and my best wishes to you always."

She hung up very quickly.

"Oh, God," I groaned out loud—and then all went black.

Twenty-Five

I LOOKED UP.

The clock showed that I had barely ten minutes before boarding time.

I sank down into a chair at the end of an empty row and stretched out my legs, still a little out of breath. It had been nothing short of a miracle that I had made it to the airport.

Suddenly I sat up, thinking that I'd forgotten my briefcase in the car.

No—there it was on the seat beside me. Marged's diaries were still safe inside, each one carefully wrapped in Clarkson stationery. Edna had taken them out of her room only minutes before Ava Stewart's lawyer had searched through Marged's things.

"He was very rude, Garth. He kept asking, 'Did anyone come to see her?' And something about a painting."

"What did you tell him?"

"Not a damn thing, of course!"

"Edna, couldn't you keep these journals for me? After the funeral, I'm headed straight to the airport."

"I think you'd better take them. Listen, it looks like you and I will be the only ones at the service."

One of the flight attendants picked up a handset and announced that my flight would be delayed by thirty minutes. "Maybe I should find something to eat," I thought, but I felt too exhausted to get up and start a search.

I let myself sink deeper into the chair and thrust my hand into my pocket, anxiously fingering my phone and then feeling the envelope that Edna had waved at me as I rushed to my car.

"Garth! I almost forgot. Marged said you're to have this letter."

I had practically grabbed it from her, stuffing it into my jacket. "Edna, you're okay to watch Mars until my friend Doug comes to get him?"

"Oh, yes—but don't expect me to ever give Farley back."

I heard her call out "good luck" as I tore out of the driveway.

I was going to need some luck, I thought.

Had Donna given Clare my message by now?

I looked down at the envelope. Marged had scrawled my name and the date across the front, adding below: *To be opened after my death.* It had been written the day before she died.

Dear Garth,

I am growing weaker and weaker by the hour, but I am truly delighted by this. I am sure that this must be my death approaching, and I can only trust that I will not be disappointed.

I strongly suspect, however, that we might not be granted time for another interview, and so I have decided to take matters into my own hands.

I have had a solicitor come, a very nice man who merely glanced at my birth certificate and didn't seem at all interested in my age. He just drew up a will for me without any fuss. It is a very simple will. All I really have is what I brought with me in that trunk.

I have left you in charge of everything. I hope that this was not a great presumption on my part, but I do not think you will disappoint me in accepting this trust.

Perhaps you will wonder why I have chosen you. But you must not think—not for an instant—that this is the last and desperate act of an old woman, abandoned by all her friends and family. In the very last days of my long, long life, it is you who have been a true friend to me. It is you who have listened to me with an open heart despite the great differences in our ages and despite all the slanderous things that have been said about me.

Dr. Latham once told me that the Greeks believed that there were special kinds of storytellers: bards who became not just the carriers, but the gatherers of stories. Hesiod, he felt, was one such bard, but I think that you are another. Perhaps this is why you took the time to listen to the story of a very old woman. You might have "abandoned ship," so to speak, after that first visit and never come back. Indeed, for a few anxious days I greatly feared this, but you did return. I believe you returned because you are part of my story, but this means that I also must be a part of *yours*.

Our beautiful Peninsula is filled with stories, is it not?

Not just with people's stories, but with the stories of all the forests, the stones, the sky and wind and waves. Mine is just one story, but I haven't known how to tell it—until I met you. And so, if somehow we do not meet again, I want to tell you about my beloved Perdita, my little one. How it breaks my heart to leave her! Yet I know I must. It is an inexpressible comfort to me to know that you will take care of her. Don't ask me how I know that you will, but I do.

Before I came to this Home, I thought that Perdita

must have come to me because of George and Andrew, that perhaps she was there to help me understand the nature of my connections to each of them. I was partly right in this. She came to me because the mortal loves of my life have indeed been intricate. But, as the wonderful Greeks knew so well, there are so many kinds of love—so many possible threads.

For all the years that Perdita has been with me, I have felt that she has connected me to something else: something that has made all my mortal loves possible and yet has offered me the possibility of a *great love*. It may seem a very strange statement, but this is something that I have known is true because I have felt it so deeply in my very soul. It is only now that I think I finally understand why Perdita came to *me*.

You see—it was the Bay who was with me that night, the night that I might have stepped out into its stormy embrace and ended my life forever. To this day, I don't know how George pulled me back, except that there was a powerful thread that we shared and he wouldn't let me go to it, not alone.

But there was another thread, and it was between the Bay and myself. We had made it—strange as it may seem—in that moment between life and death, between the Bay's form and mine. We made it as we acknowledged our affinity, as we acknowledged our impossible connection to each other.

I think the Bay has always understood the nature of my love for it and has returned it. But I think that ours must be a love that comes of the fourth thread—*biophilia* as the Greeks called it—Perdita's special province.

I have come to understand that I have much more

than a sentimental connection to this Peninsula and the Bay—that my heart holds far more than fondness for home and family and familiar surroundings. The wind, the sky, the water and the waves, the stars at night and the endless shore of rocks—all of this beautiful Peninsula. They are no mere backdrop to my human passions, no mere objects of my affection.

Dr. Latham would have said that we are *hypodoche* to each other: myself and the Bay. *Hypodoche,* or what the ancient philosophers called the co-principles of each other's becoming.

I don't know if there are other people who might understand this aspect of myself. George certainly did, and Andrew may have in his way—but it was George who truly knew it. Perhaps that is why he came to find me—to find me after we had become so lost to each other.

But even so, even if I am the *only* human being on all the earth to have this love, then Perdita has the thread. In all that vast anonymity—in all that vast blindness—there is a thread. My love of the Bay exists and Perdita keeps it.

To this day, I find it remarkable that the Greeks understood all of this. But it has been the trees who have tried to teach me of it, returning to me over all the seasons of my life and trusting that I might one day understand that I am but one being in an immense communion of hearts.

And so now, at last, I can acknowledge that I am in love with Georgian Bay and all that is here. I have loved it all my life, and I love it still. I think that I will love it even in my death.

This is the wellspring of all my other loves: for Tad and Mother, for Auntie Alis and Uncle Gil, and for Dr. McTavish. Andrew began to know this about me. How I am not sure, but he sought my heart understanding this aspect of myself.

And George—he always knew it because he shared it. At last he came to recognize it. George came to fully know it because his painting has always been his best teacher. Now I see it much more clearly: *it was Perdita who came to him, too.*

And you, Garth. You do not know your own well-springs fully yet. But I think you are a kindred spirit, kindred to the Bay. As such—and if you choose—your capacity to love is a great one. You are capable of great risks, especially the risk of a love in all its fullness. I believe that you will pick up the thread, the thread that *is* Perdita.

You will wonder how I know this, but all that I can say is that I recognized you. I *saw* you—for what and who you are. And then, of course, Perdita knew you immediately. That first day when Perdita brushed past you and you thought she was the cat—how we laughed about that together!

You see, I was asking the trees to help me when you came in through the door that first time. You came in so quietly, and it startled me. It was very terrible to be put in a Home so suddenly! Edna was so kind—everyone was so kind—but I felt so forlorn and lost… so without a true friend.

I feel a great compassion for old people, Garth! Sometimes we are but a hairsbreadth away from being locked up and put out of the way. Often we are treated like children again: very, very young children without words, and then everyone feels they can speak for us. Sometimes we are lucky—as I was when Allan and Gregory took care of me. But what happens when we are not? Haven't I been left to die here? How can I speak out against that lawyer's letter? It seems even my own birth certificate is no match for that document. And hasn't Ava left me here with a bag of gold—gold to secure Edna's silence? Ah, if you only knew how many bribes—how many little bags of gold—are left here, day after day, because one of us is not wanted.

It is a shepherd who rescues Perdita in Shakespeare's play, and I have been blessed by many shepherds here at this Home. My Perdita, too, has need for shepherds. Hers is a story as old as the Greeks, and yet she has truly been the lost child of many, many successive generations. Who will rescue and preserve her now? I know she will go back to her sisters—but ever will she return to us, offering us the fourth thread of her bundle.

I am growing very tired, and this frustrates me terribly, because I have much more that I wish to say. You have been so remarkable both to me and to those who reside in this Home. Even in my short time here, I have heard so much gratitude and thankfulness expressed for you, especially for your kindness and for your gift of listening. Ever shall I be grateful for that afternoon when I heard your voice calling out to me. I believe even now, in what I know are my final moments—I believe that it was the Bay who sent you to me.

I have no strength for more, but I close this letter trusting you will understand the fullness of my heart.

May God always bless you.

May the wind and the trees always carry your name—branch to branch, breath to breath—across my beloved Bay.

Marged Brice

I folded the letter and carefully put it back in its envelope, quietly wiping my eyes. An elderly man with a walker was trying to sit down next to me, and I quickly stood up, taking his bag and setting it down beside him.

"Does this airline let seniors board first?" he asked querulously.

A silver-haired woman sitting on his other side quickly assured him they did. He began to complain that "seniors" shouldn't include everybody over sixty-five. "There's a big difference between me and a sixty-five-year-old," he announced.

"I'm not quite there myself, but how old are you, sir?" the woman asked conversationally.

"Eighty-two and still travelin' on my own. Goin' to see my daughter. You married?"

Before she could answer, the airline announced early boarding. The woman kindly offered to assist him, and together they cautiously made their way toward the gate. She deftly got him positioned close to the attendant taking boarding passes and then blocked the stream of first-class passengers with her body.

Suddenly I thought of Edna—

Something was wrong with the man's documents. I could see the other passengers growing impatient behind him. Half a minute later, the woman stepped back, and the elderly gentleman pushed his walker forward, the woman waving encouragingly at him.

Edna.

She had been the real heroine in all of this. Edna had told Marged Brice that she could trust me.

Marged sitting in her room at the Clarkson, her long, slender fingers reaching out toward the trees outside her window.

"What would you have done if you were George?" That had been her question to me, but I hadn't been able to answer her—not at first.

Was I answering her now?

I looked out the window and across the tarmac, watching a long line of suitcases moving up a conveyor belt.

George must have gone to Marged, I told myself. His paintings were so remarkable. Wasn't she there in his brushstrokes and in the inimitable quality that made his work timeless?

But had George Stewart and Andrew Reid been the only ones involved? I watched as the last of the suitcases disappeared into the belly of the plane. Hadn't there also been Marged's wild and *beloved* Georgian Bay? Was that why Perdita had come to her?

Suddenly an image rose before me…there on the beach at night, shivering in a towel, I had heard a woman's voice calling from out of the darkness for her dog…

Perdita knew you immediately…

There on the rocky shore, Clare had appeared, moments after my swim in the Bay's bracing waters, just as the stars began to appear across its rippling surface…both of us returning to a place we loved…

That first day when Perdita brushed past you and you thought she was the cat—how we laughed about that together…

I felt my phone vibrating in my shirt pocket.

"Clare!" I exclaimed.

"Yes," she said quickly. "I just talked to Mum. She said—well, she said she had a nice talk with you this morning. But that number you were calling. That isn't my phone. That's Stuart Bretford's phone. You see, I'm always losing mine. I'm—I'm not using that number anymore. I'm so sorry for the confusion."

"Never mind about that. I'm so glad you called."

"Where are you? There's a lot of noise. I can barely hear you."

I got up and moved away from the crowd now pushing up toward the counter.

"I'm in the airport. I'm just about to board my flight. I'm flying into London tonight." She caught her breath. "Listen, I don't have much time, but can you meet me at the airport?"

"Of course I'll come!"

The airline began to announce the first rows for regular boarding.

"I've got to board, but I'll try to call you from the air. Will you be at this number?"

"Yes, I'll wait for you to call me." Then she added hurriedly, "But just in case you can't, where are you flying into?"

"Heathrow. It's not too far for you, is it?"

"Oh, no. It's not far at all. But, Garth—"

"Yes?"

"It's such a huge, busy airport. You know how crowded it can be. And it's so easy to get lost…"

"I'll find you. I'm absolutely certain I'll find you."

The flight attendant took my ticket, looking at me curiously. I stepped away and quickly moved through the gate.

"Clare, you know what I'm saying, don't you?" But I didn't wait for her answer. "This isn't another loose end. This time I'm coming to *see* you."

Epilogue

Do you wonder who we are?

There were three of them, that first time. We saw them coming down the deep wound that had been cut into us: a woman, a man, and a young girl. The woman sat next to the man at the front, her body heaving as the wagon lurched and pitched along the path. Sometimes she leaned against him, clutching his arm, but when the wheels caught and stuck, she would draw back to let the man step down and guide the horse. Then as the man took his seat, his form would come together with hers, only to part again, for the road was deeply rutted. They were quiet, these three—especially the little girl.

Marged.

But at first we did not know her name. She was sitting on the woman's lap, her eyes staring out into the forest. We were intrigued by her face—pale and smooth—and her quiet, luminous eyes. Her hair was hidden beneath a gray cloak and we wondered at it. We thought that it must be dark: dark like the clouds shading the stars, because they, too, sometimes gaze so brightly at us, just as her eyes seemed to be searching.

Was it for us?

And so we threw a branch across the road to catch her hood and pull it back.

It was then that the man reached forward, and with his hand he broke us, throwing the branch to the ground. We winced, chastened for our foolishness. To be sure, it was there again—the senselessness.

The violence. We did not trust them. And yet—the girl. She seemed to be listening intently, as if she could discern our voices in the growing darkness, her eyes gathering light even in the shadow of her hood. They will not escape the storm…

We laughed and thought that this might be our revenge for the violence. The violence of their hands, relentless as they touch us, again and again as they have touched us.

They will be surprised by the storm… But the man knew. He could tell from the heavy stillness and the whisper of the leaves as they sped along before him—for as such did he hear us. The man saw our treachery in the soft, winding pathway and in the quiet, heavy day that the morning had promised. This was to be his uneventful journey: his journey to the lonely light tower and the strange beast that they have imprisoned there.

We have seen the restless creature in the place where he is going. During the nighttime we have seen it, casting a silent, livid beam of light across us, pacing through the darkness to probe the bars of its enclosure. Always it turns, circling its cage with a fearful hope always it finds the bars still intact.

Did the man know our fear of his hands?

It was the girl who spoke to us.

Marged. We felt her soul leaning toward us, toward the wind and water and trees, just as her body shrank back, a little afraid. She huddled deeper into her cloak, and then, as the wind rose, she felt us push against her, pressing her back.

How then did she know to bend forward, just so, to catch us and turn our waywardness against us? She made us hold her, cushioning the sharp jolts and dips as the wagon rumbled on. Trust us, we whispered, amazed at her innocence, and then wondered at our own deviousness.

But again she caught us unawares. "Why, you are like me sometimes," the girl thought at us, and far away we heard her mother's hands smoothing her hair. "You are playful and rough all at the same time." Was the girl speaking to wind? She smiled, the curve of a line so faint that all of us strained to see it.

And then we remembered—holding her almost against our will—that in some stories there was a child, and that it was she who wept for Prometheus during his travails.

Perdita.

It is true that some of us were beguiled by Marged.

Only wind would not be charmed by her and blew harder, pushing her cloak back and seizing her around the waist. I am no child, wind warned, before releasing her and moving ahead along the path. And then Marged sent out her fear after us, down the wound and after the wind, holding it out in tiny hands that trembled with a shy reserve. Out of her eyes and face, out of her cloak and hair, her fear followed us, becoming a tender, fragile thing, softly feeling our face as a blind creature might, touching our lips to read what our face might tell.

This astounded us, for her fingers were not unlike those of our inquisitive branch reaching for her hair, and we too—we, too, sometimes have the power to settle a score.

Do you still wonder who we are?

What should be our answer?

We can only say that it was in the coming of these three that the thought of Perdita came to us. It was there, in the discovery of Marged sitting between the two other forms. It was in the way she wound her arms around our neck, fearful, trusting—that we dared to hope.

To be sure it was a foolish and wonderful thought.

Did we do the right thing?

There are some of us, to this day, who disapprove of what we did. Yet there is not a blade of grass, a bird, or a cloud in these parts who does not know of Perdita. It is the men and the women who live here who do not know her.

Now it is our turn to wonder, for it is only to one of them that Perdita will return.

Reading Group Guide

1. How did you find the transition between past and present voices within *Perdita*? Did you find differences in the language and pacing of Garth's narrative in contrast to Marged's journal? Were you interested in both the modern and historical periods, or were you more drawn to one?

2. Clare tells Garth she is attracted to the idea that the "threads" of love are never discarded but always preserved by Perdita. Why does this make Clare an "incorrigible romantic" in Garth's view? What does it mean to be a romantic person in our contemporary society? Do you consider yourself a "romantic"?

3. In Greek mythology, Perdita is the child of Hephaestus and Pandora. She is hidden among the Fates and she keeps a "bundle" of four different kinds of love: *philia* (affection and friendship), *eros* (passion), *agape* (unconditional love), and *biophilia* (the love between humans and nature). If Perdita were to show you "your bundle"—i.e., all the different kinds of love relationships you have experienced in your life—would *biophilia* be present?

4. The notion of threads and "loose ends" runs throughout the novel. Which "threads" or aspects of the story came full circle for you, and which were left open? How do you respond to the

parts of the story that are left open-ended? Do you think Marged is trying to convey something about the nature of love to Garth, as well as the "risks" of being in love?

5. Marged's last entry in her diary has her drifting out into the Bay's open waters, "way out beyond the buoys and their markings of safe harbor." She writes that even the lighthouse has disappeared from her sight. Does she make a choice between her two suitors? Is there anything that occurs in the novel to suggest she does make a choice?

6. When deciding if she can trust Garth, Marged asks him, "What would your trees say about you?" Why does she ask this? What if you were asked the same question? What do you think your trees would say about you?

7. Who was your favorite character and why? What is your favorite scene in the novel and why?

8. How did you respond to Marged's face and her eyes, especially when she first encounters Garth?

9. What do you think the significance of the great horned owl is? Where does it appear in the novel?

10. Do you have a special place in Nature where you go to collect your thoughts? How does this relate (if at all) to Marged's relationship with Georgian Bay?

Acknowledgments

The writing of *Perdita* was made possible by the many who have given so much of their time, energy, and lives to preserving the wild beauty of Georgian Bay, Lake Huron, and the Bruce Peninsula. Among these, I especially acknowledge Ron and Rita Baker, Wilmer Nadjiwon, Rod Steinacher, Ted Cheskey, Ned and Mary Crawford, Louise Weber (in memoriam), and Bob Lesperance. I also gratefully acknowledge the Bruce Peninsula National Park, the Friends of Cabot Head Lighthouse, the Bruce Peninsula Bird Observatory, the Bruce Trail Association, Bruce County Libraries, the Cove Island Lightstation Heritage Association, and all the other "friends" of our precious lighthouse history.

Heartfelt thanks go to my editor, Deb Werksman of *Sourcebooks*—especially for her warm and generous encouragement, as well as her skillful editorial direction. Many thanks also go to Susie Benton, Heather Hall, and cover designer Amanda Kain, as well as to mapmakers Paul Barker and Elizabeth Whitehead. Perdita's "bundle" owes much to Tim Ingold's *entanglements,* E.O. Wilson's *biophilia,* Eric Hobsbawn's *invention of tradition,* and Tom Berry's *communion of subjects.*

I am also deeply grateful to Jane Price, Shangeetha Jeyamanohar, Mary Jo Leddy, John Fraser, Elizabeth MacCallum, Alison Clarke, Laura Shin, and my remarkable literary agent, Beverley Slopen.

My son's joyous embrace of life has always been a great inspiration to me. Nolan's gentle prodding to keep me attentive to the "present" has been equaled only by his disciplined and tenacious commitment to the "classics." There were many nights when we were both up working into the wee hours of the morning—me writing this novel and Nolan translating a passage from Virgil's *Aeneid*. Somehow my difficulties always seemed to pale in comparison!

My husband, Stephen Scharper, has been an extraordinary companion to and steward of *Perdita.* Always so magnanimous in bringing his many literary gifts to bear upon the story, he has helped me to navigate the many choppy seas of writing fiction through his magical and infectious delight in the novel. Perhaps most precious of all has been his deep, steadfast belief in me as a writer—it is really with him and through him that *Perdita* has evolved.

Lastly—there is Georgian Bay. It's cold, wild waters; its moody, unpredictable skies—and the wind. Always the wind. How does one acknowledge and thank such a coauthor? As Marged Brice might say, the Bay will know the fullness of my heart.

About the Author

Hilary Scharper, who lives in Toronto, spent a decade as an assistant lighthouse keeper on the Bruce Peninsula with her husband. She also is the author of a story collection, *Dream Dresses*, and *God and Caesar at the Rio Grande* (University of Minnesota Press), which won the Choice Outstanding Academic Book Award. She received her PhD from Yale and is currently associate professor of cultural anthropology at the University of Toronto.